THE CAVALIER
of the APOCALYPSE

ALSO BY SUSANNE ALLEYN

A Far Better Rest
Game of Patience
A Treasury of Regrets

THE CAVALIER
of the APOCALYPSE

Susanne Alleyn

MINOTAUR BOOKS
NEW YORK

This is a work of fiction. All of the characters, organizations, and events portrayed in this novel are either products of the author's imagination or are used fictitiously.

A THOMAS DUNNE BOOK FOR MINOTAUR BOOKS.
An imprint of St. Martin's Publishing Group.

www.thomasdunnebooks.com
www.minotaurbooks.com

Library of Congress Cataloging-in-Publication Data

Alleyn, Susanne, 1963–
    The cavalier of the apocalypse / Susanne Alleyn.—1st ed.
        p. cm.
    ISBN-13: 978-0-312-37988-9
    ISBN-10: 0-312-37988-9
    1. Ravel, Aristide (Fictitious character)—Fiction. 2. Private investigators—France—Paris—Fiction. 3. Paris (France)—History—1715–1789—Fiction. 4. Freemasons—France—Paris—Fiction.
I. Title.
    PS3551.L4484C38 2009
    813'.6—dc22

                                                                    2009007933

First Edition: July 2009

10 9 8 7 6 5 4 3 2 1

To the memory of my grandmother,
Lillie Vanderveer Albrecht,
with love

ACKNOWLEDGMENTS

Thanks are due to Professor Sarah Maza, for helping me with some details of eighteenth-century domestic life, and especially to Professor Alan Williams, for his kind patience in reading the manuscript and answering my questions about the prerevolutionary Paris police (as well as directing me to the right parts of his excellent book on the subject).

I owe thanks, also, to Katie Gilligan, Cristina Concepcion, Pamela Thrasher, and—as always—Berenice McDayter, for their ever-valuable comments and criticism. To Erika Vause, for hospitality in Paris. And to K. A. Corlett, for the precious book!

AUTHOR'S NOTE

The first two Aristide Ravel novels, *Game of Patience* and *A Treasury of Regrets*, took place in 1796 and 1797, during the Directoire period of the French Revolution. *The Cavalier of the Apocalypse* is a prequel to these, taking place ten years earlier in 1786, during the last years of the *ancien régime*.

I have followed general European practice in the naming of floors in buildings; the first floor is one flight up from the ground floor, and so on.

Many of the tiny medieval streets in the heart of Paris disappeared during Baron Haussmann's extensive rebuilding of the city in the 1860s. Other streets have had their names, or the spelling of their names, changed during the past two centuries. All streets and street names mentioned in this novel, however, existed in the 1780s.

TERMS

Commissaire: A high-level official of the eighteenth-century Parisian police force, above the inspectors, combining the functions of an investigator and a preliminary judge. Prerevolutionary commissaires served as examining magistrates, questioning witnesses and suspects and determining whether or not a case should be pursued; they reported directly to the royal lieutenant of police (the city's chief of police).

Faubourg: A suburb or, less precisely, a neighborhood at the edge of the medieval center of a city; areas of Paris such as the faubourg St. Germain, the faubourg St. Marcel, and so on, were so named in the Middle Ages, when they were parishes lying outside the twelfth-century walls, but by the eighteenth century they were well within the city limits. Neither they, nor the numbered administrative districts of prerevolutionary Paris, bear any relation to the modern arrondissements.

Guard: Prerevolutionary Paris had several separate companies of foot soldiers and guardsmen, each with a different title, status, and function, who maintained small posts throughout the city and were supposed to patrol the streets at night. For simplicity's sake, I have used the general term of "the Guard" for all of them.

Hôtel: Can mean a hostelry, a large public building (*hôtel de ville*, city hall; *hôtel-Dieu*, charity hospital), or a large private town house or mansion (*hôtel particulier*). To avoid confusion, I have used the French form, with the circumflex over the *o*, whenever referring to a mansion or municipal hall, and the unaccented English word when referring to public accommodations.

Inspector: In prerevolutionary Paris, a police official in charge of maintaining a district of the city, under a commissaire; an inspector usually had some particular specialty in city administration and/or regulation, not necessarily related to crime or investigation.

Lèse-majesté: High treason, specifically a malicious attempt on the person (by physical attack) or the character (by insult, slander, or libel) of the king or queen.

Maître d'hôtel: A high-ranking house servant, equivalent to butler or steward.

Money: The standard unit of prerevolutionary French currency was the livre, although there was no one-livre coin. Twenty sous (which were further divided into the small change of copper deniers and liards) made up a livre; three livres a silver ecu; twenty-four livres a gold louis d'or. The franc, introduced in 1795 during the Revolution, was worth about the same as the livre and eventually replaced it.

Monseigneur: "My lord" (more formal and deferential than "monsieur" used as a form of address, which is equivalent to "sir").

Police: The duties of the police of eighteenth-century Paris, particularly before the Revolution, extended far beyond the prevention and investigation of crime, the maintenance of public order, and the system of covert informers and enforcers necessary to an absolute monarchy. Essentially city administrators, they supervised all kinds of public affairs that today, in a large European or American city, would be managed by various departments of health, sanitation, public welfare, housing, trade, the fire department, and more, directing even public morals (regulation of prostitutes) and censorship of printing and publishing.

Subinspector: Before the Revolution, a police agent, often recruited from among petty criminals, who worked either openly or clandestinely and reported to a district inspector; roughly corresponding to something between a confidential informant and an undercover investigator assisting a detective in a modern police force.

PROLOGUE

Monday, 31 October 1785

Aristide Ravel stumbled upon the first fire early on All Hallows' Eve.

The rising sun at last allowed him to see his way past the gutter that ran down the center of all the streets, thick with the black slime that Parisians politely called mud—a trampled stew of horse manure, night soil, rotten rinds and parings, ashes, and every other sort of muck and filth that the inhabitants of a vast city could produce. He strode on toward the center of Paris, trying to ignore his squalid surroundings in the outskirts while anticipating, with some pleasure, the four gold louis he would receive for a handful of manuscript pages he had written for a printer-bookseller on the Quai des Augustins.

His lodgings lay, in the autumn of 1785, on the sixth floor of a dilapidated tenement at the edge of the city, not far from the prison-hospital of La Salpêtrière, which he could smell from his room whenever the wind was right, and unpleasantly close to a pair of slaughterhouses and the desolate paupers' graveyard of Clamart, all of which he could smell all the time. To reach the printers' district by the Seine, he had first to pick his way along the refuse-strewn cobbles on the slopes of Rue Mouffetard and the neighboring streets, past the butcher shops, abbatoirs, and tanneries that crowded the landscape and poisoned the air of the neighborhood with the vile stench of soaking hides and stale blood.

He was approaching the steep hill, avoiding the scraps of offal that littered the streets near the slaughterhouses, when a large, unruly crowd and a plume of smoke caught his attention. Made up of the usual assortment of early-rising day laborers, journeymen, fishwives, errand boys, and ragged vagrants that one encountered in the seamy faubourg St. Marcel, the crowd streamed toward the church of St. Médard.

Fifty years before, a mad sect of religious fanatics had gone into convulsions there over purported miracles. Curious, he followed them, pushing the lank dark hair that spilled to his shoulders and whipped in the breeze away from his face, and wondering if new miracles had manifested themselves. As he approached, he found the spectators equally divided between those who—eager for any free entertainment—were hooting, shouting, and stamping their feet, and others, mostly women, who were on their knees, praying and sobbing. Above them all, gray smoke drifted from the church's porch, muddying the overcast sky above.

"What's this all about?" Aristide asked the nearest man.

"Don't know," he said. "Only that there's some ruckus at the church."

"Somebody set a fire!" another man exclaimed, near them. "Right in the church, by the altar!"

"God save us all!" a woman wept, dropping her market basket and fervently making the sign of the cross.

"What's the world coming to?" said another.

"You mark my words," said the second man, "there's something afoot. Something's up. It's a plot."

"A plot to do what?" Aristide said.

"Why, to profane churches and kill Christians."

"They can burn all the priests to cinders in their own churches, for all I care," growled a third, a sturdy young man of twenty-five wearing stained and scarred sabots—probably a worker in one of the slaughterhouses, Aristide thought—and a laborer's loose striped trousers and belted blouse. "Or in Hell, for that matter. What have the cassocks ever done for us in exchange for all the tithes they squeeze out of us, except feed us lies and fairy tales, and tell us how we ought to live our lives?"

"May God forgive you!" the woman with the market basket cried, crossing herself again and edging away from the blasphemer.

"Well?" demanded the young laborer, glancing truculently from side to side. "What *have* the damned priests and bishops done to earn their fat incomes? Don't tell me you never saw the bishops and the cardinals swanning about in their fancy carriages with their jewels and their fancy women. They're no more than lickspittles and courtiers. Gut them all, I say."

"Now how can you say that," a plump woman retorted, "when the Church does plenty of good for the poor." She nodded in the direction of a pair of nuns who were making their way down the street, carrying a large hamper between them. "They tend the sick in the hospitals, don't they? And many's the fellow down on his luck, or the poor widow with hungry children, who's gotten a hot bowl of soup and a bit of bread from the holy sisters." The people around her nodded and muttered in agreement.

"It's a plot, I tell you," the second man insisted. "A plot against good Christians, to bring down the Church. They arrested Cardinal de Rohan, didn't they?"

"The cardinal!" the slaughterhouse worker exclaimed. "Hah! The bastard's a lecher, a fraud, and a thief! He and his whore stole that diamond necklace, and who knows what else he was up to?"

Since August, people spoke about only one diamond necklace. The creation of the royal jewelers, worth a million and a half livres—the price of a battleship in the king's navy—it had vanished in the most mysterious and scandalous of circumstances.

"*I* heard the Austrian bitch got him to steal the necklace for her by inviting him into her bed," another man declared, with an obscene gesture, "because Fat Louis wouldn't dip into his purse for it!"

"And we all know Louis can't get it up anyway," jeered another, "so she has to feed her unnatural lusts where she can—"

"Don't you talk about the king and queen like that!" a burly fish-wife snapped, and backhanded him with her basket.

"Cardinal de Rohan's family's the richest in the land, I hear," the slaughterhouse worker continued, over the commotion, "and they say he doesn't even pretend to behave like a priest should. D'you think he's poor? A Rohan? Not likely. And if he's chaste, then I'm a Turk. He's got half a dozen mistresses, I hear . . . holds orgies, most likely, in his fancy palaces."

"He's still a prince of the Church!" said the second man. "Why, I think the king would have feared for his own soul, arresting a cardinal. They must have told him to do it, whoever it is has it in for the Church. And now this!" he concluded, gesturing vaguely at the thinning plume of smoke.

Aristide almost smiled, for everything he had ever heard about Louis XVI indicated that the king was deeply, genuinely, and obstinately devout. Such a man would scarcely have ordered the arrest of Cardinal de Rohan—a prince of the Holy Roman Empire and cadet of one of the most powerful families in France—two and a half months earlier, on charges of theft and lèse-majesté connected with the matter of the infamous necklace, without believing himself entirely within his rights to do so.

"You think, then," he said, "that a fire in a church and the cardinal's arrest are all part of the same anti-Catholic conspiracy?"

"Why not?" The man turned to scowl at Aristide from beneath heavy brows. "There are plenty of ungodly folk out there, you mark me. They want to do away with good Christians and turn us all into pagans. Jews and Protestants, and—and Mohammedans and Freemasons and Turks . . . and all those heathen aristos with their wicked temples and high priests of what-you-may-call-it, whatever you like. Plenty of them," he repeated, for emphasis.

He would learn nothing more, Aristide decided, from this crowd of ignorant gawkers. Curious, he elbowed his way through to the porch. Smoke still wafted outward, though it was thinner than before. Behind him, the clustered neighborhood folk pointed and whispered, not daring to go further.

He stepped inside the church. At the far end of the nave, half a dozen figures scurried about in the dimness, the smoke obscuring the wan, pearly morning light of late autumn that was beginning to filter down from the upper windows. As he drew nearer, he could see the fire was contained in one spot, lying like a bonfire before the communion rail, merrily consuming a few kneelers.

"You!" a man cried, spotting him. "If you're here to help us instead of to stare, go line up in back!" He pointed to the door on the north side. Aristide followed the gesture and soon found himself in a bucket line that led to a well in the corner of a narrow passage behind a row of dilapidated houses. The police maintained several crews of firefighters with pumping carts, but there was no sign of them; no doubt it would take them more time than it was worth to arrive at this remote corner of Paris.

It was over within a quarter of an hour, with little harm done; the fire had, in truth, been small enough. At last the priest appeared and announced that the fire had been quenched, thanking profusely all who had helped, as he blotted away sooty sweat with a rough handkerchief. After offering thanks and blessings all around, he retreated inside once again and Aristide discreetly followed him.

The charred, smoldering remains of the blaze still lay in the middle of the church, at the center of the two rows of classical columns that seemed strangely out of place amid the medieval stonework. As he drew closer, he could tell the sticks, tinder, and paper scraps—scavenged from the layers of advertising bills that were pasted every day on half the walls in Paris—that had made up the base of the fire had not been laid out randomly, heaped in a loose pile. Rather, the fuel had been arranged in something resembling a hollow square, or a diamond shape, with one acute angle pointing directly at the altar.

"That's odd," muttered a voice behind him. Aristide glanced over his shoulder to see one of his companions from the bucket line, a big, broad-shouldered man, somewhat older than he. Though grimy with dust and smoke, the man's clothes clearly indicated that he was not one of the many day laborers, butcher's boys, and tannery workers who populated the edge of the neighborhood; he was pulling on a frock coat that was part of the plain, neat black suit of a respectable bourgeois civil servant, much like Aristide's, though far less shabby.

"Odd?"

"Peculiar shape, that is."

"Why not just heap it all together?" Aristide agreed.

"Would have been harder to light it this way, too," the man said, musing aloud. "Easier to just make a pile and throw a little lamp oil on it. Here you'd have to pour oil all the way around."

"Yes, I was wondering about that myself."

"Peculiar," he repeated. "Like perhaps he wanted to do something in the center of the square of flames."

"Do something?" Aristide echoed him. "Do you mean, perform some outlandish ritual, or something of that sort?"

"There are some funny people about," the big man said, without further comment. He shrugged and turned away, pulling out his watch.

Suddenly Aristide recognized him: He, and his wife and small daughter, lived in an apartment on the first floor of the house in which Aristide had lived until two months ago, when the state of his finances

had obliged him to find cheaper lodgings. At the same instant, the
man, too, seemed to find Aristide vaguely familiar, and looked him up
and down.

"You don't belong in this district. You're no hide-scraper."

"Neither are you," said Aristide. "You're my former neighbor, from
the first floor, on Rue des Amandiers, aren't you? Did you come this
far to satisfy your curiosity?"

"I'd say I have a better reason than you do, monsieur, for being
hereabout." He reached into an inner pocket of his coat and pulled
out a printed card embellished with a signature and an official-looking
seal, which he briefly held up before putting it carefully away. "Inspector Brasseur, of the Eighteenth District. And you are, monsieur?"

Aristide realized suddenly that the inspector probably thought he
was a fellow member of the police. The commissaires, one step below
the royal lieutenant of police who was in charge of all Paris, wore official robes, caps, and wigs like magistrates; inspectors and their subor-
dinates, however, commonly wore plain black suits, like many other
civil servants.

"I'm not one of you," he said pleasantly, extracting his identity
papers from his pocket-book and handing them to Brasseur, "if that's
what you were wondering. Merely a private citizen and man of letters."

"Man of letters, eh?" the inspector echoed him, with a dubious
glance at him. The police and most respectable folk viewed authors,
playwrights, and poets—unless they had found patronage and become
household names—as seedy vagabonds, scarcely better than actors or
street-corner charlatans.

"A writer, monsieur, who presently can afford no better lodging
than a garret at the edge of this unwholesome quarter of Paris."

The ghost of a smile crept across Brasseur's broad countenance.
"Why the black suit, then?" he inquired. "You're not any kind of civil
servant?"

"Saints preserve me," Aristide said, thinking of the many dull hours he had spent in his uncle's law office before resolving to escape Bordeaux, and bitter memories, and move to Paris.

"Surely you're not an abbé! You don't have the look of a priest."

"It's the only suit I have, monsieur; black serves for all occasions."

Brasseur nodded and said nothing, though he continued to eye Aristide appraisingly. At last he handed back the papers, with a cordial word, and Aristide gratefully made himself scarce.

1

Family-minded bourgeois Parisians spent New Year's Day attending Mass, exchanging gifts, and hosting convivial dinner parties. Bachelors, students, and the literary cliques, on the other hand, tended to spend the holiday in taverns or cafés, which were invariably crowded and lively with those who had not yet settled down to respectable marriages and the producing of heirs. More than that, Aristide thought, as he hurried toward the Cordeliers district with an icy wind at his back, the cafés would be far warmer than his attic room—which had no fireplace and was heated only by a small charcoal brazier—in the midst of a miserably cold winter.

He was feeling unexpectedly wealthy, having earned another ten louis for a political pamphlet, with nearly sixty livres still at his disposal after clearing up accounts with his landlord. Giving way to an extravagant impulse, he established himself, with a demitasse of strong coffee, at a corner table in the Café Zoppi, wondering if anyone he recognized might come past.

He recognized a few faces, though no one whom he knew intimately, and at last he contented himself with pulling out the manuscript upon which he was currently working, and scribbling notes to himself with a battered pencil. Around him, the coffee drinkers came and went and clustered about the tall heating stove, conversing earnestly about the sad state of literature, and the even sadder state of current affairs. Inevitably the gossip would turn to the continuing delicious scandal of what people were calling "the queen's necklace," though it had never, it seemed, been hers. By now the chief characters in the drama—Cardinal de Rohan; his avaricious mistress, Jeanne de la Motte; and the notorious alchemist, soothsayer, and mystic Cagliostro—were safely locked away in the Bastille, awaiting trial. Though all legal proceedings were supposed to be conducted in the greatest secrecy, leaks, from time to time, oozed from the fortress to enliven the thousands of illegal handbills, pamphlets, and satirical songs that circulated around the city without benefit of the censor's stamp of approval.

"But it's impossible to be bored in Paris," a young man declared, some hours later, in loud, offhand tones to his companion, as they seated themselves at the table next to Aristide's. "Can't be done."

Aristide cast a sideways glance at him. He wore his hair long and unpowdered, following the careless fashion of the younger generation who patronized Zoppi's; but his clothes, well cut and crisp, betrayed him as a pampered young sprout from a comfortable bourgeois family, playing at the literary life in Paris.

Aristide glanced at his own frayed cuffs and immediately loathed him.

"There's so much to do, so much to see," the young man continued, for the benefit of his friend, who as clearly, by last year's cut of his redingote, was a country cousin. "The theater, the opera, the Italian comedy . . . Why, even if your purse is feeling a bit light, you can get cheap tickets to seats up in Paradise and go to the theater every night if you want. Or you can buy tickets to the costume balls at the opera house and perhaps find yourself dancing with a duchess."

"A duchess?" echoed the country cousin, impressed.

"Or a prostitute. You'll find both there. They say even Antoinette goes sometimes."

"My word!"

Aristide could have told him that the queen hadn't been spotted at the opera balls for years; her giddy days as the spoiled, thoughtless, pleasure-seeking young princess were behind her, now she was past thirty and the mother of three children, though popular opinion was ready to believe anything of her, the more scurrilous the better. The salacious details that had been turning up in café talk and the gutter press about the diamond necklace affair, and the queen's alleged sexual relations with both the cardinal and the so-called Comtesse de La Motte, the adventuress behind the notorious theft, had been titillating Parisian scandalmongers for months.

He signaled to a waiter, who elbowed his way across the crowded, candlelit room toward him—insolently slowly, Aristide thought, acutely aware of his threadbare clothes.

"Yes, monsieur?"

"Another coffee." He stifled a yawn and glanced at his watch, the only thing of value he presently owned. Twenty past eleven. "With sugar."

"Three sous."

Nearby a pair of earnest-looking young men were looking furtively about them as they talked, a newspaper lying forgotten on the table between them.

"You know anyone with any sense wants the Duc d'Orléans on the throne, even if it's just as regent for the boy, but first you'd have to ensure that the king's brothers were out of the running."

"How do you get rid of Louis, though? Certify him as an imbecile?"

The first man smiled sourly. "Please. He's not *stupid*, no matter what people say: just inept at the role he's forced to play. I heard he has his own private library on mechanics and the sciences. Of course, it's a tragedy of fate that he had to be a king; I expect he'd have made an excellent professor of natural philosophy instead."

"Like Father Houdelot at school," said the other man, grinning.

"Exactly. The woolly-headed sort of intellectual monk—"

" 'Monk' is right. He must be the first king of France in about five hundred years who's never had a mistress!"

"—not blessed with too much practical sense—"

"What does *that* say about him?"

"—who's vastly knowledgeable about just one or two abstruse subjects and knows nothing at all about any others."

"Or indeed about much of life."

"But instead he had to be king, and concern himself with administration, power, and politics, which he obviously has no talent for, and probably detests . . . the duke's far better suited to the part—"

"Lord, nearly anyone would be . . ."

"Or of course you can go to the Palais-Royal," the young man at the next table continued, raising his voice above the din.

"What's that?"

"Oh, it's quite new, and it's the latest sensation! We ought to visit tomorrow. It's part of the Duc d'Orléans's *hôtel particulier*, you know, the family's Paris mansion."

"Orléans? The king's cousin?"

"They say he was badly in debt by the time the old duke finally breathed his last and Philippe inherited; at any rate, he knocked down the old walls and houses about the garden—it's immense—and he's building new houses with covered arcades all the way around on three sides, and *collecting shop rents*."

"But he's a *prince*," protested the younger man. "A prince of the blood!"

"That's what makes it so delicious. They say the king, when he heard about it, said 'I hear, cousin, that we'll only see you on Sundays, now you've turned shopkeeper.' But that's beside the point. The gardens are simply the latest rage. Ever hear of Vauxhall or Ranelagh in London? Well," he continued, as his companion nodded, "it's much the same. You can stroll through the Palais-Royal and visit a dozen different gaming houses or brothels within a hundred steps. And there are plenty of cafés and theaters and luxury shops and bookstalls if your tastes are tamer," he added, with a dismissive shrug.

"Is it expensive?"

"Well, yes, of course. It's fashionable. But the police aren't keeping watch over your shoulder, saying what you shouldn't do and shouldn't read. Orléans keeps them out—of course, someone like him can get away with doing that—because he believes people should be able to think and read as they please. If they're reading satires about the king, at any rate!"

"Father said I wasn't to spend all—"

"Oh, if you just want to see the sights for a fortnight, and you haven't much money, you can admire the royal art collection—that's at the Louvre Palace, but anyone properly dressed can get in—or the queen's formal court gowns . . ."

The fellow prattled on. Aristide endeavored to ignore him and leaned on the tiny table, chin balanced on fists, drowsily surveying the room from his dim corner. Zoppi's prices were outrageous—coffee was only two sous elsewhere, even at the Palais-Royal—but it was a good place to meet people; everyone in the lively Cordeliers district eventually turned up there. You were also paying for the privilege of drinking your coffee or hot chocolate beneath the same gilded chandeliers under which, twenty or thirty years ago, Voltaire and Diderot had once sipped theirs and discussed the philosophy of the day. Zoppi kept a bust of Voltaire on the mantel to remind his customers of this fact, although people said that when the canny Italian had bought the Café Procope and renamed it after himself, Voltaire was in no condition to visit his favorite café, having already been dead for several years.

His coffee arrived at last. He sipped it, slowly coming awake again. Coffee for wakefulness and as much sugar as you could stand for a burst of energy: that was the trick to keeping late hours. That night he had to finish copying Maître Carriau's brief before the next morning. Only two or three hours' work left on it, thank God!

"It's all about privilege," said a man to a companion as they passed and found a table. "What about the frustration of the ambitious, talented commoner who knows he'll never rise past a certain level in the army, the government, the Church, because all the top positions are reserved for sons of the nobility—plenty of whom are brainless fops who have done nothing besides being born into the right families?"

"You sound like Figaro: 'You took the trouble to be born and that's all.'"

"Exactly."

"Or," continued the young man beside Aristide, raising his voice again to be heard over the increasing noise—would he never shut up, Aristide wondered—"you can visit the Place de Grève."

"What's that?"

"It's the square in front of the Hôtel de Ville. But it's what goes on there, now and then, that's exciting."

"Hangings?" said his companion.

"Better," said the young man, lowering his voice. "Ever seen a murderer broken on the wheel?"

Evidently the country cousin had not, for he paled and mutely shook his head.

"Oh, then we must go, if we're lucky enough to have a breaking while you're here. We have one or two a year, when there's a particularly notorious crime. Usually they hang murderers, but if it's certain circumstances—parricide, or multiple murders—I saw Derues broken, you know, a few years ago. The poisoner. Fascinating stuff. Drama right before your eyes—the best sort of theater."

Theater? Aristide repeated to himself as the strong coffee he had just drunk on an empty stomach abruptly nauseated him.

"Some of my friends at school once sneaked out to see a man broken," the country cousin ventured. "They—they talked about it for weeks."

"I'm sure they did. Much more impressive than a hanging."

. . . Condemned to be taken to the scaffold, and his limbs and body there broken, and his living body shown on the wheel, staring at the sky, for as long as it pleases God to grant him life . . . and the corpse burned and the ashes scattered to the winds . . .

Aristide could bear no more. He pushed his coffee aside half drunk, snatched up the pages of his manuscript and thrust them into his worn leather dispatch case, and launched himself across the room past laughing, chattering customers bent over newspapers, literary journals, and games of chess or dominoes.

Someone turned as he shouldered his way through a group of half a dozen men who had just entered. Aristide thought he heard his name but dismissed it as a trick of the clamor all about him, until he heard it again and abruptly paused a few steps from the back door.

"Ravel?" Someone was approaching him, impatiently pushing past the loitering newcomers. "Aristide Ravel? It is, isn't it?"

"Derville?" Aristide said after an instant's hesitation, suddenly recognizing him.

"Faith, I didn't think I could have mistaken that mug of yours! It's been years!"

They embraced, whooping. Olivier Derville looked much the same as he had when they were schoolmates, Aristide thought, somehow drawn together despite the three years' difference in their ages: pale watery-blue eyes, sandy hair, a good-humored, sarcastic expression. His redingote, cut simply in the latest English style, hung well on his lanky frame, and the cloth was good, and looked new.

"You're not going?" Derville said when he had stepped back and taken a look at Aristide. "No, I demand that you sit down and take something with me. What'll it be?"

"Chocolate?" Aristide said, feeling unable to consume another mouthful of Zoppi's robust coffee.

"Hot chocolate it is. Sit, sit."

"What are you doing with yourself?" Aristide asked as Derville nudged another patron out of the way and seized a vacant table. "Do you live here in Paris?"

"Of course I live in Paris," the older man said. "Where else would one live? And you?"

"Right now, in the faubourg St. Marcel," Aristide said, grimacing. "Only temporarily, of course. Tell me, what do you do these days? Does your family still own *Parnassus?*"

Parnassus was a literary journal that Derville's father, a wealthy dilettante and patron of the arts, had begun a dozen years before. Subsidized by Derville senior's fortune, it had lasted long enough to gain several thousand subscribers and become profitable.

Derville nodded. "Yes, I've still got it around my neck. It's a frightful bore. The censors have the journals tied up so tightly you can't print anything interesting, just the muck they consider proper . . . poems about flowers, you know, and fawning tributes to minor royalties. Waiter! A half bottle of red over here, and a cup of chocolate. I really only keep on with it to spite my uncle," he continued. "Uncle Albert is a complete stick-in-the-mud and hates the way I run it. He thinks he could do better, of course."

"God, I'd give my teeth to have my own paper!"

"The last time I saw you, you were a couple of years shy of getting out of St. Barthélemy, and you were talking about taking a degree in law. Shouldn't you be in Bordeaux in a wig and gown?"

"I preferred to come to Paris," Aristide said. "Bordeaux finally became unbearable."

Derville nodded, without speaking. He had known about Aristide's family since their years together at school, where it was impossible to keep secrets. Unlike the great majority of the other boys and their parents, however, he had been broad-minded enough to ignore the scandal and treat the solitary, taciturn, furiously touchy boy Aristide had been at thirteen with a certain amount of careless kindness.

"Besides," Aristide added, "I thought there must be more to life than my uncle's law practice."

Derville grinned. "I don't blame you! What about that friend of yours Alexandre—have you seen much of him? Is he in Paris, too?"

"No, he's still at home. Family business." Mathieu Alexandre, his closest friend at boarding school, was the son of a wealthy merchant and shipowner, and had returned to Bordeaux to join the family firm. "He's already married and respectably settled down."

"While you're living—if you can call it living—in the wilds of the faubourg St. Marcel?" Derville clucked sympathetically. "Oh, Lord, Ravel, you didn't decide to try making your fortune in Paris as a scribbler—you haven't become a backstreet hack, have you?"

"Well . . . not exactly . . ." He summoned a smile. "All right, then, I do write . . . though to pay the rent, with a background in law, frequently I do drudge-work for lawyers. Copying and clerking and such."

"But you call yourself a writer, I suppose?"

"I think I have some talent for it," Aristide confessed, avoiding Derville's eyes.

"What kind of writing?" The waiter arrived and Derville poured himself a generous glass of wine while casting a cynical eye at the three men loudly discussing literature two tables away. "Please, please, *please* tell me you're not a poet."

"I do a little of everything. Poetry now and then, but mostly essays. Literary pieces." He tried the chocolate, scalded his lip, and set down the cup. "I write some satirical verse, and I've thought of trying a play or a novel."

"That doesn't pay much," Derville said, shaking his head.

"Don't I know it! I need a patron. You wouldn't know of anyone, would you?"

"Sorry. The few bigwigs I know personally already have stables of writers sucking up to them. Let me read some of your pieces and I might be able to fit a few of them in *Parnassus*; though it's been a bit dry lately, and I can't pay you much. However . . . I do know a few people who'll pay good money for good writing," he added, lowering his voice, "but it won't get you into the *Mercure*, and it might easily get you into trouble."

Aristide almost smiled again, for he knew exactly what his friend meant. Half the books and journals published in France—perhaps more—were illegal, printed on miniature presses in back rooms and attics all over Paris, or smuggled over the frontier from Amsterdam and Brussels. The lesser portion that was not pornography consisted of books and seditious pamphlets mocking, criticizing, or vilifying the court, the king's ministers, the royal family, the Church, and all the other venerable institutions of France. If you knew where to go, you could buy banned books from beneath the counter at dozens of otherwise respectable bookshops, many of them in the Palais-Royal, where—as the young man at the next table had said—the police were not allowed and the ambitious Duc d'Orléans made the rules.

"I already know a few people in that business," Aristide said, nodding. Illegal or not, scribbling *libelles*, political tracts, and catchy, venomous verses set to popular tunes was a living, and he, like the duke—though for different reasons—had no great love for the king, or for France's medieval laws.

Derville laughed. "I ought to have known you'd already be in the thick of it." He glanced from side to side, on the lookout for anyone who might be one of the ubiquitous police spies, and continued, his voice still low in the clamor. "Do you know Joubert?"

"No."

"Ah, well, then, I'll introduce you to one of the publishers who cranks out the most, and pays the best. Where did you say you lived?"

"Rue de la Muette, near La Salpêtrière." Aristide scribbled down the address and Derville pocketed it before raising his glass.

"To old friends met again."

Aristide could hardly toast him with a cup of hot chocolate, but he nodded in a half bow. "To old friends." He cautiously sipped at the thick, creamy brew and looked his friend over. He wore two gold watches, the new fashion. "Despite your complaints about *Parnassus*, you can't be doing too badly."

"Oh, I'm not! The thing always sells at least well enough to break even. The rubbish in it, however, is worse than it was when Voltaire enraged my dear late papa by calling it the literary equivalent of fertilizer: material that may someday produce something of value, but which is, at present, composed mostly of horse manure." He raised his glass in an ironic salute to the bust above the fireplace.

"Don't complain; at least you make a living from it." Aristide finished the chocolate and rose to his feet, apologetic. "I have to go and finish copying a brief by eight tomorrow morning, or a certain lawyer will have my skin. But if you could talk me up to any of the publishers you know . . ."

"I'll see what I can do. Meanwhile, come and dine sometime," Derville suggested. "The house at the sign of the scissors, Rue des Bons Enfants, just around the corner from the Palais-Royal. Second floor. Tomorrow—no, that's no good. Sunday, Monday . . . Tuesday? We'll make a day of it. Come by my lodgings on Tuesday morning and we'll visit the shopping arcades. I'll introduce you to Joubert, and we'll have dinner—on me, of course—and if we've time later, we'll walk a bit in the gardens, and make eyes at the pretty girls. What do you say?"

"All right." Aristide suddenly smiled. "Faith, it's good to see you again, Derville."

Monday, 2 January

There had to be something wrong, Aristide thought sourly for the hundredth time, with a kingdom that enriched courtiers, merchants, and money-grubbers, and let writers and artists starve in the streets.

Like him.

He shivered and stared into the dark corners of his garret room, lit by a single stinking tallow candle that assaulted his senses with the odor of rancid grease. Encountering Derville had not, he admitted, done much good for his general mood. He still liked him—it was impossible to really dislike Derville, after all—but meeting him after the passage of ten years or more had reminded Aristide just how much Derville's nonchalant arrogance and casual condescension could irritate him. Above all, he thought, it was the simple fact that everything seemed to have come to the man so *easily*: his family fortune, his literary career, his connections.

Derville had been born to money, and had inherited his father's bourgeois fortune, his father's friends, and his father's journal without having to lift a finger for them. Could such a man ever understand what it was like to be poor, shabby, and unconnected, to wait hungrily at the gates of literary success with a thousand others all fighting to pass through, and know you had nothing, beyond your own talent, to give you the tiniest advantage in that merciless battle for patronage, recognition, and celebrity?

He moved the candle closer, squinting in the gloom and wishing he could afford to burn more than one at a time.

God, how I hate this life.

Living in freezing, tatty furnished rooms, taking your meals from food stalls or peddlers on the street and at dirty chophouses among a lot of rough workmen, scrounging drinks from friends whom you knew you couldn't repay because you owed three months' rent to your bloodsucking landlord. Cracked plaster, dirty bed linens, rats in the walls, ice in the washbasin, fetid outdoor privies—and you'd have to tend to your own chamber pot if you preferred not to hurry down six flights of stairs at midnight—and it all cost two or three times what it would have cost anywhere else in France. And scribblers in the provinces sighed and wished they were in Paris, like you, living the literary high life!

But would you give it up to go home forever to Bordeaux?

A comfortable situation . . . was it worth the boredom, the stifling dullness of a provincial lawyer's life?

Pleading for some crofter whose neighbor's pigs had broken his fence down and devastated his garden, or taking a side in a boundary dispute that had gone on for six generations between a couple of penniless country squires—by God, no, he couldn't!

He took a swallow of the watered, vinegary red wine before him, making a face, and read through the poem he had just completed as he flexed his fingers to warm them. Perhaps, he admitted reluctantly to himself, he wasn't quite meant to be a serious poet. Prose and satirical verses flew from his pen speedily enough, while he struggled over each line whenever he attempted poetry. But his essays and satires always seemed to end as biting indictments of the way France was mismanaged, and such commentary, no matter how clever and graceful, was destined only for illegal books and, if he was unlucky, the royal censor's bonfire, lit by the public executioner.

Perhaps he would try a play; though probably, he thought with a grimace, he would end by writing something as inflammatory as *Figaro's Marriage* and the censor would ban it before it ever reached the stage. *Hell,* he said to himself, *you might as well just give up serious literature and poetry altogether, and commit yourself to a career of writing trash, producing reams of cheap satirical hackwork and savage libels, and always keeping one step ahead of the police . . .*

He sighed. No doubt he would think of something better in the morning.

The attic room was icy. He tried rubbing his hands together over the candle's flame, thinking of his aunt's warm kitchen. Stew bubbling in a big iron pot, or a goose turning on the spit—oh, hell, and all he'd had for supper was a dish of bean soup and a mouthful of bread and cheese at a cheap eating-house!

The commotion in the street outside shook him from his gloomy reverie. The bells of a nearby church began to sound—what would it be now? Two in the morning? But the peals were quick and sharp, not the measured tolling of the hours. Curious, he dragged a stool beneath the skylight that served as his window, climbed upon it, hauled open the casement—it was nearly as cold inside as out, anyhow—and leaned out. Though the sloping roof obscured his view of the street, the moon gave a little light and he could just see a handful of dark figures hurrying past, toward Clamart. He caught the word "fire" amid the shouts and realized that what he heard must be alarm bells.

First St. Médard, now the paupers' graveyard. Was it some madman, intent on setting fires, who had found that churches and cemeteries provided ideal concealment? Or, as the suspicious man outside St. Médard had said, back in October, was it something deeper and darker, a conspiracy against the Church?

Aristide sighed. Going against the Church was a dangerous business; twenty years ago, or less, you could have been beheaded, like the Chevalier de La Barre, for putting a toe out of line and denying its authority. Casual talk in cafés and on street corners, even within earshot of the ever-present, ever-vigilant police spies, was one thing, usually dismissed with a warning and an offhand reference to the Bastille, but a material act of defiance was quite another.

He thought briefly of descending the six flights of stairs and joining those who were on their way to fight the fire, but decided against it as he lost his balance and nearly fell off the stool while trying to stifle an enormous yawn. If the blaze was like the one at St. Médard, then they would soon have it in hand, with little harm done.

Get to bed, he told himself, *and don't waste the candle; you can't afford it.*

God, what a life.

2

He called on Derville on Tuesday morning as they had arranged. Derville's manservant, with a dubious glance at Aristide's well-worn overcoat and black suit, led him through a small, octagonal ante-room to wait in the salon. He occupied the time by wandering about, inspecting the objects on display.

Derville's taste, at odds with the prevailing fashions, ran not to bronzes in the classical style, sentimental paintings, or dainty porcelain figurines, but to the bizarre and risqué. A small terra-cotta figurine—ancient Roman, Aristide thought, either genuine or counterfeit—proved to be the god Priapus, boasting an enormous phallus and a suitably cheerful grin. Reaching a corner, he pushed aside a small velvet curtain to discover a framed engraving of three women and two men—nude, but with their hair perfectly dressed—engaged in athletic and anatomically improbable activities that left nothing to the imagination.

He hastily dropped the curtain back into place as Derville entered, half dressed, and the manservant brought morning coffee for them. At last Derville threw off his dressing gown, examined with a critical eye the three exquisitely tailored coats and four waistcoats that the servant presented to him, condemned all of them as unwearable, finally shouldered himself into an elegant striped silk coat and warm woolen overcoat, and pronounced himself ready to depart for the pleasure gardens.

The new construction at the Palais-Royal, surrounding the open grounds, was, in fact, not quite completed. One long row of arcades receded northward into the distance before them, as perfect in its perspective as a draftsman's architectural drawing. On the far side of the gardens, however, beyond the lawns, the fountain, and the severely clipped rows of young lime trees, skeletons in midwinter, the houses were still merely stone shells. Winches strained and workmen shouted as, below them, fashionable shoppers and their servants scurried to avoid any possible falling beams or limestone blocks.

Derville's conversation that morning consisted mostly of advice about fashions and tailors as they passed the shops and he declared this one to be the best glover, or that one to be a hatter to avoid. Aristide, uninterested in the latest mode, nodded when he felt it was appropriate and tried to recall whether or not Derville had always been so concerned with trivial matters.

"Have him make your culotte," Derville added, pointing, as they passed a particularly opulent-looking tailor's workroom, "but not your coat or your waistcoat, and if you want a complete suit of clothes, then you should probably go elsewhere. Ah, here we are." He steered Aristide toward an arcade with the legend JOUBERT FRÈRES above it, halfway down the row of crowded, colorful shops and doorways. "That bookshop."

They strolled toward it, dodging the crowds, numerous even on an icy January day: chattering ladies, swaggering dandies, footmen laden with parcels, and pert young shopgirls selling ribbons, paper flowers, trinkets, tobacco, and other such fancies from trays. The boutiques and businesses they passed ranged from the most elegant of perfumeries, jewelers, and dressmakers' shops to cafés, grand or modest, small hotels, and a tiny theater or two, little more than sideshows. Here and there discreet signs pointed to upstairs establishments offering, Aristide guessed, the amusements of the roulette table or the bedroom or both. Interspersed with the expensive luxury shops were more prosaic enterprises selling books, pamphlets, sheet music, and kitchenware. It being only noon, Derville announced, the whores were not up yet.

Joubert's shop was lined from floor to ten-foot ceiling with shelves of books, some already bound in gleaming gilt-stamped leather, but most still in coverless *broché* form, so that the customer could have his purchases bound to order, matching the other volumes in his library. Before the counter stood racks of respectable periodicals, from the *Journal de Paris*, the official daily newspaper, to literary weeklies like the *Mercure de France*, *L'Année Littéraire*, and Derville's own *Parnassus*. Behind the counter or in a back room, Aristide knew, would be a much greater number of books, pamphlets, and one-page handbills, every kind of banned literature from political satire and anticlerical tirades to the most lurid pornography, complete with illustrations.

His experience with other Parisian printer-booksellers had colored his expectations, Aristide decided, for he was surprised to discover that Pierre Joubert was not the dry, elderly little man whom he had come to expect when introducing himself to a bookseller. Joubert proved to be a handsome, conservatively dressed man in his late thirties. He invited Derville and Aristide into a tiny parlor at the back of the shop, where another, younger, man was sitting sprawled in an armchair, booted feet to the fire.

"My brother, Nicolas-Antoine," said Joubert. "He's merely stopped in for a friendly word; haven't you, Nico?"

"I take it I'm being dismissed," said Nicolas. He swung himself around, dusting ash from his boots with his handkerchief, and stood up. "Oh, good day to you, Derville. Pierre, want me to look in at the printing works on my way home?"

"If you're not headed home at three in the morning, as usual," the elder brother said, holding open the door for him. "Don't forget you're leaving for Lyon in two days, so you'd better have your trunk packed by tomorrow!" Nicolas grinned, bowed, and went out.

"Nicolas hasn't improved?" Derville asked dryly as they took seats.

"I suppose he's sowing his wild oats," said Joubert with a sigh. "*I* was already managing the business for our father by the time I was twenty-nine . . . ah, well, he'll grow up eventually, and stop throwing away his money on expensive whores and married women. What can I do for you today?"

"My friend here, Ravel," said Derville, indicating Aristide. "He's an old schoolfellow, looking for work in the literary line."

"I expect you're not too fussy about the sort of thing I might be willing to buy from you?" Joubert inquired, after they had exchanged commonplaces.

"Not at all," Aristide said. "I've already written a few gossip sheets for some other people: Demonville, for instance, and Royer. 'The True and Genuine History of Madame de Polignac, Dear Friend to Antoinette,' was mine, and a few songs, and so on."

"Oh," said Joubert, pursing his lips, "that was yours? I heard it sold fairly well. Honestly, I think you were a bit too kind to the slut, but then there's something to be said for keeping within the bounds of reasonably good taste, isn't there?"

Derville hooted. Aristide smiled slightly.

"Frankly," he said, "I don't much like writing the vicious sort of rag, full of invented slanders, that gives authors a bad name."

"Squeamish?"

"Not in the least. But I'd rather point out, with devastating precision, all the ills besetting the kingdom, including, of course, the king's lack of will, the queen's ignorance, the court's avarice, the ministers' shocking incompetence, a thousand antiquated laws and taxes that make corruption far too easy . . ."

Joubert smiled. "Go on."

"Go on? All right then . . . all of these, combined with a treasury depleted from an expensive war; a played-out old nobility with nothing left to it but poverty and arrogance, but which will fight to the last man before giving up the least of its medieval privileges; a despotic, corrupt church, most of whose bishops are either frauds or fanatics; a church, moreover, that dictates to the state, owns a quarter of the land in France yet pays no taxes, and all the while keeps our books and our minds as chained as a lunatic in a madhouse; all of it amounting to such greed, deceit, superstition, intolerance, stupidity, and fear, that it strangles every attempt at reform . . . need I go on? Oh, yes, and whatever the actual facts may be behind the affair of the diamond necklace, and whether it's the Comtesse de La Motte or the cardinal who's telling the most lies, and what the king and queen might have had to do with it. Monsieur Joubert, why waste time with silly, vulgar inventions about silly courtiers when you can make your point so much more effectively with the simple truth?"

"Monsieur Ravel," Joubert said promptly, "you're hired."

Aristide left Joubert's shop with five louis in a pouch in his pocket, as partial advance payment, and a request for three essays, of suitable length for duodecimo pamphlets, to be written on the state of France and what might be done about it—in a lively and entertaining manner, to be sure. He and Derville enjoyed a good dinner near the Palais-Royal before he headed southward again for the Left Bank.

A fine, frigid rain was falling by the time he crossed the Pont-Neuf, the Seine below him dark and choked with slabs of river ice. With money in his pocket, he had no great desire to return yet to his cold and dreary garret. A house farther east where half a dozen pretty, scantily clad women gazed out the windows and giggled coquettishly soon promised an evening's diversion.

Though he had never considered himself particularly handsome, neither had he lacked willing girls when the mood struck him; at present he was spending the night, once in a while, with a simple, cheerful laundress in the faubourg St. Marcel. But real Parisian sophistication—not to be found in laundresses, milliners, and shopgirls—was tempting, and a house in the Latin Quarter, he reasoned, could not possibly cost as much as one in the Palais-Royal.

The rain abruptly swelled to a sharp shower and he hastily decided which young lady most appealed to his fancy. As he reached the door he felt someone bump up against him, and with a queasy jolt in his belly, found his money pouch was gone.

"Hell!"

He caught sight of a fleeing figure at the end of the street and with a shout pursued him.

In the murky streets of Paris, Aristide soon discovered, people did not pay so much heed to shouts of "Stop, thief!" as they did elsewhere. Heads scarcely turned as he sprinted after the pickpocket, who was rapidly leading him into the ever darker, ever narrower and more tortuous streets that converged upon the seedy Place Maubert. Despite the cloudburst and the treacherous patches of dirty ice that lay here and there, Aristide increased his pace, seeing the distance between them diminish. He sped on, rounded a corner, and promptly cannoned into a shadowy figure in his path, sending them both tumbling to the cobblestones.

Aristide scrambled to his feet, with an oath and a muttered word of apology, and launched himself after the thief, but realized he had lost him. Disgusted, and dripping with slimy mud, he turned back to the stranger.

"What the devil do you think you're doing, you damned fool?" the other man roared. He made a halfhearted attempt to brush himself off. "What do you mean by blundering into a fellow and sending him into the mud? Look at my overcoat!"

With a qualm, Aristide recognized the voice and face as that of his former neighbor, Brasseur, the police inspector. "Forgive me, monsieur," he said, fetching Brasseur's hat from where it had rolled into a torrent of dirty water. "But I've just had my pocket picked, and I don't know my way about this quarter too well—"

"Don't I know you?" the inspector demanded, thrusting out a hand for his hat.

"Your ex-neighbor, monsieur: Ravel, formerly from the fifth-floor attic."

Brasseur peered at him through the gloom. "So you are. Put out any more fires lately, have you?"

"Only if they were on my person this evening," Aristide said, indicating his dripping coat. Brasseur stared at him for a moment and abruptly burst into a loud guffaw.

"Well, after all, what can you do but laugh?" he exclaimed. He shook himself and spat into the running sewer before them. "Damn these foul streets—Paris mud's like nothing else anywhere. This overcoat's pretty near ruined." The fact did not seem to upset him greatly, for his overcoat and three-cornered hat had seen better days long before their dip in the gutter.

"I would offer you what recompense I could," Aristide said, "if I hadn't just lost a month's worth of earnings—"

"Had your pocket picked, you said?" Brasseur interrupted him. "Hmm, where did it happen?"

"In front of a house on a street paralleling the river—Rue de la Huchette, I think it was."

"Oh, *that* house. Yes, the cutpurses often hang about there. They profit by the distractions, you know."

"That house," Aristide agreed, a trifle embarrassed. "It *was* distracting . . ."

"Come with me, lad," Brasseur told him, shaking the water out of his hat and clapping it firmly back on his head. "Let's see if we can't find your purse."

"But . . . he's long disappeared. I'm afraid my purse is gone for good."

"Maybe not, if you're lucky; maybe not. Come on, let's go back to Rue de la Huchette, the way you came."

Shrugging, Aristide surrendered to his companion's demands. He led the way back, as well as he could remember, along the route he had taken from the brothel. At last Brasseur paused before a church and stood studying it for a moment. "You passed this way, you say?" he asked. "You're sure?"

"Yes, I remember noticing the steps."

"Hmm. Well . . ." He prowled about the steps for a moment. "Not much in the way of hiding places here . . . no, wait!" Casting a glance about him like an eager hound, he strode into the alley between two of the tall, rickety houses that huddled about the church.

Aristide watched him, completely mystified. "Were you gaining on him before you ran into me instead?" Brasseur demanded, emerging once more from the depths of the alley.

"I think so; I'm not a bad runner."

"Ah, then I must be right . . . where the devil . . ."

"Monsieur the inspector," Aristide said, impatient to be on his way to the nearest guardpost, "I thank you for your trouble, but perhaps—"

"Got it!" he exclaimed. Beckoning Aristide on, Brasseur proceeded to the far side of the church, where a barred iron gate closed off a second alley between two sagging buildings. "There."

"There, what?"

"Your purse. Somewhere in the alley, just out of the light." He gestured at the lantern glimmering sullenly overhead from a rope stretched across the narrow street.

"What would my purse be doing in a locked alleyway?"

"Monsieur," he said patiently, "think it out. The pickpocket lifts your purse and runs this way. You follow him at a pretty fair pace, and get him thinking that you have a good chance of catching him and turning him over to the Guard, which means—with you present to testify against him—branding at best, or even hanging if he has a record. Maybe the sight of St. Séverin here"—he indicated the church—"set his guilty conscience to pricking him. So what does he do? Why, he gets rid of the evidence, of course—but in a way that, if he does lose you, he can return and retrieve the swag at any time he pleases. So he tosses your purse through the nearest iron gate, hoping no one else will find it before he has the chance to creep back here. After all," he added, "collaring him's no good if we don't find the loot on him."

"Isn't that quite a lot of 'maybe'?" Aristide said.

Brasseur sighed and planted his fists on his hips. "My dear young gentleman of letters, you ought to know people better if you're going to write about them. Human nature. All you need to do, to succeed as a thief-taker, is to know how they think, and be smarter than they are. Now if I'm wrong, and you've lost your money, I give you my word I'll make amends, and even forgive you muddying my clothes, by buying you supper."

"All right, then," Aristide said, not altogether convinced. He doffed his overcoat, coat, and hat, thrust them in Brasseur's arms, and clambered up and over the gate—just like climbing a tree in the abbey gardens at school, he thought.

It was black as Paris mud inside the alley. Not far beyond him, a rain gutter emptied itself from four stories above onto the cobbles. He felt his way along, carefully edging past the worst of the torrent from the waterspout, until his foot struck something soft. Eagerly he reached for it, only to find he was clutching a squashy, slimy object that could have been anything from a rotten melon (had it been the season for melons) to a sheep's stomach, or worse. He flung it away with a curse and continued on his quest.

It took him little time to find his purse, once he investigated the sides of the alley more thoroughly. He snatched it up, after ensuring that it was, indeed, a leather pouch and not another handful of offal, and to his pleased astonishment felt the familiar weight of four gold louis and a handful of silver ecus within. He turned back toward the gate, brandishing his prize overhead, and, giddy with his triumph, stepped directly into the path of the rain gutter.

3

The sole advantage of his icy drenching, Aristide thought, between curses, was that it instantly washed the greater part of the mud off him. Sputtering, he returned to the gate, climbed it with rather less speed than before, and dropped soggily to the pavement.

"Lord help us," Brasseur said, eyeing him as he pushed the lank, dripping hair from his eyes and shook himself. "You're a sorry sight, aren't you? Did you find your purse?"

"Thanks to you, Monsieur Brasseur."

"Hmm, that's all very well, but from the look of you I'd say I do owe you that supper after all, since you've spoiled your clothes. Come on, then. Papillon's cabaret isn't far, if Papillon can spare a seat beside the fire, and out of this damnable rain."

"Don't let me keep you from your own fireside," Aristide began, but Brasseur waved him away.

"Trust me, friend, with a three-year-old child just back home from the wet nurse, I'd much rather be sitting at somebody else's fireside!"

He led Aristide through the streets to a large establishment that combined the functions of wine shop, workingmen's café, and cheap eating-house. Aristide ordered half a bottle of good Burgundy wine for him, as amends for his dip in the gutter, and stepped in front of the fire to warm his own sodden backside.

At last, in the flickering firelight, he had a good look at his companion. Brasseur was a big man in his late thirties, two or three inches shorter than Aristide, but broad and muscular enough to make two of him. He must have been in the war at one time, Aristide thought, noting the scar—probably the work of a bayonet—that slashed from eyebrow to hairline, and another that had glanced across his jaw, seaming a face that had never been handsome but which radiated a stolid good humor.

"So, Monsieur Ravel," he inquired, when the wine arrived, "what part of the kingdom do you hail from?"

"From Bordeaux—"

"Bordeaux, eh?" he echoed him. "Thought I recognized the accent. We're countrymen, then, or almost—I'm from Libourne, myself."

"But I've been living in Paris for the past year."

"Pursuing a literary career," Brasseur concluded, shaking his head. He poured out a glass for each of them, despite Aristide's protestations. "Like forty thousand other ambitious young scribblers. What else is new, I wonder?"

Aristide took a cautious swallow of the Burgundy, savoring the warmth of it on such a frigid evening. He did not quite know what to say to Brasseur; one did not, as a rule, freely volunteer information to the police. Brasseur saved him the trouble of thinking of something to say by continuing.

"If you really want to make a living as a writer—what is it you're aiming for? Poetry, plays, novels? Or essays?"

"A little of each," Aristide confessed.

"Well, then, as I told you earlier, you ought to go out and study people more. You can't write successfully about them until you know why they do what they do. Now, you might have been wondering what I was doing in the back streets alone after dark?"

Aristide nodded and he continued. "To be sure, I was on my way home; but I generally take a roundabout route. See, we inspectors are each in charge of a district of Paris, but we also each concentrate on a particular category of police duties, and mine and that of three other fellows is crime. Criminals, vagabondage, thievery, arson, assault, murder . . . crimes against property and against persons . . . you get my drift. So as I said earlier, in order to ferret out the right people, you need to know them, to know how they think."

He took a swig from his glass, settled more comfortably into his chair, and went on. "I met a curious little fellow a couple of years ago, wandering the streets alone after midnight, and I was ready to take him in, because he looked suspicious to me, going about so late. But one of the other inspectors told me that he's a writer, a bit eccentric of course, writes naughty novels and such, and one of his favorite subjects is what he sees while he's strolling through the city at night."

"That wouldn't be Restif de la Bretonne?" Aristide said, surprised. "The author of *Les Contemporaines*, and so on?"

"That's the fellow. Well, the next time I ran into him, I struck up a conversation with him, and he said something to me I've never forgotten: 'I like to think of myself,' he said, 'as a student of mankind. I observe people, all manner of people . . . in the streets, in the lodging-houses, in the churches, and in the slums of the faubourgs . . . I observe them in the gilded salons of St. Germain, when I get the chance . . . I watch them in the workshops, at the carnivals, at the cabarets, at the processions on holy days, and in the middle of the Pont-Neuf. I observe their joys, their woes, their vices, their virtues, their amusements, their disasters—in short, everything. You'll never learn so much about mankind and all the aspects of human nature, monsieur, as from taking a stroll through Paris between six in the evening and six in the morning on any night of the year.' And he was right. It's the best way to learn about people, and knowing about people is the most useful tool in your bag of tricks when you're trying to catch them out at their misdemeanors. Or, I expect, when you're trying to write novels about them, eh?"

He stretched and brushed some of the drying mud from his culotte and stockings. "That's better . . . what about you? Are you drying off? I'd hate to be the cause of your ruining your only suit of clothes."

"It'll do," Aristide said ruefully, glancing down at the spots and creases in the woolen fabric that had already been fading from black to a dingy dark green.

"You'd better take some of that chink in your purse, lad, before it gets lifted again, and bespeak yourself a new suit." Brasseur leaned forward and shook a finger at him. "It's high time. I may not dress fashionably myself, but I've lived in Paris long enough to know when a coat is two years behind the times."

"It's not two years behind the times," Aristide retorted, "it's at least half a dozen years behind the times."

"Touché! Well, something in black wears better than most, doesn't it. I should know. Could it be you're following the useful vogue of always claiming to be in mourning for some deceased foreign royalty or other?"

"I wear black by choice," Aristide said stiffly. "For my parents. I care little for fashion . . . and even less for the opinion of spoiled, shallow fools who can think of nothing else."

"For your parents?" Brasseur said. "Forgive me. My sympathies, monsieur." He fell silent for a moment. Aristide took a few more sips of wine and, deciding his coat and culotte were as dry as they were likely to get, pulled out a chair.

"Ravel," Brasseur said suddenly. "From Bordeaux, you said?"

"Yes," Aristide said, with a chill feeling in his vitals that Brasseur knew exactly who he was. He glanced about, expecting all eyes in the smoky café to be fixed greedily upon him, but the workmen at the tables and benches nearby were absorbed in their wine, their card games, and their pipes.

"Relation to Étienne Ravel, by any chance? The fellow who shot his wife and her lover and created a thundering scandal? Twenty years ago it must have been."

Aristide seated himself and took a long swallow of wine, without looking at Brasseur. "Eighteen years ago," he said at last. "He was my father."

"Hard luck on you," Brasseur rumbled. "You must have been pretty young."

"I was nine."

"Only child?"

"I have a sister. She wasn't yet three when it happened; she remembers nothing. Except, of course, what it's like to grow up as the child of an adulteress and of a double murderer who died on the scaffold. That, neither of us will ever forget."

He stole a quick glance at Brasseur. He was so accustomed to seeing people shrink away from him, as if they might catch some foul disease, that he was surprised when the other man said nothing, only shrugged and felt in his pockets for a pipe and tobacco pouch.

"It must have left you with a few scores to settle," Brasseur said at last, after filling the pipe, lighting it with an ember from the fire, and puffing gently at it for a moment.

"A few."

"Mm."

"Have you learned who lit the fire at St. Médard?" Aristide inquired, eager to change the subject.

"Ah, that . . . no, we've had no luck. There've been half a dozen more, you know, since then. Middle of the night, early morning always. All on the Left Bank."

"I heard some commotion a few nights ago, near Clamart."

"You're living in that quarter now?"

"Rue de la Muette. It's quite disgusting."

"Yes, Clamart was the latest. Whoever it was, he climbed the wall and set a fire in the middle of the cemetery . . . and then he daubed some of the walls and a cross or two with blood—which I hope came from the slaughterhouses nearby—and threw a few bones on the fire, for good measure. *Not* pigs' bones."

"Good God."

"Well, if the churchyards are so full of rotten stinking corpses that you've bones lying about, falling out of the charnels and sticking out of the ground in front of you, what do they expect? Some madman comes along, gets ideas, and thinks he'll do a spot of devil worship or what have you—it began on All Hallows' Eve, which is suggestive. Or it may just be people who've got it in for the Church. Heathens and freethinkers, you know."

"What do you mean by 'heathens'?" Aristide said.

"Like I told you the other day, there are a lot of funny people about. And in the big cities, they disappear in the crowd; a lunatic or a troublemaker'll stick out a mile away in some little village, but in Paris, he's just one of the mob. And even the aristocracy's joining the fun these days, playing at outlandish rituals and secret societies; Freemasons, you know, and folk even madder than that." Brasseur shrugged again. "Ah, well, there wasn't much damage done. Fire's soon put out and the mess scrubbed away. Trouble is, folk who get away with such nonsense a few times, they keep on with it."

"But the more often he does it, the more likely you are to catch him in the act."

"Yes, indeed." Brasseur suddenly grinned at him. "And we *will* catch him, of course." He sucked a few more times at his pipe and at length knocked it out in the hearth and pocketed it, with a sigh. "Well, I should have been home an hour ago, and my wife'll be wondering where I've got to. I'll have to come up with some convincing story for her."

"Perhaps you pursued a pickpocket, caught him, and had to drag him off to the Guard and make a report."

"Yes, that's pretty likely, isn't it?"

They exchanged glances and Brasseur chuckled. "Are you on your way home yourself, then? I'll go with you as far as Le Plessis; we may as well fend off the footpads together "

4

Aristide saw nothing more of Brasseur over the next few days, but the following Tuesday a brisk knocking roused him not long after the winter dawn. He opened the door to a rough-looking, black-clad man whom he did not recognize.

"Monsieur Ravel? I work for Inspector Brasseur, and he said you're to come with me."

Aristide stared at him, rubbing the sleep from his eyes. "Are you sure you have the right man? What have I done?"

"You're not under arrest, monsieur," the man said woodenly. "But Inspector Brasseur believes you might be of some help to him."

"Let me dress, then." He broke the skin of ice in the washbasin, splashed some frigid water on his face and hands, and pulled on his clothes, mystified. Brasseur would just have to find him sleepy-eyed and unshaven, he thought grudgingly. Whatever could the fellow want from him?

In his shabby black suit, he realized he must have looked as if he were merely one more police official. A few early-going laborers gave the two of them sour glances as they climbed into a waiting fiacre; in the opinion of many, particularly in the poorer quarters, the police existed to make trouble for ordinary folk who wanted only to be let alone. Let their house catch fire, however, Aristide mused, or let them be cheated at the horse market or learn that their unmarried daughter was expecting, and they would avail themselves of the services of the police quickly enough.

The morning was foggy and gray, with an icy breeze that bit through his thin overcoat. The fiacre rattled northward, toward the heart of the city. Aristide recognized the dome of the Sorbonne as they passed. At last they alighted near one of the bridges to the Île de la Cité, by the high iron gates of a small, dismal churchyard. Six- and seven-story apartment houses rose up all around the church, the walls facing the cemetery blank and windowless to keep the inhabitants from emptying their chamber pots onto consecrated ground. Below them, a narrow rectangle of gabled stone arcades, the charnels, surrounded the half acre of stony earth.

The gates, usually chained and padlocked at that early hour of the morning, stood open. A ragged beggar woman crouched beside them, mutely thrusting out an open palm.

"Where are we?" Aristide said, dodging the beggar.

"Churchyard of St. André des Arts," said his escort, stepping back and gesturing him inside. "If you please, monsieur." Aristide glanced dubiously at him, but the man merely pointed toward a few figures moving about.

He carefully picked his way forward across the uneven ground, past dog droppings, limp tufts of last summer's weeds, a few yellowed bones poking through the frozen soil, and a handful of mossy, weather-beaten stone crosses and monuments that leaned drunkenly, a fine glaze of ice glistening on them. The usual pungent smell of decay was absent here, though the oldest cemeteries of Paris were disastrously overcrowded from five or six hundred years of constant use; in the past century, they had been packing in the burials far too close to the surface of the rancid earth. This churchyard, Aristide thought, small, central, and ancient as it was, had probably been closed to burials for decades for reasons of public health.

Brasseur's voice rose nearby and he moved a few paces closer, curious.

"See, I don't give a damn whether you're in league with a band of thieves or with every pervert in Paris," Brasseur roared at a glowering sexton, thrusting his police card into the man's face. "Last chance: Who paid you to leave the gate unlocked last night?"

"I didn't mean no harm," the man said sullenly. "It wasn't no thief. Thought he wanted to meet one of his fancy boys here, didn't I? Thought maybe he wanted someplace quieter for his indecent doings than the public gardens."

"You thought he wanted to arrange a tryst in a cemetery in the middle of the night, did you, when it's been cold enough all month to freeze your balls off?"

"I didn't know and I didn't care. I've got four brats to feed, and the price of bread's gone up half again what it was a month ago." The sexton jerked a thumb backward at the stone monuments. "And they're past caring what goes on at night. Where's the harm?"

"Describe him."

"It was dark. Didn't get a good look at him."

"Well? You must have seen something."

"He wore a cloak and a wide-brimmed hat."

"What else? Young, old, tall, short, what?"

"Tallish, youngish, sounded high-class."

"High-class clothes?"

"Couldn't tell under the cloak. He didn't want to be seen, see?"

"When?"

"Day before yesterday, in the evening. He came by as I was locking the gates and said there was forty sous in it for me if I'd do him a favor by forgetting to do it next day. I lock the churchyard up at sunset, like the law tells us to—"

"Except when somebody greases your palm to forget," Brasseur finished for him. "All right, get out of here. And if I hear you've been forgetting to lock the gates again, I'll have your skin."

The sexton shambled off toward the church, spitting behind a tombstone as Brasseur turned away. A moment later Brasseur saw Aristide and approached him, offering a hand, a silent subinspector clutching a notebook dogging his footsteps. "Good morning, Monsieur Ravel. It's kind of you to come at this hour."

"Your agent gave me little choice, monsieur the inspector," Aristide said. "What is it you want from me?"

"Ah. Well, to be honest, I wanted your opinion on something. You're an educated man . . ."

"I don't know how I could help you," Aristide said, looking about. Brasseur pointed toward the rows of covered charnels, fourteen feet high, that formed the walls of the cemetery. Every Parisian churchyard that was still admitting burials excavated hundreds of decades-old bones each year from the old mass graves and systematically moved them into the charnels, to make room for the fresh corpses of the city's poor that soon refilled the twenty-foot-deep trenches.

"There, monsieur. The western side. Maybe you could give your opinion as to what the devil those signs mean?"

Aristide followed him to the charnels. Before him, roughly daubed on the stone arch in dull reddish brown, was a symbol he thought he recognized.

"Would you know what that is?" Brasseur inquired, behind him.

"It . . . it's a compass and square, I believe," he said. "It's a symbol the Freemasons use, or so I've heard."

"You're not a Freemason yourself, monsieur?"

"No. I'm not one for ceremonies and rituals."

"A Masonic compass and square," Brasseur repeated, jotting down a few words in a small notebook as the subinspector began furiously scribbling his own notes. "I thought so, too, but I might have been mistaken. Come to think of it, that fire at St. Médard, it was laid out in something like a hollow square, but it could have been that compass-and-square pattern just as well, with the two sets of arms overlapping, don't you think?"

Aristide thought about it, surprised, and at last nodded.

"That's very helpful, monsieur," Brasseur continued. "Those Freemasons, they don't often like the police, you know, and they wouldn't spare the time of day for the likes of me. What about that, then, monsieur?"

Aristide followed his gaze and discovered, to his shock, a five-pointed star laid out on the ground, a crude circle ringing it, the lines composed of long human bones. "Good God!" Irresistibly he raised his eyes to the open charnel behind it. Near the peak of the roof, it was obvious the neatly stacked bones had been disturbed.

"Would you say that's a Masonic symbol, too, monsieur?" Brasseur said.

"I . . . I believe so. A pentagram. Monsieur, as I said, I'm no Mason. Wouldn't it be more useful to ask a genuine Freemason for his opinion, or a scholar well versed in ancient mysticism and so on?"

"Maybe, maybe not. If a Mason is behind this nasty bit of work, they won't be too willing to lend us a hand, will they? What I hear is, they protect their own." He turned about and gestured Aristide onward. "One more thing, monsieur."

Aristide followed him and the secretary to a nearby section of the charnels that was clear of bones but crowded with several uniformed guards of the city watch. The arcade reminded him strangely of the Palais-Royal and he glanced away, fixing his gaze on a battered old stone cross bearing the nearly illegible name of some noble family that had probably died out a century or two before.

"Here, monsieur. If you'd just take a look at this and tell me what you think."

Steeling himself for another macabre display, Aristide turned back to the charnel. At a word from Brasseur, the men moved aside to reveal a rough square of cloth on the ground. Brasseur strode forward and with a single swift movement flung aside the sheet.

"Any ideas?"

Aristide stared. Before him lay, not dry bones, but the sprawled, supine body of a man, his throat cut, shirt drenched in blood.

Though he wanted to look away, Aristide's gaze was drawn irresistibly to the wound, gaping obscenely like a vast grin, and the severed vessels of the neck. After an instant, he spun about, pressing his hand to his mouth.

"For God's sake!" he exclaimed, after drawing a deep breath and deciding he was not, after all, going to be sick. "Was that necessary?"

Brasseur said nothing, but gazed at him, meeting his eyes. Aristide stared back, indignant. After a moment, Brasseur looked away, sighed, and muttered to himself, "Ah, well, it was worth a try."

"What was worth—" Aristide began. Suddenly the meaning of it all—Brasseur's bringing him there, his casual questioning, his sudden revealing of the corpse, and his searching gaze—became clear to him. "You bastard," he said, before remembering it was not wise to insult the police. "You think *I* did this, don't you?"

Slowly Brasseur nodded. "It crossed my mind."

"I never—"

"What I said about there being a lot of funny sorts about," Brasseur calmly interrupted him, "freethinkers and such . . . well, they're usually young, educated, thwarted fellows like yourself, with a lot of ambition and nowhere to go, who have a bone to pick—if you'll excuse the expression—with the folk in charge. And often they're Freemasons, even if they joined only to make the right connections and find a patron. With you so handy at one of the fires, and living right in the quarter near a couple of them, and then what you told me about your father—I thought I'd keep my eye on you."

A frigid breeze gusted across the cemetery and Aristide shouldered himself more snugly into his overcoat, feeling a chill from more than the breeze. "Because I might hold a grudge against the Church and the king."

"That's it, monsieur."

"And now you don't think I do?"

"Oh, no, lad, I'm pretty sure you do. But I'm pretty sure, also, that you didn't kill that fellow. You see, Monsieur Ravel," he continued pleasantly, turning away from the corpse, "when you have your suspicions of somebody and you put him right in front of what you think he's done, if he really did do it he usually reacts in one of two ways. He either flinches back and changes color and can't help looking guilty, because he thinks we know everything and we're just about to nab him; or else he smirks and looks terribly pleased with himself, because, like most criminals, he's a conceited little prick, and he thinks we're fools and that he's going to get away with it."

"And I did neither."

"That's right."

"I might be one of the few who can manage not to betray themselves either way."

"Yes," Brasseur said, "you might be, at that. But I'm willing to give you the benefit of the doubt. Just for the record, though, where were you last night around midnight?"

"Arriving home from the Café Manoury," Aristide said promptly. "I left at half past eleven."

"And you live down by La Salpêtrière, don't you? That's a good half-hour walk. Any proof you got home when you say you did? Anybody see you who knows you?"

"No, of course not; not at that hour."

Brasseur eyed him. "Well, it's no worse an alibi than I'd expect. Now if you were suddenly to give up your lodgings and disappear, I'd begin to wonder. But if you stay put and don't give me any cause to ask questions, then I think we can afford to let you run along home now."

"I'm free to go?"

"Lord, yes. Or—wait—I'd been meaning to ask you about something else. Know if the skull and crossbones means anything besides a pirate flag?"

"I've no idea. Why?"

"Because those little heaps of bones," Brasseur said, pointing to the bones at the corpse's head and feet, "got dislodged while those fools from the Guard were tramping around the place, looking for a murderer who'd been gone for hours—"

"When . . . did it happen?"

"The sexton found him at about five, but he was already stone-cold. Sometime in the middle of the night, I gather. I'd guess those bones were arranged at first more like a pattern of a skull and crossbones, wouldn't you say?"

"It's possible."

"Another Masonic symbol, maybe. But if you say you don't know . . . well, you've no need to stand about in this miserable cold. Get along home."

Aristide took three steps toward the gate before pausing and glancing over his shoulder. Something about the horrid corpse fascinated him, despite his qualms. "Who is he?" he said suddenly. "Do you know?"

"Our victim here?" Brasseur said, half amused at his sudden curiosity. "No. Hasn't any papers on him, and he's been robbed, maybe by the murderer, or else some passing lowlife saw the open gate and just seized his moment to strip him down to his waistcoat."

The scavengers would probably have taken the shirt and waistcoat, too, Aristide thought, if they had not been so sodden with blood.

"No overcoat, hat, pocket-book, jewelry, peruke, or shoes," Brasseur continued. "Those are the first things to go, of course, since they're easy to lift." He sighed. "They got the coat and culotte, too, even though it takes a bit more time and effort to undress a corpse. But what's left seems to indicate a bourgeois with some means, or a gentleman; that should make it easier. Eventually he'll be missed, and his family, if he's got any, will come looking for him at the morgue. If he's from out of town, then heaven help us. Might never be identified."

After the first shock had passed, Aristide found he could look at the corpse, though he avoided glancing at the bloody throat. As Brasseur had mentioned, the man wore no wig, coat, breeches, or shoes and the sight of his underlinen and stockinged feet seemed oddly pathetic on such a cold morning.

"Why . . ."

"Why kill him? I've no more idea than you do, monsieur. Though I'd make a guess that he interrupted our madman in the middle of his deviltry." He pointed at a small pile of kindling that lay at the base of one of the old stone crosses. "See the flask there? It's half full of lamp oil. Looks as if the fellow who's been setting these fires was just about to light another, and the other man came to the churchyard and stumbled on him, and got killed for his pains."

"But why slit his throat?" Aristide objected. "Surely, if you're interrupted while you're setting a fire, and you have to stop the man before he raises the alarm, you're not going to take the time to pull out a knife from beneath your coat. You'd snatch up the first thing at hand, a stick of wood, say, and knock him senseless with it. And you wouldn't kill him, necessarily. Cutting his throat seems . . . excessive."

"Unless he recognized you, of course," said Brasseur.

"All right, unless he knew you and recognized you. But still, you'd want to act quickly. He could be gone by the time you got hold of your knife. And if this madman is an educated man, as you suggest, then he's not of the class who would normally carry a knife at all. A pocket pistol, perhaps, or even a sword, but not a knife."

"You've a point there," Brasseur conceded. He gestured to the secretary to continue taking notes. "All right, then, say it happened your way. You're kneeling over a pile of kindling and fiddling with a tinderbox or a pot of hot coals. Stranger walks in and bumps up against you and demands to know what the devil you're doing on top of his family monument."

"Why does he walk in? What would a bourgeois be doing in a graveyard in January in the middle of the night?"

"You're suggesting they planned to meet here?"

"Especially if one of them bribed the sexton to leave the gate unlocked after dark."

"That might have just been to make it easier for himself."

"Were there gates left unlocked at the other cemeteries, or do you think someone climbed the wall?"

"No, he seems to have climbed the wall the rest of the time," said Brasseur. "Go on: You're the madman and the other fellow sees you. Maybe he was just passing by and noticed the flame, and came in to satisfy his curiosity."

"I jump to my feet," Aristide said, suiting the action to the word, "and grab whatever's nearest. A stick, my firepot, a broken piece of stone . . ."

"Or even a bone, I daresay."

"Yes, or a bone . . . and I go for him. He mustn't escape to raise the alarm and get me arrested. I take a good swing at him and perhaps we struggle for a moment." He examined the stony ground and found a few blurred, trampled footprints amid the pebbles and dead weeds. "Were those there, or did your men make a mess of the place?"

"A bit of both, I expect," Brasseur said, nodding. "Go on, then."

"We struggle. Finally I get the better of him and stun him with a good blow to the head." He paused. "Though if all I want to do is make my escape . . ."

"Then, as you said, why cut his throat?"

"Why, indeed, unless I have some other motive?"

"Well," Brasseur said, "you're absolutely right about what happened. The police surgeon was here about half an hour ago, and what he told us was, once you took the medical Latin rubbish out of it, that the man had bled to death, but he had a fine bloody bump on the side of his head that would probably have knocked him out before his throat was cut." He stopped and looked hard at Aristide. "You may be too clever for your own good, Monsieur Ravel."

"If I were the guilty party," Aristide retorted, "do you think I'd hang about, explaining to you what must have happened?"

"You might," said Brasseur, "if you were one of those smug fellows who thinks the police are fools. But," he added glumly, "I don't think you are. For one thing, the man who committed this murder would have got some blood on him, and here you are still wearing your only suit of clothes, with no bloodstains to be seen."

"Thank you . . . I think."

"So that leaves us," Brasseur mused, "with the alternative. The victim wasn't murdered because he had the bad luck to stumble over our fire-setting madman; the madman meant to do for him all along. That would fit with the unlocked gate. This time, he wanted the gates unlocked so that the other man could get in without any fuss. Yes, I think the meeting was prearranged, and our man knocked the victim out and then cut his throat to be sure."

"Or what if," Aristide said abruptly, "the dead man was actually the man who was setting the fires?"

Brasseur wheeled about and stared at him for a moment. "Death of the devil. Never thought of it that way. You're saying he could have been killed to stop him from setting his fires and smearing his daubs on the church walls."

"Why not?"

"That throws a whole new light on it, doesn't it? Looking at it the other way round, if these symbols are Masonic, like you suggested, then either he's doing it because he's a fanatical Mason and free-thinker and hates the Church and the king and everything they stand for—"

"Or else he hates the Freemasons and wants to throw suspicion on them, destroy their reputation, brand them as sacrilegious heathens," Aristide finished for him. "And either way, other Masons might have killed him in order to defend their reputation."

Brasseur grinned and clapped him on the shoulder.

"You've a fine head on your shoulders, Ravel! We could use you in the police."

"Thank you, no. I have other plans." And, Aristide thought, they did not include hanging about a gory corpse in a churchyard on an icy January morning. "Good day, monsieur."

"Right, you're going to be the next Voltaire, aren't you."

Aristide heard Brasseur softly chuckling behind him as he bowed and strode out to the street.

5

Aristide met Derville in the afternoon for a few hours of dining and sightseeing at the Palais-Royal. He returned to his room late in the evening and, with a sigh, dropped onto his bed. He had had more wine than he knew was sensible, and wanted only to lie back in the darkness and settle his stomach after an overrich supper. His faintly rancorous musings about Derville's patronizing generosity were abruptly cut short, however, when someone rapped on the door.

His first thought was to ignore the caller, for it was past eleven o'clock. Few people had unexpected callers after ten o'clock, for by law the street doors were locked every night at that hour, to keep fleeing criminals from bolting into the nearest house, and so late a visitor was probably his landlord with some demand or other. But the rapping sounded again, rattling his aching head, and he dragged himself to his feet and unlatched the door.

Brasseur stood on the landing, large, solid, and apparently immovable.

"Could we have a talk?"

Aristide stared. "What?"

"I'd like to talk."

Brasseur, he supposed, must have used his authority as a police inspector to get himself admitted at such an hour, and to demand and receive a candle to light himself up the stairs, too. "Look, this isn't the best time," he began, but Brasseur strolled in past him, set the candlestick down amid the litter of papers on the writing table, pulled out the chair, and seated himself.

"You're a clever fellow, Ravel."

"So you said." Aristide eyed him, wary. What on earth did the man want from him?

"As I said, we could use a man like you in the police."

"And I said I had other plans. I've no interest in a career of patrolling the streets and reminding tradesmen to sweep in front of their shops. Monsieur Brasseur, is this really necessary? It's late, and I'm a little unwell—"

"There are other ways of working for the police besides strutting about giving orders," Brasseur said. "Have you thought about that?"

"What do you mean?"

"A police force lives on information. Two-thirds of the people who work for the police never put on a black suit or fill out an official report."

Aristide knew immediately what he meant. Covert informers, often nicknamed *mouches*—flies—were the backbone of the Paris police; they supplied everything from court gossip to intelligence about the sordid doings of the pickpockets, housebreakers, confidence artists, quacks, and pimps who swarmed from the filthy and teeming warrens of central Paris to profit from the weaknesses of their more prosperous neighbors.

"Monsieur Brasseur, are you suggesting I should become a police spy?"

He smiled slightly. "What would you say if I did suggest it?"

"I'd tell you to go to the devil, of course." The average Parisian grudgingly tolerated the police, who kept the city running more or less smoothly, but detested their spies.

"Oh, I've no doubt you would. But you know what they say, that the police know everything about everybody. Why, they even know a bit about *you*. How do you think I got your address?"

"Me?" Aristide echoed him, the queasy feeling in his belly abruptly swelling. "What are you talking about?"

"I went and looked you up at the office of Control of the Book Trade, Monsieur Ravel. They keep dossiers on men like you, the hungry young literary fellows, once you've attracted a little attention." He extracted his notebook from a pocket and glanced through it. "Nothing much here . . . they seem to think you're pretty harmless. Though I copied this bit down: 'Ravel, Aristide-Chrétien-Marie, native of Bordeaux, son of a felon broken on the wheel for murdering his adulterous wife and her lover. Physiognomy tall, thin; hair and eyes dark brown; aspect not unhandsome, though habitually with a dour and sarcastic demeanor. Most recent known address a shoddy sixth-floor attic on Rue de la Muette, near La Salpêtrière. Reported to be a malicious and mediocre hack writer—' "

" 'Malicious and mediocre hack'?" Aristide repeated indignantly.

" '—suspected of producing various indecent and seditious writings for known publishers and disseminators of illegal works.' " Brasseur closed the notebook and beamed at Aristide. "What do you think?"

Suddenly the full import of what Brasseur had recited to him sank in, and Aristide abruptly sat down on the bed. "Are you arresting me?"

"Good Lord, no. Just making a little proposition. You see," Brasseur continued when Aristide said nothing, "I really do want a fellow like you on my side. Our conversation this morning proved to me that you've a talent for investigation. Now investigating crimes is only a portion of what the police do, of course, and sometimes it gets short shrift. My superior, that's Monsieur Le Roux, the commissaire, he's a good honest gentleman and all, but he's getting along—he's been commissaire for twenty years—and his talents run more in the administrative line. He doesn't like criminal matters, unless they're the easy ones like a vagrant stealing sheets off the washlines, or a drunk beating up his girlfriend in the wine shop, in front of half a dozen witnesses. A thorny problem like this morning's murder, with peculiar evidence and no eyewitnesses, is going to put him completely out of countenance, and I'd like to make it nice and clear for him when I finally put the case in front of him."

He paused and Aristide gathered his wits sufficiently to ask a question. "You want me to become a spy—"

"Not a spy, monsieur. A subinspector, say. Working openly with me."

"—to help you investigate this murder?"

"That's it precisely, Monsieur Ravel. I knew you were quick on the uptake. I thought I'd seize my opportunity before Delahaye, that's the inspector in charge of the book trade, saw you were an educated fellow who'd be useful to him, and nabbed you for himself."

"And what if I refuse?"

"Well," Brasseur said placidly, "in that case, I'm afraid I might feel it was my duty to alert Delahaye that this particular 'malicious and mediocre hack writer' was continuing to produce seditious writings. Which you are, of course, aren't you? A bit of filth about Antoinette and the cardinal in bed together pays a whole lot better than getting an ode respectably printed in the *Mercure*."

What choice do I have? Aristide thought. Loathsome as his present room was, he had no desire to find himself in new lodgings in the Bastille. He nodded and Brasseur grinned.

"Splendid. We start tomorrow morning. You know where I live."

Wednesday, 11 January

The house where Brasseur lived, and where Aristide had lived until some months before, was notable chiefly for the sign in the shape of an enormous boot that hung out over the street; a cobbler's shop occupied the rear of the building, behind the two small ground-floor rooms that served as the inspector's headquarters. Aristide arrived at Brasseur's apartment at half past seven and soon learned that the inspector, while he might be a redoubtable enemy, was a congenial enough ally. After a quick breakfast of bread, butter, and strong coffee that he insisted Aristide share, devoured under the suspicious eye of his plump wife, he led the way downstairs to his office. Aristide waited while he glanced over a few reports, briefly conferred with a subinspector and a seedy-looking individual who had "spy" written all over him, and at last led him out toward Rue St. Jacques, where he flagged down a fiacre.

"The Châtelet," he told the driver, and gestured Aristide inside. Aristide found a spot on the grimy leather seat that was not too lumpy and looked at Brasseur, beside him.

"What's at the Châtelet? That's where the police courts are, isn't it?"

"Yes, but we don't want those. We're going to the Basse-Geôle de la Seine."

"The what?"

"The morgue, Ravel. The attendants might be able to tell us a bit more about our corpse. The first thing you need to know in a case of murder is, of course, the victim's identity."

Aristide did not fancy reexamining the body from the churchyard, but knew he had no choice and said nothing.

"Then you need to learn who benefits from his death," Brasseur went on as the cab got under way. "People kill other people for just a few essential reasons: gain—that's the most common. Gain covers everything from a bandit who shoots a traveler to rob him, to some young wastrel poisoning his father for the inheritance because the old man's taking too long to die. Then there's jealousy—" He stopped short and glanced at Aristide, not without sympathy. "I expect you know all about that."

Aristide did not reply and Brasseur continued. "Also revenge, self-preservation . . . those are pretty simple to understand . . . and love."

"Love?"

"Oh, yes."

"Wouldn't that fall under 'jealousy'?" Aristide said, resolutely thrusting away the sudden sharp memory of the smell of gunpowder, and his mother's body, and blood.

"No, I mean love. Jealousy is just a form of selfishness; it's some-body who can't bear the knowledge that he's lost something he thought was his. But murder for love . . . that's a person acting com-pletely against his usual nature because he has such an intense love for somebody, or something. If what he loves is an idea, then you call it a murder for principles, but it's all the same in the end. Gain, jeal-ousy, revenge, self-preservation, love," he repeated, ticking them off on his fingers. "Remember that."

The cab made its way down the long, congested stretch of Rue St. Jacques, and across the Seine directly to the forbidding gray bulk of the Châtelet.

Brasseur paid off the cabman and strode down a dim, chilly public footpath, past a few laborers trudging with handcarts, to the magis-trates' stairway, which led up to the judicial chambers at the heart of the medieval castle. Opposite the foot of the staircase, he paused at an inconspicuous door and gestured Aristide inside. "You might want a handkerchief handy."

The sickly, butcher-shop odor of slowly decaying flesh rose to Aris-tide's nostrils as they entered the Basse-Geôle and a taciturn clerk ad-mitted them past an iron grille. He fumbled for a handkerchief and pressed it to his nose. Brasseur, he noticed, seemed unaffected. He guessed the other man had visited the place in far warmer weather and thus was inured to what must have been, for him, only a mild stink.

Aristide followed him down a flight of stairs to a frigid, dank cellar with a single small window. Somewhere in a corner, beyond a dozen stone slabs where a few sheeted figures lay, he thought he saw a rat scuttle past.

"You're here for yesterday's murder, I suppose?" the attendant inquired, appearing from the shadows. Aristide tried not to stare, for the man was all one might expect the concierge of a morgue to be, pale and hollow-cheeked, with the long, doleful face of a bloodhound, made yet more bizarre by a gloomy, pop-eyed gaze.

"Morning, Bouille," said Brasseur. "Yes, that's the one. What can you tell us?"

"He had a contusion on his head but died of the throat wound, bled to death, probably within a few seconds of the attack. No surprises there. Let me see, he was found at half past five yesterday morning, and was already quite cold . . . though that's nothing astonishing, in this brutal weather we're having . . . I'd say he was killed between, oh, some time after sunset the night before, say nine o'clock, and the small hours of the morning, judging from the rigor mortis, just as your police surgeon said. Have you found the weapon?"

"No."

"It was an ordinary sharp blade of some kind that made a clean cut, a kitchen knife or a hunting knife, or even a razor . . . nothing you couldn't find in half the households in Paris, I fear. Angle of the cut indicates a right-handed murderer standing behind him, which isn't of much help to you."

"A man, of course," Brasseur muttered.

"Oh, yes, absolutely. With this knock on the head, the victim was probably on the ground or on his knees, and the murderer had to pull him partially upright to reach his throat, and I doubt a woman would have had the strength for that; or else he was standing or staggering, dazed, and in that case the murderer must have been at least the same height as his victim, or ideally a little taller. Definitely a man's crime."

"He'd have gotten blood on his clothes, wouldn't he?"

"Undoubtedly; the great vessels would—"

"But not very much," Aristide said, "if he was standing behind his victim. Wouldn't the victim's body itself have shielded him from most of it?"

Brasseur abruptly strode to Bouille and, to the attendant's surprised indignation, seized him from behind and mimed cutting his throat. "Yes, I see what you mean. A bit of blood spraying on your cuffs and sleeves, maybe, but not much more than that. Strip off your coat, toss it in an alley where some beggar will find it and disappear with it, and there goes any evidence."

"So, a man who can afford to throw away an otherwise wearable coat."

"I wasn't done," Bouille said, with a cough and a glare at Brasseur. He reached beneath the long apron he wore, brought out a pocket flask and took a swallow from it, then gestured them to one of the tables and drew back the sheet covering the nude corpse. "First, have a look at that."

Aristide reluctantly peered over Brasseur's shoulder, trying to avoid looking at the broad bandage loosely wrapped about the man's throat. Brasseur whistled.

"Now how did we miss that?"

A compass and square, crude but unmistakable, had been slashed into the man's chest. Aristide winced but forced himself to take a closer look. The cuts were not deep, though they looked as raw as meat on a butcher's counter.

"I don't imagine anybody looked beyond the slit throat when they examined him," Bouille said. "You know Dr. Touret never takes more than five minutes when it's outside and the weather's bad. These cuts were undoubtedly done after he was dead. The murderer pulled open his shirt—which was already soaked with blood, of course—slashed him, and laced him up again."

Brasseur glanced at Aristide. "Freemasons again. And it looks like the matter's getting very, very personal. Would *you* slash something like this into a dead man's flesh?"

"God, no."

"Well, then. Something nasty's going on here."

"There's something else," said the concierge. The pocket flask reappeared and he took another generous swallow. "Dr. Touret didn't put this down in his report, either."

He unknotted the linen bandage tied about the corpse's head to keep the mouth from falling open, and gently pried the jaws apart. "I didn't find this until the rigor mortis began to pass off. Look."

Gingerly they peered into the dead man's mouth. Aristide saw, at first, nothing but a set of good white teeth, missing one toward the side, until he realized he was looking at only a stump of raw flesh where the tongue ought to have been. He jerked backward and quickly pressed his handkerchief once again over his mouth and nose, praying he would not be sick.

"His tongue's been cut out?" Brasseur said incredulously. "What sort of madman would do that?"

"Lord knows," said Bouille. "Though that, also, was done after he was dead. I don't suppose you found it?"

"The rats probably got it." Shaking his head, he turned to Aristide. "Are you all right there, Ravel?" Aristide nodded and Brasseur turned once again to Bouille. "Got a report on the clothing and effects? Any clue at all to who he is?"

The attendant took another swallow from his flask and dolefully shook his head as he handed Brasseur a sheet of paper covered with tiny, precise handwriting. "Only the obvious. He's a well-nourished man of about forty to forty-five, average height and build, hair medium brown turning to gray, slightly receding hairline, eyes brown, no significant identifying marks or scars aside from one missing tooth in the left side of the upper jaw. His clothes and the state of his apparent health would suggest he's a well-off bourgeois: a merchant or manufacturer or a professional man. Not the sort that usually ends up here."

"Corpses from the river, mostly," Brasseur said, in response to Aristide's curious glance. "Accidents with the dock workers, the boatmen and bargemen, people watering horses that get out of control . . . and suicides. Some in better condition than others."

"We had just a single leg in, a few days ago," Bouille announced, to no one in particular, with a glance toward the far side of the cellar. "From upriver, apparently. No one's claimed it yet."

Brasseur ignored him and glanced through the report, abruptly pausing to tap a finger on the paper. "Let's see his things."

Bouille vanished into an adjoining room and returned, clothing draped over one arm. "Clothes, what was left of them, of good quality. Underlinen, new thread stockings, shirt, waistcoat, cravat. Whoever stole his outer garments must have left the rest because they were worthless; of course the shirt and waistcoat, and especially the cravat, received the full flow of blood from the throat . . ."

Aristide made himself look more closely at the dead man's hands. They were clean and well kept. A pale band, slightly chafed, around the little finger of his right hand indicated that he had habitually worn a ring.

"Well," he said at last, "I don't know who or what he was, but I can guess what he wasn't. He wasn't a writer, a lawyer, a clerk . . . a man who used a pen for a living, the sort of man who regularly spent a long time writing manuscripts, or letters, or working in ledgers or anything of that sort."

"Not a writer?" Brasseur echoed him. "Why not?"

For answer Aristide held out his own right hand. "See the ink stains? He has scarcely any. If you spend your time holding a quill for hours, day after day, you're going to get stains on your fingertips that never go away. And that little callus on his middle finger, where the pen rests, is no more pronounced than anyone else's, while mine is obvious."

"Not bad," Brasseur said, with a slow smile. "What else can we learn about him? What about the clothes?"

Bouille handed them over to Aristide. He shook out the shirt, relieved to find that the blood had been washed out of it, save for some lingering reddish-brown stains. "Good quality linen, well made. Same for the cravat; fine muslin, tiny stitches."

The striped silk waistcoat was a sad sight; the washing had removed the worst of the blood but ruined the cloth, although it had obviously been of fine quality before the dyes had bled and the blood and water had stained and puckered it. Aristide looked it over and turned to Brasseur. "I'm no judge of fashion, as you know. But he dressed well, and he liked the English style." English men's fashions, with their plainer, slimmer silhouette, had eclipsed the fussier French style of the 1770s for the past several years, and had grown so popular that the trend was known as "Anglomania."

"Think you could name the tailor?"

"From one waistcoat? Not in a hundred years. But," Aristide said suddenly, "I know someone who might be able to. Could we take these with us for a few hours?"

Brasseur and Bouille exchanged glances. The attendant shrugged. "It's your business, monsieur."

"I don't imagine your friend would be willing to come here to look at the clothes?" Brasseur inquired. "No, I didn't think so. All right, I'll take responsibility for them. Wrap them up well, would you, Bouille?"

6

They learned nothing more from the corpse and left soon afterward, the parcel of clothing under Brasseur's arm. Aristide hoped Derville would be sufficiently awake, at nine o'clock in the morning, to receive them. His manservant admitted them and ushered them into the salon to wait, where Derville joined them, yawning, a quarter hour later.

"How can I help you, then, Monsieur Brasseur?" he inquired warily, after Aristide had introduced his companion. "I'm sure I know nothing about any sordid criminal matters."

"We wanted only to take advantage of your particular knowledge," Aristide assured him. "You know all about the latest fashions, and I'm sure you're acquainted with the best tailors in the city—not socially, of course."

Derville smiled. "I expect I could recognize the work of a few of them."

"Perhaps you could identify the tailor who cut this waistcoat or shirt."

Brasseur untied the parcel and laid out the clothes across the two dainty armchairs. Derville inspected them, rubbing the cloth between his fingers and frowning. "Hmm . . . bad stain there across the front, of course. And what idiot thought he could wash silk, and ruined the fabric completely? What a pity."

Aristide opened his mouth to tell him that the marks were the remains of a vast bloodstain, but he caught Brasseur's minuscule shake of the head from out of the corner of his eye, and said nothing as Derville continued.

"Well, the shirt is new enough, perhaps made by a doting wife who's good with her needle, but it's certainly not from some common backstreet tailor shop; I could name you three or four good tailors, including my own, who would make a gentleman's shirt of this quality."

"What about the waistcoat?" rumbled Brasseur.

"Ah, yes, the waistcoat; that's a different story. That's a fine piece of work, and good fabric. See how well the stripes are aligned at the seams, and how stiffly the collar stands up? And the buttons." He pointed to the self buttons covered with the same silk fabric whose narrow stripes subtly shaded at one edge, thread by thread, from wine-red to a deep rose-pink against the pale cream background. "Those are excellent. A bit staid overall for my taste, but you can recognize the quality immediately. Where on earth did you get these, monsieur?"

"Off a dead man, Monsieur Derville."

"Dead!"

"Yes, monsieur. We were hoping you could help us identify him through his clothes. A fine master tailor ought to recognize his own work right off, and he'll know who bespoke it."

Derville thought for a moment. "I see . . . well, I know of only a couple of tailors who do waistcoats as fine as this one: I should think it's Noguier's work. He has an establishment on Rue du Faubourg St. Honoré."

"Noguier," Brasseur muttered, scribbling down the name.

"Be sure to mention my name when you visit. I fear you wouldn't get past the front door, otherwise."

"A police card does wonders, monsieur," Brasseur said woodenly. "Even for a fellow in a shabby black suit two years old."

Half an hour in a fiacre brought them across the city to the fashionable faubourg St. Honoré, a suburban district of comfortable stone houses belonging to the prosperous bourgeoisie. Here and there, amid the private houses, stood the reception rooms and workshops of a fashionable dressmaker, milliner, or tailor, or an elegant apartment house, or the high walls surrounding a great nobleman's mansion with cobbled front courtyard and spacious gardens and stables at the rear.

They found Noguier's shop without difficulty. At the front door a footman clad in powdered wig and velveteen coat gazed haughtily upon them, ready to suggest that two such unimpressively dressed individuals could not possibly be seeking the services of the great Noguier. Brasseur's police card, however, as he had foreseen, startled the lackey into silence.

Withindoors, the establishment seemed in a perpetual state of barely controlled pandemonium. In a small chamber at the left of the foyer, a languid, exquisitely dressed young man lounged on a sofa while inspecting colored fashion plates, occasionally making a comment to the thin, harassed-looking man hovering over his shoulder. In another room farther down the central hallway, a brisk male voice related snippets of court gossip in an endless stream of patter, frequently punctuated with "Now if you would raise your left arm *so*, monsieur the vicomte," "I believe we'll have to add just one or two more stitches to that buttonhole," and "If you would be so good, monsieur, as to walk a few paces—but mind the pins, if you please." Far down the hall, a subdued murmur rose from the journeymen busily stitching in the workroom, interspersed with the treble voices of boy apprentices running errands back and forth.

The haughty footman vanished into the left-hand chamber and shortly the harassed-looking man emerged. "Messieurs?"

"Monsieur Noguier?" said Brasseur.

"I am he."

"It's likely a certain piece of clothing we have here, evidence in a crime, was a creation of yours. If you'd kindly take a look at it, monsieur."

Noguier led them into an empty reception room and shut the door. "Well?"

"This waistcoat, Monsieur Noguier."

"That's not one of mine," the master tailor said, as soon as Brasseur had lifted it out of its muslin wrapping and laid it on a side table. "Gracious God, what happened to it? It's scarcely fit to pass on to a kitchen boy."

"Are you sure it wasn't made here in your workshop, monsieur?" Brasseur inquired, ignoring Noguier's questions.

"Of course. I'd recognize the fabric, and I know every item we've sewn in the past two years, at least. If you wish proof, I'll show you." He summoned the lackey and told him to fetch the order book. "You see?" he continued, when the thick folio, a foot wide and half again as high, had been presented. He opened the book in the middle and leafed past a few pages. "Now this waistcoat of yours is in the latest style—it certainly wasn't cut before late summer." He stabbed a finger down on a page containing a pair of rough sketches, several paragraphs of notes, measurements, and calculations, and half a dozen fabric samples. "Ah, yes, here are the two dress suits, with embroidered waistcoats complementing them, for Monsieur de Gamache, delivered on the eighteenth of September; our first order of the autumn. We *might* have cut this waistcoat of yours any time after that, but we didn't. Look through the orders for yourself."

"We'll have to take your word for it, monsieur," Brasseur said, after Aristide had leafed through the massive book for several minutes, shaking his head. "But if you didn't create this suit of clothes, then who did?"

"A gentleman assured us," Aristide added, "you made the best waistcoats in Paris."

Noguier permitted himself a dry smile. "I don't flatter myself that I stand entirely alone in the tailors' guild, above the rest. Monsieur Yvon could have made this waistcoat, I admit. He's the only other master tailor whom I would consider my equal, at least in the matter of waistcoats. His establishment is on Rue de Beaujolais, near the Palais-Royal."

Armed with a note of introduction from Noguier, they flagged down another fiacre and set back eastward along Rue St. Honoré. Rue de Beaujolais, bordering the northern edge of the Palais-Royal, was a short street and they quickly found the tailor shop. Inside, they encountered the same sort of wealthy and aristocratic customers and deft, glib fitters, but the chatter of the cutters and sewers was upstairs, rather than at the back of the building, and more muted. Yvon, a brisk, gray-haired, middle-aged man, recognized the waistcoat immediately and seemed almost ready to break into tears at the sight of his creation.

"What fool *washed* this? The very best Lyon silk—it's a crime, monsieur, a crime!"

"You wouldn't have wanted to see it before it was washed, monsieur," Aristide said dryly. "You can take Inspector Brasseur's word for it that it was already ruined."

"Now, Monsieur Yvon," Brasseur said, "you definitely acknowledge this article as one made in your workshop? Yes? Could you then, if you please, give us some particulars?"

"Yes, to be sure. The bolt of silk was new . . . arrived in August or September . . . so let me see . . ." Yvon fetched his own order book and pored through it for a moment. "We've made six waistcoats with that fabric, and another's still back being stitched . . . popular pattern.

Now . . . hmm . . . this certainly isn't Monsieur Latouraille's waistcoat, it's far too small. And Monsieur d'Inville likes his waistcoats cut long. So it must be one of the other four." He turned a few pages and jotted down some notes. "These, with their addresses in town, are the four gentlemen to whom this waistcoat might belong: Messieurs Wendelin, Saint-Landry, Leforestier, or de Beaupréau. They are all frequent customers of mine."

"You haven't seen any of them in the past few days, perhaps?" Aristide inquired.

"No, no, the last one to call was Monsieur Leforestier, when he came in for final fittings on . . . let me see . . . Tuesday the eleventh of October. Monsieur de Beaupréau's valet came in a fortnight ago, or so, with an order for half a dozen shirts, but that's all. What's this about, messieurs?"

"Police business, I'm afraid," said Brasseur, "but I expect you'll find out eventually. Are all four of these gentlemen naturally dark-haired?"

"Yes, I believe so . . . except for Monsieur Wendelin; I fear he's quite bald, though he can afford an excellent wigmaker, of course."

"You can scratch Wendelin off your list, then. What about the other three? Can you describe them?"

"Their persons? Average build, all three. I can provide you with their measurements, if you wish."

"We were hoping for something a bit more individual than their measurements," Brasseur said gently. "What do they look like?"

"Oh." Yvon rubbed his nose. "I'm more concerned with their figures than their faces, understand. I would say that none of them, either in beauty or in ugliness, is a particularly striking individual, though Monsieur de Beaupréau is, I suppose, a good-looking young gentleman."

Aristide sighed. "At least their ages, monsieur?"

"Oh . . . thirty to forty, all of them, more or less; medium height or a little over, dark hair, though Monsieur Leforestier often wears a wig in public. They are, of course, more individual when wearing a fine suit of clothes cut to measure." Yvon smiled slightly, with a dubious sideways glance at Aristide's coat. "If I might interest you gentlemen . . ."

Aristide nearly laughed. They escaped, after assuring Yvon that their fortunes were far too humble to allow them to patronize his establishment. It was nearing midday and Brasseur led Aristide to a modest eating-house a few streets to the north, away from the high-priced district surrounding the Palais-Royal, for a dish of pot-au-feu and a glass of rough red wine.

"What now?" Aristide asked, after wolfing down most of his portion of the stew. "I suppose we have to visit all these addresses."

"Of course," said Brasseur, crumbling the last of his slab of black bread into his bowl. "Only three of them; that's nothing."

"Is this your usual police work, then? Endless rounds of asking the same questions over and over?"

"Afraid so," Brasseur said pleasantly. "Consider yourself lucky; we might be working something tricky like a poisoning, in which case we'd be wearing out our shoes and our voices asking the same very dull questions of every apothecary in Paris, until we found the one who admitted to selling the stuff. But that's the only way it gets done: patient, methodical investigation. Eventually, with common sense and enough shoe leather, you'll find the answers you need."

Aristide looked at the last few swallows of wine in his glass and decided against finishing it; he preferred the alertness that coffee brought, and the wine, in any case, was nearly undrinkable.

Brasseur, oblivious, tossed off the last of his own wine. "Are you done, then? Brace yourself, Ravel. One of these three on Yvon's list is probably our corpse, and breaking the news to the family is never a pleasant job."

Monsieur Leforestier lived only a few minutes' walk away from Yvon's workshop, in a luxurious apartment in one of the new houses surrounding the Palais-Royal. He quickly proved to be alive, and none too pleased at having the police interrupt his dinner party. Brasseur's request to see the striped waistcoat recently made for him by Monsieur Yvon was met with a puzzled scowl and the irritable summoning of Leforestier's valet before the master of the household vanished once more into his salon.

"You never know who might have lent his new suit of clothes to a visiting friend," Brasseur said, with a shrug, as they descended the staircase to the street. "But Leforestier's alive and kicking, and his waistcoat's in his wardrobe drawer where it ought to be." He took a stubby pencil from a pocket and drew a line through another name on Yvon's list.

"Now," he continued, "these last two, luckily, live not too far apart, and one's on Rue de Savoie, not at all far from St. André des Arts, so I'd wager he's our man. But we'd better call first on the Marquis de Beaupréau, on Rue St. Dominique, if you please, so that it's at a suitable hour."

"In the faubourg St. Germain?" Aristide said. "Heaven help us." Wealth and power had migrated, during the past half century, from the Marais—in the ancient eastern portion of the Right Bank—across the Seine to the Left Bank, in the much more spacious and more recently built-up area west of the Latin Quarter, surrounding the once-rural Abbey of St. Germain des Prés. The high walls and carriage gates to the grand mansions of the wealthiest of the aristocracy now lined many of the long suburban streets in the district. "Will they even let us in the door?"

"Strictly speaking, they have to, since we answer to the Royal Lieutenant of Police," Brasseur said, "but we'd better not arrive during his lordship's dinner; his high-and-mighty lackeys'll give short shrift to a humble police official if we inconvenience them. Let's go."

The Hôtel de Beaupréau stood, surrounded by tranquil, formal gardens, in the center of the fashionable district, within sight of the

Hôtel des Invalides and twenty minutes' brisk walk from St. André des Arts. Brasseur strode past a porter and an idling groom at the porte cochère and across the broad courtyard to the imposing front doors.

Monsieur de Beaupréau was not at home, the footman protested, after Brasseur had presented his police card and requested entry into the marble foyer. Monsieur de Beaupréau was truly not at home, not merely "not at home to visitors"; neither was madame. The maître d'hôtel, sent for, confirmed the fact. No, monsieur the marquis had not said where he would be going.

"What about his manservant?" Brasseur inquired.

"His valet? I believe Moreau is present," said the maître d'hôtel stiffly.

"I'll speak to him, then."

"I'll have him sent for."

The footman showed them to a well-concealed door leading to the servants' hall and kitchens in the cellars, where they waited beneath an arched, barred window that let in light from the terrace above. A few minutes later a slender, dark-haired young man clad in the neat blue livery of an upper servant approached them.

"Messieurs? How may I be of service?"

"You're the Marquis de Beaupréau's valet?" said Brasseur.

"Yes, monsieur, Gabriel Moreau."

"I understand the marquis is not at home. Would you have any reason to believe that his absence was unexplained?"

"Unexplained?" Moreau smiled. "No, monsieur the inspector. Monsieur de Beaupréau comes and goes as he pleases."

"I expect he has a dear female friend somewhere, doesn't he?" Aristide said.

Moreau nodded. "I would imagine," he added, lowering his voice, "that he could be found with his mistress. He nearly lives there; often he won't come home for two or three nights in a row."

"As his personal servant," said Brasseur, "I expect you're in charge of keeping the marquis's clothing in order?"

Moreau looked politely nonplussed, but responded nonetheless. "Yes, monsieur."

Brasseur gestured to Aristide, who unwrapped the waistcoat. "Monsieur Yvon, the master tailor, said Monsieur de Beaupréau has a waistcoat like this one. Do you recognize it?"

The young man stared, then reached for the garment. "If I may?" Brasseur nodded and Moreau scrutinized it for a moment before handing it back to Aristide. "My master has a waistcoat very similar to this. The same fabric, surely the same tailor. But I couldn't swear that it's the same article. Monsieur de Beaupréau is a trifle longer in the waist than the gentleman who wore this, I should think."

Brasseur frowned. "When did you last see your master?"

"Monday, monsieur. He dined at home at three o'clock, quite as usual, with family and friends—"

"Family? Madame the marquise, you mean?"

"No, Madame de Beaupréau's in Rouen for the month, visiting her mother. Monsieur's youngest sister was here, Mademoiselle Désirée that was, though she's the Comtesse de Saint-Aubin now, and Monsieur de Castagnac—that's his father's cousin, who lives here. Four or five friends of the family were present, as well."

"What about after dinner?"

"After dinner Monsieur de Beaupréau usually goes out to socialize, or to the theater, or to his mistress's apartment."

"Any idea who his mistress might be?"

"Yes, monsieur, of course. Mademoiselle Sédillot, the actress, of the Montansier Theater. Her lodgings are on Rue d'Amboise, near the theaters, in the house above the locksmith's shop with the sign of the crossed keys. Unless mademoiselle has a performance tonight," Moreau added, "I expect that's where you'll find Monsieur de Beaupréau."

"Was Monsieur de Beaupréau wearing that waistcoat when you saw him last?" Aristide inquired.

"I don't recall . . . He wouldn't have worn it at dinner, of course; it's not formal enough for a dinner party. But he'd have changed if he went out that evening for an informal engagement, and Monsieur de Beaupréau doesn't always ring for me when he changes; he frequently dresses himself, you see, having become accustomed to living rough during the American war. But if it's so important, messieurs, I'll fetch down his waistcoat and you can see it for yourselves."

Brasseur nodded and the valet hurried away. They waited silently while chattering chambermaids, laundresses, and footmen passed them, casting inquisitive looks in their direction. Moreau, Aristide thought, seemed a cut above the other servants in voice and manner; his speech was probably as refined as that of the family he served.

A tempting aroma of roasting fowl drifted from the kitchen, without doubt someone's informal midday dinner. If neither the marquis nor the marquise were present, then simple meals were being prepared only for the servants and for the other members of the family who called the Hôtel de Beaupréau home.

Moreau returned shortly, empty-handed. "Messieurs? I can't find the rose-striped waistcoat in monsieur's wardrobe. It's entirely possible he left the house wearing it on Monday evening, though honestly I can't recall. The coat he wore would have been a good match for it, though."

Brasseur scribbled down a final note and nodded. "That'll do. Thank you, Moreau. Come on, Ravel. It might be Beaupréau, at that," he added to Aristide as they retraced their steps to the front door, "though these grand gentlemen keep whatever hours they please. I expect, if we look, we'll find him in the actress's bed. But first we'll look up Monsieur Saint-Landry and see if he and his waistcoat are where they ought to be."

7

The address on Rue de Savoie proved to be a well-kept stone house with a small courtyard opening onto the street and large, luxurious bourgeois apartments on the lower floors. A pretty, auburn-haired young woman of about twenty answered the door to them on the first-floor landing. "Messieurs?"

"Is this apartment the residence of Monsieur Saint-Landry?" Brasseur inquired.

"Yes, it is." She smiled, revealing enchanting dimples in a softly rounded, rosy-cheeked countenance. Aristide caught himself staring, and hurriedly blinked and looked hard at the doorframe. "May I ask who's calling for him?"

"Inspector Brasseur, mademoiselle, of the police of—"

"Police!" she exclaimed, her smile fading.

"—the Eighteenth District, and Monsieur Ravel, my associate. Are you one of the family, mademoiselle?" Brasseur continued.

"I'm Monsieur Saint-Landry's half sister; I live here with him and his wife."

"Is Monsieur Saint-Landry at home?"

She slowly shook her head. "No, he's not. What's this about, monsieur the inspector?"

"Might we come inside, mademoiselle? Are other members of the household here . . . Madame Saint-Landry, perhaps?"

"Yes, my sister-in-law's here, and also Marguerite . . . that's my cousin, Madame Fournier." She stepped aside slightly to allow them to pass. "What do the police want with *us*? Is it something to do with my brother?"

"Why would you say that, mademoiselle?"

"Because he went out late in the evening, two days ago, after receiving a letter that he wouldn't show to us, and he didn't come back. He hasn't been seen all day yesterday, nor has he sent us any message. Has something happened to him?"

"It's possible."

"You'd better come in, monsieur the inspector. Eugénie—my sister-in-law—is in the salon."

"And your name is, mademoiselle?"

"Sophie, monsieur, Sophie Saint-Landry."

"Keep your eye on the wife," Brasseur muttered to Aristide as they followed Sophie through an anteroom to a sunny parlor trimmed in pale yellows and greens on the wallpaper and upholstery. "Two-thirds of the domestic murders I've seen have been wives murdering husbands and husbands murdering wives. Usually to make way for a lover or a more advantageous marriage."

Two women sat in the salon, one working at a piece of embroidery, the other reading aloud. Sophie coughed discreetly.

"Eugénie, this is Inspector Brasseur, from the police. He's asking for Lambert."

"Lambert?" the younger woman echoed her, looking up from her embroidery hoop. "Why, what's the matter? Is he—is he in your custody?"

Aristide covertly glanced at Brasseur. How did you tell a respectable, sheltered matron that her husband might be lying in the morgue with his throat cut?

"Now why would you say that, madame?" Brasseur said. "Your sister-in-law just told me your husband hasn't been seen since Monday evening. Why would you assume the police were holding him?"

"I—I don't know. But he has been behaving quite out of character during the past few months. Going out at all hours without telling us where, shutting himself up in his study with visitors . . . I hope he isn't involved in anything irregular?"

Aristide gazed discreetly about the room, but took her measure out of the corner of his eye. Eugénie was a petite, slender, waiflike woman of about thirty, with soft features, a fresh, fair complexion, pale golden hair, and enormous gray eyes. Her companion, presumably Marguerite Fournier, was older and more sturdily built, with a plain, intelligent face.

Brasseur cleared his throat. "No, madame, we don't know anything against your husband. But I fear we've found a dead man who answers roughly to Monsieur Saint-Landry's description . . . to the best of our knowledge."

Aristide wondered if she would burst into hysterics or a flood of tears, but she merely stared at Brasseur, speechless, the gray eyes widening. "I'm afraid," Brasseur continued, "that someone will have to come to the morgue at the Châtelet, and identify him."

Eugénie Saint-Landry continued to stare at him, as if she had not quite taken in what he was saying. "Identify him?" she whispered at last. "Oh, no! You can't be right, monsieur."

"I fear it's possible, madame. Do you have a portrait of monsieur here in the house? We might be able to spare you—"

"No," said the other woman, "I fear there's no portrait of Lambert. He says it's an unnecessary luxury."

"But—what—was it an accident, then?" Eugénie said. "On the street? Those horrid carriages—they go much too fast—"

"No, madame. I'm afraid this man was murdered. Have you not heard about the dead man who was found yesterday at St. André des Arts?"

"Murdered!" the other woman exclaimed. "I heard rumors on the street yesterday, from the peddlers, about a dead man—but who'd want to murder Lambert? He's the most amiable man alive."

"My . . . my husband's cousin, Madame Fournier," Eugénie said mechanically. "She lives here with us."

"Tell me, madame," Brasseur persisted, "do you recognize this waistcoat?"

Aristide untied the parcel again and laid the waistcoat out before her. She gazed at it, at last reaching out a hand to finger the stained silk.

"Lambert bespoke a new suit and two waistcoats from Yvon this autumn," she said softly, looking up from it to gaze first at Brasseur and then at Aristide. "He's not an extravagant man, but he does like to dress well, befitting his station. This is certainly the same fabric as one of the waistcoats."

"You identify it as an article belonging to your husband?"

"No! No—I didn't say that. It might be his . . . but I refuse to believe that my husband is dead, Inspector."

"Monsieur Yvon gave us a list of gentlemen who—"

"But some other tailor, not Monsieur Yvon, might have cut and sewn this," Eugénie said, her eyes pleading. "There must be more than one bolt of this fabric in existence, and at least a few other waistcoats, don't you think? A tailor doesn't use an entire bolt of silk on one waistcoat!"

"It's always possible," said Brasseur, "but I suspect Yvon's the most likely one. And since you say your husband is missing, madame, the quickest way to settle this is for you to come to the morgue with—"

"No!" she cried, paling until her fair skin seemed translucent as alabaster. "No, I couldn't. Please."

"Madame Saint-Landry is very sensitive," Marguerite told him, as she rose and laid a hand on Eugénie's shoulder. "It's all right, dear; he can't force you to go. I'll go, if I must."

"I'll go," Sophie said, behind Aristide. He had almost forgotten her presence, though he abruptly wondered, as he turned and cast an admiring glance at her, how that was possible.

"Mademoiselle?"

"I'll go with you," she repeated.

"It's not a pleasant experience, mademoiselle. I visited the morgue myself for the first time this morning," he added, with a faint smile. "It's no place for young ladies."

"I don't mind," she said. "I'm harder than I look."

He realized he must have smiled again, for "hard" was not an adjective he would have thought of in connection with the blue-eyed, dimpled Sophie. She darted him a stern glance that he found completely charming.

"Not all young ladies are languishing little creatures prone to fainting, you know. We can go now, if you want. I'd rather get it over with."

Brasseur nodded. "As you wish, mademoiselle. Tell me, might Monsieur Saint-Landry be in the habit of lending his clothes to visiting friends or relatives? Perhaps a dress suit for a night at the theater, or something of that order?"

She stared at him. "No, Lambert is most particular about his clothes; he wouldn't lend them to anyone. And we haven't had any houseguests for at least a fortnight."

"Did anyone else see the letter Monsieur Saint-Landry received on Monday evening?" Brasseur inquired, as Sophie went out to fetch a cloak. The two women shook their heads.

"I brought it in to him," said Marguerite. "It arrived sometime around supper, perhaps half past eight. He glanced at it—it was only a brief note, I think—and he told us he had to go out later—"

"When did he leave?"

"About eleven, perhaps a little before. He told us not to stay up for him, that he would let himself in."

"What did he do with the note?"

"He . . . he folded it and put it in an inner pocket of his coat," she said, after a moment's thought. "You didn't find anything in his pockets?"

"No, madame," he said, without elaborating. "Do you remember who delivered it?"

Marguerite shrugged. "Some errand boy off the street. I might have seen him in this quarter once or twice before."

"What was Monsieur Saint-Landry wearing when he went out?" Aristide inquired. "Does either of you remember?"

"I never remember what other people are wearing," Eugénie said, with a fleeting, self-deprecating smile, and fixing her gaze on him once again with a flutter of eyelashes. "It's dreadful, I know . . ."

It occurred to Aristide that Eugénie was flirting with him just a little, inviting him, with those great, sad eyes, to rush to her side and comfort her in a crisis. Perhaps, he thought, she was a woman who, without even thinking about it, no matter what the circumstances, played the coquette with every man she encountered. He gravely nodded and stepped back, behind Brasseur, thinking that he much preferred the forthright Sophie.

"I certainly couldn't remember what Lambert was wearing two days ago," Marguerite agreed, "though of course he had his overcoat well buttoned up against the cold when he left. A dark gray-blue overcoat and a tall hat, gray, in the English style, with a small silver buckle on the band. Does that help?"

"It might," Aristide said, to reassure her. He suspected that, if Saint-Landry was indeed the man, the hat and overcoat were, together with the rest of his effects, by now in the back of a pawnshop or old-clothes dealer's shop. He glanced at Brasseur, fervently hoping that the inspector would not send him out to question every ragman in Paris in search of the missing articles.

Sophie returned with her cloak and a maid, a taciturn, middle-aged woman who was evidently a formidable chaperone, and together the four of them left the apartment. She turned to Brasseur as soon as they had reached the bottom of the stairs to the courtyard.

"Monsieur the inspector, I didn't want to say more about it and upset my sister-in-law, because she hasn't been feeling very well lately . . . but just now, while I was fetching Victoire, I slipped into Lambert's dressing room and looked in the chest of drawers where I think he keeps his waistcoats." She paused for an instant and then continued, her voice trembling. "I didn't see the rose-colored striped one anywhere."

"You mustn't give up hope yet, mademoiselle," Aristide said quickly, seeing the first glint of tears in her eyes. "It still may be nothing more than a coincidence. Your brother may yet return unscathed, together with his waistcoat."

She blinked away the tears and managed a smile. "Thank you. You're very kind, Monsieur . . ."

"Ravel." He offered her his arm. As the porter closed the gate to the courtyard behind them, a fiacre came rattling up.

"Derville!" Aristide exclaimed, recognizing the passenger who climbed out, a fashionable long walking stick in one hand.

"Oh, good Lord," he said, glancing from Aristide to Sophie. "Do you know the Saint-Landrys, Ravel?"

"Not socially." Aristide drew him aside and lowered his voice. "What are you doing here?"

"I, er, I thought I recognized that waistcoat. I've seen Saint-Landry wearing one like it this past autumn. And when your inspector said it had been taken from a dead man," Derville added, growing serious, "I couldn't help thinking the worst—you know how one gets—and I thought I ought to pay a visit to reassure myself that he was well." He paused, with a smile. "But I see you got here before I did. What's this you're up to with the police, anyway? You haven't turned spy, have you?"

"Long story," said Aristide.

"Is Saint-Landry upstairs, then?" Derville said, tucking his stick carelessly under his arm and turning to the gate.

"No, I fear he's not."

"You're not saying he *is* missing?"

"According to Mademoiselle Saint-Landry, he's been missing since Monday evening. She's accompanying us to the Basse-Geôle to tell us whether or not the corpse that was found yesterday is that of her brother. I'm sorry, Derville."

"My word," Derville said softly. "I'd hoped I was just being foolish. All right then, I'd better be the dutiful friend and call upon Eugénie, to offer a shoulder if needed."

"Monsieur Derville, I strongly suggest you don't say anything to madame until the body at the morgue's been identified," Brasseur said, approaching them. "If the corpse is not her husband's after all, we don't want to upset her for nothing."

"Yes, of course. As you wish, Inspector." He bowed to Sophie and pulled the bell chain. "Mademoiselle, gentlemen."

Aristide and Brasseur escorted Sophie and her maid out to the Pont St. Michel. The Châtelet was only a few minutes' walk away on the other side of the river, across the Île de la Cité. Sophie shivered and pulled her hood more securely about her face, against the chilly breeze that whistled among the half-timbered wooden houses that lined the bridge. Below them, great slabs of ice drifted slowly in the current, sluggishly wedging against each other beneath the stone arches.

"I see you're acquainted with Monsieur Derville," Sophie said to Aristide as they crossed. "How on earth does he know a police official?"

"I'm not really in the police, mademoiselle," he said, with a sur-
reptitious glance at Brasseur, who surely would have said otherwise.
"Derville's an old school friend of mine."

"You were at school together?" she echoed him, with a soft laugh.
"How droll."

"How so?" he inquired.

"Why, Lambert and I have known Monsieur Derville's family for
ages, even before my parents died. He's always calling on us and coming to dinner. He used to tease me when I was a child." She glanced
up at him, smiling. "It's very amusing to imagine him as a schoolboy of
twelve; you must have some tales to tell. Where do you come from,
Monsieur Ravel? I don't think he's ever mentioned you."

"From Bordeaux, mademoiselle."

"Bordeaux? I think we have some distant cousins there, or somewhere nearby," she said. "Their name is Tourtier; they're more closely
related to the Ducos family. Perhaps you know them?"

"I—I've heard of them," he said tersely, vividly remembering the
Tourtiers, wealthy merchants and clients of his uncle the lawyer, who,
despite that, had pointedly not invited Aristide and his sister, Thérèse,
to their daughter's engagement ball two years previously. The un-
pardonable scandal of murder, adultery, and public execution in the
family did not easily fade from the long memories of the respectable
bourgeoisie.

Sophie looked puzzled but said little else as they passed the Law
Courts. He saw her take a deep, bracing breath as they reached the
Right Bank and stood before the looming Châtelet.

Sophie's maid refused to go farther than the public passageway
and remained outside, grimly huddled in her cloak against the cold.
"Why don't you take mademoiselle inside?" Brasseur murmured to
Aristide. "I expect she'd prefer your company to mine, you being
more appealing to young ladies and all. Go on with you. I'll wait out
here."

No one was on duty at the desk in the close, chilly antechamber of the morgue. Curious, Aristide edged his way closer to the iron grille that led to the stairs, and there heard excited voices. A moment later two men, one clad in black, appeared and stopped short upon seeing him.

"Monsieur?" he said tentatively, addressing the man whom he recognized as having admitted them that morning. "I'm Ravel, Inspector Brasseur's associate . . . we were here earlier . . ."

"Yes?" he said impatiently as Aristide paused.

"I've brought this young lady to identify the corpse that arrived here yesterday, the murder victim."

The two men both looked at him. "*Who* did you say you were?" said the black-clad man at last.

"Ravel . . . Monsieur Brasseur has asked me to assist him in this matter."

"And where, pray, is Brasseur?"

Aristide abruptly realized that this stranger must be another police inspector. "He's outside, but sent me—"

"Well, then," the man snapped, "he's wasting his time. The corpse with throat slit, male, found in the churchyard of St. André des Arts early yesterday morning . . . that's the one you mean?"

"Yes, monsieur."

"It's been stolen."

8

Stolen!" Sophie and Aristide exclaimed in the same instant. The man nodded, still gazing skeptically at Aristide.

"About an hour ago, when Monsieur Daude here and the man who performs the menial work were both out eating their dinners, three men entered, overpowered Monsieur Bouille, and absconded with the corpse."

"I returned twenty minutes ago," Daude interrupted, "and found poor Bouille bound, gagged, and blindfolded in the cellar. Resurrectionists, no doubt!"

"No doubt," the police official echoed him. "Meanwhile, Monsieur . . . Ravel, obviously there is no further need for your presence."

"No, monsieur."

"But I—" Sophie began. Aristide whispered "Let's go" in her ear and hastily escorted her back to the public passage, where Brasseur was waiting with the maid.

"Monsieur Brasseur," Aristide said, "you won't believe what's happened—"

"The body's been stolen!" Sophie interrupted him.

"The body's . . . been . . . stolen," Brasseur repeated, after a moment of stunned silence. "Death of the devil!"

Aristide nodded. "Some men overpowered the concierge and made off with it, about an hour ago. A police inspector is with them still. He and the other concierge are saying it was resurrectionists."

"What is going *on* here?" Sophie demanded. "What on earth is a resurrectionist?"

"It's argot for a body snatcher, mademoiselle," said Brasseur. "They dig up fresh corpses from the churchyards to sell to anatomists, or sometimes medical students do it on their own."

"It's illegal to dissect any corpse except that of an executed criminal," Aristide said, with a glance at Brasseur for confirmation, "and there aren't nearly enough of those to go around to all the professors of medicine who need them for their lectures, so the resurrectionists step in and make a profit out of it." He paused, hoping she would not turn faint or queasy upon hearing of such a disagreeable subject, but she merely grimaced and said nothing.

"Occasionally they even save a life," he continued, recalling an anecdote he had heard on good authority from a physician acquaintance. "A few years ago, some students dug up a girl who'd been buried the day before; on the way back to their laboratory, they discovered she was alive, revived her, and brought her back to her family."

"Gracious!" she exclaimed, wide-eyed.

"Well, that's neither here nor there," Brasseur growled. "Damnation! I suppose it's just possible," he continued, after a moment's gloomy silence, "that some resurrectionist heard about a fresh corpse at the morgue that hadn't been rotting in the river for a week, and took advantage of the fact."

Sophie grimaced again, but seemed remarkably undistressed. "That's a horrid thought, but surely it's not the only explanation? Are body snatchers usually so bold, monsieur?"

"I've never heard of them tying up someone and stealing a body from the morgue in broad daylight," he admitted. "Why take the risk, right here at the Châtelet, where it's swarming with magistrates and guardsmen?"

Aristide nodded. "I should think it would be much safer and easier to bribe the guard or the sexton and creep into a churchyard in the middle of the night, just as the murderer did. Those mass graves must be brimming with fresh corpses."

"But why else would anyone steal my brother's body? And if it's not he, then where *is* my brother?"

"I'm afraid we don't know any more than you do, mademoiselle," Brasseur said. "But you shouldn't become alarmed quite yet—"

"You don't know my brother, monsieur. Lambert is a very good, respectable man, and the best of brothers, but he's utterly dull and domestic, and quite predictable."

"Madame Saint-Landry told us he had been behaving oddly of late," Aristide said. "Might this disappearance of his be—"

"But he *never* goes out without telling us when he'll return," she insisted. "To disappear for two days, without a word—it's completely unlike him. Please—don't dismiss this. It should be a police matter."

Brasseur thought it over for a moment and at last nodded. "All right, mademoiselle, I'll try to return when I can, to interview the household further. That's the best we can do today, I'm afraid." He hailed her a fiacre from the square beyond. "Or perhaps I'll send Monsieur Ravel, shall I?" he added, as Aristide handed her into the cab.

"That would be most satisfactory, monsieur," she said primly, though Aristide thought he caught a hint of a blush and a quickly hidden smile.

"Want to hear what the ghouls have to say?" Brasseur added, to Aristide, as the cab rolled away and he turned toward the door to the Basse-Geôle. Aristide followed him, his curiosity overcoming his reluctance at visiting the morgue yet again.

Bouille, he of the grotesquely comic, melancholy visage, was sprawled on a chair in the antechamber when they entered. Daude fussily poured out a glass of brandy while the other inspector stood stolidly to one side.

"I hear you've had an unexpected bit of trouble," Brasseur said as he approached. Bouille's eyelids flickered.

"Never in all my days! I was manhandled, monsieur, seized bodily by three men, and tied up!" He seized the glass that his colleague handed him and gulped it down.

"Can you describe these men?"

"I've already questioned Monsieur Bouille," the inspector said. Brasseur glanced at him.

"Good afternoon to you, too, Marchand. If you don't mind, I'll ask my own questions, seeing as it's *my* corpse that's disappeared. Make yourself useful, if you would, and station yourself outside so we're not interrupted."

Marchand shot him a sour glance but did as he was requested. "Marchand would think it was a resurrectionist," Brasseur muttered, when he had gone. "The man has no imagination at all." He turned back to Bouille. "Well, what about it? You're not hurt, are you?"

"No . . . I confess they did no more than handle me roughly. But—"

"How much did you see? Can you describe them?"

"Monsieur Brasseur, I never pay much attention to the living; they're not my business. A little more brandy, if you please," he added faintly to Daude.

"Come, surely you can remember something about them. How many?"

"Three men," said Bouille, his outraged expression further distorting his clown's face. "Two were young, early thirties perhaps. The third man was older. One of them came in alone, and said he'd come to look for a groom who might have had an accident at the water's edge; and then they grabbed me, all three of them, when I turned my back to unlock the grille. They blindfolded me and forced me down to the cellar and tied me to a chair."

"Can you describe these men?"

Bouille had another swallow of brandy, thought for a moment, and at last reluctantly divulged that the man he had seen had clearly been a gentleman, well-bred and well-spoken. The color of his hair? Brown, carelessly dressed, without powder.

"I did notice his clothes," Bouille said suddenly. "In our line of work, you notice that. A corpse is a corpse, but you have to take detailed notes on the clothes and effects, and we rarely see anything near as fine here."

Aristide could well believe him; the great majority of the corpses that arrived at the morgue would have been those of laborers and paupers.

"This gentleman wore a good silk suit," Bouille continued, "plain but excellent quality, with the redingote in solid deep blue and an admirable waistcoat. Patterned silk . . . let me see . . . white and . . . tawny gold. Yes, that's it. Blue coat and patterned silk waistcoat, beneath a gray wool overcoat. It's not often," he added, with a mournful smile, "that we here have the opportunity to set eyes on such outstanding examples of the tailor's art, especially twice in one day."

"Twice?" Aristide said. "Why, were the others who attacked you also well dressed?"

Bouille shook his head. "No, I scarcely saw them, though I recall the second man was more plainly dressed, like a clerk. And the third man was quite ordinary-looking, though his clothes were passable. But a gentleman arrived in the morning—"

"I remember the gentleman who came in earlier," Daude interrupted, "on a separate errand. I was on duty here at the desk; he came in at about ten o'clock. Quite fashionably clad. He was looking for his valet and feared the man—who evidently had an unfortunate weakness for gambling and bad company—might have fallen afoul of some villain."

"I showed him the only two males who fit the description," Bouille agreed, "but he said that neither was the man he sought, and took his leave. The second gentleman, with the others, the ones who attacked me, they arrived later, at about half past one."

Aristide glanced at Brasseur, thoroughly puzzled. Surely, he thought, among so many other peculiar occurrences, the two visits must be related.

"Monsieur Bouille," he said, struck with a sudden idea, "when you assisted the first man, do you remember which corpses you showed him?"

"Ah, let me see . . . I showed him the body of a male who had drowned in the river four days previously, but he said it wasn't the man. Then he asked me if I had no others that could possibly fit the description. I told him that my only other male of the right age had been dressed like a gentleman, not a lackey, but he explained that he himself frequently gave his valet his castoff clothing, some of it still quite new, so the fellow might be clad above his station. So I showed him the new one, the cut throat, but he said that that wasn't his man, either, and left, and I saw no more of him."

"So you showed him our mysterious murder victim, did you?" Brasseur said. "And three hours later that particular body disappears. That's very interesting."

"He came in looking for one particular man," Aristide said. "And perhaps he found him, but he didn't wish anyone to know that."

"He wasn't accommodating enough," Brasseur said to Daude, "to give you his name?"

"No, monsieur. They're only required to give us their names and addresses if they identify and claim a corpse."

"And later, three other men steal the corpse . . . well! It's a pretty problem we have here, isn't it?" He looked at his watch and thrust it back into his pocket, with a gloomy glance at the outer door. "Half past three . . . I have to be off, Ravel. We inspectors who concentrate on criminal activity have a meeting most days at four, and, unfortunately, Marchand—who you may have guessed doesn't like me much—is one of them, and he'd love to see me turn up late. Why don't you go back to the Saint-Landrys and interview them, learn what you can about the man and the household?"

"If you wish," Aristide said, unable to quite suppress a smile, and wondering what police officials normally asked the relatives of presumed victims.

"Leave the waistcoat—oh, by the way. Here." Brasseur extracted a card from his pocket-book and thrust it at Aristide, together with a handful of copper coins. "Cab fare in case you need it in the next few days. And show this card to anyone who demands to know who the devil you are. You're not quite on the books yet as a police agent, but it'll do. Go on, then—I'm sure Mademoiselle Saint-Landry is looking forward to your visit!"

9

The forbidding, middle-aged maid who had accompanied Sophie to the Basse-Geôle opened the door to Aristide and brusquely told him to wait in the foyer. A few minutes later she returned and led him to the salon, where Sophie jumped to her feet at the sight of him.

"Monsieur Ravel! I didn't expect . . ." She hastily bobbed him a decorous curtsy. "Have you learned anything—"

"Have you had any word from your brother?" Aristide asked at the same instant. He paused, feeling sheepish, and asked again: "Your brother's not yet returned?"

"No. And I'm worried to death. What about the body that was stolen? What have you learned about that?"

"Very little," he told her, "but we don't know yet that your brother was the dead man, do we? The theft may have nothing to do with him."

"Yes, of course you're right," she said, though he could tell that her thoughts were far away. "Please sit down."

As he pulled a chair forward, he belatedly noticed Marguerite

Fournier, perched on a hassock in a corner. She smiled and gave him a brief nod before returning to the knitting in her lap.

"Is Madame Saint-Landry not here?"

"She retired to her boudoir after Monsieur Derville left us," said Marguerite. "The inspector's news distressed her more than she'll admit; she's delicate, and I don't think she'll be able to see anyone else today. Will you take some refreshment, monsieur? Some coffee or hot chocolate?"

Marguerite had a beautiful voice, Aristide realized, low and rich. Most men, he thought, would pay little attention to her if they passed her on the street, but the sound of her voice might make them turn.

"I must tell you," he said to Sophie, after agreeing to coffee, "that I'm here in place of Inspector Brasseur. That is, I need to ask you some questions the police might ask, but since I'm not a police official, only one of their . . . er . . . authorized agents . . . you needn't speak to me if you don't want to."

"But of course I will," Sophie said promptly. "I was nearly about to send for the commissaire, I'm so concerned about Lambert. Have you any news at all?"

Aristide shook his head. "I fear not. Mademoiselle Saint-Landry, I know there's no portrait of your brother here, but have you anything at all that could help us to identify him . . . whether living or dead?"

"The miniatures!" she said, after a moment's thought. "I'd almost forgotten. Lambert felt that having a full-sized portrait painted was far too expensive—he's always one for little economies—but he agreed to have a pair of miniatures done when he married Eugénie." She hurried to the mahogany buffet against the wall and brought out a small velvet-covered case from a drawer. "That was nine years ago. I hope these are of some use?"

He inspected the tiny portraits that nestled within three-inch frames. Both sitters had worn their most formal clothes for the occasion. Eugénie he recognized immediately by the enormous, wistful gray eyes, which captured the viewer's gaze, even when overshadowed by a looming, powdered coiffure of the past decade, when the prevailing fashion in hairdressing had demanded height and two or three rows, at least, of stiffly pomaded curls. Eugénie's taste, it seemed, had run toward the elaborate. Her bridegroom, on the other hand, an agreeable-looking man in his early thirties, neither handsome nor ugly, looked out at the viewer from beneath a simple, crisp peruke with one neat row of side curls above each ear.

"I don't know," he said at last, shutting the case, not wishing to distress her, though he suspected that the missing Saint-Landry might indeed be the dead man of the churchyard. "He was older. It's difficult to tell; the portrait is so small, and your brother is younger in it, of course, and the powdered wig changes the appearance so much. The man I saw might have been your brother, mademoiselle, but I couldn't swear to it. You mustn't give up hope of finding him, not yet."

"I'll do whatever you say, Monsieur Ravel," Sophie said. Reaching for the case, she inadvertently brushed his hand with hers.

"Tell me more about Monsieur Saint-Landry," Aristide said quickly, groping at something useful to do, as she clutched the velvet case to her, blushing. He fumbled with his notebook, found his stubby pencil at the bottom of his pocket, and began to scrawl down notes. "His full name: Jean-Lambert Saint-Landry? Age?"

"Forty-one."

The point of the pencil abruptly snapped in his fingers and he muttered an oath that, he remembered belatedly, was unsuitable in the presence of young ladies. Sophie gave a nervous giggle. He felt again in his pocket, realized he must have left his penknife at home, and muttered, embarrassed, "If you would be so kind . . . a—a pen . . ."

Marguerite silently went to the writing-table in the corner and brought him a small lap desk with a sheet of paper and a newly cut quill.

"His description," he continued, when he had gathered his wits and dipped the point of the quill into the inkwell, praying that he would not lose his head completely and manage to spill the ink into his lap. "That's to say . . . beyond what I can tell from the miniature?"

"Oh . . ." She had been staring at him, he realized, and abruptly hoped that his frayed cuffs were not too conspicuous.

Quickly she recovered herself. "Er . . . medium height, dark brown hair with a little gray in it, brown eyes. You can see he has a nice kind face, but I wouldn't say he's particularly striking. Really, he looks a great deal like any other man of his age."

"His profession, mademoiselle?"

"Gentleman . . . property owner or man of finance, I suppose. Lambert was the sole heir to his family business, a paper manufactory. It was small at first, but he made it quite profitable, and then he discovered that he had even more talent for investing the profits than he did for running the mill itself. So he sold it, years ago, and has been speculating with the capital ever since. Usually successfully; he's doubled or tripled his fortune, I should think." A maid entered with the coffee tray and Sophie busied herself with pouring.

"I'll put him down as 'property owner,'" Aristide said. "Mademoiselle Saint-Landry," he continued, "if your brother was, indeed, implicated in something dangerous or illegal, to whom would he be most likely to open his heart, if anyone? His wife?"

She set down the coffeepot and thought for a moment. "No, I think he would probably speak to me. Eugénie isn't . . . well . . ." She paused for an instant, handed him a cup, and then continued. "She isn't precisely overendowed with brains, if you know what I mean. She's very lovely, and she's gracious and she entertains and is a fine hostess at the dinners Lambert gives for business gentlemen and their wives, and she's quite good at all that, but I wouldn't depend on her for anything that involved *thinking*. She never reads anything except sentimental English novels."

"Is that a crime, mademoiselle?" Aristide said, as she made a face.

"Well, I tried reading two or three of them, before she took them back to the lending library. I thought the first one was quite amusing and romantic. But then the rest were all just the same! Endless variations of weepy, contrived drivel about insipid heroines, who always have to be rescued from the castle of the wicked and debauched nobleman who's threatening their virtue." She added sugar to her own coffee and gazed down with a sad smile at the tiny cup in her hands. "Honestly, I think Eugénie's a little bored, because she has no children to keep her occupied, and she reads those things for a bit of fantasy. Marguerite and I—we prefer the theater. Comedies—I adored *Figaro's Marriage*—or good, lively adventures with swordfights and Turkish sultans and depraved courtesans, and handsome heroes and lots of blood."

"Hardly appropriate entertainment for young ladies."

"Oh, please, monsieur, you sound like my brother! 'It's not the sort of play a young lady should be seeing.' Fiddlesticks. Perhaps it's not the sort of thing he enjoys—he hardly ever goes to the theater—but I'll attend the plays I want to, and he's never yet stopped me."

Her tone, despite its cheerful mockery, was so evidently full of affection for her straitlaced elder half brother that Aristide looked away for an instant, blinking. Sophie quickly tugged a handkerchief from her bodice and blew her nose. "Oh, poor Lambert. It just can't be true. I can't believe anyone could hurt him. He's the best man I know!"

"Mademoiselle, the dead man was found in rather extraordinary surroundings. Was—is—your brother a Freemason, or does he have anything to do with Freemasonry?"

"Oh, yes," she said instantly. "I believe so. Those are the gentlemen who wear little aprons when they assemble, aren't they? He's been a member of something or other for years and years, because he frequently goes out to meetings."

"Yes," said Marguerite, "Monsieur Saint-Landry is a Mason."

"Do you know where he, er, meets with . . ."

"His lodge, you mean? As a matter of fact, I don't," she said thoughtfully. "He's very closemouthed about that."

"He scarcely ever talks about it," Sophie agreed, "and I never pay much attention when he does. Clubs and select societies are really so dull, don't you think?"

Aristide nearly smiled. "My opinion has nothing to do with it, mademoiselle."

She blushed and clapped a hand over her mouth. "Oh, have I said something dreadful? I do apologize if I've offended you. You're not a Freemason yourself, are you?"

"Far from it."

She glanced over her shoulder, with a flash of a wicked smile. "Because between Lambert, and Eugénie and Marguerite, sometimes all you hear is endless claptrap about 'the society' and so on."

"I thought the Masons didn't admit women," Aristide said.

"They don't," Marguerite said. "French lodges don't, at least in theory. But there are other societies besides the Freemasons."

"Eugénie and Marguerite are both members of ladies' societies just like them, devoted to ancient rites and doing good works. Giving soup to the poor and collecting donations for widows and orphans."

"There's more to it than that," Marguerite said, with a tolerant smile.

Sophie shrugged. "They won't tell me much about it, but Marguerite drops mysterious hints sometimes, and tells me I must join once I'm married." Marguerite smiled again and bent over her knitting.

"Eugénie's society—I think they call it the Sacred Order of the Dove—they meet every Wednesday and Saturday afternoon," Sophie continued, "and wear white tunics and colored sashes and pretend to be ancient Roman priestesses or something of that kind, and I'm sure they have all sorts of rituals and incantations invented to make themselves feel important, just like the men. But if that's how you spend your time once you're married, then heavens, let me remain a spinster!"

She laughed, and her sudden merriment was so contagious that Aristide could not help smiling for an instant before moving on to weightier matters.

"If you're truly convinced that your brother is a good man," he said slowly, "with no dark secrets, then it would follow that it's unlikely anyone would murder him because he committed some crime against the Freemasons, or betrayed them."

Sophie vigorously shook her head. "No. Absolutely not."

"He is—it sounds trite, but it's true—he is completely honorable and upright," Marguerite said slowly. "When he owned the manufactory, he was an excellent employer and took good care of his workers. He hates waste and prefers to live rather simply, and he'll drop the money he's saved from some little economy into the poor box instead. And if he'd taken an oath, he would stand by it, no matter what." She abruptly replaced her cup and saucer on the table between them and gave him a hard stare. "Why should the Freemasons have something to do with it?"

Aristide was silent for a moment, remembering how and where the dead man had been found. "Have you heard about the fires and desecrations that have occurred in and near some churches on the Left Bank recently?" he asked them at last. Marguerite nodded.

"I heard a few rumors from our cook, who had it from the market women. People are saying the oddest things. I've heard a few of the symbols described, and they sound to me like Masonic symbols. But that simply can't be true. The brotherhood is composed of good men like Lambert, whose intent is to do good deeds."

"Well," Aristide continued, "the dead man was discovered in the churchyard of St. André des Arts, surrounded by Masonic symbols, just as you say, and it looked as if he had either interrupted the vandal in his work, and recognized him, and was murdered to keep him from denouncing the perpetrator; or else he had been setting the fires himself and was murdered to stop him—"

"Lambert would never do something so horrid as desecrating a church!" Sophie exclaimed. "He's a good Catholic."

"Then it must be the other way round, *if* your brother was the murdered man, which we don't yet know, of course. Either he was killed by someone who bears a grudge, real or imagined, toward the fraternity; or else he died because he had discovered that someone else, some fellow Mason, probably, had betrayed the others, and that other person killed him to keep him from talking."

"That sounds much more like something Lambert would do," Marguerite agreed. "If he discovered that something wasn't right, he would go straight to the person in charge, and report whatever had gone wrong. If he'd learned something dangerous, anyone who knew him would have known he couldn't be bought."

"So what do we do about it?" Sophie demanded. "Can't the police help us?"

Aristide sighed. "I don't know what the police can do about missing individuals, or about the murder of a man with no name and, now, no corpse. I'll see what Inspector Brasseur can tell me, but I suspect that nothing will be done until the body is found."

"But we have to *do* something. I can't just sit about and wait, when my brother is missing, perhaps dead, and his murderer might be as free as you please."

"Perhaps, for a start, you could advertise in the newspapers for any information on your brother's whereabouts."

"That seems so . . . inadequate," Sophie said.

"Well, if it's something to do with the Masons, we'll have to wait until Inspector Brasseur and I learn a little more about his connections to them. Meanwhile, we'll try to discover what happened to this man's body. If it wasn't stolen by a resurrectionist, which seems highly unlikely, then surely its disappearance must mean something." He folded the notes he had taken and thrust them into a pocket of his coat before setting the lap desk aside and rising. "Brasseur will be investigat-

ing that, I'm sure; the police can do that sort of thing much better than
you and I could."

After taking leave of Sophie and Marguerite, Aristide turned his steps
toward the Café Zoppi, which was only a short walk away. The main
entrance was on Rue des Fossés St. Germain des Prés, but regular customers frequently used a smaller, less busy, back door on the Cour du
Commerce, a prosperous bourgeois enclave boasting several new stone
apartment houses amid the workshops of master artisans in the luxury trades. He wandered down the narrow street, past a fashionable
milliner's shop and a maker of harpsichords, and idled by the café, oc-
cupying himself with the advertising bills and public notices pasted
everywhere on the walls. Hoping to see someone he knew amid the
parade of literary lights and pretenders, he waited twenty minutes
until an acquaintance slipped out. Christophe Lefèvre would do quite
well, he decided.

"Lefèvre, do you have a moment?"

"Oh, good day, Ravel," Lefèvre said, pausing. "What's up?"

"I need your help."

Lefèvre's face took on the usual expression of someone who expected to be asked for a loan. Unlike most of the impecunious young
men Aristide knew in the quarter, Lefèvre was reasonably well off; the
illegitimate son of a long-dead banker, he had always enjoyed a modest but regular income from his father's estate that allowed him to live
a comfortable bachelor existence.

"I don't need cash," Aristide said, before Lefèvre could grope for an
excuse. "What I need is information. Lefèvre, are you a Freemason?"

"Sorry, no. What of it?"

"Do you know any Masons?"

"I'm sure I know dozens," he said, laughing. "Everybody who's
anybody is a member of something or other; didn't you know?"

"Then perhaps you could find me one or two of them who'd be willing to answer some questions—people who aren't as secretive as most Masons seem to be. Can we meet tomorrow, somewhere that's less public than Zoppi's?"

Lefèvre promised to do what he could, and suggested a humbler café not far from Zoppi's, on a small side street off Rue des Cordeliers, which catered to a less prominent and intellectual crowd. They parted, Aristide turning his steps toward an eating-house for a quick supper before heading homeward to ponder what he had seen and learned that day.

10

Aristide returned to Brasseur's office on Rue des Amandiers early in the morning. As he approached the hanging sign of the boot, a small boy detached himself from a handful of urchins who were hanging about the nearby baker's shop, hopefully eyeing the passersby, and darted up to him.

"You Ravel?"

"Why?"

" 'Cause the police inspector, he said you'd be coming here. Tall and skinny and a bit gloomy-looking, he said, and a black suit under a shabby overcoat. You him?"

"Yes."

The boy thrust a folded note at him and looked expectant. Aristide parted with a few deniers and retreated to the shelter of a doorway.

> *Ravel* [the note read],
>
> *Unfortunately something's come up that I didn't expect. My superior, M. Le Roux, has learned about you from Inspector*

Marchand of the 11th District, whom you met yesterday and who is no friend of mine. The commissaire has plainly taken a look at your dossier and the present case file and taken it— most unreasonably—into his head that you may have had something to do with this unidentified man's death and the theft of his corpse. I expect nothing will come of it; but for the moment it would be safer, and would spare you a good deal of inconvenience, if you took yourself off for a while. Don't go to a hotel; the hotelkeepers have to show their registers every day to the police. Can you lodge a few nights with your friend, M. Derville? I will find you there, or will send the next message to you in care of M. Derville in the hope that he will forward it to you.

G. Brasseur.
The 12th January.

Aristide stared at the note, his stomach tying itself up in knots. At last, getting hold of himself, he quickly turned and walked the half mile back to his lodgings. To his relief, no suspicious strangers seemed to be about. Returning to his room, he threw a change of linen and all the money he had into a satchel, as well as any pamphlets, manuscripts, and scrawled notes he thought would get him into trouble if the police searched his room and perused them, and crept down the stairs. Fortunately it was midmorning with few people about—the house was too poorly maintained to have a resident porter—and he escaped unnoticed.

Derville, as he had hoped, was at home, though barely dressed. "I didn't come here for a stroll through the Palais-Royal," Aristide told him, as Derville welcomed him and called for his manservant to lay two places for breakfast. "I may be in some hot water. Could I presume upon your hospitality for a few days?"

"Of course you may," Derville said, "but what sort of scrape have you gotten yourself into? Don't tell me you've already been unmasked as the author of one of those seditious pamphlets of yours! Will I be forwarding a change of body linen to the Bastille?"

"Don't joke about it." Aristide sat gratefully on the chair Derville pulled out for him and rubbed his eyes. "It's worse. The dead man—the man with the striped waistcoat—Brasseur's superior thinks I may have had something to do with his murder."

"You!"

"Because they already know that I'm probably the author of some of those seditious pamphlets, and they also know whose son I am, and so obviously I'm an unsavory character. But I don't even know who the man was."

"It wasn't Saint-Landry, then, after all? Because Madame Saint-Landry told me he hadn't been home for two days. She's growing very worried."

"I don't know where Saint-Landry may be, alive or dead, but we can't confirm anything, because the corpse has vanished."

"Vanished!" Derville echoed him. He sat down hard on a sofa, with a hoot of laughter, and leaned back, crossing his arms. "How does a dead body just 'vanish'?"

"It's been stolen, Derville. And I don't know why, and I don't know who he was, and I never saw the man before in my life, and yet the police think I may have murdered him!"

"Surely that inspector—Briseur—Brissot—"

"Brasseur."

"Surely Brasseur doesn't think so."

"No, he was the one who warned me. He's on my side . . . I think."

"Well," said Derville, "you can certainly stay here until this is cleared up. I'll have Renauld make up a bed for you."

"Derville," Aristide said abruptly, "are you a Freemason?"

"Good Lord, no," he said. "Why do you ask?"

"Because I think this affair has something to do with the Masons, and I need to know more about them. On the dead man's body . . . someone had cut a symbol, which I think was a Masonic compass and square, into his chest after he was dead."

"Good God." Derville looked away for a moment before shrugging. "I know a few people who are Freemasons, certainly. They're perfectly respectable, decent people. If you think any of them would do such a thing—"

"I don't think anything, at this point. I'm just baffled, and I want to get to the bottom of this. If you say that no Mason would commit such an outrage, then who would? Someone who doesn't like the Masons?"

The servant entered with coffee and rolls on a tray and Derville gestured Aristide to the breakfast table. "Come on; I always think better after a decent meal." He took a seat, poured coffee into the two bowls, passed Aristide the jug of hot milk, and began spreading anchovy butter onto a roll. "Are you sure," he added, "that what you saw really was a compass and square?"

"I'll draw it for you."

Sighing, Derville fetched a sheet of paper and an inkwell from his writing-desk and returned. Aristide sketched the symbol, an acute angle, with a short arc connecting the two arms near its point, and crossed by a right angle below. Derville frowned at it.

"Well, it *might* be a compass and square, but really it could be anything, Ravel."

"What about this one?" Aristide said. He drew the pentagram in five swift strokes and surrounded it with a circle. "Someone laid this symbol out in lines composed of human bones, not ten paces from the body."

"*Bones?*" Derville echoed him, incredulous.

"Bones. Old dry ones, out of the charnels in the cemetery. Also a skull and crossbones laid out at his head and feet. Don't tell me it's not all linked, and that something extremely nasty isn't going on here."

"All right, I grant you that anyone who thought of that must have a remarkably bizarre imagination." Derville sighed and reached for another roll. "Look, Ravel, I don't know what sort of superstitious nonsense you may have heard, but the Freemasons are devoted to bettering themselves and their fellow men. There's nothing sinister about them."

"What about the rituals—"

"Half the bored gentry of Europe plays at mysterious rituals, for something to do, and charlatans like Saint-Germain and Casanova egg them on with a lot of sleight of hand and hocus-pocus. The Masons have their rituals, I've no doubt, but plenty of well-known people are members. For God's sake, even the Duc d'Orléans is a Mason; everybody knows that. He's Grand Master, in fact, because he's the king's cousin and First Prince of the Blood. People whisper silly rumors because the Masons consider themselves a secret society, but if they use some passwords or hush-hush gestures among themselves, it's only because most of them are in the same business you are."

"Business?" Aristide said.

"Championing liberty and free thought, my friend. The political pamphlets you write, the hot stuff that has to be sold out of Joubert's back room because it tells the truth that the people in power don't want to hear. The sort of writing and talk that'll get you thrown into the Bastille if you get too noisy. That's why they use passwords and secret handshakes and so on: it's just a way to get around police spies."

Aristide nodded and busied himself with adding hot milk and sugar to his coffee bowl as he felt himself blushing.

"You know what sort of calamitous, ill-governed mess this country is in," Derville continued, between bites, apparently oblivious to Aristide's discomfort. "Even though it's the biggest, wealthiest kingdom in Europe. Well, everyone I know who's a Mason knows it just as well as you do, and I know that what they want is nothing more than what *you* want, and what you've been writing about: reform, tolerance, doing away with the old, outmoded, unfair laws and privileges. The usual catchword is, I believe, 'Freedom from the tyranny of priests and kings.'" He smiled suddenly. "I expect you'd find yourself quite at home, you know, if you applied to join them."

Aristide shook his head. "I'm really more the sort of person who prefers to work alone and be left alone." Perhaps it was owing to the harshness of his childhood after his parents' deaths, but he had found long ago that he rarely made friends easily, and much preferred solitude to compulsory camaraderie. "I'd rather choose my friends as I wish, not flock together with a lot of strangers in some sort of hearty brotherhood."

"As you like," Derville said, pushing away the dish of anchovy butter. "But don't forget that any Mason you meet is likely to be your ally rather than your enemy. Is that the apricot jam there by your elbow?"

"So who would slash a Masonic symbol into a dead man's flesh?" Aristide said, handing over the jam pot.

"Certainly not a Mason. I can't conceive it; it's completely barbaric."

"Someone who hates Freemasons, then. Who would hate them that much?"

"Plenty of people. Anyone who doesn't like what they stand for." Derville refilled his coffee bowl and leaned back in his chair. "Anyone who'd have a lot to lose if we loosened the grip of those in power. A courtier. Some idiot third son of a nobleman who got his pension by sucking up to a government minister. Any of those parasites. Or . . . what would you say is the greatest obstacle to the advancement of reason, science, and liberalism? What institution ruthlessly crushes dissenters and has fought, tooth and nail, every step of the way, whenever someone tries to explain the mysteries of nature in a rational manner? When they first tried to publish the *Encyclopedia*, for instance?"

"The greatest obstacle to reason?" Aristide said. "That's easy: the

Church. Keep people ignorant, and you keep them credulous, chained to their superstitions, and dependant on their priests."

"Well, I know more than a few liberal priests, but I'm sure there are just as many fanatics who think the Inquisition is a wonderful thing, and that it's a natural and desirable state of affairs to have the power of the king ready to enforce religion. Perhaps you should look for a mad monk or curé who believes the Freemasons are agents of Satan."

Aristide groaned. "How do I do that?"

"Search me. I never said it would be easy."

Aristide finished his breakfast, mulling over what Derville had told him. "You said you had friends who were Masons—could you introduce me to some of them?"

"I didn't say 'friends,'" Derville said hastily. "Just acquaintances."

"Still, if you could—"

"I can't just go barging in on them with a companion who wants to know about the deepest secrets of Freemasonry, Ravel. Though if you can allow me a few days, I might be able to arrange something . . ." The gilt clock on the mantel chimed the half hour and he glanced at it. "Lord, is that the time? I'm rather busy today; I've an appointment with my bootmaker this morning, then I'm meeting people later for the opera and supper afterward. Come to think of it, a fellow who might be at the opera tonight . . . I could try to wheedle a dinner invitation out of him."

"Dinner?" Aristide said, with an involuntary glance down at his threadbare suit.

"Hmm, that may be a snag . . ." Derville looked him over, with a critical eye. "Do you *have* any other clothes?"

"No. Just a change of linen."

"Well, maybe we can find you some decent clothes to wear. I do know a first-rate dealer in secondhand gentlemen's clothes . . . perhaps we can find a proper dress suit that would fit you, and get it altered in time."

Aristide agreed, having plans of his own for the rest of the morning while Derville was busy with his bootmaker. When Derville had departed, he slipped out and walked to the Left Bank. Lefèvre was waiting at the café they had agreed upon the previous day. Aristide followed him inside and he pushed past the clientele standing about the counter, which at midday seemed to consist mostly of unemployed *petits-bourgeois*, clerks and the like, as well as the usual complement of shabby literary men who could not afford the higher prices at Zoppi's.

"I thought I might find him here at Vachon's," he said to Aristide, as they reached a table at the rear, with a glance at the young man busily scrawling away at a few sheets of ink-blotted paper. "Desmoulins!"

The scribbler, a year or two younger than Aristide, raised his head. He had remarkably fine dark eyes, though the rest of him was unprepossessing; he was very much a type Aristide recognized, young, untidy, and earnest.

"Good day," the young man said, uncertainly. He glanced at Lefèvre with a flicker of recognition in his eyes, but said nothing more. Lefèvre stepped forward.

"Lefèvre. We've met a few times at the Café de l'École."

"Oh, yes, of c-course!" The young man halted for an instant in the midst of his sentence and Aristide sensed that he was struggling with a slight stutter.

"You're a Freemason, aren't you?" Lefèvre inquired.

Desmoulins nodded. "Of the Lodge of the Nine Sisters. Why?"

"I haven't the faintest idea why. But Ravel here needs to talk to a Mason, and you were the first one who turned up." He performed brief introductions.

"You never saw me, by the way," Aristide said, as Lefèvre retreated. "If anyone should ask."

Lefèvre grinned and excused himself, talking vaguely of a prior engagement.

"Why do you need to talk to a Mason?" Desmoulins inquired,

turning his gaze back to Aristide, who ordered two cups of hot chocolate and settled himself at the table. "Some things about the C-Craft I
can't tell you, you know."

"I . . . I'm not sure what I need to ask you," Aristide confessed.
"But something damned peculiar is going on, and Freemasons seem
to be involved."

"Peculiar?"

The waiter arrived with their chocolate and Aristide took a swallow and proceeded to recount, in a low voice, the tale of the mysterious fires, the symbols daubed in blood, and finally the anonymous,
murdered man lying in the churchyard. Desmoulins nodded when he
paused for breath.

"I heard about the murder at St. André des Arts. Didn't hear the
details, though. You say there was a pentagram composed of *bones*
nearby?"

"What meaning do pentagrams have?"

He shrugged. "None I know of. They're not mentioned in any ritual I've ever taken part in. Maybe as an ancient symbol of wisdom, or
signifying the five wounds of C-Christ, but . . . no, I'd say pentagrams
really have no particular meaning to Masons. But I've only been an
initiate for about six months," he added. "I joined the lodge at about
the same time as I was called to the Paris bar; frankly, I hoped to make
some useful acquaintances out of it."

"You're an attorney?" Aristide said, hoping he did not sound too
incredulous, for Desmoulins, aside from those sparkling black eyes,
looked no different from most of the penniless, ambitious writers he
knew, including himself.

"I don't look much like a proper lawyer, do I?" Desmoulins said, as
if reading his thoughts. Suddenly he flashed Aristide a quick impish
grin. "Getting briefs in Paris is nearly as difficult as getting published.
I should know. Actually, I earn most of my living from copying, or
clerking now and then—"

"I ought to tell you something else about the dead man," Aristide interrupted, lowering his voice again. "At the morgue, they discovered that a compass and square had been slashed into his flesh after he was dead . . . and that his tongue had been cut out."

"Good God!" Desmoulins exclaimed. "That's barbaric." Abruptly his eyes widened and he caught his breath.

"Monsieur Ravel . . . how was this man k-killed?"

"His throat was cut. That is, he was stunned first, then the murderer . . ." Aristide broke off as he realized that the young man had gone very still.

"His throat was c-cut?"

Aristide nodded. Desmoulins drew a deep breath and was silent for a moment, leaning on his elbows, fist pressed to his chin.

"I don't know if I ought to repeat any of this," he said at length, "but do you know the oath an initiate must swear when he joins the Freemasons?"

"I know exactly nothing about Freemasonry except what I've picked up in the past day and a half."

"Well . . . you swear to uphold the tenets and never reveal any of the mysteries of Freemasonry . . . under penalty of having your throat c-cut and your tongue torn out by its roots."

They stared at each other, paling.

11

His throat cut and his tongue torn out," Aristide said at last.

"It looks bad, doesn't it?" said Desmoulins "I mean, I sup-posed it was just a formula. Anyone would. You don't expect anyone would really take an extravagant oath like that seriously, to the letter. It's mostly rituals and trappings."

"Tell me, do all of you Masons know each other?"

"Know each other?" Desmoulins echoed him. "Maybe you've been listening to hysterical rumors, monsieur. We're not a vast web of secret c-conspirators who want to overthrow the Church and establish our own heathen religion. Of c-course we don't all know each other."

"But members of a lodge would?"

"To be sure; not intimately perhaps, if it's a lodge with qu-quite a few members, but at least by name and sight."

"Do you know a Mason named Saint-Landry, who lives in this quarter on Rue de Savoie?" Aristide said.

"No, I'm sure I don't. Who is he?"

"He might be the corpse, except we don't know it absolutely, because now the corpse itself is missing." Desmoulins's eyes widened at that and Aristide forged ahead, not wishing to spend time in explanations. "Monsieur Desmoulins, if you're willing to help me, you could do me a great service by asking among your fellow Masons and learning something about this man Saint-Landry, or simply his present whereabouts. You can leave a message for me with my friend Derville, if you need to." He scrawled Saint-Landry's name and address and also Derville's address on a scrap of paper the other pushed toward him. "I think it better if you tell no one any details, though."

"We've a lodge meeting tonight," Desmoulins said. "I c-can ask a few questions then."

They agreed to meet there, in the same modest café, the next day, and Aristide returned to Derville's apartment. Derville arrived shortly thereafter and whisked him away to the Palais-Royal and the establishment of a certain Monsieur Baudry who was, Derville told him, a most excellent and discreet reseller of fine clothing.

After selecting a handsome burgundy silk suit for Aristide, and ordering the appropriate alterations, Derville invited him to dine and took him to a nearby restaurateur's. Cheap taverns, eating-houses, and food stalls were plentiful, meeting the needs of the working class who often had no way to cook in their overcrowded tenements, or of *petit-bourgeois* bachelors living alone, but a dining establishment that served fine dishes and was as comfortable and elegant as a rich man's own salon was a fashionable novelty. They enjoyed a good dinner, though Derville refused to respond to any reference Aristide made to the dead man and his possible ties to Freemasonry, claiming that he did not wish to lose his appetite.

At last they returned to the apartment, for Derville had to change clothes for his evening at the opera. After the hairdresser and his assistant had left, and Derville had dressed to his satisfaction in a fine *demi-gala* suit of embroidered green satin and gone out, Aristide settled himself in the salon with a book. Some while later, after night had fallen outside, Renauld, the manservant, entered.

"Monsieur, a visitor has arrived who wishes to speak with Monsieur Derville. I've told him monsieur is out."

"What, he won't take no for an answer?" said Aristide.

"It's not that, monsieur," Renauld said, looking uncomfortable. "He's known to me, you see, as his master has called here two or three times, and he says it's most urgent. In Monsieur Derville's absence, I thought I had better consult you before asking him to return later."

"Who is he?"

"The Marquis de Beaupréau's man."

"Moreau?" Aristide said, intrigued, wondering if any link could be forged between Beaupréau and Saint-Landry.

"Yes, monsieur, Moreau."

"I know him. You'd better let him in."

The manservant bowed and slipped out, and a moment later the valet entered, hat in hand. He frowned for an instant at Aristide, as though trying to retrieve a memory, and then his face cleared.

"I know you, monsieur. You came to the house yesterday, with the inspector of police, did you not?"

"Yes." He imagined that Moreau was attempting to decide who and what he was. After an instant's deliberation, he decided to tell the young man as much of the truth as he dared. "I'm a friend of Monsieur Derville's, but I'm also assisting Inspector Brasseur. What was it you wished to see Derville about?"

"Well, monsieur, as you know, my master is the Marquis de Beaupréau, and Monsieur Derville is one of his many acquaintances."

"Good friends?"

"I wouldn't say that, though they're on more than civil terms. Sociable, you might say. Monsieur de Beaupréau has brought me here with him from time to time, when he's come calling with other gentlemen.

So I thought perhaps Monsieur Derville might know something of my master's whereabouts."

"His whereabouts?" Aristide echoed him. "You mean he hasn't returned yet?"

"That's just it, monsieur. Monsieur de Beaupréau's nowhere to be found, and I'm beginning to worry. He didn't come home yesterday evening when I expected he would, and he sent no message, nothing."

This can't be a coincidence, Aristide thought, with a sinking feeling in the pit of his stomach. *Two men missing now, one of them likely dead . . .*

"Moreau," he said slowly, suspecting he already knew the answer to his question, "is Monsieur de Beaupréau a Freemason?"

"Yes, monsieur."

"Has he been behaving out of character lately?"

Moreau hesitated for an instant before replying. "You might say that. He's been spending a good deal of time, recently, off with some other gentlemen who, he's told me, are members of his lodge. He hasn't taken me along, and there's not much that he doesn't share with me, so they must want whatever they're doing kept very secret. Do you think that could have something to do with all this?"

"Do you know the name Saint-Landry?"

"Saint-Landry? Yes, he's one of the gentlemen from monsieur's lodge."

"You're sure that Monsieur de Beaupréau is really missing," Aristide said, without much hope, "and not just occupied elsewhere?"

"It's been too long, monsieur; he'd have sent word by now. He's considerate that way, and wouldn't have left the household at sixes and sevens like this."

"There's no chance he could be with a friend who unexpectedly turned up in Paris, or . . . spending a few days with a fascinating new mistress?"

Moreau shook his head. "Not without sending me a message, which is what he always does if he's detained. This morning I went to all the places where I thought he might have been, but I couldn't find any sign of him. Mademoiselle Sédillot, his mistress, she said he'd visited her on Monday evening, and he took his leave toward midnight, and then he might have vanished into thin air, for all the traces I can find of him. Now I'm trying to call on all the gentlemen he knows, in the hope that one of them might have seen him since."

"I'm sorry, Moreau," Aristide said, "but Monsieur Derville is out and won't be back until three or four in the morning, I suspect. If you came back tomorrow, not too early—"

"Monsieur," Moreau said suddenly, "I hardly like to ask it, but . . . that waistcoat you and the inspector showed me . . . it must have been connected to a police matter?"

"Yes, I fear so."

"I saw stains on it that hadn't quite washed out. They were bloodstains, weren't they?"

"Why do you say that?"

Moreau smiled slightly. "Monsieur, I've been taking care of Monsieur de Beaupréau's wardrobe, among other things, since I was sixteen. I've cleaned up his riding clothes—and mine—after a day's hunting, many times, and I know very well what an old bloodstain looks like. Was that waistcoat off a dead man? Was that why the inspector was asking about it?"

Aristide nodded, wondering if Brasseur would approve of how much he was disclosing, although Moreau seemed perfectly capable of working out the facts for himself.

"You remember, monsieur," the young man continued, "I couldn't find Monsieur de Beaupréau's waistcoat in his wardrobe. It's foolish, I know, but I fret about his safety sometimes, and I do get all sorts of wild ideas. Monsieur Alexis—Monsieur de Beaupréau, that is—he's a bit reckless. He's the finest man that ever lived, but he is one to take chances, and he's never feared anything in his life. So he might be anywhere, you see."

"How old is Monsieur de Beaupréau?" Aristide inquired.

"Twenty-nine, monsieur."

"The dead man was older, I'm sure of it."

"You saw this dead man for yourself?" Moreau said, excited. Aristide nodded. "Monsieur—I pray you—you could do me a tremendous service, if you would, by easing my mind. Come back with me to the Hôtel de Beaupréau and take a look at monsieur's portrait, and tell me if that's the man you saw or not." He clapped a hand to his forehead and shook his head. "I might have shown the portrait to both of you when you called, but it was early yet, Monsieur de Beaupréau had only gone out Monday evening and I wasn't so concerned about him then . . ."

"Of course I'll come," Aristide said. He shouted to Derville's servant that he might be out rather late, and hurried down the dark staircase after Moreau.

"You're Monsieur de Beaupréau's valet," he said, after they had seated themselves in a chilly fiacre for the ride to the Left Bank. "Surely a man has no secrets from his valet?"

Moreau smiled in the gloom beneath the lantern that swung above them. "I probably know him better than anyone, monsieur. As I said, there's not much he doesn't share with me. That's why this has me so troubled."

Aristide covertly took his measure. Moreau seemed about the same age as his master, a good-looking young man in his late twenties. "Are you very close, then?" he inquired.

"Like brothers, monsieur. We grew up together, he being an only son with four sisters. I'm an orphan; my father was the coachman at the estate, and then both my parents and my sister died of the smallpox when I was seven, and monsieur's father, the old marquis, he brought the two of us up together, so Monsieur Alexis would have some company. I played with Monsieur Alexis, went riding and hunting with him, shared his lessons, everything."

"Everything?"

"They treated me like one of their own. I ate with Monsieur Alexis in the schoolroom, and my bedchamber was next to his at the château at Andrezé. We even played together at amateur theatricals with his sisters, when we were lads, before the young ladies went off to school at the convent. Monsieur Alexis was as good as any actor I've seen on the stage in Paris."

Aristide nodded. He had been wondering why the valet, whose cheerful, open, courteous manner made him instantly likable, spoke and carried himself like a man of much higher station. "So you're friends, then, as well as master and servant."

"As much as a nobleman's son and a servant's son could ever be. Brothers in the country, you might say, where it's informal, and we rag each other over everything . . . and master and servant in city society, and I'm not ashamed of it. I went with him to America, even."

"To the war?"

"He was an officer, though he's resigned his commission now. He didn't want me to come; he said it would be dangerous, and that I had no need to risk my life over there. But I wasn't going to be separated from him. He's my family, you see . . . my brother," he repeated softly.

They alighted in the broad, cobbled front courtyard of the Hôtel de Beaupréau. Moreau led Aristide around the side of the mansion to a terrace and an inconspicuous, narrow flight of steps that led down to a sunken path and a door below ground level. "This way, monsieur; we'd better go through the kitchens and up the back stairs. Though nobody's likely to see us; madame is in Rouen, and we won't be having any visitors, not till tomorrow afternoon anyway." He gestured at the windows high above them, which were draped in black.

"The household is in mourning?" Aristide said, trying to recall if he had seen any black draperies the day before.

Moreau let out a soft chuckle. "Just since early today, but only for form's sake. It's Monsieur de Beaupréau's cousin, the Vicomte de

Castagnac. I'd wager everyone in the family heaved a great sigh of relief to learn Castagnac finally breathed his last. Black sheep of the family," he added, in response to Aristide's curious glance, "spendthrift, runs up gambling debts, drinks too much, picks up nasty diseases from whores, forever a burden and an embarrassment . . . you know the sort." He pulled a ring of keys from a pocket and unlocked the door.

Aristide followed him inside and through a short tunnel that ran beneath the terrace above and into the dark corridors of the kitchens, storerooms, and servants' halls in the cellars. Faint cracks of light flickered from beneath a few doors, where he could hear servant girls gossiping, amid splashing and the clatter of cooking pots. After Moreau had paused to light a few candles on a pewter candelabrum, they climbed a bare, narrow stone stairway and emerged from a door camouflaged by cleverly carved woodwork into a twilit foyer. Moreau continued through a salon, in which Aristide could make out the silhouettes of a harp and various pieces of graceful Louis XV furniture, and onward into another, smaller parlor that the servants had not yet swathed in mourning black.

"There," Moreau said, crossing to a full-length portrait of a young officer in uniform, hanging above a sumptuous buffet topped in green malachite. "That's Monsieur Alexis." He raised the candelabrum higher to illuminate the portrait.

Aristide took the candelabrum and examined the painting. The Marquis de Beaupréau, posing beneath an enormous, gnarled tree and resting one hand on the hilt of his sword, had an intelligent, pleasant face and looked lean and athletic. Behind him stretched a wild landscape that did not look like anything Aristide had ever seen.

"He had that painted four years ago, before we returned from America," Moreau said, behind him. "It's the countryside in Virginia. He loved America . . . thought it was like no place else on earth."

"I'm sorry," Aristide said at last. "Or rather, I'm glad; for your sake.

This is not the dead man I saw. They're little like, and the man I saw was older."

"Thank God," whispered Moreau.

So the dead man was most likely the absent Saint-Landry, as he had suspected, Aristide decided. He looked again at the painting, and then abruptly back at Moreau. Something about the eyes, the shape of the mouth and chin . . .

His curiosity must have evidenced itself, he realized, for the young man quickly nodded, with a hint of a self-conscious grin.

"Yes, monsieur. I've wondered about the resemblance, myself. The old marquis was always good to my family, more generous than he needed to be. But they're all of them dead now, so there's no use asking awkward questions."

"But when you say that you and Monsieur de Beaupréau are like brothers . . ."

"I expect it's truer than we know. But no two brothers could be closer, monsieur, and Monsieur Alexis feels just the same way. He's always said to me that even though he pays me to shave him and take care of his wardrobe and run his errands, I'm his friend first of all, and I shouldn't consider myself any less of a man than he is. 'You're as good a man as any other, Gabriel,' he says sometimes, 'and should deserve the happiness every man deserves.' And I think he truly believes that. He's very well read in all the modern thought, you see, and he believes all men ought to be equal, equal in rights and under the law." He abruptly paused and looked away, blinking hard.

"Forgive me, monsieur," he said a moment later, self-possessed once more. "I've no other family—he means the world to me. So if anything has gone ill with him . . ."

Aristide was spared having to fumble for a reply when Moreau continued. "Monsieur, do you think it's possible that these two matters are connected—the dead man, and Monsieur Alexis's disappearance?"

"I'm beginning to fear it's not a coincidence," Aristide agreed.

"The waistcoat you showed me . . . this dead man who wore it ordered his clothes from Monsieur Alexis's tailor, I've no doubt at all about that. It's possible they knew each other. Society's not large. And with this man dead, and Monsieur Alexis missing . . . maybe Monsieur Alexis . . ."

"Murdered him?" Aristide said as the young man's voice trailed off.

"No!" Moreau exclaimed. "No, monsieur, I'd swear by all the saints that he did not. He couldn't do such a thing. But I'm beginning to fear that somehow he might be mixed up in this affair, that . . . that the same person who killed the owner of that waistcoat might have murdered him—God will it isn't so," he added, hastily making the sign of the cross, "—or tried to. Maybe he's hiding from these people."

"Why might he hide from them?"

"Because they know something, monsieur? Something they shouldn't? Or they're mixed up in something crooked and he found out about it? Or *he's* mixed up in something?"

Aristide was silent for a moment as he pondered the young man's words, but Moreau raced onward.

"Are you thinking, monsieur, that the dead man was Monsieur Saint-Landry that you asked me about? I know he bespoke his wardrobe from Monsieur Yvon, just like Monsieur Alexis."

"It's possible."

"Then we ought to consider that they were both caught up in something dangerous, monsieur. After all, they're members of the same lodge, and who knows what some of those Freemasons might be up to?" Moreau put a hand to his waist and Aristide heard a muffled jingle. "I have the keys to Monsieur Alexis's private study. Perhaps if we were to take a look around . . . if we could find any letters, any clues to what might be going on . . ."

Heaven only knows what I'm supposed to be looking for, Aristide thought as he followed Moreau through more shadowed salons. The faintest glimmer of light showed from beneath a pair of double doors as they passed, and Moreau paused to cross himself. "Monsieur de Castagnac," he whispered, as Aristide glanced at him. "In there, with Madame de Saint-Aubin keeping vigil, since Monsieur Alexis isn't here. He's to be buried tomorrow. This way, if you please."

Beaupréau's study was lined with books, many by authors who Aristide knew were often banned for their criticism of the monarchy and the Church. He spotted finely bound copies of *The Social Contract*, *In the Year 2440*, *The Picture of Paris*, *The Private Life of Louis XV*, *Christianity Unveiled*, *The System of Nature*, *The Philosophical Dictionary*, *The History of Madame du Barry*—the latest scandalous, subversive bestseller—and *The Spirit of the Laws*. Sharing space with works on natural history by Buffon and Daubenton, a complete set of the *Encyclopedia*, including the volumes printed without royal approval, took up an entire wall.

They glanced over the bookshelves and sorted through half a dozen papers on Beaupréau's desk and in a drawer, but found nothing of significance. Moreau tried the keys he carried in the other drawers, but they would not turn.

"I suppose he must have a few things he'd want kept private, even from me."

Aristide did not answer him. A tiny, windowless antechamber led off from the study and the recessed, mirror-backed shelves that lined it seemed to hold at least a dozen objects that glinted in the flickering light of their candles. "What's this?"

"What's what, monsieur?"

"This anteroom."

"That's Monsieur Alexis's private collection. He's interested in scientific curiosities."

"'Scientific curiosities'?"

"Well . . . if you have a strong stomach, monsieur, I'll show you."

He stepped close to Aristide and raised the candelabrum high above his head, then slowly passed it across the shelves. Aristide stared.

"God's death!"

The shiny objects were tall glass vials. Within each one a monstrous creature—a two-headed grass snake, a tiny piglet with a stunted fifth leg dangling from its shoulder, a hideously deformed human fetus with almost no head—floated in clear liquid. He glanced up and down and saw a few more monstrosities, including a malformed calf's skull boasting a single enormous eye, that set his stomach to churning before he quickly stepped backward.

The specimens on the next row of shelves were less bizarre. The ivory-white, perfect skeleton of a snake, spiraled about a leafless branch, seemed ready to slither out of its glass case. In another case, a pair of mummified bats stretched their leathery wings wide, tiny sharp teeth gleaming in half-open mouths.

"Where on earth did all this come from?"

"The old marquis bought most of them, over the years. He liked studying natural philosophy. Monsieur Alexis and I spent some very interesting lessons, when we were boys, looking over those creatures! This one's more recent, though. Monsieur Alexis bought it himself, or rather he paid to have it preserved." Moreau turned and pointed to a bell jar, which appeared to hold a dun-colored, shriveled doll.

Aristide peered into the jar and saw a tiny, desiccated mummy, frozen forever in the midst of dancing a macabre jig. Little more than a foot and a half tall, it gaped at him with blank eyeballs the color of a dead leaf, and a wide, ghastly, lipless grin full of yellowed teeth. Its skinless flesh peeled away from it in papery flaps, revealing shrunken tendons and muscles, bluish veins, and the traces of bone beneath. It could have been, he thought, an image straight out of an anatomist's textbook, if there happened to be schools of surgery in Hell.

"That's Coco," Moreau said, behind him. "Ingenious, isn't he?"

"*Coco?*" He looked more closely and realized a moment later, at the sight of the thumbs on the withered little feet, that the thing had once been a monkey.

"He belonged to Mademoiselle Isabelle—that's Monsieur Alexis's favorite sister. He bought her the monkey. The poor creature suddenly took cold and died a few years ago. Monsieur Alexis was fond of him, and he'd paid quite a lot for him, so perhaps he didn't want to simply dispose of him on the nearest rubbish heap. He hired a man who makes specimens for surgeons to preserve him."

"Well," said Aristide, turning away thankfully from the shelves of vials, "I don't think we can learn anything more here. You'd better let me out before one of the other servants finds us."

"If they did," Moreau said, "they wouldn't have anything to say about it. They know Monsieur Alexis trusts me." He locked the study door behind them and guided Aristide back to the servants' entrance.

"I'm sure Monsieur de Beaupréau will return safely," Aristide said, lingering a moment in the doorway at the end of the tunnel. "But if you should need help, look for me, or leave a message for me, at Monsieur Derville's lodgings; or you can always try to reach Inspector Brasseur at his headquarters on Rue des Amandiers, in the Eighteenth District, near St. Étienne du Mont. All right?"

"Yes, monsieur. You've taken a lot off my mind; I thank you." They shook hands and Aristide hastily crossed the courtyard and dodged out through the wicket gate before the porter could inquire his business.

The street beyond was empty and almost completely dark, but for the wan moonlight. A few thin cracks of light spilled from curtained windows in the mansion across the way, and a pair of swinging lanterns glimmered faintly from a carriage that was retreating northward into the gloom, toward the amusements of the Right Bank. Aristide had gone only a few steps when a thickset, shadowy figure abruptly loomed up before him and seized him, thrusting him backward against a wall.

"Drop it, monsieur."

"What?" Aristide gasped.

"I said, drop it," the man repeated in a guttural whisper, keeping hold of Aristide's lapels. "Shut your trap and disappear. Keep your long nose out of things that don't concern you. Understand?"

Aristide could see almost nothing of his attacker, except for a hat well pulled down above a muffler and a heavy overcoat. "Who are you?"

"You just can't stop asking questions, can you? Well, if you keep on, it'll be the worse for you."

"But—"

"Nobody wants to see you hurt, monsieur, but you ought to stay away from the Hôtel de Beaupréau."

He emphasized his words by giving Aristide a rough shove against the stone wall behind him, before melting into the darkness.

12

B rasseur called at Derville's lodgings at quarter to nine the next morning, while Derville was still, as far as Aristide knew, sound asleep. Renauld let him in and silently laid another place at the small breakfast table.

"Well," Brasseur said, after a few appreciative swallows of coffee, "I've not gotten too far with anything. Some men of mine are still questioning the neighborhood around St. André des Arts; nobody on patrol seems to have seen anything out of the ordinary around midnight . . . not that you could see much in those ill-lit streets . . . and of course most folk are safe inside with their shutters closed. But if the fellow who delivered that letter to Saint-Landry is still about, we'll find him sooner or later." He sighed and reached for the plate of rolls. "What the devil's this? It smells like the fish market."

"Anchovy butter."

"Saints alive, the tastes of the rich . . ."

Aristide pushed the dish of sweet butter toward him. "One of my men did find a local beggar," Brasseur continued, "name of Lame

Barnabé, who, with a little persuasion, owned up to coming across a bloodstained coat abandoned in an alley near the cemetery."

"Does he still have it?" Aristide said, brightening. "Does it tell you anything?"

"No, curse it, he says he sold it to a man with an old-clothes cart, for enough silver to keep him drunk for a month. Claims it was just an ordinary coat, darkish brown, a year or two out of date as far as he could tell, but in decent condition; nothing special. The sort of thing a clerk or a grocer would wear on Sundays, he said."

"Nothing special? What about the blood on it?"

"Blood, mud, what would he care?" Brasseur said, shrugging. "I think his words were, 'There might have been some stains about the cuffs, but it was still fit to wear, wasn't it?'"

"A drab brown coat," Aristide mused, "an unremarkable coat you would wear if you didn't wish to be noticed at night. And it brings us not a step further to the killer's identity. Is it even worth going after the *fripier* to whom Barnabé sold it, to try to find the coat?"

"Probably not, because when we find it, it'll prove to be the sort of thing that any third-rate tailor makes dozens of in the course of a year. Though I suppose I'd better put somebody onto it anyway, for more of those endless rounds of asking the same questions over and over."

Aristide glanced at him, found the older man was looking studiously into his coffee bowl, but with the faintest of grins, and suddenly decided that, despite his high-handed methods and his deceptively stolid manner, he could not help liking Brasseur.

"I've learned something, at least," he said, as Brasseur buttered a roll and hungrily bit into it. "Moreau, Beaupréau's valet, came looking for his master—Beaupréau's been missing since Monday—"

"Eh?"

"Moreau was concerned, though there's no evidence at all—yet—that Beaupréau's in any trouble. But Moreau had the bright idea of showing me Beaupréau's portrait when he learned that I'd seen the dead

man before he disappeared. The corpse certainly wasn't Beaupréau, Brasseur. So by elimination, I'd say it has to be Saint-Landry."

"Excellent," Brasseur muttered, pulling out his notebook. "See, you do have a talent for investigation . . ."

"That was just luck. But between that and the clothes . . . which Moreau swears are Yvon's tailoring . . . it can't be a coincidence. And furthermore," Aristide added, "Saint-Landry was a Freemason, and so is Beaupréau, and Moreau told me they knew each other."

Brasseur stared at him for an instant as he reached for another roll. "That's interesting, isn't it?"

"Very interesting. Especially since, as I was leaving the Hôtel de Beaupréau, somebody's flunky tried to frighten me off with a bit of rough handling."

"Did they, by God!"

"I don't suppose that's something the police would have done?"

"No, we'd have just nabbed you and taken you in," said Brasseur. "We don't waste time with threats."

"Then it seems someone doesn't want me hanging around the Hôtel de Beaupréau, inquiring into the marquis's business."

"Beaupréau's flunky, you think?"

"I've no idea. He didn't introduce himself. But it makes me wonder, certainly, about Beaupréau's role in all this."

"Oh, Lord, I hope you're wrong," said Brasseur. "Arresting a nobleman for murder's a messy affair. Any guesses why Beaupréau might have wanted Saint-Landry dead?"

"None at all. Though perhaps I can get nearer to the bottom of this Freemasonry business," Aristide said. "An acquaintance, a Mason . . . he's promised to help me if he can. I'll meet him at the Café Vachon—do you know it, on Rue du Paon?—at eleven, if you should happen to be in the quarter."

"Good work," Brasseur said indistinctly, around the roll. "I'll leave that to you, though; they wouldn't talk to an inspector of police."

"What about the corpse?"

"The corpse? Well, so far, all my underworld *mouches* say they've heard nothing about any plans, anywhere, to steal bodies from the morgue. As you said, it's a lunatic thing to do; it's safer to rob the graveyards."

"So it was stolen for a reason. A reason other than an anatomy lecture, I mean."

"Yes, I think we can conclude they wanted this particular corpse, though I'm damned if I know why somebody's made off with the remains of this—this inoffensive ex-papermaker. As to how—I've questioned any number of people in the neighborhood of the Châtelet, and nobody'll admit to seeing anything out of the ordinary."

"But what's to see?" Aristide said, remembering the public passage at the fortress. "It's pretty dim by the door to the cellars."

"Exactly." Brasseur gulped down another swallow of coffee. "Probably the men who took the body had a cart waiting right outside, seized their moment when no one was nearby, shoved it into the cart, and covered it up with a bit of canvas and some turnips. How the devil do you find a cart that looks just like the hundred other market carts that go past the Châtelet every day?" He rose, slipping a last roll into his pocket, and grasped Aristide's arm. "Look here, Ravel, I owe you an apology. I know I've put you in a tight spot by drawing attention to you. Probably it would never have crossed the commissaire's mind to suspect you of this murder, if I hadn't been dragging you around Paris with me."

"You deduced that, did you?"

"But you're safe enough here, and no real harm done," Brasseur continued, paying no heed to Aristide's sarcasm. "This is going to blow over, I promise you. Now since we've no body, it's going to be damned difficult to pursue this case. The one advantage we do have is that we're pretty sure that the murdered man was Monsieur Saint-Landry. But no one else in the police knows that. So if you were to keep on with the Saint-Landry household, and pursue this Masonic

angle, and why someone might have wanted to kill him—the police, in their happy ignorance, wouldn't be around to interfere with you. As far as they're concerned, the dead man has no name yet, and you've gone to ground somewhere and you're not giving them any trouble, and that's all that matters for the moment."

"In other words," Aristide said, "you're leaving this investigation up to me, because if you were to question the Saint-Landrys in your official capacity, that would lead the police my way."

Brasseur nodded. "More or less."

"Thanks so much."

"I'll do what I can at my end, of course," Brasseur assured him. "If I don't stop by in the morning, meet me at Delonge's eating-house between one and two tomorrow. And by the way," he added, turning back in the doorway, "I hope I don't have to tell you not to share everything you learn with Monsieur Derville, no matter how friendly you are. Understood?"

"How much of what we already know can I tell him?"

"Use your best judgment. If, by chance, he murdered Saint-Landry himself—"

"Eh?" Aristide said.

"The possibility hadn't crossed your mind?"

"He does know the family," Aristide said slowly, "but what motive could he have for murdering Jean-Lambert?"

"Is Monsieur Derville a Freemason, by the way?"

"No. Though he seems sympathetic to their goals."

Gain, jealousy, revenge, self-preservation, love, he swiftly repeated to himself. "I don't see why he might have wanted Saint-Landry dead. Revenge and self-preservation seem unlikely. He'd gain nothing materially by Saint-Landry's death; and he has no cause for jealousy . . . does he?"

"Could he be in love with Madame Saint-Landry?" Brasseur suggested. "She's quite a handsome lady."

"I can't see Derville committing a crime of passion, though; he's much too cynical. He might seduce her and carry on a discreet affair with her, but he wouldn't commit murder for her."

"Well, you might find out, if you can, where Monsieur Derville was at the time of the murder. As I was saying, use your judgment about what you let slip to him."

Aristide slowly finished his breakfast after Brasseur had left. Derville appeared, yawning, at a few minutes to ten. "Was I dreaming, or did I hear voices in here?" he inquired, after calling for fresh coffee.

"It was Inspector Brasseur, bringing me up to date."

"Learned anything more?"

"Not much," Aristide said, remembering Brasseur's final remark. He rapidly made up his mind what course to pursue, reasoning that if Derville was innocent, there was little harm done; and if he had indeed committed the crime, then the grisly details of the murder would be nothing new to him. "Listen, those friends of yours who are Freemasons—"

"Are you still going on about the Masons?" said Derville. "Really, I think you're worrying too much about them—"

"I didn't tell you before, did I, that the murdered man's throat was cut?"

Derville blinked. "Well," Aristide continued, "I've been told throat-cutting figures symbolically in a Masonic ritual. Derville, this is ugly. I have to find out more. Any help your friends can give me, any hints in the right direction . . ."

Derville was silent as he seated himself at the breakfast table and began spooning preserves and anchovy butter onto his plate. "That's beastly," he said at last. "Forgive me if I've been taking this a bit too lightly."

"A man named Desmoulins, a lawyer . . . though he looks as if he'd rather be a scribbler like me . . . has promised to help me. I'm meeting him in a couple of hours. But who knows if his information will be any good at all? I need to find all the Freemasons I can."

"Would you mind if I came along with you to see this fellow?" Derville said abruptly.

"You?"

"Well, we need to get you out of this fix, and they say two heads are better than one, don't they?"

Aristide shrugged. "I doubt Desmoulins would object. If he's willing to talk to me, then why not? Perhaps you have some Freemason acquaintances in common, and you could introduce me—"

"Oh, Lord," Derville exclaimed, waving him away, "please, no more, not until Renauld's brought the coffee!"

Aristide, with Derville in tow, arrived at the Café Vachon shortly after eleven o'clock. Desmoulins signaled to him from the back of the crowded common room and gestured to an open doorway.

"I g-got us a private room for an hour—hope you don't mind the expense."

Derville hung back a moment to order coffee from a passing waiter while Aristide followed Desmoulins into a small, unheated, dismal chamber. A few tallow candles smoked and sputtered from wall sconces. Two men were waiting for them at the table inside, a young, fair-haired man of Desmoulins's age, wearing a neat black suit with frock coat and clerical cravat, and an older man in his forties. Desmoulins introduced them as Varenne and Étaillot, both junior members of his own lodge. Derville sidled in a moment later, after hesitating at the door, introduced himself, and pulled out a chair.

"You wanted to know about someone named Saint-Landry," said Étaillot, when the waiter had brought their coffee and Varenne had made sure the door was securely closed behind him. "Well, I don't know him personally, but I believe that Saint-Landry is the name of the Worshipful Master—that's the president, so to speak—of the Lodge of the Sacred Trinity."

Aristide stared at him. "So he's not only a Freemason, but a highly placed one?"

"Very highly placed."

"And yet he has no claims to nobility, has he?"

"Freemasons elect their officers without regard to social rank," Varenne said, with a smile. "Pure democracy. That's one of the reasons why we're considered so subversive."

"The Lodge of the Sacred Trinity," Aristide repeated, intrigued. "It sounds more like the name of a religious order."

"You'd think that, wouldn't you? And plenty of ecclesiastics like me, the ones who aren't narrowminded traditionalists, are Masons. Officially the Church forbids it, of course, but if you keep it quiet . . ."

"But the Sacred Trinity doesn't have anything to do with the Holy Trinity," Desmoulins interrupted, "unless you like to c-call it the holy trinity of Masonic ideals. You could say our sacred trinity is liberty, equality, and brotherhood; ask any Mason. That's what the lodge name means—it's nothing to do with the Church."

"And I've heard it whispered," said Étaillot, "that the Sacred Trinity people, at least the higher ranks, are a little dodgy."

"Dodgy?" Aristide said.

"Well . . . questionable." Étaillot pushed aside his empty coffee cup and continued, keeping his voice low, despite the clamor in the outer room. "The Lodge of the Sacred Trinity, according to all I've heard, is concerned less with charitable works and the general improvement of mankind than it is with having a clandestine finger in all sorts of pies, if you know what I mean."

"For one thing," Varenne broke in, "they don't have a set lodge, an official meeting place, like us. The Lodge of the Nine Sisters, which concerns itself with the arts and sciences, is ten years old now, and quite respectable; we meet in the old Jesuit novitiates' hall on Rue du Pot de Fer—"

"Excuse me?" said Aristide, who was moderately familiar with the narrow and squalid Rue du Pot de Fer, which led off Rue Mouffetard. "Jesuit buildings on Pot de Fer?"

"The former novitiates' hall, near St. Sulpice."

"St. Sulpice! But that's nowhere near Rue Mouffetard."

"I think we're talking about two different streets with the same name," Desmoulins suggested with a grin. "Aren't there about three Rue Traversines and half a dozen Rue Pavées scattered about Paris?"

"Anyway," Varenne continued impatiently, "it's no secret where our lodge meets, nor is it with most lodges. The Sacred Trinity, though, is a relatively new lodge, and they don't give out details. Only the members know where they meet—perhaps in a back room at Zoppi's, or in the house of one of the members, or upstairs in one of those new houses at the Palais-Royal—the Duc d'Orléans might have offered it rent free, he being Grand Master and sympathetic to liberalism—or heaven knows where. For all I know, it could be in this very room."

Étaillot nodded. "The point being that they're extraordinarily secretive about themselves and what they're up to. But I gather they're probably responsible for quite a lot of the filthier libels and the nastier political broadsheets and pamphlets that have been spread about lately."

"You mean they're actively working against the government," Aristide said.

"I wouldn't say that. Working to reform the government. We're all loyal subjects of the king here, aren't we?" Étaillot glanced about him, with a quick look in the direction of the door as someone outside bumped against it, and continued. "Nobody wants to see Louis dethroned or assassinated; he's a decent enough fellow."

"Maybe *you* don't," said Varenne. "If it were up to me, and quite a few other people, we'd happily put Louis out to pasture in favor of Orléans."

"But not if everything else stays the same," said Desmoulins. "Absolutism is a c-crime against nature. We need a c-constitutional monarchy, and the laws have to be reformed; privilege has to end, the nobility has to start paying taxes, the Church has to stop dictating to the state—"

"Understand, please," Étaillot added hastily, before Desmoulins could continue along what was undoubtedly a well-trodden path, "that we're not asserting any of these things at our own lodge. It's only what we've heard from rumors about members of the Sacred Trinity."

"And some lodges—meaning the Sacred Trinity first of all—are working harder for reform than others."

"And if the only way to bring about reform is to stir things up a bit—if you have to tear down the house before you can rebuild it— then that's what they'll do."

"Easy, Étaillot!" Varenne muttered, with a sideways glance at Aristide and Derville. "You don't know either of them."

"Desmoulins vouches for Ravel."

"How well do *you* know this fellow, Desmoulins?" Varenne demanded. Before Desmoulins could stammer out a response, Aristide raised a hand.

"Before you conclude that my friend and I are police spies, let me be perfectly honest with you. I'm working with a inspector of police—"

"What did I tell you?" hissed Varenne.

"—but all we want to do is investigate a murder. I'm not interested in what goes on in Masonic meetings, except as they might relate to the crime; and I am not, and will never be, a spy and informer."

"And just how do we know that?"

Aristide had come prepared for such a circumstance. "Have you ever read 'The True and Genuine History of Madame de Polignac'? I wrote that for Royer's press." He pulled from his coat pocket a dozen creased and folded sheets of paper, which, luckily, he had removed from his garret room before fleeing to Derville's, and tossed them onto the table. "That's the first draft of it. Do you want me to sign my name on it so you can compare the handwriting?"

Étaillot snatched up the pages and glanced through them, his lips occasionally twitching into a smile. "I've a copy at home, Varenne," he said at last. "It's genuine enough. So what else have you written, Monsieur Ravel?"

"A few unimportant things, and Joubert at the Palais-Royal will be coming out with a couple of pamphlets shortly. But I'm not concerned about that. As I said, I'm aiding in the investigation of a murder."

"So who's been murdered?" Varenne inquired.

"I think it was this man Saint-Landry."

"You *think*?"

Aristide was about to say "the body's been stolen," but thought better of it. "We . . . we haven't positively identified the body yet. But something mysterious is going on. You wouldn't happen," he added impulsively, "to know the Marquis de Beaupréau, would you?"

"Beaupréau?" said Varenne. "Well, the Beaupréaus are distant cousins of mine."

"C-cousins?" Desmoulins said.

"Distant." Varenne suddenly grinned. "I can't help it if my grandfather is the Baron de Mardeuil, can I? Beaupréau's a third cousin or something on the wealthy side of the family . . . not that we ever see any of it beyond dinner once a year at the Hôtel de Beaupréau. And I wouldn't swear to it, but I'm pretty sure I've heard his name in connection with the Sacred Trinity, too."

Aristide nodded. Varenne's information confirmed what Moreau had told him about Beaupréau and Saint-Landry. "What else do you know about Beaupréau?"

"Oh, the usual. Full of advanced ideas. Became a soldier because it was his father's dearest wish, but then he went off to America in 'seventy-nine to join La Fayette. He came back worshiping liberty and announcing that Washington was the next thing to God, and La Fayette was his prophet. It made his father so angry that the old man finally died of an apoplexy. So now Alexis is the head of the family, even though he can't be more than thirty."

"I hear he's got a few headaches, though," said Étaillot. "Doesn't he have an appalling black-sheep relation of some sort, a hopeless drunk, whom he's always hauling out of trouble?"

Not any more, Aristide thought, as he scribbled down a few notes. "What else can you tell me about the Lodge of the Sacred Trinity?" he inquired. "Do you know any other members, who might talk to me?"

Étaillot shrugged, but Varenne looked thoughtful. "Well, I don't know anyone besides Beaupréau personally, but I've heard that some fishy people are connected to it: Cagliostro, for one."

"Cagliostro!"

The name brought forth a plethora of images, of alchemists and wizards bearing vials of shimmering elixirs, of enigmatic robed priests, of mystical figures as old as time. Everyone had heard of the great Count Cagliostro, even those who despised superstition and dismissed such self-styled masters of the occult as mere conjurors, quacks, and charlatans.

"Cagliostro!" Derville echoed him, speaking for the first time. He leaned forward into the candlelight. "What about him?"

"Surely you don't believe all that nonsense about him being a thousand-year-old sorcerer," Aristide said, with a glance at his friend.

"No, of course I don't—I leave that to silly women who want their fortunes told—but I do know he's a Mason."

Étaillot nodded. "That's common knowledge. Pretty high up, too, from what I hear. He claims to be the Great Copt of the Egyptian Rite himself, though I expect that's pure claptrap."

"Cagliostro—highly placed Mason, linked to members of Lodge of S Trin-

ity, possibly member himself," Aristide scribbled down. The thought that the man who called himself Count Cagliostro, mystic, alchemist, and seer—or confidence artist and adventurer, as many people styled him— was somehow involved in the murder and the disappearance of the corpse was intriguing. The only flaw in such a theory was that Cagliostro had been locked up in the Bastille since August, accused of complicity with Cardinal de Rohan and Madame de la Motte in the diamond necklace affair.

"No one else?"

"No one I'm sure of," said Varenne. "They keep themselves to themselves."

Aristide nodded and was silent for a moment before glancing about the table. "Do you think," he said at last, "that a member of that lodge would be more likely than most, if provoked, to slit a man's throat, and then cut out his tongue?"

"What?"

"You heard me."

"No one would take that oath literally!" Étaillot exclaimed.

"What about someone a little unbalanced, who believed a fellow Mason had somehow broken a law or betrayed a secret of the fraternity? Do you think members of the Sacred Trinity would be more capable of committing such an act, in order to keep their secrets, than, say, the common run of Freemasons?"

Étaillot looked away, frowning. "We—the Freemasons—are supposed to be honorable and charitable men who spread enlightenment among others. The thought that one of us could go so far wrong . . ."

"But do you think that members of that lodge might be capable of it?" Aristide insisted. "Are they that extreme?"

Varenne exchanged glances with the others and slowly nodded. "They might be."

13

I think," Aristide said, as he and Derville walked northward, buttoning their overcoats against the chill breeze, "that the person I'd most like to talk to right now is Cagliostro."

Derville burst out laughing and stopped in the middle of the narrow street as pedestrians and street vendors pushed past them. "What the devil for?"

"Because he's a high-ranking Freemason, and he must know both Beaupréau and Saint-Landry, if he has connections to the Lodge of the Sacred Trinity."

"Why would he talk to you and not to the police or the magistrates?"

"I haven't the faintest idea. But if someone, somehow, could pull strings and get me in to see him—"

"Ravel, have you gone mad? People don't just go inside the Bastille on a whim! Unless they're aristocratic friends of the cardinal, of course, but I don't think either of us moves in such exalted circles—"

"You know people." Aristide seized Derville's elbow and steered him to the side of the street. "You have connections, you know everybody."

"I *don't* know anybody who could get you an interview with a prisoner in the Bastille. Give it up." Derville strolled on, chuckling.

"Where were you around midnight, Monday night?" Aristide said, without moving. Derville stopped short and spun about.

"What the devil?"

"Where were you on Monday night?" Aristide repeated. "Inspector Brasseur's growing curious about that."

"He thinks *I* murdered Saint-Landry?"

"He doesn't discount the possibility."

"Oh, please. You ought to know me better than that."

"Knowing you at school a dozen years ago doesn't mean I know you now. Why do you seem to be stalling me?"

"I'm not stalling you. Of course I want the murderer brought to justice. The Saint-Landrys are great friends of mine."

"Then where were you Monday night?"

Derville sighed. "If you must know, I picked up a girl outside the Comédie-Française and spent the night at her lodgings."

"Her name and address?" said Aristide.

"Lord, you're sounding far too much like a police inspector yourself, Ravel. How should I know?" He grinned, with a shrug. "She called herself Mélisande or Mirabelle or some such nonsense; but those elaborate professional monikers are always just covers for plebeian names like Agnès or Marthe. I'm sure your inspector can run her to earth, though. She had a ghastly little room on the fifth floor somewhere, a house just north of the Luxembourg, I think it was." He clapped Aristide on the shoulder and strode on, saying, "Now enough of this foolishness. If you want to learn more about Saint-Landry's secret activities with the Masons, I suggest we call at the house, which isn't far, and try to find out if the ladies know anything."

Evidently Eugénie was convinced that her husband was still alive, for the apartment bore no signs of formal mourning and she wore a stylish indigo-blue day dress, though Aristide thought that her pallor and the dark smudges beneath her eyes betrayed her anxiety over his whereabouts. She did not rise from the divan on which she was reclining, but gestured them to chairs in the green and yellow salon, where Sophie and Marguerite sat sewing beside the comfortable fire burning in the hearth. The pale winter sun shone in the windows, burnishing Eugénie's golden hair into an aureole about her head.

"Have—have you any news about my husband?" Her gray eyes rested on Aristide for a moment before moving to Derville.

Aristide shook his head. "No, madame, I fear any news I might have is probably bad. He's not appeared, or sent you any word?"

"No. Nothing."

"Madame," said Derville, "do you have any idea what Monsieur Saint-Landry might have been up to . . . something connected to his status as a Freemason?"

"Up to?" she said blankly, looking from one to the other of them.

"He might have been part of—of some sort of plot."

Her eyes widened. "But Lambert has always insisted that the Masons were a benevolent society."

"We've no reason to think otherwise," Aristide said. "But it's possible, don't you see, that your husband committed some offense against them, real or imaginary, and some madman among them murdered him."

"Lambert?" she echoed him. "I don't know what he could possibly have done to offend anyone."

"He's the most inoffensive of men," said Sophie, looking up from her sewing. "He's kind and domestic and dull. I don't think he's ever been in a quarrel in his life. Or, at least," she added, with a quick smile, "not since he got in a fight as a schoolboy and had one of his teeth knocked out. I expect he learned his lesson—"

"He was missing a tooth?" Aristide exclaimed. "Just the one?"

"Yes. Just there," she said, pointing to her left cheek. "One of the upper ones. You can't see it, thank goodness, unless he laughs." Suddenly her smile faded and she looked straight at him. "You saw the—this man before he . . . disappeared. He had a tooth missing, too, didn't he?"

"I fear so. In the same spot as you describe; I noticed it at the morgue."

Sophie squeezed her eyes shut and stifled a sob. Derville half rose from his chair, but Marguerite was quicker and hurried to her with a handkerchief. She shot Aristide a baleful glare before pressing Sophie to her and letting the girl weep into her shoulder.

"No," said Eugénie. She half rose from the divan and propped herself up, her back rigid. "No, it's simply a coincidence. I won't believe it."

Aristide turned to her. "Madame, all the evidence we've—"

"No!" she cried. "He's not dead! He must be away on some secret errand—something having to do with all the meetings he's had with Monsieur de Beaupréau and the rest. Lambert will come back—you'll see! He *will* come back!"

Derville took a step toward her, but she abruptly clapped a hand to her mouth, scrambled from the divan, and fled the room. For a moment the salon was silent but for Sophie's muffled sobs.

"I'm all right, Marguerite," she said at last, drawing a long breath. She clasped her cousin's hand and gave her a weak smile. "I'm all right."

Marguerite nodded. "If you'll excuse me, messieurs, I'd better see to Madame Saint-Landry."

"Monsieur Ravel," Sophie said, after Marguerite had quitted them, "how did my brother die?"

Oh, Lord, he said to himself. "He, er, his—"

She sat up straight and faced them, her small chin set at a determined angle. "I want the truth, please. You needn't hide it from me."

"His throat was cut, mademoiselle," he said. He looked away as she gave a little gasp of horror. "The morgue attendant said he would have—it would have been over almost at once. He didn't suffer."

"That's a blessing, I suppose," Derville said at last, in the silence.

"What must we do now?" said Sophie.

Aristide looked at her, hoping the sudden panic he felt did not show in his face. Brasseur was far too optimistic about his talents as an investigator, he thought, and now Sophie seemed to think he was in charge of finding her brother's corpse, and perhaps even his killer, when in truth he had no idea what to do next.

A maid entered, bearing tiny glasses of liqueur on a tray. Aristide took one and stared at the crystal facets, wondering what Brasseur would do. Collect further information about the household, he decided, now that it seemed certain—despite Eugénie's stubborn insistence that her husband would return—that the murdered man had been Saint-Landry.

"How many are you in the household, please?"

"Only the four of us," said Sophie, staring at her clasped hands. "Lambert, Eugénie, Marguerite, and myself. No children. And the servants, of course." She counted them off on her fingers. "Marie-Anne, the cook; Jacques, the man of all work; Victoire and Babette, the maids."

"No coachman or housekeeper?" he said, scribbling notes. He had remembered to carry an extra pencil with him this time, and a penknife for sharpening it.

She smiled slightly. "We're not *that* grand. Lambert likes to—liked to economize where he could, despite his wealth. He flatly refused to bear the expense of keeping a carriage and pair."

"Even though Eugénie tried her best to cajole him into it," Derville added.

"Yes, he'd always insist that a carriage hired by the day, when needed, was quite sufficient. And Marguerite manages the servants."

"I like to earn my keep," Marguerite said, returning and overhearing, "and I believe I'm good at it."

"And you, mademoiselle—"

"Madame," Derville corrected him.

"Madame Fournier. I'm a widow."

Aristide nodded. "I'm sorry."

"You needn't be," she said. "My husband spent all my dowry, and gave me a black eye whenever he was drunk, which was most of the time."

"The only thing he did properly, I hear," said Derville, "was to die quickly."

"He treated her very badly, indeed," Sophie said indignantly, looking up, "and left her with practically nothing. Lambert took her in, as a companion for Eugénie and me. It was just kindness. She's my mother's cousin, not his."

"Couldn't you have joined a religious order, madame?" Aristide said, curious. That was, he thought, what most women in such a situation would have done; the convent provided them with shelter, security, companionship, and useful work.

Marguerite shook her head. "It's not the life for me."

"Marguerite had already entered a convent when she was a girl," Sophie said, "but she left before taking final vows."

"It didn't suit me," the older woman said simply.

"So her mother arranged a marriage for her, and—well, you can see how successful *that* was."

"And you all—here in this household—get along well enough?" Aristide said hurriedly, before the conversation turned entirely to women's gossip.

"Of course," said Marguerite. "Nothing worse than the usual bickering at times."

He glanced at his notebook, in which, at the morgue, he had scrawled *"Died between 9 in the evening and early morning."* "Where were you—all of you—on Monday night, when Monsieur Saint-Landry left the apartment? He left at about eleven, is that right?"

"Yes. Marguerite and I played cards that evening," said Sophie, "while we waited for Lambert to return, but finally, since he'd told us not to stay up for him, we went to bed. That must have been a little after midnight. Say quarter past twelve, or half past."

"And Madame Saint-Landry?"

Sophie looked blank, but Marguerite nodded. "She went to bed just a little while after Lambert left the house."

"Forgive me for asking," Aristide said, "but could anyone have left the apartment, late at night, without the rest of the household knowing?"

"You suspect Madame Saint-Landry?" Derville said quickly.

"No, this was a man's crime, not a woman's."

"I certainly agree," said Derville. "Can you really imagine Eugénie attacking Saint-Landry with a knife?"

Aristide shook his head. Eugénie Saint-Landry was small and slender; such a woman would never have had the sheer physical strength to commit such a murder.

"At any rate, I think it would be impossible for Eugénie to have left the house so late, unnoticed," Marguerite said, as if reading his thoughts. "Poor Lambert was murdered in the middle of the night, wasn't he?"

"They do keep separate bedrooms," Sophie broke in.

"Yes; that's my point. Eugénie is rather delicate. She's subject to nightmares and nervous fits, and so she insists that her maid sleep in her boudoir, just a few steps away. Babette's a light sleeper. She could never have gone out in the middle of the night without Babette knowing. And if any of us had left the house at that hour, surely someone would have noticed a woman alone on the street, wouldn't they?"

"Yes, I imagine so." Anything so unexpected and unseemly as a woman who was neither a laborer, a beggar, a professional midwife, nor a prostitute, on foot alone in the streets after midnight, would have been remarked upon, and remembered, by the Guard or late-going passersby. "Er, what about the servants?"

"Babette sleeps in Eugénie's boudoir," Marguerite said. "Marie-Anne and Victoire share a room off the kitchen, and Jacques sleeps in the kitchen. I don't think any one of those three could have crept out without rousing the others. But what earthly motive could any of them have had to murder Lambert?"

"Are any of the women young and pretty?" he said, thinking of angry fathers, brothers, or sweethearts.

"Nonsense," she said briskly.

"Saint-Landry wasn't that sort of man," Derville agreed. "Sober and domestic, all the way. I don't believe he even kept a mistress. And what sort of man would want a chambermaid when he was married to a beautiful woman like Eugénie?"

"Marie-Anne and Babette are both fairly young," Marguerite said, "but they seem happy and content here. If either one of them was carrying on with Lambert—which I find most unlikely—then there were no hard feelings, as far as I can tell."

"Even if he'd . . . well . . . gotten one of them into trouble?" he inquired, with a glance at Sophie, hoping he was not shocking her.

"As I said, they both seem content. I think I'd have noticed if one of them were worried or upset."

"How old is your male domestic?" he said suddenly, remembering that the sexton at the graveyard had mentioned a young man.

"Jacques? Oh, perhaps fifty."

Think, he said to himself, staring down at his notes, which seemed extraordinarily inadequate.

Gain, jealousy, revenge, self-preservation, love.

"Who benefits?" he blurted out. "I mean—where does Monsieur Saint-Landry's fortune go?"

"To me, I suppose," Sophie said, after a moment's thought. "Eugénie brought quite an adequate dowry to the marriage."

Which she would receive back, of course, when the estate was settled, always assuming the Saint-Landry fortune was intact. But a wealthy man with a well-dowered wife would not have needed to make any special provisions for her possible widowhood.

"And they've never had any children," Marguerite said, nodding, "so I think Sophie would indeed be his only heir."

"Got any fortune hunters hounding you, Sophie?" Derville inquired.

"Only a few very respectable young men with excellent prospects," Sophie said. "That's how Lambert described them, at any rate."

"And how do *you* describe them?"

Aristide could have sworn that her glance flicked toward him for an instant before she replied, with a sad smile, "Very respectable, and very boring."

"No wedding bells in your immediate future, eh?"

"Oh, no. Not with one of *them*."

"So no one you know of would have realistic hopes of marrying you for your fortune," Aristide said, "and . . . and murdering your brother to hurry matters along?"

"No, certainly not."

Again he sensed that her glance was sliding toward him and he hastily looked down at his notes.

From what he had learned of the late Jean-Lambert Saint-Landry's character, jealousy as a motive for murdering him seemed unlikely. But if, as Brasseur had claimed, spouses were the most likely murderers . . .

"Forgive me for asking, mademoiselle, madame, but since we've concluded that Madame Saint-Landry couldn't have committed this murder herself, is it possible she might have a lover who—"

"No," Marguerite interrupted him. "Eugénie's reputation is spotless."

"She certainly made it clear to me that it was nothing doing, about a year ago, when I tried to make a pass at her," Derville said ruefully. "Sorry if that's a bit coarse, but you might as well know."

"Besides," Marguerite added, with a chilly glance at Derville, "I spend much of my time in her company. When would she have the chance to see a lover?"

So much for the domestic side of things, Aristide thought. But revenge and self-preservation were still to be explored . . .

Saint-Landry's connection to the Lodge of the Sacred Trinity, it seemed, was well worth examining.

"Er . . . Mademoiselle Saint-Landry . . . are you acquainted with the Marquis de Beaupréau? I know your brother knew him."

"Oh, yes," Sophie said, with a faint smile. "We know him, a little. He's twice done us the honor of dining with us. He and Lambert are—were members of the same lodge, or whatever it's called."

"Sometimes he also calls informally on Lambert," Marguerite said.

"Does he? What did they talk about?"

"I couldn't say; they'd usually go into Lambert's study and shut the door."

Sophie giggled. "Babette and Marie-Anne are always thrilled when Monsieur de Beaupréau comes to call, because he usually brings along that handsome valet of his! They flirt with him like mad."

"A superior young man," Marguerite said. "I've seen him now and then in the kitchen, when I've been speaking with Marie-Anne. He never pays any attention to those silly girls' coquetry, though he's invariably polite."

"So you've no idea what these conversations between Monsieur de Beaupréau and Monsieur Saint-Landry might have been about?" he inquired.

Both women shook their heads. "None at all," said Marguerite. "Although they were extraordinarily careful to avoid being overheard," she added. "Often they'd encourage us to go out for the afternoon, and sometimes Lambert would even give the servants a few hours off. And Lambert would laugh it off after Monsieur de Beaupréau had gone: 'It's nothing you need concern yourselves with,' and so on."

No doubt Brasseur, accustomed to investigation, would have known better what to ask, Aristide thought, as he took a final sip from his liqueur glass. He could not think of anything else to ask them. "Thank you for your patience," he said, rising. "If either of you thinks of anything helpful, please send me or Inspector Brasseur a message."

"Good day, Monsieur Ravel, Monsieur Derville," Sophie said. "Thank you both." She curtsied as Marguerite showed them out of the salon. Aristide could not help a brief, admiring glance backward at Sophie as he reached the door, and was rewarded with a similar glance and a blushing smile.

Eugénie appeared in the foyer as the manservant fetched their overcoats. "Monsieur Derville . . . a moment of your time, if I may?" She dismissed the servant with a glance and carefully seated herself on a cane-backed, upholstered bench. "You've always been such a good friend to our family; pray tell me, what should I do?"

"Do, madame?" Derville inquired.

"I've been behaving like a child, I know, and refusing to listen to reason. I hate to consider it, but I must be sensible and at least accept the possibility that my husband is dead." She gazed sadly up at him, the great gray eyes shining with tears. She looked ill and exhausted, Aristide thought. "You've known us both for so long; can you really offer me any hope that he's alive?"

"I fear not, madame," Derville said. He took her hands in his and stood gazing down at her. "But Saint-Landry was a good man and he's undoubtedly left you well provided for. Your man of business can advise you; he'll be more useful than I could be."

"Yes—yes, of course you're right. I ought to consult Maître Ouvrard. But how on earth can we be sure that my husband really is dead, without a body?"

"Your notary would know more about that than I. I'm sure there are legal measures . . ."

Eugénie smiled for an instant. "Of course there must be. I'm so ignorant about such things. You'll visit us often, won't you, Monsieur Derville, to help us weather this difficult time?"

"Of course, madame."

"I—perhaps I should warn you that I do not intend to wear mourning for my husband until the day I've seen his body. Imagine what he would feel if he *did* return, to discover everything draped in hideous black, and to realize that I'd given up hope so easily!"

"You must do as you think best, of course." He raised her hand to his lips and bowed. "Good day, madame."

"Good day, madame," Aristide echoed him, following Derville out. She murmured a perfunctory good-bye and turned away.

"Private conversations, making sure everyone was out of earshot?" Aristide said, after they had descended the staircase and crossed the little front courtyard to the street. "Saint-Landry and Beaupréau were certainly up to something."

"Saint-Landry?" Derville said dubiously. "I don't know . . . as the charming Sophie says, he was almost tediously honest and respectable."

"And Beaupréau?" Aristide said, thinking of the faceless man in the street outside Beaupréau's mansion. "Does he share Saint-Landry's principles?"

"He's perfectly decent, as far as I know. Though he's little more than a cordial acquaintance."

"But they were members of the same lodge. You heard Desmoulins and his friends; members of the Lodge of the Sacred Trinity aren't as scrupulous as most about their activities."

"Really, I doubt they'd stoop to murder. And you don't need a dark, secret conspiracy to publish illegal political tracts," Derville added, with a chuckle. "After all, everybody does that."

He fell silent until they had gone the length of the short Rue des Grands Augustins and were walking westward along the quay, their collars turned up against the frigid breeze. Dozens of small boats lay idle at wharves or on the stony shore, where the river had frozen solid twenty feet out into the channel, and from bank to bank around the islands, where the Seine was narrow. Elsewhere, great slabs of ice, which could block or even endanger the barges that delivered grain and firewood from the countryside, still floated below them, drifting slowly with the current. The prices of essentials, already steep this year, would be rising again soon, Aristide thought; there might once more be food riots in the poorer quarters by spring.

"And speaking of the charming Sophie," Derville said suddenly, "I imagine you noticed how she was looking at you?"

"Looking at me?" Aristide said.

Derville paused, leaned against the balustrade that edged the riverbank below, and raked his gaze over him. "My dear idiot, you really don't have much of an opinion of yourself, do you? It's true you're a glum sort of fellow—though some ladies find that intriguing—and of course you dress atrociously, but obviously Sophie seems to find something about you beguiling."

It was true, Aristide realized, with an unexpected jolt of satisfaction, that not only had Sophie given him a pink-cheeked, playful smile, but she had scarcely glanced at Derville during their interview, family friend though he was.

"Don't change the subject," he said.

14

Saturday, 14 January

A messenger arrived with a letter for Derville in the middle of the morning. Derville cracked the seal, glanced through its contents, and cocked an eyebrow. "It's for you, actually."

"Me?" said Aristide. "From Brasseur?"

"No, from Sophie Saint-Landry. She's asking me to forward this on to you, since she doesn't know your address. Here." He tossed a second sealed letter, which had been enclosed inside the first, over to Aristide. He opened it to find a note in a neat feminine hand.

> Dear M. Ravel,
>
> You asked us yesterday about the visits that M. de Beaupréau paid my brother, and about their conversation. Something has occurred to me, which I hope will be of some use to you. Would it be possible for us to meet in the garden of the Luxembourg, by the central fountain, today at noon?
>
> I remain your servant,
> S. Saint-Landry.

"I have to go out shortly," Aristide said, hoping he did not look too pleased. Whatever Sophie had to tell him could have just as easily been written down in her letter. And the Luxembourg palace gardens, with their trees, lawns, and formal flowerbeds, were an agreeable spot, even in winter, for courting couples to meet under the watchful eyes of mothers and chaperones. "Could Renauld give me a shave before I leave?"

"Want to look your best, do you?" Derville said, eyeing him.

The weather was pleasant enough, for January, Aristide thought as he hurried into the gardens past the Palais du Luxembourg, the Paris residence of the Comte de Provence, the king's brother. A gatekeeper, there to keep the riffraff out of the grounds, stared dubiously at his shabby clothes, but at last nodded him through. A few chinks of blue showed here and there in the pearly gray skies that were an ever-present part of a Parisian winter; perhaps a thaw was finally on the way.

Sophie was waiting for him beside the fountain's wide basin, the ever-watchful, middle-aged maid Victoire hovering a few paces away. They exchanged greetings and Sophie gestured to a bench. Aristide took a seat beside her, taking care to sit neither too close for propriety nor too far away.

"It's really the most trivial thing," she said apologetically when they had settled themselves. "I completely forgot about it until last night, just as I was falling asleep. But you wanted to know what Lambert and Monsieur de Beaupréau might have been talking about when they were together."

"Yes?"

"You see, I heard something once . . . ages ago . . . I didn't mean to eavesdrop, but the door to Lambert's study wasn't quite closed and I just caught a little of what they were saying as I passed. Lambert said something like 'I'm not sure it's a wise course of action,' and Monsieur de Beaupréau said 'I defer to your judgment as my superior, naturally—'" She paused abruptly. "Though it's odd: why would the Marquis de Beaupréau call a bourgeois like Lambert his superior?"

"Because they're both Freemasons, I imagine," Aristide said. "I suppose," he added, when Sophie still looked puzzled, "since your brother was the master of his lodge—"

"Was he? I didn't know that. How remarkable."

"Yes, mademoiselle, I heard it on good authority. And since the Masons seem to consider all men equal in society," he continued, "then among Freemasons Monsieur Saint-Landry held the higher rank."

Sophie nodded. "I see now. Lambert didn't talk much about being a Freemason, but sometimes he would remind us that nowhere else could members of different levels of society mix so freely, as brothers."

In previous centuries holy orders had offered that opportunity, Aristide mused, but for decades the higher ranks of the Church in France—and the authority, influence, and lavish incomes attached to them—had been firmly closed to everyone but the nobly born, whether or not they had the least aptitude or desire for the priesthood. More than a few prominent ecclesiastics, he reflected cynically, not for the first time, were notorious for their extravagance, loose conduct, and utter indifference to their religious duties.

"Go on," he said, feeling Sophie's eyes upon him. "What else did you overhear?"

"Oh! Yes. Monsieur de Beaupréau said, 'I defer to your judgment as my superior, but I do strongly feel that the master must be brought into it. His is the first voice the man listens to, and you know he has nothing but horsehair stuffing beneath that pretty hat of his.'" She paused, blushing charmingly. "Then I heard one of them moving to the door, and I thought I'd better leave before they discovered me and were cross with me."

"Have you any idea what they were talking about?" he inquired. She shook her head.

"None at all. Though I know exactly when it was," she said suddenly. "It must have been the fifth of January, just a year ago. Because that was the first time Monsieur de Beaupréau came to dinner, rather than just calling and paying a brief visit to Lambert, and it was a special dinner that day, for Eugénie's birthday. I hope that's of some use to you, Monsieur Ravel?"

"It might be," he said, summoning a smile. Something was teasing at the back of his mind, something to do with holy orders—

"Rohan!" he said suddenly. Sophie stared.

"I beg your pardon?"

" 'Nothing but horsehair stuffing beneath that pretty hat of his'!" he repeated, with a dry chuckle.

"I don't understand."

He turned to her and, almost without realizing it, seized her hand. "Mademoiselle, can you tell me what's the most popular fashion in ladies' hats lately?"

She smiled at him, baffled but eager, without snatching her hand away. "Of course. Red with yellow ribbons. I'm thinking of ordering—"

"What do they call it?"

" 'Cardinal on the straw—' " She broke off, the blue eyes round. "Oh. Oh, my."

"Cardinals wear red hats. Yes."

Not, of course, that a son of the most puissant and princely house of Rohan was sleeping on a heap of straw in his comfortable apartments in the Bastille . . .

"Do you think that Lambert and Monsieur de Beaupréau were referring to *him*?" said Sophie.

" 'His is the first voice the man listens to . . .' Rohan has absolutely nothing to recommend him except for the fact that he's a cadet of one of the most powerful families in the kingdom. By all accounts, he's a dissipated fool who certainly has 'nothing but horsehair stuffing' between his ears. It's far-fetched, I admit, but it's not impossible . . ."

"But why would they have been talking about him?"

"I scarcely want to say it, because it seems too fantastic . . . but I wonder if they might have been talking about the diamond necklace."

"The necklace!" Sophie exclaimed.

"But listen. As highly placed Masons, they both knew Count Cagliostro. Perhaps I'm jumping to conclusions here, but if 'the man' they mentioned was Cardinal de Rohan, then they could have meant Cagliostro when they spoke of 'the master,' the man whose advice Rohan trusted implicitly. The master of magic and spirituality, who claims to be the high priest of some sort of exotic Eastern Freemasonry. And the police already believe he's mixed up in the theft! Couldn't your brother and Beaupréau have been talking about something having to do with the diamonds?"

"But that was a year ago," Sophie protested, "when I heard them, and nobody knew anything about the necklace until just this past summer . . ." She broke off and stared at him, her mouth a little open in astonishment. "You're saying they were involved with it, aren't you? With stealing the necklace, I mean?"

"They might have been."

"But Lambert would *never* have done anything like that, something so dishonest and underhanded, especially not with anyone like that awful La Motte woman." Swiftly she withdrew her hand from his and folded both hands decorously in her lap. "He was the most honest man I know."

"Perhaps this was something else," Aristide said quickly.

"I don't even understand half of what everyone says about this beastly necklace."

"That's because everyone says something different."

"I wish someone would explain it to me," she said, glancing at him once more. "Eugénie's not interested, and Marguerite says it's not fit for young ladies."

"What did your brother say about it?"

"He always changed the subject when it came up in conversation," she said slowly. "That's a little peculiar, isn't it?"

Aristide nodded. "I could explain some of it to you," he told her, "although your cousin is right about there being some indelicate parts to the story."

"I don't mind that." Sophie shivered. "Let's walk a bit, though; it's getting chilly here."

He rose, offering her his arm, and together they strolled around the basin, past the leafless lilacs. "The root of it began in Vienna," he said, thinking back to the various illegal pamphlets he had read about the affair, all of which had breathlessly promised to reveal the entire scandalous story, just as police officials with secret liberal sympathies had disclosed it to the gutter press. "Rohan was ambassador to the Austrian court fifteen years ago or so, before Princess Antoinette married the Dauphin. And Empress Maria Theresa didn't like him one bit; she considered him a disgrace to his cloth."

"What did he do to offend her?"

"Well, he already had a reputation for vice, and rumor had it that in his retinue, in his private carriage in fact, he had a number of handsome young abbés traveling with him. But a closer look would have revealed that they were not priests at all, but attractive young women in disguise." Sophie gave a shrill giggle and quickly stifled it with a small, shapely hand.

"Not only that," Aristide continued, as they waited a moment for Victoire to catch up to them, "but it's possible he insulted the princess, as she was then, by taking liberties with a few indiscreet remarks. Whatever the truth of it, the queen has always hated Rohan, and has probably been behind his lack of advancement at court. He may be a cardinal, a prince of the house of Rohan-Guemenée, a prince-bishop of the Holy Roman Empire, Grand Almoner of France, and lord of who knows how many abbeys and manors, but he's never been one of the king's ministers. And despite his really astounding lack of brains, I'm sure he's always believed he ought to be a minister by right of birth, because aristocrats like the Rohans are brought up to believe that they can and should have anything they want." He paused, hearing his voice grow bitter at the mention of unearned privilege.

"And that's how matters would probably have remained, if Madame de La Motte hadn't gotten her claws into him."

"Isn't she just a—a lady of bad reputation?" Sophie said.

"She's that, certainly. But she claims to be a descendant of the Valois kings."

"But the Valois lived centuries ago! Who cares?"

"Oh, silly people at court care, because they're the sort of fools who believe that one's ancestors are much more important than one's personal merit. Prove you're the great-great-great granddaughter of some medieval king's illegitimate whelp, as she did, and they'll fawn all over you and give you money, entry into the right houses, introductions to the right people . . . even if you're actually a scheming trollop who'll sleep with anyone who will help you on your way to the top." He stopped short, feeling his face grow hot. "Forgive me, mademoiselle. That was extremely coarse of me. I ought to watch my language more."

"You're forgiven," she told him, squeezing his arm. "You're very refreshing, Monsieur Ravel, because you speak your mind. Much more interesting than those respectable young men who call on me."

"I'm glad to hear it," he said gravely. He gazed around them at the shrubs and empty flower beds. The ground was frozen hard beneath their feet. Despite the eventual thaw, it would be another month at least before the Comte de Provence's gardeners would be able to re-plant the formal beds.

"Er . . . Madame de La Motte. Well, she managed to catch Rohan's eye, and became his mistress. She would sooner or later have been discarded like all his other mistresses—he's had dozens—"

"That's disgraceful," Sophie said, making the sign of the cross. "A prince of the Church; he ought to be ashamed of himself."

"—except she was clever enough to realize that his thwarted ambition to shine at court was the key to keeping hold of him and profiting from his generosity. So she began to hint that she was a close personal friend of the queen, and that a word from her in the royal ear might do him a great deal of good. She probably told him that Antoinette was ready to forgive him, and so on . . . anything she knew he most wanted to hear. And she backed it all up with letters to him from the queen. Forged, of course, but he was too much of an ass to suspect anything."

"Wasn't there something about a woman impersonating the queen?" Sophie inquired. "Did Madame de La Motte do that?"

"No, it wasn't she, though it was all part of her scheme for keeping hold of the cardinal's favor. She and her husband found a girl, some ignorant seamstress or milliner, who looked rather like the queen. They paid her to go to the palace gardens late one evening, dressed up in a gown like the ones Antoinette was wearing that season—that was in the summer of 1784—and say a few words to the gentleman she would see there. The gentleman, of course, was Cardinal de Rohan, who by that time was convinced that Madame de La Motte was the queen's dearest friend." He nearly said "Or even something much more intimate, according to some rumors," but decided that that particular bit of salacious gossip was nothing Sophie needed to know.

"Now that the cardinal had actually seen Antoinette ready to offer him her favor, or so he thought, and was certain that advancement lay just around the corner, he trusted La Motte more than ever. Of course she took advantage of that in every way she could. But it would have gone on being just another instance of a foolish man being fleeced by a greedy mistress, until the royal jewelers approached her. They'd heard the rumors that she was one of the queen's intimate friends, you see—the Valois connection helped—and they offered her a percentage of the sale, if she would speak to the queen about the diamond necklace that they had been hawking for years to every royal court in Europe. The thing was so enormous, expensive, and vulgar that even Antoinette, with her immoderate taste for diamonds, hadn't wanted it. But they thought it was worth another try, and so Madame de La Motte heard about the necklace for the first time."

"And decided to deceive the cardinal into buying it."

"More or less. She produced a few more of those supposed letters from the queen, and now suddenly Antoinette was asking Rohan to do her a great service. She wanted to buy the necklace, but knew the king wouldn't approve of such reckless spending, and so if a trusted friend would buy it for her—to be discreetly paid back in installments—then she could say nothing about it until it was an accomplished fact, and she was already wearing the diamonds at a court ball, and by that time the king wouldn't be able to forbid the purchase."

"But it was all lies?" said Sophie.

"Yes, apparently it was lies from start to finish. But Rohan, being an ass, ate it up. He imagined that such a great favor must naturally deserve another great favor—say, that of being made prime minister—in return. So he told La Motte to arrange matters with the jewelers. And finally, on the strength of the cardinal's word, they delivered the necklace to Madame de La Motte's house and into the hands of one of the gentlemen of the queen's household—except that actually the man was La Motte's husband or lover, I don't know which."

"So the La Mottes got hold of the necklace and immediately sold it?"

"Naturally. They broke it up and her husband took most of the stones to London."

"And then the jewelers expected to be paid."

"Yes. But Rohan didn't pay up when the time came, because *he* was expecting that the queen would send payment to *him*. And when no one came forward with any gold, the jewelers went to the king and asked for their money, and then the whole scheme blew up like a faulty firework. The king had Rohan arrested for theft and fraud, and Rohan tried to explain, and in denying he had intended to steal the jewels, he managed instead, like a fool, to imply that the queen had behaved in a shameful and immoral manner; and that's high treason, to insult the sovereign."

"So the queen never actually had anything to do with the necklace."

"No," he admitted, "I don't think she did. But the king made a mess of things, too. If he'd hushed it up and simply made Rohan pay the jewelers everything they were owed, as punishment for being such a credulous imbecile, it wouldn't have become such a roaring scandal. Instead he arrested him and made the whole thing public in a feebleminded attempt to clear the queen's name from the insinuations Rohan had made. But people are always eager to believe the worst of someone they already dislike, and now everyone assumes that the queen did have a hand in it."

"Oh, my. What a dreadful muddle." Sophie sat on the nearest bench and arranged her skirts. "But didn't you say that Count Cagliostro had something to do with it," she said suddenly, looking up at Aristide, "and that Lambert and Monsieur de Beaupréau were connected to him somehow?"

"They arrested Cagliostro because he was the cardinal's chief adviser, and Madame de La Motte—after *she* was arrested—accused him of having planned the whole thing."

"But you said that Madame de La Motte—"

"Ah, but the mysterious Cagliostro makes an excellent scapegoat, doesn't he? These shady foreign adventurers might be up to anything." Sophie switched her skirts aside and he seated himself beside her again. "All he'll admit to doing, though, is having given his blessing to the cardinal's enterprise, without the least idea that the purchase was a fraud engineered by others. He says he first tried to dissuade the cardinal from such an expensive gamble. Then, because the spirits had guided him or some such claptrap, later he changed his mind and announced that the ancient prophets had foreseen that Rohan would have a brilliant future because of his services to a very great lady. All of it nonsense, of course."

"Well," Sophie said, "if the cardinal was as stupid as you're saying, then of course Count Cagliostro would have said something like that to him. You don't need to be a magician to know that. If you depend on somebody to keep you, then you keep them happy by telling them what they want to hear. I was doing that with my own nurse," she added with a wicked smile, "when I was six years old. I knew she'd bring me extra sugar for my bread and milk if I told her that I'd overheard Jacques, the manservant, saying she was good-looking."

Aristide stared at her. "Maybe that's it."

"What's it? What's what?"

"Telling him what he wanted to hear. Maybe that's the connection between your brother and Cagliostro and the cardinal."

"Buttering up my nurse?" she said, laughing.

"Buttering up the cardinal. Making sure they did everything they could do to persuade him to purchase that necklace."

"But I told you," Sophie insisted, "Lambert was not a thief! It's completely against his character. He would never have gotten mixed up with horrible people like that La Motte creature."

"Not so they could steal it," Aristide said. Suddenly a great deal was becoming clear to him. "What if . . . what if they *wanted* the queen to have it?"

"While poor people are starving?" she said indignantly.

"Exactly. Don't you see? That's it—that must be it!"

Scarcely knowing what he was doing, he reached for her with both hands and kissed her hard on the mouth. He felt her start and shrink back for an instant and drew away, afraid he had offended her, but found she was staring at him with more surprise than displeasure.

Abruptly she seized his hands in hers and smiled at him. He needed no further invitation. The feel of her soft lips beneath his banished all thoughts of occasional laundresses in the faubourg St. Marcel.

"Sophie—lovely Sophie . . ."

A dry cough interrupted them and they reluctantly separated. "That's quite enough, ma'm'selle," said the maid, emerging from the shadow of a nearby tree.

"Oh, Victoire!" Sophie exclaimed.

"You know very well, ma'm'selle, any more of that in public and you'll get the wrong kind of reputation for yourself."

Sophie rolled her eyes. "Chaperones!"

"I quite agree with Victoire," said Aristide. He found he was smiling. "For the sake of your reputation, I'll restrain myself, difficult though it is."

A distant church bell tolled one o'clock. Sophie heaved a great sigh, and gazed up at him through her lashes. "I suppose I ought to go. Though I don't want to."

"Can I see you again? Soon?"

"Here?"

"Anywhere you like."

"Here, then. No—wait—not right at this spot. People might notice."

"By the Medici Fountain?" he said, glancing at the stone arch visible through the bare trees.

"All right. Tomorrow, at noon, after Mass."

"Tomorrow, at noon." Impulsively he lifted her hand to his lips. "I—I've never done that before," he said, as she giggled.

"I've never had my hand kissed by someone who meant it," she told him, smiling over her shoulder at him as Victoire beckoned her away. He watched her stroll toward the gates, with an occasional backward glance at him. She was taking her time about it, he thought.

15

You look pleased with yourself," Brasseur said, in the eating-house near his office where they had agreed to meet. A slatternly serving girl thumped down a dish of pork and stewed haricots and a bottle of red wine in front of him. "Here, another glass for my friend, love."

"I *am* pleased," Aristide said, after ordering a portion of pot-au-feu for himself from the girl. "I think I can make a good guess as to what Saint-Landry and Beaupréau were up to."

"You think—"

"And Mademoiselle Saint-Landry has asked me to meet her in the Luxembourg gardens again, tomorrow morning," he added, unable to resist.

"Oho," said Brasseur, busying himself with his dinner. "Well, since the love affairs of my subinspectors are none of my concern, I'll go first and tell you that my men have found the errand boy who delivered that note to Saint-Landry."

"Have they?"

"He says the man who gave him the note was youngish, tall,

looked like a gentleman, though he kept out of the light. Sounds like it could be the same man the sexton described Monday morning, the one who paid him to leave the gate unlocked."

"It could have been Beaupréau," Aristide said, thinking back to the portrait.

"Could have been Monsieur Derville, at that," said Brasseur. "Have you found out whether or not he has an alibi for the night of the tenth?"

"He claims he was with a prostitute all night."

"At a brothel?" Brasseur said, brightening. "That's easy enough to confirm—"

"No, some girl with her own lodgings." He repeated the details and Brasseur scribbled down a few notes.

"Well, I'll set someone to asking questions in that quarter. I can't say it's a terribly good alibi, but it's no worse than most—no worse than yours, come to think of it," he added dryly.

"The errand boy could give you no other details about the man who hired him?"

"No. These street boys often deal with a couple of dozen people a day, of course."

"My money's on Beaupréau, Brasseur. It's possible he feared that Saint-Landry was going to betray them—"

"Yes?" Brasseur said quickly, looking up from his plate. "Over what? What's this you've guessed about the two of them?"

"Well, we already know that both Saint-Landry and Beaupréau were—are—Freemasons. They were also both members of the Lodge of the Sacred Trinity. Saint-Landry was evidently its president. Ever heard of it?"

Brasseur nodded. "Just barely."

"I've been told it's the most liberal and militant of all the Masonic lodges in Paris. Other lodges hold respectable meetings about the arts and sciences, and politely discuss reform and equality, and go about drumming up subscriptions for deserving widows; while the Sacred Trinity isn't much concerned about the arts and sciences, and doesn't give out the address of its meeting place." The serving girl arrived with his stew, a chipped wineglass, and a basket containing a few hunks of heavy dark bread. "Mademoiselle, a pitcher of water, if you please."

"Water," she repeated scornfully.

"Water, please. They're rumored to subsidize illegal books and pamphlets in order to effect reform," he continued as she trudged off, "but that's probably the least of it. My guess is that they'll do anything they can to undermine what they call the tyranny of priests and kings."

"Sounds like they do a good deal more than talk," Brasseur agreed. "I've heard the commissaire muttering about lodges like that, saying they're up to no good. But politics is none of my business, is it?" he added blandly.

Aristide drew a quick breath and continued, speaking softly, the words tumbling out of him in a rush. "I think it possible that they were involved, at least indirectly, in the necklace affair."

"The *what?*"

"The matter of the diamond necklace," Aristide repeated, lowering his voice further as the girl shoved an earthenware pitcher onto the table. He added water to the wine Brasseur had poured out for him and took a swift sip. "This is what Sophie overheard a year ago . . ."

"It's a stretch," Brasseur said, when he had done, "but I suppose it's not altogether impossible . . ."

"You see, she overheard that conversation on the fifth of January, last year. She's quite definite about it." Aristide scraped the last of the stew from his bowl and washed it down with a final swallow of watered wine. "Brasseur, you must know more about the necklace affair than an ordinary fellow might. Wasn't it said that Rohan received the necklace and had it sent on to the queen—or thought he sent it—around that time last year?"

Brasseur nodded. "On the first of February, I think, according to his statement."

"'The Master must be brought into it.' Rohan was obsessed with Cagliostro's parlor tricks. He would certainly have asked his pet prophet for advice before investing so much of his own money for the queen's sake. Now if you wanted Rohan to agree to the scheme, the most fool-proof way would be to induce Cagliostro himself to assure Rohan that a rosy future awaited him if he bought the necklace."

"Under interrogation, he did admit that he advised the cardinal to buy it," Brasseur said thoughtfully, "after first warning him off it; but obviously that's because the La Motte woman dragged him into the plot."

"But we don't know that for a fact. What if Cagliostro wasn't working with La Motte at all, but with his fellow Freemasons Beaupréau and Saint-Landry?"

"You're not saying that *they* were party to the theft?" Brasseur shook his head. "To fund their efforts, pay for printing and so on? Wouldn't a proper Freemason find that disgraceful?"

"No—not theft, not at all. I think they were pursuing their own ends. If the Lodge of the Sacred Trinity is striving to bring about reform by any means necessary, then there are other ways of subverting the monarchy, perhaps more speedily and effectively, than simply cranking out endless complaints against privilege and corruption . . ."

Brasseur frowned at him over his wineglass and abruptly set it down untouched.

"You know people are whispering that Antoinette's mixed up in the necklace affair," Aristide continued. "What if lodge members have been the ones deliberately spreading it about since August that she—or the whole royal family—is behind it? They could say almost anything, and people would believe them: that Antoinette's a whore, that she's a foreign spy, that she's still loyal to Austria, that she cooked the whole thing up in order to make the king look like a fool, or to destroy Cardinal de Rohan. Everybody knows that Antoinette's loathed Rohan for years." He paused and gazed into his empty glass, marshaling his thoughts. "What if Beaupréau and Saint-Landry, using their Masonic connection, asked Cagliostro to persuade the cardinal to buy that necklace, simply in order to cause a scandal that would be too great to be contained, that would inevitably find its way into every foul gutter rag? That would cause such an outcry against the queen, and royal extravagance, and corruption at court, and even the king, that it might rock the entire monarchy?"

"D'you think they could have known it was actually a swindle?" Brasseur said slowly. "That Madame de La Motte intended to steal the diamonds for herself all along?"

"I doubt it. All they believed, probably, was that it was a genuine, though secret, transaction; and they also knew that if the queen were really to acquire that outrageous necklace and dare to wear it at court, then the scandal would be immense. It would be one more blow to absolutism; it would imply, perhaps, that her relationship with the cardinal was an improper one, and it would revive all the old tales about Antoinette being a heartless, depraved spendthrift ready to spread her legs for anyone who'll favor her or flatter her; and moreover, it would confirm the rumors that Louis is a pathetically weak ruler who can't even control his own wife."

Brasseur nodded. "But La Motte and her little gang steal the diamonds, and the jewelers demand their money, and Rohan, being a prize fool, repeats La Motte's lies; and then the king, being almost as much of a prize fool as Rohan, brings the whole mess out into the open."

"And what Beaupréau and Saint-Landry actually get for their efforts, of course, is a much, much bigger scandal that can't possibly be kept quiet, with a tangle of forgery and lèse-majesté and corruption in high places—not to mention a fresh airing of every vile insinuation against the queen that Madame de La Motte can think of. I expect they seized their unexpected opportunity then, and have been fanning the flames ever since. Isn't that a secret Beaupréau might be willing to kill for, if he thought Saint-Landry was going to have second thoughts and betray them?"

"Well," Brasseur admitted, "it's a fantastic story, but it could make sense . . ." He emptied the last few drops of wine in the bottle into his glass and scowled at it.

"Brasseur," Aristide said, scarcely daring to look at him, "we need to talk to Cagliostro."

"I was afraid you'd say that."

"Can you get us inside the Bastille for an interview?"

Brasseur snorted. "I'm only an inspector, not the Royal Lieutenant of Police!"

"But you must have some connections . . ."

"All right, all right." Brasseur was silent for a moment, absently watching the wine dregs wash back and forth at the bottom of his glass. "Perhaps . . . I was in the war with a fellow who's a captain of the guard there now. I'll write to him. We might arrange something discreet."

"Arrange it. As soon as possible. We need to get to the bottom of this before anyone else is murdered or goes missing."

"All right! As soon as I can get back to my desk. Satisfied?"

"Thanks . . ."

"You really think that talking to Count Cagliostro is going to help us find out who murdered Saint-Landry, and where Beaupréau can be if he didn't murder Saint-Landry himself, and why?"

Aristide shrugged. "Whatever he tells us can't confuse us any more than we're already confused, can it?"

He took a small detour to revisit the church of St. André des Arts as he walked northward toward the Right Bank. The gate to the cemetery hung open and he strolled through, avoiding the ever-present beggar—a man with a withered arm, this time—crouching by the wall. Only a few rusty stains remained on the stones where Saint-Landry's body had lain.

"Were you here the night the gentleman was murdered in the charnels?" he asked the beggar when he returned to the gate, handing over a coin. "Did you hear anything?"

"I sleep over there sometimes," the beggar said. He pointed a dirty finger at the church porch, which provided some slight protection from the elements. "Didn't hear nothing more than usual."

So Saint-Landry must have known and trusted the man who had lured him out, if they had met near the cemetery gate, and gone inside, with only a few soft words exchanged.

Beaupréau . . . but where *was* Beaupréau? And if he, too, was dead, then who had murdered them both?

Aristide dropped another sou in the beggar's hand and left the cemetery, only to discover that he had, without thinking about it, wandered down Rue St. André des Arts and was nearing Rue de Savoie.

I'm behaving like a smitten schoolboy, he thought, turning his steps toward the house where the Saint-Landrys lived, *and I don't really care.* He stopped in the courtyard and gazed up at the first-floor windows until the porter finally came outside to inquire his business.

"Police business," he said brazenly, pulling out his card. The man bowed and hastily retreated to his room by the stairs.

Sophie appeared in the window a moment later and caught sight of him. Aristide nodded to her and she smiled down at him, blushing. A moment later she glanced over her shoulder as if someone inside had called her away, then brought her fingertips to her lips, blew him a kiss, and vanished.

He was scarcely aware of the cold, or of anything else, as he turned and made for the gate. Another pedestrian collided with him as he reached the street and he muttered a word of apology without being aware of anything but Sophie's smile.

"My word, you have got it badly," said a familiar voice. "I know I'm no beauty, but I thought at least I'd stand out in a crowd when a friend cannons into me."

"Derville?"

"Visiting the Saint-Landrys again, are you?"

"No, I . . . I was merely passing by."

Derville looked at him, tapping the head of his walking stick gently into his palm. "You know," he said at last, "you're running the risk of becoming quite the cliché. Somebody'll put you in a third-rate comedy if you're not careful."

"I've been meeting with Brasseur," Aristide snapped. "I was merely on my way back to your lodgings."

"Well, why not come upstairs with me? I felt I ought to pay a call on them and see how they were bearing up. Eugénie still refuses to go into mourning, I see," he added, with a glance upward at the windows, which were free of any black draperies. "A visit might cheer her up."

Aristide nearly agreed, but thought better of it. Suddenly he knew he did not want to share a half hour in Sophie's company with anyone.

16

Aristide had no idea whether or not Derville went to Mass on Sundays, though he rather suspected that, in midwinter, his friend preferred a warm bed to a frigid church. Rising early, he washed, begged a shave from Renauld, threw on his clothes, and left the apartment before Derville woke.

The Luxembourg gardens were still and empty at that hour; the mothers with marriageable daughters and the decorous, fashionable couples would not appear until the afternoon. He spent the time strolling about in a daze, oblivious to the damp chill.

He was waiting beside the Medici Fountain by the time a nearby church bell tolled noon. There was no sign of Sophie or Victoire in the distance. Of course it was a lady's prerogative to be late, he told himself, and occupied ten minutes with a turn around a grove of trees, kicking aside the last of the fallen horse chestnuts and rehearsing what he would say to her when she arrived.

At half past twelve, he ceased pacing and threw himself down on the nearest bench, staring into the rippling surface of the fountain's little pool. A lady's prerogative was all very well . . .

One o'clock.

Perhaps she was ill. Or perhaps Eugénie was ill; she had not looked well when he had last seen her.

At last he strode off, past the first of the fashionable matrons, and walked swiftly northward. A quarter hour later he entered the courtyard on Rue de Savoie once again and hurried up the stairs, ignoring the porter.

The maid Victoire opened the door to him. "Is anything wrong?" he blurted out, before she could even say "Good day" to him. "Is something the matter?"

"Beyond the master being gone, probably dead, and the household at sixes and sevens, monsieur?" she said tartly.

"I—I meant Mademoiselle Sophie. She didn't come to the gardens as she promised."

"No, monsieur, she said yesterday evening that we wouldn't be going after all."

"But she never sent word to me. Has anything gone ill with her, or with Madame Saint-Landry?"

"They're both in good health, monsieur," she told him, avoiding his gaze, "though madame's been feeling out of sorts lately, and no wonder. Other than that, I couldn't say."

"Might I come in?" he inquired, when she made no move to let him past her.

"Begging your pardon, monsieur, but Mademoiselle Sophie . . . she told me she wasn't to be at home to you."

He stared at her, baffled. "I don't understand. Did I—did I overstep myself yesterday? Is that it?"

"I couldn't say, monsieur," she repeated woodenly.

"I insist upon seeing mademoiselle," he said, and pushed past her. "I'm not leaving until she agrees to meet me face-to-face."

"But monsieur—"

"Tell her that. Ten minutes—that's all I ask."

He strode into the salon, which was empty, and wandered over to the fireplace. Someone—Sophie, he guessed—had set the two miniatures on the mantelpiece. A few daintily crafted paper flowers stood in a vase next to the portrait of Jean-Lambert.

A long while later, he became aware of another presence. He turned and saw Sophie in the doorway. She was very pale and he thought the tiny gasp he had heard was the sound of her drawing a deep breath. He took a step toward her and she raised a hand as if to keep him away.

"No," she said, "please—"

"Sophie? What's the matter? How could you refuse—"

"I—I do like you," she said abruptly. "Truly."

Aristide found himself smiling, despite his confusion. "And I like you. Quite a lot. Is that something to be sorry or ashamed about?"

She shook her head, mute.

"I waited in the gardens . . . why didn't you send me a message?"

She shrank back a pace as he stepped toward her, her cheeks suddenly crimson. "You don't understand."

"Understand what?"

Her pretty eyes, he saw now, were red and puffy, with dark smudges beneath them. "Mademoiselle—you've been crying. What's the matter? Please tell me."

"Were you going to tell me that you adore me and have the greatest regard and respect for me and all the rest of it?"

The directness of her question startled him, but he swallowed his surprise and slowly nodded. "Yes," he said, "I suppose I was. Should I not?"

"No. I—I can't hear such things from you, Monsieur Ravel."

He stood quite still for a moment, until he decided that she had not, after all, thrust a dagger between his ribs. "Because—because you're a wealthy heiress and I'm just a provincial scribbler?" he said at last. "Do you think I'm a fortune hunter, and that I only want to make empty promises to you so I can marry you for your money?"

"I . . . no . . ."

"I don't want your money, mademoiselle. I barely know you, but you can't deny an attraction exists between us. And if we grew to know each other better, and matters reached a certain point . . . I would have told you to arrange a marriage contract any way you wished, for all I cared. I do care about *you*; because you're a lovely, clever, intelligent young woman and I think we could make each other happy."

She shook her head. "No . . . no, it's not that. It's because . . . because if I let myself fall in love with you, and married you, it would be disastrous. No matter what we did, or where we went, someone would be sure to find out. Somehow they would learn. And the truth would come out about me, that I've been mixed up in a case of murder; and about you . . . about your father."

Aristide stared at her, thunderstruck. How on earth could she know about his father?

"And then what would become of us," she continued, "when people knew that my brother had been murdered, and that I'd married the son of a murderer who—who was broken on the wheel? You know exactly what they would think, what they would say. What sort of outcasts would we be, no matter where we were?"

"You—I never—how could you—" he stammered.

"Monsieur Derville told me," she said, without looking at him. "Yesterday afternoon."

"*Derville?*"

"And he's asked me to marry him."

And yet, he realized, how clear it was. Derville, who had known— and, he saw it now, admired—Sophie for years, and who was the only man in Paris, besides Brasseur, who knew his secret. How better to win her, than to tell her the one damning fact that would poison her against him forever?

"Are you . . ." he whispered at last.

"I don't know. I think I may. I do like him, and he's funny and charming."

"I thought perhaps . . . it's not the same, of course . . . but still, a murder in the family brings unwanted scrutiny. I thought you might understand my own situation better now."

"I do. Far too much— Oh, be honest," she said suddenly, with a quick glance up at him. "You and I . . . both tainted by the crimes of others . . . it would be doomed before it began. Even if you and the inspector discover who murdered Lambert, some people will always wonder if that was really what happened, and they'll start vicious rumors. How could the two of us ever be more than pariahs?"

He knew she was right, and said nothing.

"If I marry Monsieur Derville, it should be all right. He said that if rumors start, we can go to Brussels and live there—"

"Derville? Leave Paris?" he interrupted her. "He must love you more than I thought, to make that ultimate sacrifice for you!"

"I think he does," Sophie said, ignoring his angry sarcasm. "He told me he's loved me for years, since I was only a child. He must, mustn't he, if he's willing to ally himself with me now? We can go to the Low Countries, if we have to, where no one knows us, but his family has some property, and with luck, no one will ever know about me. And if they should learn, his money and his family connections should be able to shield us from the worst of it."

"While I'm worse than a nobody, with no money, and a taint of my own," Aristide finished for her. "What can I offer you, except the name of a felon, and shame and heartbreak?"

"You can offer me love," she said softly. "I know that. But you must know, as well as I, that sometimes love isn't enough."

"Do you love Derville?"

"I'm fond of him . . . and I've known him for ages, long enough to believe he'll be a good husband to me."

"After he betrayed a friend in order to possess you," Aristide said, "do you think he'll never betray you, as well?"

She did not answer. The expression in her eyes was sufficient. He bent and kissed her forehead. "Good-bye, Sophie."

He thought he heard her whisper "Adieu" to his back as he left the room, strode blindly out of the apartment, and hurtled down the staircase. Hailing the first fiacre he saw, he threw himself onto the dirty seat, seething.

"Where's Derville?" he demanded as Renauld opened the door of Derville's apartment to him.

"He's already gone out, Monsieur Ravel. Would you care to wait for him?"

Aristide shouldered his way past the man and stood glowering in the salon. "Where is he? Where's he gone?"

"He did say something about meeting a friend for luncheon at a café in the gardens, monsieur," Renauld said imperturbably. "May I bring you some refreshment?"

"No, you can pack my bag. Everything that's mine, understand— I'll never be coming back here. Send it—leave it downstairs with the porter." He turned about and slammed the door behind him as he left.

Half an hour later he found Derville in the Café de Foy, laughing over after-dinner coffee with three companions, a man and two women. "You're going to talk with me right now," he said, without preamble, as he seized Derville by the shoulder of his elegantly tailored coat and dragged him around in his seat. "How could you?"

Derville's smile faded abruptly. "I won't insult you by pretending I don't know what you're talking about—"

"How could you?" Aristide repeated. "You bastard—all through your life, you've had everything you ever wanted. You've never lacked for anything, never known what it's like to be without money, family, connections, the lot! Couldn't you have restrained yourself from grabbing away the one thing I wanted? Couldn't you have accepted the fact that she cared for me more than she cared for you? But no, you had to have her, and you used a low, dirty trick to get her!"

"Perhaps I did," said Derville, rising. His companions, embarrassed, muttered excuses and sidled away. "But you can't say I lied to her."

"You could have minded your own business! Since school—I always thought you were my friend. You kept quiet about my—my father. I trusted you! And now this!"

"Do keep your voice down," Derville said. He threw a few coins on the table and strode out to the arcade, where he turned to face Aristide amid the thin stream of shoppers that came strolling past.

"All right, I don't deny it. I told Sophie about your father and mother. But can you possibly believe that it was for her sake that I told her, just as much as for my own sake?"

Aristide felt his fists clenching and resisted the urge to break Derville's jaw. "Oh, yes, because you're so damned altruistic!"

"Don't be an idiot, Ravel. You would have had to tell her some time, you know. Better now than later, don't you think?"

"And what damned business was it of yours?"

"Somebody had to do it. Did you ever stop to think of how an alliance with you would affect Sophie? I was selfish; I admit that. But what about your own selfishness in allowing her to cultivate a fine crush on you because you're so intriguingly melancholy and secretive—and in letting yourself think you could have her, and damn the consequences? Did you think that nobody in the circles she moves in would ever entertain a gossipy cousin from Bordeaux? It would take only one person to learn whose son you were, start up the rumor mill, and make both of your lives hell. And, for God's sake, do you imagine you've improved your reputation, now that you've turned police spy?"

Aristide stared at him, knowing that Derville spoke the truth, and hating him for it. At last, unable to speak, he swung a wild punch at Derville, which the other man countered easily.

"Ravel," Derville said softly, still gripping him by the wrist, "you probably won't believe me, but I swear to you on all that's holy that if your father hadn't been—what he was—then I'd have stood aside. I know she prefers you to me. She told me so. And if the only thing anyone could hold against you was that you were poor and without connections, and that you did a little work for the police now and then, I'd have been a gentleman, for the sake of her happiness. But marrying you, taking that taint on herself, that taint which will cling to you for the rest of your life, even though I know it isn't remotely your fault— that would have made her very unhappy, in the end. No one can keep a secret like that forever. You know that. Are you finally ready to admit it?"

"None of what you've said," Aristide said at last, his voice low and tight, "makes you any less of an unparalleled bastard. You thought you'd save her from me, so you snatched her up for yourself?"

"Yes, if you want to put it plainly."

"Those two girls who were here with you and your friend—were they the afternoon's entertainment? If you love Sophie so much, why don't you go and spend the afternoon with her, instead?"

"Perhaps I will," Derville said evenly. "If you've just come from an interview with her, I expect she's upset."

"Go on, then. Get out of here. Show her you really do love her—"

"I've loved her since she was fourteen years old!"

"And if you end by treating her as you eventually treat everyone else—as someone who's only worth anything to you as long as he amuses you—then by God I'll—I'll—"

He could think of nothing to say that would not be hopelessly hackneyed, and at last turned and strode away without further words. He had passed a dozen shop windows when he heard Derville call his name. Aristide ignored him and strode on, stopping only as Derville caught up to him and tugged his elbow.

"Ravel—I have to tell you something."

"More excuses?" Aristide said without turning around.

"No—it's not that. Something you ought to know."

Aristide turned halfway. "What, then?"

"I've been a cad—I admit it. I owe you this, at least." Derville paused, looked away, and fidgeted for an instant before rapidly continuing. "You should know that I told Monsieur de Beaupréau on Wednesday that Saint-Landry was lying dead in the morgue."

17

Aristide stared at Derville as he abruptly fell silent.

"*You* told Beaupréau?"

Suddenly great pieces of the puzzle began to fall into place. He seized Derville's coat collar and forced him backward until he was up against one of the square stone pillars that supported the arcade.

"It was *you*, wasn't it? The man who came to the morgue. The first one, who came in the morning, looking for the body of a mythical servant. Because you recognized that waistcoat when Brasseur showed it to you and told you it belonged to a dead man. But Saint-Landry was more to you than just a family friend. You're a Mason, too, aren't you? You've been lying to me all along!"

"For God's sake," Derville said, "let's not stand here quarreling in the midst of the traffic." He twisted away and marched to the half-dozen empty tables that stood in front of the nearest café. "Yes, I'm a Freemason," he declared, flinging himself down in a rickety basket-seated chair. "After seeing Saint-Landry's body, and what was done to it, I thought it would be safer if you didn't know."

"Are you a member of the Lodge of the Sacred Trinity?" Aristide demanded, suddenly enlightened. A waiter approached them and he gestured the man away with a glare. "Is that how you knew Saint-Landry? No wonder you kept stalling me when I asked you about friends who were Masons—and I suppose that's why you wanted to come along with me and find out what Desmoulins's friends might know."

"I knew Saint-Landry long before I became a Mason and joined his lodge."

"And when Brasseur showed you the waistcoat, and you realized it might belong to a friend—either Saint-Landry or Beaupréau—you sent Brasseur and me off on a wild-goose chase to the wrong tailor, to buy yourself some time while you went to the Basse-Geôle to see for yourself if that corpse could be one or the other of them. Am I right?" Derville nodded infinitesimally and Aristide continued.

"And you knew it was Saint-Landry right off. What's more, the attendants could hardly hide the manner in which he died; and you, being a Mason, and recognizing the dead man as the head of your own lodge, feared that the throat-cutting, the tongue, and the marks in his flesh were significant. That's what happened, isn't it?"

"All right, all right," said Derville. He slouched down into his chair, scowling, and thrust his hands into his pockets. "It was for Eugénie's and Sophie's sake; I only wanted to know who the dead man was. I just wanted to slow you down for a couple of hours, while I made sure, so if it was Saint-Landry, I could break it to them gently . . . but when I saw those wounds, I panicked. So I went to the lodge—which isn't far from here—and looked for the most senior member—"

"Beaupréau."

"Yes. He's Senior Warden, under Saint-Landry. That means he's second in command."

"I should have known." Aristide tugged his notes from a pocket and glanced over them, disgusted. "Beaupréau must have been the well-dressed man in the blue coat and silk waistcoat whom Bouille described."

Derville nodded. "He was wearing a blue coat that day."

"So you found Beaupréau at your lodge. And you told him Saint-Landry was dead, with a slit throat, what's more, and a Masonic symbol carved into his flesh, and asked him what ought to be done. And then Beaupréau, for his own reasons, must have gone off to the morgue like a shot, with a couple of friends, and stolen the body." He paused, with a glance at Derville, who shrugged.

"I expect so. He didn't say anything to me beyond 'I'll take care of it.' I'm a very junior member, Ravel—he wouldn't have included me in whatever it was he was hatching."

"Do you realize what a damned mess you've made of everything?" Aristide demanded. "Obstructing a police investigation into a murder—"

"Understand my position, will you?" Derville said. "Look . . . I told Beaupréau that Saint-Landry was dead, in the morgue, with a cut throat, because I didn't know what else to do. If Saint-Landry had been run over by a carriage or stabbed by a footpad, it would have been different . . . tragic, but accidents happen. I'd have told Sophie that her brother was dead, because I thought she ought to hear it from a friend rather than from some police official, and that would have been an end to the matter; but that cut throat scared me more than I want to say. His throat cut from ear to ear . . . I took that oath when I was initiated, and you saw for yourself how Étaillot and Varenne reacted when you spoke of what had been done to him. Any other Mason you care to question would be just as uneasy as I am to hear that someone may have taken the oath literally."

"And what has Beaupréau done with the corpse of his friend and fellow Mason?"

"I haven't the faintest idea." Derville leaned back in his chair and stared at him, one eyebrow slightly raised. "That's your job, isn't it, to unravel this pretty mess?"

Aristide shot to his feet and shoved his chair aside. "Oh, go to the devil," he snapped, and stalked off.

He threw aside caution and went straight to Brasseur's headquarters, striding through the anteroom with his satchel and flinging the door to the office wide. To his annoyance, Brasseur found Derville's confession highly entertaining.

"What a merry dance they led us on!" he exclaimed, after he had ceased chuckling. "Despite all, Ravel, you have to laugh . . ."

Aristide, thinking of his last glimpse of Sophie, did not feel in the least like laughing, but at last permitted himself a faint, sour smile.

"I really ought to have Monsieur Derville up before the commissaire for hindering the investigation," Brasseur said at last. He blew his nose and sat up straighter in his chair. "Although, as you say, he couldn't possibly have known that Beaupréau was going to make off with the corpse. And, I suppose, that lets Derville off as a possible murderer. He wouldn't have done all that nonsense if he'd cut Saint-Landry's throat himself."

"At least we know Beaupréau's alive, or he was on Wednesday, at any rate," Aristide said absently.

"So what the devil is he up to? Why steal the body? What good does that do anyone?"

"Perhaps he wanted to keep it from being identified."

"After you and I, and my men, and the morgue attendants, had all seen it? And with the clothes, we were already halfway to identifying it. He'd have done better to steal the clothes, not the corpse."

Aristide reached for one of the glasses of red wine that Brasseur had poured out for them. "You're perfectly right. So why do you steal a body if it's *not* to prevent identification?"

"Because . . . because something about the victim could identify his killer?" Brasseur suggested.

"What? How? And that would mean Beaupréau knows, or suspects, who the killer is. Unless he did it himself."

"That's scarcely likely," Brasseur pointed out, pouring himself another half glass, "after the murderer went to such trouble dressing up the scene with occult symbols and such. Why do all that, just crying out for attention, and then go to even more trouble stealing the corpse?"

"No, no, of course you're right." Aristide clawed at his hair and pushed it impatiently away from his face. "Unless . . . unless he killed Saint-Landry—or thought he killed him with a blow to the head—and then someone else, after Beaupréau had gone, had come in and finished him off, with the slit throat and the tongue and and the symbols and so on? We still don't know who's been setting those fires."

"Masonic symbols . . ." Brasseur growled. "Beaupréau's a Mason of high rank . . . it can't possibly be a coincidence, can it? Curse it, if Beaupréau didn't do it, he must at least suspect who did . . ."

Aristide thought for a moment, staring at the glinting of the firelight as it reflected off the decanter on the desk between them, and suddenly looked up. "Brasseur—what if Saint-Landry's body wasn't stolen to prevent identification, but to prevent anyone else from seeing and recognizing those Masonic symbols that were left on him? We suspect they were mixed up in something dangerous together—fanning the flames of the diamond necklace affair—and it probably got Saint-Landry murdered."

"And Beaupréau is doing his best to conceal the Masonic connection by stealing Saint-Landry's body?"

"Exactly. He must have disposed of it somehow, so that it won't be seen again. He may be the only one who knows where it is, not to mention who actually committed the murder."

"Yes, and he's got a title, too," Brasseur grumbled, "so he's practically immune from prosecution unless we have rock-solid evidence against him, and without the body we've got no proof at all; Commissaire Le Roux probably wouldn't even let me try to put him in front of poor Bouille for identification, unless Beaupréau agreed to it himself. I can't just go to the Hôtel de Beaupréau, with nothing but a wild theory, and start digging up the garden for lost corpses."

"He couldn't have buried Saint-Landry in his own garden, or anyone else's," said Aristide. "It's been too cold; the ground is frozen solid."

"But if he hasn't been buried, he ought to have turned up before now, in the river, in a ditch, in a cellar, in a public privy, *somewhere!*" Brasseur pushed his wine glass away and sighed. "I'd also like a theory about Saint-Landry's murder that I could put before the commissaire, without worrying that I'd end up in the Bastille myself . . ."

"But if you did have the body, and proof that Beaupréau stole it, would that be enough to bring Beaupréau in for questioning, if you can find him?"

"It might be, though a fellow with money and a title can get away with quite a lot," Brasseur grumbled. "But where in the name of all the saints *is* it?"

18

M adame Brasseur, still casting a suspicious eye at Aristide, at last
agreed to give him a bed for a few nights in their small daughter's room, and ordered the child's bed to be moved into their own
bedchamber. He fell asleep on a lumpy, hastily stuffed straw mattress,
surrounded by half-finished children's gowns.

A letter arrived for Brasseur the following morning. "You're in
luck," he said, tossing it across the dining table to Aristide as they ate
their midday dinner. "Grimaud—the captain at the Bastille—says the
police interrogated Cagliostro just a couple of days ago."

Aristide winced; though the judicial torture of accused prisoners
had been abolished half a dozen years before, he suspected that, in
pursuit of matters involving the royal family, the police could be both
persuasive and thorough.

"After that," Brasseur continued, oblivious, "he might be more
willing to cooperate with anyone who looks more like a friend."

"But can Grimaud get us in to see him?" Aristide said, scanning
the note.

"For a short visit, perhaps." He looked gloomily at Aristide. "I suppose you'll want to go right away?"

The driver of their fiacre muttered a few sullen words at hearing their destination but made no other complaint. They clattered down Rue St. Honoré, the driver adding his cries and insults to the din of the street as they maneuvered past pedestrians, cabs, the occasional private carriage, and peddlers carrying enormous barrels or bundles on their backs and shouting wares of every description. On Rue St. Antoine, as they approached the Bastille, the congestion grew worse, as market gardeners' handcarts, tradesmen's wagons from the many furniture workshops, apprentices running errands, and countless wallowing pigs continually blocked the way.

Aristide swallowed hard as the fortress loomed ahead of them and a chill gust of wind suddenly rattled their carriage. "You look like you're coming to stay," Brasseur muttered in his ear as they passed through the open gates of the outer courtyard. "Keep cool, all right?"

They continued unhindered to the drawbridge, where Brasseur imperiously announced to the soldiers on duty that he was a police inspector and a friend of Captain Grimaud, and wished to be taken to the captain at once.

"Your name, monsieur?" a guard inquired.

"Brasseur."

"And your companion?"

"My subinspector."

"His name, monsieur the inspector."

Brasseur hesitated for an instant. "Joubert," Aristide said, blurting out the first name that came to mind. The guard instructed them to wait and sent a man inside. A few minutes later a smartly uniformed officer emerged from the inner courtyard and, upon seeing Brasseur, bowed slightly.

"Brasseur, old man, I didn't expect to see you quite so soon as this—but come in, come in."

Aristide followed them unobtrusively as Grimaud led Brasseur through the broad passageway into the keep. It was far less alarming than he had expected, more a military stronghold than a prison. The courtyard of the keep was busy with soldiers, servants, and carters hauling in supplies, and littered with the usual foul-smelling accumulation of straw, ashes, kitchen scraps, waste, and assorted manure that could be found on any street in Paris.

"He's in Tower Block D," Grimaud said, breaking into Aristide's thoughts. "This way. What's the matter—want your fortune told?" He dug Brasseur in the ribs and guffawed. Brasseur politely chuckled.

"Actually I'm here on some unofficial police business, with some questions about Madame de La Motte's doings. I'd rather ask the cardinal, but since I'm not important enough for him to see me—"

"Oh, you'd be surprised. His Eminence has had so many visitors since he was lodged here, what's one more or less?"

"Still, I'm not here under orders, and I doubt I'm distinguished enough to keep company with a Rohan . . . Cagliostro will do nicely, thanks."

Grimaud led them into one of the eight massive towers and began to ascend a spiral staircase. Aristide was slightly dizzy by the time they emerged onto the fourth level and continued down a frigid corridor. At last the captain stopped at a barred door and peered through the spy hole.

"He looks pretty well, I'd say. A guard's in there with him; would you rather be private?" Grimaud unlocked the door and gestured Brasseur and Aristide inside. "You there—these gentlemen want a word alone with the prisoner. Fifteen minutes!" he added to Brasseur.

"Well, go ahead," Brasseur said, when the attending guard had left the cell and the spy hole had been shut with a hollow thump behind them. Aristide cautiously stepped forward. Though the cell had a low, domed ceiling, it was spacious—about the size of his own room on Rue de la Muette—and the walls were plastered and whitewashed. A fire crackled on the hearth, banishing much of the January chill, and the bed linens, though the mattress was of straw, seemed clean enough. Undoubtedly Cagliostro was able to pay for his comforts. Also for his distractions, Aristide realized, noticing a table at one side bearing signs of a card game suddenly interrupted, and a few silver coins.

"Messieurs?" the alchemist inquired, turning away from the fire. He glanced over Brasseur and Aristide and tilted his head, looking faintly puzzled. "I have already spent some hours with the police, the day before yesterday. I have told you everything I know."

"Perhaps not everything," Aristide said. He could see more clearly as he approached the hearth. For all his famous reputation, the self-styled sorcerer Cagliostro was an ordinary-looking man of early middle age, with a slight paunch and the smooth, bland face of a successful, though not entirely scrupulous, lawyer. His clothes, lacking any vestiges of the flamboyant robes and jewels that he reportedly wore during his elaborate ceremonies, were plain and neat, as was the modest wig he had donned to keep out the cold. His most remarkable features were his voice, which bore a distinct foreign lilt, and his eyes, deep, dark, and brilliant.

"Who are you, pray?"

"My name is . . . Joubert," Aristide said, remembering the alias he had adopted just in time.

"And what may I do for you . . . Monsieur Joubert?" Cagliostro moved forward a step, giving Aristide a swift appraising glance.

"You are a Freemason of high rank, Count."

Cagliostro blinked. "I am an *Egyptian* Freemason," he conceded, after an infinitesimal pause. "I adhere to the Egyptian rite, far more ancient, and superior to, these bastard European offshoots."

"But you consider yourself to be a brother to all other Freemasons, no matter what rites they may practice, don't you?"

"Naturally."

"And if a fellow Mason asked you to do something, something innocuous, which might bring about an outcome that would be consistent with Masonic ideals, you would do it, would you not?"

Cagliostro shook his head. "I have no idea what you mean, monsieur."

"We're speaking about your convincing Cardinal de Rohan to buy the diamond necklace," Brasseur said, stepping forward from the shadows.

"*No!*" Cagliostro snapped, smacking a hand down on the table beside him and making the coins rattle. "For the fortieth time, no! I know nothing more about this plot, this theft, than anyone else. I have told the police, over and over again, I had no part in this. I am merely His Eminence the cardinal's mystical advisor. I looked into his future and saw great things in store for him. When he summoned me and asked me whether or not he ought to enter into this great purchase for, as he sincerely thought, the queen, I advised him to do so."

"After first advising him not to, I believe," said Aristide.

"But it's common sense, monsieur. I thought it over and changed my mind on the matter. What else should I have done? After all, His Eminence needed little persuading from me. Any fool knows that if you do a favor for royalty, you're likely to be rewarded. The theft, though, was all the doing of that woman, a mere swindler and adventuress, a creature with whose name I would barely soil my mouth."

"So you had nothing to do with her plans?" said Brasseur.

"Nothing. I have said it before, and I say it again: nothing at all. Oh, she deceived me, I confess it, but not for long."

"Deceived *you*, Count?"

He drew himself up, and for an instant Aristide caught sight of the charismatic miracle worker who had enthralled jaded aristocrats and played high priest at so many rumored secret rituals. "She tried every avenue that might lead her to joining my Supreme Council of the

Egyptian Rite, which is open only to those, both men and women, of high birth and superior qualities. And—since she has neither fortune, breeding, nor morals, nothing more than a thin claim to the vestiges of a royal house by way of the wrong side of the blanket—naturally she failed. So she set up an elaborate little piece of theater in order to induce me to trust her. I should have seen through her when she brought forward her own niece as the virgin through whom the good spirits would prophesy."

"Prophesy what?" Aristide said, making an effort to remind himself that, no matter how fascinating, the man was nothing more than a brilliant charlatan.

"The happy results of the queen's pregnancy last year, of course. And when the queen was brought to bed of a healthy prince, I was . . . shall we say . . . more inclined to believe Madame de La Motte's claims." He paused, smirking slightly. "She is also quite a handsome lady, and knows how to exploit her charms. But she took me in, messieurs, she took me in as she did everyone else. I was never her intentional confederate in any of her schemes, neither to hoodwink His Eminence nor to steal those cursed diamonds. And now the whore denounces me as a conspirator, or even as the author of the plot, but it is false, false, false!" He strode to the fireplace and turned his back to them. "*Basta!* I will say no more, messieurs."

"You misapprehend us, Count," Aristide said, feeling it was time for a bluff. "We know, in fact, that you weren't conspiring with Madame de La Motte. Tell us, rather, about your connection with the Marquis de Beaupréau."

He watched Cagliostro and smiled to himself as he saw the alchemist suddenly go rigid. "I am slightly acquainted with him," Cagliostro said coldly, without turning around. "But surely that's no crime, monsieur."

"It is if it has to do with a plot to discredit the monarchy . . . in short, to commit high treason. Not to mention murder."

"Murder!" the alchemist exclaimed, jerking about. He dragged out a chair and clutched at the back of it. "I know nothing of any murder."

"Jean-Lambert Saint-Landry, Worshipful Master of Beaupréau's lodge, had his throat slit a week ago," Aristide said, watching Cagliostro. "Do you deny knowing anything about it?"

"I most certainly deny it! *Dio mio!* Monsieur . . . I am a simple mystic, whom supernatural forces have blessed with certain talents. My mission is to aid and advise those who need me, not to enter into conspiracies."

"Then tell us what happened between you, Saint-Landry, and Monsieur de Beaupréau."

"Beaupréau and Saint-Landry came to me in secret," Cagliostro said, after a moment's hesitation. "At the beginning of last year. Some weeks before, I had let slip a few imprudent words to Beaupréau about His Eminence's intention to enter into a purchase with the royal jewelers, on behalf of the queen. At that time, I had little notion that the La Motte woman was even involved with the matter, for I knew of her only as His Eminence's premier mistress, though I had heard some rumors that she claimed to be intimate with Her Majesty and sometimes took letters back and forth between the queen and the cardinal. I had not the least idea, of course, that the letters from Her Majesty were all forged, but I did believe the investment of so much money for a mere bauble to be somewhat risky, and I told His Eminence as much."

"What did Saint-Landry and Beaupréau say to you?"

"Saint-Landry simply gave me to understand that I could do my brother Masons, and our sacred principles, a great service. He suggested I change my mind and prophesy a successful outcome to the cardinal's enterprise—in short, I was to do all I could to encourage him to go along with the purchase after all. Where was the harm in that? Why would I have refused?"

"You didn't suspect a political plot in this 'great service' he spoke of?" Brasseur demanded.

Cagliostro slowly straightened and fixed Brasseur with the intense gaze that, Aristide thought, must have won him hundreds of adoring converts. "Monsieur, I am not a fool. I keep my finger on the pulse of the times. I never thought it would be wise for Her Majesty, given her past reputation for extravagance and selfish frivolity, to be buying a jewel worth a million and a half livres while the treasury is nearly empty and the poor go hungry. But what does it matter to me? Why should I care a jot what she does, or what calamity she brings upon herself? The movement of the stars, the influence of the spirits, the fate of nations, is my concern; not the popularity of stupid people whom chance has made kings and queens."

"Signor Cagliostro cares about royalty and nobility only to the extent that he can dazzle them into fawning over him and showering him with gifts," said Aristide, turning to Brasseur. "He has the deepest disdain for them, otherwise. Isn't that true, Count?"

Cagliostro glared at him with the same piercing gaze, but said nothing.

"I've heard all kinds of rumors about him," Aristide continued, "that he's thousands of years old, that he's actually the Wandering Jew of legend, that he's been initiated into the darkest secrets of the occult, that he studied magic and healing with the greatest minds of history. Also that he's nothing but a fraud, and certainly not any kind of nobleman. Just a common adventurer, a smart swindler from the slums of Naples or Alexandria, who knows how to use impressive words and gestures and parlor tricks to dupe bored, empty-headed aristocrats."

"The La Motte woman, naturally, has been disseminating slanders against me," Cagliostro said calmly.

Brasseur snorted. "Well, 'Count,' I think the truth is closer to Madame de La Motte's version; it usually is."

"And someone who's clawed himself up from nothing," Aristide continued, "usually harbors a deep well of resentment toward those who never had to lift a finger to get where they are. So if you deduced that Saint-Landry's and Beaupréau's harmless little favor was actually part of a plan to allow the king and queen to make themselves look as contemptible and odious as they possibly could, I think you'd have closed your eyes and gone along with it." He paused for a moment and they exchanged level stares. "I would have."

"You may believe what you wish," said Cagliostro, after a moment. "And I have nothing more to say. Good day to you."

19

"Well?" Brasseur said, once they were safely away from the Bastille and jolting westward in another fiacre along Rue St. Antoine. "I don't know that anything he said brought us one step closer to learning who murdered Saint-Landry. Do you?"

"He was more forthright with us than I'd expected," said Aristide thoughtfully. "In his position, would you have admitted to someone you'd never met before that you didn't give a damn about the monarchy's reputation? Something about us caused him to trust us, at least a little."

"Perhaps he's read some pamphlet of yours," Brasseur suggested.

"You don't think I put my name to those, do you? Anyway, I didn't give him my real name."

"That's right, you called yourself Joubert—"

"Joubert!" Aristide exclaimed.

"Who's Joubert, then?"

"My—a publisher. Keeps a bookshop at the Palais-Royal."

"I thought it sounded familiar," Brasseur said, nodding.

"Derville's friendly with him; that's how I met him. And—just keep it under your hat, will you?—Joubert, like most publishers, puts out a line of illegal books, mostly political, but Derville told me he turns out more than most. Who's to say that he's not also one of the Sacred Trinity fraternity? For all we know, he prints every screed they distribute. And if he's a member of the lodge, perhaps Cagliostro recognized the name. Joubert may have been hand in glove with Beaupréau all the time."

Brasseur thumped on the roof and leaned out the window. "Driver, a change of route: my friend is going to the Palais-Royal before you take me to the Left Bank."

Only a girl of twelve was behind the counter when Aristide entered the bookshop. "Papa's in back," she said, curtsying, when he asked for Monsieur Joubert. He went on to the tiny sitting room, where he found Joubert, brow puckered in concentration, jotting annotations in a manuscript beside a comfortable fire.

"Monsieur Ravel!" he exclaimed, upon seeing Aristide. "Don't tell me you have something for me already."

"Actually," Aristide said pleasantly, taking a seat next to the fire and stretching out his hands to the warmth, "I hoped you could tell me who murdered Jean-Lambert Saint-Landry, and what's become of his body."

The shocked stare with which Joubert met Aristide's statement was enough to tell him that the bookseller knew something. "I've no idea what you're talking about," he protested feebly, when he had recovered himself.

"Yes you do. You're not a very good actor, monsieur."

"I will never trust Derville again," Joubert muttered as he rose to his feet. "You were a spy all along, weren't you?"

"No, Monsieur Joubert, I'm an honest-to-God scribbler, who doesn't think much of our government and our monarchy, and who just wants to earn a little money with his pen. But whether I like it or not, I'm stuck investigating this business, and at this point I wouldn't be beyond sending a hint to Inspector Delahaye that you're one of the most prolific clandestine publishers in Paris. But if you'll just tell me what you know about Saint-Landry's murder, I'll keep my mouth shut and be on my way."

With a shaky hand, Joubert poured himself a splash of brandy from a decanter on a side table and drank it off. "I know nothing about his murder."

"No?"

"Word of honor."

"Well? What is it you do know?"

"Monsieur de Beaupréau unexpectedly turned up at my establishment—not here, at the printing works on the Left Bank—on Wednesday afternoon, and told me that he needed to store a parcel out of sight, in complete secrecy, for some hours. He requested the favor as a brother Mason, and I didn't ask any questions. We scarcely ever need the subcellar—all that's stored down there is broken type, until it can be melted down and recast—so I gave the workmen a couple of hours off and told Beaupréau he could hide his parcel there."

"Did you see this 'parcel'?" Aristide inquired.

"I caught a glimpse of it when they were carrying it down the stairs. They had it wrapped in sailcloth, but it was quite obvious to me what it was. I felt I did have to ask questions at that point, so I demanded to know what Beaupréau was up to. He showed me Saint-Landry's face and the—the marks on his flesh, and said he had been murdered, no one knew by whom, but he feared it was something to do with—" He stopped short, flushing.

"With the matter of Count Cagliostro, and the hundreds of juicy libels and songs you've been cranking out lately about the queen's connection with the diamond necklace," Aristide finished for him. Joubert paled as quickly as he had turned red an instant before.

"Yes—yes."

"And then?"

"We hid the corpse in the subcellar. Some time after midnight, Beaupréau returned, disguised as a laborer, with his cart, and they took it away again."

"That's all?"

Joubert nodded. "Yes—that's all I had to do with it."

"And Beaupréau said to you that he didn't know who had murdered Saint-Landry?"

"Yes."

"Would you say he was telling the truth?"

"How should I know?" Joubert shrugged and poured himself another brandy. "I've always known Beaupréau to be an honorable man, though."

"Did he say where he was taking the corpse?"

"He . . . he said something to one of the others, about his own stables being good enough for a day or two, while he made further arrangements. That's all I know."

"Thanks," Aristide said, rising. "Oh, by the way," he added over his shoulder, as he reached for the door handle, "I hope you don't mind if I'm a little tardy with the manuscripts I owe you."

"So there you have it," he said, when he had done relating the interview to Brasseur. "The last known destination seems to have been the stables at the Hôtel de Beaupréau."

"But what the devil did Beaupréau do with it then?" Brasseur demanded. He strode to the window of his office and stood glaring out at the traffic on the street. "'Further arrangements.' What further arrangements? How do you arrange to rid yourself of a corpse? You could," he continued, talking half to himself, "bundle it out of the city in the middle of the night, but there's always the very good chance that some interfering toll collector at the barrier will want to see what you've got in your cart. And you can't just strip it naked and throw it in the river, because people would eventually find it and see the wounds, and even then there's always the small possibility that it would be identified, and then you're right back where you started."

"Burn it?" Aristide suggested halfheartedly.

"Not as easy as you think. You'd need a lot of firewood, and you'd hardly escape notice."

"What about surgeons?"

"What about them?"

"Surgeons and professors of medicine want bodies to dissect. We know bodysnatchers didn't steal it, but perhaps Beaupréau disposed of Saint-Landry's corpse to a resurrectionist. Who's to say it hasn't already been a subject on someone's covert dissecting table?"

"With a Masonic symbol cut in its flesh, and a slit throat just shouting out 'murder' in front of a couple of dozen medical students, or more?" Brasseur shook his head. "We agreed, didn't we, that Beaupréau probably stole the body so no one would see the Masonic marks and start putting two and two together. So that won't wash." He fetched the decanter and a glass from a cabinet and poured himself a brimming glass of wine. "Care for a drop? I certainly could use one!"

Tuesday, 17 January

"If Beaupréau wants to keep that Masonic compass and square away from prying eyes," Aristide said the next morning at breakfast, over rolls and butter and milky coffee, "he'd need to hide it where it'll never be seen again. Could he possibly conceal the body somewhere inside his own house? You've seen those cellars; there may be some hidden rooms."

"But how do you keep it from stinking?" Brasseur said. "It's January now, but corpses have a nasty habit of making themselves known when the weather turns warm." His wife cast him a disapproving glance and he smiled weakly. "Sorry, *chérie*, but this is important."

"How do you keep any meat from stinking and rotting after a few days?" Aristide said. "Salt it down, dry it, smoke it . . ."

"Oh, yes, in front of a couple of dozen servants. I am *not* going into the Marquis de Beaupréau's pantry to snoop inside a barrel of salt beef. The commissaire'd have my head."

Madame Brasseur slapped down her napkin and rose from the table. "Disposing of bodies! A nice subject for the breakfast table! I'll finish my breakfast with Jeanne in the kitchen, thank you."

"What would *you* do, madame, with an inconvenient corpse that no one must ever see again?" Aristide inquired, exchanging a malicious glance with Brasseur.

"Grind it into sausage meat, I expect," she snapped, with an exasperated swish of petticoats. "Heaven knows what they're putting into them, these days!"

"Not a bad idea," Brasseur said with a sigh as the door closed behind his wife. "Though I can't really entertain the notion that his high-and-mightiness the Marquis de Beaupréau would go that far with his friend's body, nor that he's cozy with the sort of ruffian who'd actually be willing to lend a hand." He sighed and loudly blew his nose. "Don't mind me, lad. This affair is so confused that I don't know which side is up anymore."

"But madame's on the right path, I think," Aristide said. "You don't necessarily need to get rid of the body completely, make it vanish into thin air, do you? You just need it—and the cut throat and the Masonic marks in his flesh—to be unrecognizable."

"Not in the form of sausages, I hope?"

"No, not sausages . . . at least I hope not . . . but wait . . ." He grimaced and clutched at his head with both hands, trying to retrieve an elusive memory. *Salt beef . . . dried . . . smoked . . .*

What *was* it that was nagging at the edge of his thoughts?

Dried . . . smoked . . . preserved—

"My God, it certainly was barely recognizable . . ."

"What's that?"

"I've just . . . no, he couldn't—but . . ."

"Would you care to tell me what's the matter?" said Brasseur.

"I have an idea about what he might have done—"

"Who? Beaupréau?"

"Yes—it's possible—and it's appalling . . ." He gulped down a last swallow of coffee and snatched up his hat and coat from a peg on the wall. "I may be gone for a while," he added, thrusting a roll into his coat pocket, and sped away, leaving Brasseur staring behind him.

Trembling with impatience, he set off through the crowds of workmen, street peddlers, and hurrying servants, intent on morning errands, toward the faubourg St. Germain. Twenty minutes later he reached Rue St. Dominique and the Hôtel de Beaupréau. He paused, at the gates, with a wary glance about him, but at last decided that his mysterious assailant, while he might still be spying on him, was not about to threaten or attack him in the full light of day.

Beaupréau had not yet returned, according to the porter, who waved Aristide through toward the hidden servants' entrance. An undersized scullery maid answered his knock and stood gaping at him in the shadows, not knowing what to make of him.

"I need to speak with Monsieur Moreau, the valet, right away," Aristide told her. "Is he here?"

"Yes, monsieur."

"Then could you fetch him for me?" he said, when she did not move, but continued to stare at him. She blinked. He felt in a pocket and came up with a few coppers, which he held up in front of her. "If you bring Monsieur Moreau to me within five minutes."

She hastily curtsied and scuttled away. He walked as far as the end of the tunnel that gave into the kitchens and waited, beneath the censorious glare of an elderly lackey who was polishing brasses. Moreau arrived shortly and Aristide paid off the scullery maid and turned to the valet.

"Moreau—do you know the name of the man who preserved the monkey?"

Moreau stared. "I beg your pardon, monsieur?"

"The monkey! His sister's pet monkey that died, in Monsieur de Beaupréau's collection of curiosities. Do you know whom Beaupréau hired to preserve its body?"

"Oh, that," Moreau said, his face clearing. "For a moment there, I thought you'd gone mad, monsieur! No, I can't say I remember the name, if I ever knew it. Is it important?"

"It may be vital," Aristide began, then recalled that it would be wiser to say as little as possible about Beaupréau's role in the affair of the missing corpse. "It may be the clue we need to find Monsieur de Beaupréau. Do you remember anything at all about the man?"

"Well . . . not much, monsieur . . . you see, Monsieur Alexis went himself. He didn't want to entrust the errand to a servant. So I never saw the man or talked with him. I think Monsieur Alexis said he was quite a learned gentleman, though, a doctor of some sort who'd had some ill fortune." He brightened and snapped his fingers. "That was it—he wasn't a doctor, he was a horse doctor, but not your common butcher from a livery stable. Knew everything about anatomy, Monsieur Alexis said: animals and people alike."

"A horse doctor, but a man of learning, evidently fallen on hard times," Aristide repeated, scribbling in his notebook. "Now how do I find one particular horse doctor, I wonder?"

"You could start with Godart, the coachman," Moreau suggested. "He's a fine hand with a horse. This way."

Aristide followed Moreau down an alley of sculpted trees to the far end of the garden and the stables, where they quickly located Godart. The coachman, who was idly smoking his pipe in a patch of weak sunshine by the water trough, was willing enough to sit and gossip.

"Horse doctors? What d'you want to know about those quacks for?"

"Surely they're not all quacks," said Aristide. "Doctoring domestic animals should be just as much of a science as doctoring human beings, shouldn't it?"

The coachman shrugged and pulled thoughtfully at his pipe. "Well, you might have a point there, though I wouldn't trust most of the folk who call themselves doctors for people, neither! They do say there's a proper school for horse doctors somewhere, though, in the South it might be, to train up people to look after the cavalry horses for the armies." He started forward and waved his pipe at Aristide. "Ha— come to think of it, I hear they started one here in the Île-de-France, too. Maybe they could tell you who the man you're looking for is. Hey, boy! Joseph!"

"M'sieur?" said a scared-looking stable boy, peering from a stall.

"Come out here and answer the gentleman's questions. Didn't you say something once about a school for horse doctors near where you come from?"

The boy gaped at him. "That place? They're all mad there, m'sieur; they belong in the madhouse across the river."

"Mad?" said Aristide.

Joseph shifted uncomfortably, rubbing one manure-crusted sabot against the other. "They cut up animals, m'sieur. Horses and cattle and such. Rotten carcasses out of the fields and off the roads, sometimes. Not to eat, mind you—just to look at their insides, especially when they're sick. Disgusting, my pa calls it, and sinful. God never meant us to be rummaging around anybody's innards; it's as bad as the hang-man." He hastily made the sign of the cross.

"Where is this school?"

"Alfort, in the old château, the Baron de Bormes's that was."

"Where on earth is Alfort?"

"It's my village, m'sieur, beside the Marne, just before it runs into the Seine."

"About six miles southeast from Paris," said Godart. "Just across the river from Charenton and the lunatic asylum, like the boy says. You're never thinking of paying those madmen a visit?"

20

Until Beaupréau returned, Moreau was at loose ends, and insisted upon accompanying Aristide to try and find his master. Alfort was too far for a fiacre, so Moreau persuaded the coachman to lend them a pair of the second-best saddle horses. After scribbling a hasty note to Brasseur, telling him that he was continuing to pursue his idea, and dispatching it with an errand boy who was idling at the nearest corner, Aristide set out with Moreau in the wan winter sunshine.

After an hour's brisk riding outside the city, they descended a steep hill to Charenton, paid to be ferried across the Marne, and shortly found themselves in front of a great arched stone gateway with the words ROYAL VETERINARY SCHOOL carved above them. Beyond the gates, an imposing stone edifice from the days of Louis XIV stood behind an avenue of leafless trees.

Aristide glanced back across the road at the village of Alfort and a retreating carter who had sullenly pointed the way to them and then quickly made a few ancient gestures against evil spirits. "You'd think, from their reaction," he said, "that we were entering the foulest of

slaughterhouses set amid a coven of devil worshippers; not an insti-
tute of learning."

"I never knew there were such schools for horse doctors," Moreau
said, looking about him with lively interest. "What now, monsieur?"

After a few inquiries, a student directed them to a lecture hall,
where they slipped into the rear and waited for the instructor to conclude a talk on what was, apparently, common diseases of cattle. When
the students had dispersed and the lecturer was gathering together his
notes, Aristide stepped forward. "Monsieur Thierrot?"

"Who are you?" the instructor said suspiciously.

"My name's Ravel; we were told you might be able to help us. I
need information, monsieur, about a man whose name I don't know. I
believe he was a horse doctor but also a scholar—"

"The correct term," Thierrot interrupted him, "is 'doctor of veterinary medicine,' if you please. Unless you mean some illiterate sta-
blehand who attempts to treat peasants' nags for spavins."

"Forgive me, a doctor of veterinary medicine. I hoped someone
here would know of the man I mean. All I know is that he's a man of
learning, knowledgeable about anatomy, who has perhaps lost his
original livelihood for some reason. He evidently now earns his living
preparing specimens as scientific curiosities—" He broke off as he realized the other man was slowly nodding.

"Not another word," Thierrot said, with the faintest suggestion of
a smile. "I believe I know exactly who you're talking about. Fragonard."

"The painter?" Aristide said, startled, thinking of the cheap, popular engravings he had seen for sale at bookstalls along the Seine and
at the Palais-Royal. But the dainty rococo images of young ladies in
lace-bedecked gowns, flirting in lush gardens with perfectly coiffed
gentlemen, seemed a world away from the horrid, flayed monkey's
corpse in Beaupréau's collection.

"They're related. First cousins, I believe."

"He was a student here? Did you know him?"

"He was no student, monsieur; Honoré Fragonard was professor of anatomy here, and the school's first director. He came from the veterinary school at Lyon at Monsieur Bourgelat's request when we first began here, twenty years ago. Brilliant man. He didn't last long, though."

"Why not, monsieur?" Moreau inquired.

"Because he was mad," Thierrot said succinctly.

Aristide raised an eyebrow. "Don't the countryfolk hereabout say that you're all mad?"

"Oh, no, monsieur, I assure you we're men of science and quite sane, but Fragonard—well, as I said, the man was brilliant, but he was a brilliant madman. Not a case for the lunatic asylum, of course, but . . . call it eccentricity, immoderate single-mindedness, if you wish. Monsieur Bourgelat—he's the one who founded the school—and Fragonard didn't get along at all." He thrust the last of his notes and papers into a satchel. "Bourgelat wasn't even a physician, he was a lawyer. A normal sort of dabbler in science and letters, quite erudite, a member of the Academy of Sciences, even, but not one to ever get his hands dirty in a dissection room."

"How did such a man found a school like this one?" Aristide said.

"In the usual way. Influence."

"But the greater part of the study would be in dissection, wouldn't it?"

"Bourgelat was clever enough to obtain royal patronage, of course," Thierrot said, "and to impress influential people at court; while Fragonard was obsessed with his research, and had no patience for administration or for flattering courtiers. And since much of the work that Fragonard did wasn't even the normal sort of work that was expected of him, Bourgelat finally dismissed him."

"Would it be possible to have a word with this Monsieur Bourgelat?"

"Sorry, he died a few years ago. But if you want to know about

Fragonard, you might as well talk to me. I was a student and assistant of his, for a while."

"Why was he dismissed, if he was so brilliant?" Moreau said.

"You want to know?" said Thierrot, glancing from Aristide to Moreau and back again. "I'll show you. Come along with me, messieurs. Neither of you are students of medicine, I imagine . . . I hope you both have steady nerves?"

He led the way outside and to another building on the grounds, one with exceptionally high, wide casement windows that ran the length of the walls. "Fragonard was, as I said, a professor of anatomy, both animal and human," he continued as he ushered them inside an airy, echoing two-story foyer and they climbed a broad flight of stairs to the first floor. "But he wasn't nearly as interested in lecturing as he was in dissecting and preparing specimens. You know, don't you, that most self-respecting doctors, at least all but the youngest and most broad-minded ones, wouldn't dream of touching corpses of any kind? That an assistant performs the actual dissection during a lecture, while the professor oversees him and indicates the points of interest to the students? Well, Fragonard had such a passion for anatomy that he didn't care what anyone might think of him; his favorite place was the dissecting room."

"Should that make him a madman?"

"Wait and see," Thierrot said. They reached the top of the long flight and he unlocked the door on the landing. "This, messieurs, is our collection of anatomical specimens, known as the royal cabinet of curiosities. We have nearly three thousand pieces," he added, with a touch of pride. "Normal specimens, diseased specimens, freaks of nature. Many are genuine organs and tissue; a few are models in wax or plaster. Fragonard and his students, I among them, preserved most of these."

"Lord save us," Moreau muttered, glancing about.

Aristide stared. Glass cases, eight or nine feet high, crowded a huge room, high and wide as a church. In the case nearest to him, the bloated intestines of cattle or horses, inflated and dried, looked like monstrous sausages. All around them were kidneys, lungs, stomachs, and other organs he could not name, dried or pickled, displayed like a parody of a butcher shop. A life-sized plaster model of a skinless horse, muscles neatly labeled, stood frozen in mid-step in another case. A few paces farther, row upon row of shelves held dozens of tall jars like those in Beaupréau's study, in which mysterious objects floated in spirits or brine.

" 'The royal cabinet of curiosities'?" he said. "I grant you it's fascinating, monsieur, but I doubt any king or queen would ever want to set foot within a mile of this place."

"As I said," Thierrot continued, "Fragonard was devoted to preserving anatomical specimens for scientific study. And he was extraordinarily gifted at it. These pieces are invaluable to our students." He pointed to a young man in the next room, who was perched on a stool in front of a case and busily scribbling notes. "You're about to say that all of this makes Fragonard an accomplished man of science and a talented practitioner of the anatomical and medical arts, not a madman, doesn't it?"

Aristide nodded. "I should think so."

"He was both man of science and madman, messieurs; I assure you." He strode on through the display rooms, past the glass jars and a dozen mounted skeletons that Aristide realized, as they passed, were of deformed lambs, goats, and calves, some hideously misshapen, some with two heads, some with one head and two conjoined bodies, others with extra limbs that splayed out at grotesque angles.

"You see, despite his devotion to creating and preserving anatomical pieces, Fragonard wasn't satisfied with that. A scientific specimen is a useful object, and I daresay has its own sort of beauty for the student of medicine, but Fragonard felt compelled to create more than objects of study with his cadavers. I think, myself, that within him the soul of a physician warred continually with that of an artist."

"An artist!" Aristide echoed him.

"Yes, monsieur, an artist. Perhaps he took after his cousin more than we'd like to admit." Thierrot reached another set of high double doors and unlocked them. "Take a look in here, and tell me if you don't think the man who created these was at least a little mad." He threw open the doors and gestured Aristide inside.

Beside him, Moreau muttered "Jesus Christ!" under his breath and crossed himself.

Having already seen the monkey in Beaupréau's collection, Aristide thought he was prepared for what was within, but he could not help taking a step backward at the sight of the thing that stood before him in a tall glass case. Like an angry guard at the gateway to the underworld, the creature—no, not an ape, it had once been human, a full-grown man—stood menacingly in his path, hairless head thrown slightly back, fixing him with a glassy, lidless, furious gaze.

The dissected, dehydrated cadaver had been deliberately posed, with one fist clenched, the other raised to shoulder height and forever clutching a great ivory club that Aristide recognized belatedly as the jawbone of some large animal. "Samson," he whispered, recalling the tale of the biblical strongman who had wielded the jawbone of an ass as a weapon. This was no mere scientific specimen for study, he realized immediately, though he could not bring himself to say the word "sculpture."

And yet it was, undoubtedly, a masterpiece of the anatomist's art, and more. The skin was gone; layers of dry muscle peeled delicately away from the shoulders, arms, and legs, revealing sinews and long bones beneath, all of it the dull, desiccated brownish yellow of dead leaves. Inside the gaping chest cavity, the heart, the color of old blood, hung amid a nest of swollen, twisting blue and red vessels that snaked and branched off toward the limbs and up the neck to wreathe the skull.

"He called them *écorchés*, stripped figures," Thierrot said softly, "like the ones you'll see in an anatomy book for studying muscula-ture . . ."

"I expect no one ever imagined that they'd exist anywhere but on an engraver's plate, though," Aristide said, feeling a slight tremor in his voice. "How did he do it?"

"We soaked the cadavers in warm water," said Thierrot, "and drained and flayed them. Then, after dissection, he treated the flesh and some of the organs with a special preservative mixture he'd come up with himself, a sort of varnish made of resin, spirits, and so on; and finally they were posed in a brick oven with a slow fire, to dry out. He injected the larger blood vessels with colored wax, so you can tell the arteries from the veins."

Aristide slowly stepped past the horrible figure and glanced about. More *écorchés*, animals both familiar and exotic, stood together as if in a menagerie: a goat with four horns, an African antelope, a strange, long-necked creature that seemed like something halfway between the pic-tures he had seen of both camels and giraffes. Their heads turned inquiringly toward him, their parched flesh seeming to spring away from their skeletons. The animal specimens were less unsettling, he thought, than the man with the jawbone. On a shelf behind them, a quartet of small figures resembling Beaupréau's monkey stood posed at odd angles, their tiny skulls exploding outward in bony points, arms and legs raised frozen forever, locked in a grisly dance of death.

He looked more closely and saw that these were not monkeys but human fetuses.

Above and below on the shelves were more human specimens, preserved in the same fashion: detached arms and legs, illustrating every tendon and sinew that worked the muscles and joints; a deli-cate, treelike network of the nervous system; the head and shoulders of a man, teeth bared beneath nearly fleshless lips, blackish veins bulging all across it like an overgrowth of vines, the whole looking like a travesty of an antique marble bust.

"Some are purely for study, of course," said Thierrot. "The limbs and busts and so on. But how are you to explain why he would mount others in such lifelike poses, unless he really imagined he was creating something approaching a work of art?"

"Art's forbidden in the halls of science, is that it, monsieur?" Moreau said, with a feeble attempt at humor. Thierrot coughed.

"When it's created from human remains? From the corpses of still-born infants?"

"He could still claim, I imagine, that all these figures are suitable for anatomical study," Aristide said.

"Suitable, yes . . . but there was no need, shall we say, to set them *dancing*. As a student, I admired Fragonard's knowledge and his scholarship; but I cannot quite approve of its application. And he knew exactly what he was doing." Thierrot pointed at the nightmarish face of the full-sized figure. "Do you see how the glass eyes are placed, a little askew, walleyed? He told us he was setting them that way intentionally, to make the figure's gaze more disturbing to the viewer." He shook his head and gestured toward the last room. "In there, messieurs, you'll find the final piece in the royal cabinet of curiosities, and then perhaps you'll agree with me about Monsieur Fragonard."

Not even the figure of the man with the jawbone could have prepared Aristide for what waited within. It was certain, he thought, staring, that the final and most astonishing *écorché* had never been produced for earnest medical study. Rather, it was a wild, feverish fantasy created to astound and terrify: a horse and rider, exposed tendons straining, the steed petrified in mid-stride as it galloped toward eternity.

"'And his name was Death—'" he could not help murmuring.

As a touch of realism, or black humor, or both, the figure clutched a riding whip in one skeletal hand and, in the other, a pair of blue velvet ribbons that served as reins. And his own army of the damned surrounded him; half a dozen diminutive *écorchés*, the skinned, dissected carcasses of sheep, goats, and foals, and their miniature riders—more of the grotesque, shriveled human fetuses—marched in formation around the galloping horse.

" '—and he rode a pale horse . . . ' "

"You have it in one, monsieur," said Thierrot. "Monsieur Fragonard named this piece *The Cavalier of the Apocalypse*. Though usually it goes by the less sensational title of *The Anatomized Cavalier*," he added repressively.

The Cavalier was very young, perhaps a boy. His fixed gaze stared out through the same eerie glass eyes as those of the fierce Samson figure clutching the jawbone, but Aristide thought suddenly that his face, though nearly fleshless, bore a strange serenity in the midst of so much ghoulishness.

War, Pestilence, Famine, and Death . . . the horsemen of the apocalypse. The Cavalier might have been any of them, or all of them together.

Thierrot cleared his throat. "Most of our specimens were animals and stillborn babies, of course, owing to the difficulty of obtaining cadavers. When he did get a full-grown human cadaver . . . by whatever means . . . Fragonard tended to reserve it for something special, like the Cavalier. I have never seen him so excited as on the day when this cadaver arrived," he continued, "and we had chanced to have the horse in the dissecting room, in excellent condition, the day before. Have you seen enough, messieurs?"

"Yes," said Aristide, "I've seen enough." He followed Thierrot back through the collection rooms and down the staircase, lost in thought.

"So," Thierrot said, evidently eager to be off, "can I be of further service to you, monsieur?"

"I wonder if you can tell me how I might speak with Monsieur Fragonard. He's still alive, isn't he?"

"Oh, yes. Yes, I'm sure of it. I've heard a few rumors that he's still preparing models and *écorchés* to order for private collections, and apparently doing quite well for himself."

"Any idea where we could find him?"

"Well, he's no longer there, but you might ask at the house of Eméry, the notary, in the village. Fragonard lodged with him for a few months after he was dismissed; many of his students didn't want to see him go, and they would slip out of the grounds to seek his advice. Perhaps Eméry can tell you where he went."

"Monsieur Ravel," Moreau said, after they had thanked Thierrot, "do you think, then, that we'll find Monsieur Alexis in the company of this Fragonard?"

"Possibly," Aristide said absently. He stared down the avenue of trees at the village, without seeing it, as their saddle horses stamped and blew beside them in the icy air.

The notary Eméry, who proved to be an enthusiastic amateur student of medical and scientific matters, was eager to provide Aristide with the forwarding address that Fragonard had given him when he had left Alfort. "Rue de Bellefond; that's in the north of Paris," Moreau said, glancing at the address the notary wrote down for them.

"Yes, indeed," said Eméry, beaming, "he said his new lodgings were in a house quite at the edge of the city, near the road to Montmartre, with outbuildings he could use as workshops. He seemed pleased with them. It's possible, you know, that being dismissed from the veterinary school was actually a stroke of good fortune for him."

21

It was mid-afternoon by the time they arrived back at the Hôtel de Beaupréau and returned the horses to the stables. They snatched a hasty meal of bread and cheese in the servants' hall, under the solicitous gaze of a plump kitchenmaid, and continued in a fiacre to the northern edge of the city.

Here the roads were not yet cobbled and Paris was far less congested. A number of ramshackle theaters stood among fine new apartment houses that had been built alongside the Boulevard, the broad avenue marking the traces of the long-demolished sixteenth-century city walls. Beyond the tax collectors' wall, which was still being constructed in a new, much larger ring around Paris to control trade in and out of the city, lay rambling villas, abbeys, and farms. Within the tax wall, suburban manufactories, livery stables, market gardens, and other such enterprises requiring the extra space unavailable in the crowded heart of the city, lined the muddy roads.

Aristide found Rue de Bellefond at last and asked the first workman he saw for directions to Fragonard's workshop, unsurprised when the man spat on the ground and tramped away without another word. A second man, though no less contemptuous than the first, was more helpful and pointed out the house of the mad horse doctor. "Though I'd stay away from there if I was you," he added, crossing himself and hurrying off.

A slovenly, middle-aged woman servant, wearing a stained apron and clutching a wooden spoon, answered their ring and told them that monsieur was out in the barn, as usual. "You can go out and try to have a word with him, but I don't know as how he'll see you or not," she said, shrugging.

"Is a gentleman with him?" Moreau inquired.

"A gentleman?" she echoed him, scowling. "You mean a real gentleman, the quality? Lord love you, no. Only Paul and the boy, who help monsieur with his nasty experiments."

"But gentlemen sometimes come here?" Aristide said.

"Sometimes. They come to buy those horrible things that monsieur makes out of dead animals." She swiftly crossed herself with the spoon. "No accounting for the tastes of rich folk, that's all I'll say."

"Has a gentleman visited monsieur during the past few days?" Aristide said, before she could shut the door. "A Monsieur de Beaupréau?"

"Nobody's been by for the past week except deliveries."

"Deliveries?" said Moreau.

"Carcasses for his experiments. I ask you! Any number of villainous-looking sorts come here with something dead they want to sell him. I don't ask any questions; I just point them and their carts toward the stableyard. Now did you want to talk to monsieur or not?" she added, impatient.

"Would he spare us a moment?"

The woman shrugged. "Well, you'd have better luck in the summer. Wintertime, he's always busy out there, hardly comes in for meals, even."

"Why the summer?" Moreau inquired.

She cast him a pitying glance, as though he were a particularly fee-bleminded errand boy. "'Cause of the stink, of course. You can't mess about with maggoty carcasses in July, can you? Winter's when he does all that, cutting up dead horses and dogs and the like. Now you go around the house there, through the alley, and he'll be in one of the barns out back, couldn't tell you which one. *I* don't go out there far-ther than the privy, *ever*," she added, in response to Aristide's curious glance.

They picked their way past the icy pools of mud in the alley and found themselves in a stableyard, crisscrossed with frozen ruts that led to various barns and sheds. A thin stream of smoke drifted from the smallest of the stone outbuildings. Somewhere behind a fence, a chain rattled and a dog bayed as it hurtled toward them on heavy paws.

From another direction, a powerful reek of turpentine, combined with other odors Aristide could not identify, assailed them like a sud-den gale. Following the smell, he found an open cauldron simmering over a fire, tended by a dirty faced boy who stared at them, slack-jawed, when Aristide asked him if Monsieur Fragonard was about. Aristide repeated his question, more slowly, over the dog's barking, and at last the boy jerked his thumb at the largest of the barns.

Aristide tried the high double doors, found they were barred shut on the inside, and knocked. When he received no response, he knocked again, insistently. At last he heard a heavy beam being lifted away, and one of the doors swung open halfway, revealing a short, gray-haired, untidy man in his shirtsleeves, wearing a canvas apron.

"Yes? What is it?"

"Monsieur Fragonard?"

"Yes, what do you want?"

"I want to know about the human cadaver that was recently deliv-ered to you."

The anatomist's small eyes narrowed suspiciously. "What's it to you? What cadaver?"

"You ought to have asked 'what cadaver?' first, I'm afraid," Aristide said. "So you do have a corpse in there, don't you? Male, forties, medium height?"

"Who the devil are you people?" Fragonard snapped, stepping back a pace. He seized hold of the door, ready to slam it, as his wary gaze raked over Aristide's shabby black suit. "Are you the police? I'm a man of science, I'll have you know, and that cadaver was honestly obtained."

"Honestly obtained?" Aristide said. "I hardly think so. Surely you must have noticed, monsieur, that the man had been murdered."

Fragonard eyed him, at last shaking his head. "And they call *me* mad. What are you jabbering about? Get off my premises and leave me in peace." He attempted to slam the door but Moreau shot forward and leaned his shoulder into it.

"Please listen, monsieur."

"You know what I'm talking about, monsieur," said Aristide. "The corpse that was recently delivered to you, the one you're probably working on right now, with—as a lurid novel might describe it—the throat cut from ear to ear."

"My dear young man," the anatomist said, stepping backward, "you're sadly mistaken. The only adult human subject I've had here for, oh, at least two or three years, is the body of a man who was hanged. All perfectly legal and aboveboard. Not even the Church could accuse me of impropriety."

"Hanged?" Moreau exclaimed.

"Hanged, I assure you."

"But . . ." Aristide paused, drew a deep breath, regretted it as the frigid breeze blew a strong whiff of turpentine his way, and began again. "I know that the body of a man with his throat slit must have been delivered to you during the past few days. Do you deny it?"

Fragonard bristled. "Monsieur, I am an anatomist by profession, and I can recognize the difference between a slit throat and a broken neck! Would you care to see for yourself?"

"See?"

"Come in, if you must. I've nothing to hide."

Aristide hesitated and the older man gave him a brief, superior smile. "Don't worry, I haven't begun dissection yet; the subject is still soaking in brine, and quite presentable to the layman."

"I saw your finished pieces, the *écorchés*, at the Royal Veterinary School, monsieur," Aristide said as he and Moreau followed Fragonard into the chilly barn. "They're . . . astonishing."

Fragonard, as he had hoped, was as susceptible to flattery as anyone else. The anatomist paused and straightened his shoulders a little.

"Someday everyone will appreciate the value of my work. And the Church, with its stupid, hidebound prejudices, will no longer dictate to men of science. Someday, monsieur!"

Aristide could sense a vaguely disagreeable odor, raw flesh, he realized, like the smell of a butcher shop, mingled with the strong scent of the preservative mixture. "You're still creating *écorchés*, aren't you?"

"From time to time, on commission." Fragonard gestured at a high shelf, where a handful of small animal skeletons and *écorchés* stood already mounted on stands, draped in sheeting, presumably waiting to be claimed by their buyers. Below, at one of several nearby tables, an assistant was arranging the flayed, gutted cadaver of a small animal, perhaps a dog or a fox, over a wooden framework. A few other specimens lay in dissecting trays and a neatly sorted collection of bleached bones waited to be assembled on yet another table.

"I provide *écorchés* or articulated skeletons for certain clients," Fragonard told them, "the more open-minded of our physicians, for example; or simply laymen with an interest in natural philosophy who wish a rare or exotic animal, or even a pet, preserved."

"A pet?" Moreau echoed him uneasily, as the dog began to bark again outside the barn. Aristide suddenly wondered if it, too, was destined for a dissecting tray, but Fragonard coughed gently.

"Merely a watchdog, monsieur. I receive threats now and then from the ignorant louts who live in this quarter, and I don't intend to make it easy for some band of drunken vandals to invade my workshops during the night and smash up my specimens, or set the place on fire." He gestured at a small *écorché*, an undersized human fetus like those Aristide had seen at the veterinary school. The horrid little corpse was already flayed, dissected, and posed upon a framework, though the drying tissue, each individual muscle and tendon carefully separated from the rest, was not yet parched and papery. A pot of the strong-smelling preservative sat beside it. Fragonard seized the paintbrush resting in the pot and set to work. "They believe, most of them," he continued, as he carefully brushed the varnish onto the flesh, "in their simpleminded superstition, that I'm an unholy ghoul who creeps into the cemeteries at night to dig up their dead relatives! Bah! There are plenty of unbaptized infant corpses to be had, for a few livres, from the charity hospitals, but try telling these local buffoons that . . ."

"The cadaver, monsieur," Aristide said, guessing that Fragonard had already forgotten the purpose of his visit. "You were about to show it to me . . ."

"The cadaver?" Fragonard said, without pausing in his brushstrokes.

"The full-grown male cadaver you recently acquired?"

"Dear me, of course." Fragonard set down his brush, shaking his head, and crossed the barn to a long tin tub, one of three. He jerked back the coarse sheet draped over it. "Here, messieurs, look all you want; look in all the tubs if it pleases you."

Moreau hesitantly leaned forward, drew in his breath with a sharp gasp, and quickly looked away, muttering an oath. Aristide peered into the tub, expecting the worst, but saw nothing more repulsive than the intact, nude body of a paunchy middle-aged man, submerged in salt-water. The neck bore a faint reddish imprint around it, but there was no trace of the gaping wound or the slashed symbol that Aristide had seen at the Basse-Geôle. The man, moreover, was completely unfamil-iar to him.

"Well, am I right?" Fragonard demanded. "You'll agree this man did *not* die of a slit throat?"

"Yes . . . yes, I fear so."

He examined the cadaver's features more closely, trying to fix them in his memory. The man's face was prematurely lined and pouches sagged beneath his eyes. He bore signs of overindulgence and hard living; small, shiny, unmistakable syphilitic ulcers had formed on his lower lip and genitals, while his flabby skin, though pallid, was sallow and blotchy and crisscrossed with tiny spider veins.

This was no common, habitual felon from the slums, Aristide real-ized immediately; such men would rarely have the opportunity to grow fleshy and gross. "What . . . what was his crime?"

"I've no idea."

"Don't you—"

"I don't need to know anything," Fragonard said impatiently. "I merely pay them what they ask."

By "them," Aristide guessed that Fragonard meant resurrection-ists, or perhaps assistant executioners eager to scrape a few more livres' profit from a criminal whose clothes they would already have sold to the ragman. He glanced into the other tubs, which contained only brine. "Who offered you this cadaver?"

Fragonard shrugged. "One of the usual disreputable-looking ruffians. They don't give me their names, and I don't inquire. I was merely delighted to have a full-grown cadaver, for once. I may do an-other cavalier," he added thoughtfully, "if I can get hold of a decent horse soon—not one of the starved nags they usually try to sell me, which are fit only for the glue pot—it's a splendid challenge, and any one of my wealthier clients would pay very well for that, I should think . . ."

"The man who sold you this corpse," Aristide persisted, "when did he—"

"Friday morning," said Fragonard, still looking over the cadaver appraisingly. At last he sighed and threw the sheet back over the tub. "Now, monsieur, I believe you've seen everything, and I'm busy . . ."

"Do you know a Monsieur de Beaupréau?"

"Beaupréau?" Fragonard thought a moment. "The name seems familiar . . ."

"A monkey—"

"Yes, yes, of course. Some time ago, three or four years. He commissioned a myological study of a marmoset, if I'm not mistaken, and supplied the subject himself. What about him?"

"Has he called on you lately?"

"No, certainly not."

Aristide sighed and turned to his companion, who was staring hard at the half-assembled skeleton of something with impressively sharp teeth. "Moreau? I think we're done here."

"I have an interesting theory," Aristide said, when he returned at five o'clock to Brasseur's office. "Or rather, I *had* a theory, but it seems to have reached a dead end. Would you like to hear it?"

"I'd like to hear something useful," Brasseur grumbled, as he settled with a grateful sigh into the chair at his desk, "but 'interesting' will do for the moment. What's your bright idea?"

"Beaupréau happens to have a dissected and mummified monkey in his personal collection of curiosities," said Aristide. "According to Moreau—Beaupréau's valet, if you recall—a certain eccentric anatomist named Fragonard preserved it for him a few years ago. Moreau and I went looking for him, and we learned at the Royal Veterinary School in Alfort that Fragonard, as I suspected, didn't confine his dissections and experiments to animal cadavers. He knows perfectly well how to work on human corpses."

Brasseur, with a faintly nauseated expression, stared at him in dawning comprehension.

"You think . . ."

"Beaupréau already knew who Fragonard was, and what he did, and where to find him. If you had an inconvenient corpse to dispose of, and you happened to know of a slightly mad anatomist who prepared sculptures to order that are created from flayed and dissected bodies, and who of course was eager for human cadavers to work with, wouldn't you seize your opportunity?"

"Now wait a minute," said Brasseur. "You're saying Beaupréau could have had Saint-Landry's body delivered to this Fragonard to make mincemeat of it, so it couldn't be recognized. But that body had a cut throat, a missing tongue, and a few nasty slashes on its chest. Not even a mad anatomist, if he was a reasonably law-abiding fellow, could overlook the rather obvious fact that his nice fresh subject had been murdered."

"That's where my wonderful theory falls apart with a resounding crash," Aristide said. He flung himself onto a chair and rubbed his eyes. "I found Fragonard. He had a human cadaver he was about to work on—I didn't ask him for details. But I got a look at it, and it wasn't Saint-Landry."

"Wasn't?"

"Not a bit like him. Older, taller, much less respectable-looking. No cut throat, no wounds. Moreover, Fragonard said he'd been hanged."

"Hanged!" Brasseur echoed him. "Are you sure?"

"That's what Fragonard told me," Aristide said. "Why would he lie?"

"Oh, I can think of plenty of reasons why he'd lie . . . body-snatching is illegal, after all."

"Well, the man certainly didn't die of a slit throat. Anyway, what it comes down to is that I've been following a false trail. Now what on earth do I do?"

"D'you think Beaupréau is still at the heart of it?"

"I don't know. I don't know anything anymore."

"But there's one thing *I* know," said Brasseur, "and that's the fact that we haven't had a hanging in town for at least a month."

Aristide digested this fresh intelligence in baffled silence. "But I *saw* him," he said at last.

"Of course, it's possible your corpse came from the nearest town to Paris with a public gallows," Brasseur suggested.

"But that makes no sense. Executed criminals are fair game, aren't they? Wouldn't lecturers and surgeons fight over the chance to get their hands on a fresh, legal corpse? So why," Aristide continued, as Brasseur nodded, "would a small-town executioner cart his corpse all the way to Paris when he'd have at least one local doctor ready to pay him for it, probably right at the foot of the scaffold?"

"Maybe your mad anatomist pays better?"

"I doubt he'd pay enough to cover the extra cost of cartage. And imagine bringing in a corpse past the toll barriers! You'd never get away with it—unless you bribed the customs inspector. I don't know, Brasseur . . . it scarcely seems worth it."

"So where did *this* corpse come from, then?" Brasseur shook his head, with a grimace. "That's altogether too many bodies—"

Aristide stared at him. "But that's it," he said, starting to his feet. "Dear Lord, that's it!"

"What's 'it'?"

"Too many bodies! A corpse we can't find, and a corpse that shouldn't be where it is—I think I know how it was done . . . and I think . . . oh, Lord."

"Eh?"

"Moreau . . . he looked a bit green and backed away at Fragonard's when we took a look at the cadaver. He seemed oversqueamish at the sight of what was, after all, a fresh, intact corpse; I'd expect a grown man, especially one who's used to hunting, to have a stronger stomach than that—"

"What of it? Ravel, what are you getting at?"

"I wonder—what if he wasn't revolted by what he saw there, but simply startled by something he never expected to see?"

"*What?*"

Aristide threw on his overcoat again. "Come on—we have to go back to the Hôtel de Beaupréau, right away."

He sat silently thinking it out during the brief ride to Rue St. Dominique, Brasseur fuming beside him. Night had fallen by the time they arrived at the gates of the mansion. Leaving Brasseur to pay the driver, he leaped out of the fiacre and hurried once again into the courtyard. A lackey answered the bell at the servants' entrance but, recognizing him, told him that Monsieur Moreau was busy and could not be disturbed.

"I expect you can help me instead," Aristide said as the lackey began to shut the door. "I only need the answer to one question."

"What's that, monsieur?"

"What did Monsieur de Castagnac die of?"

22

I hope you're now going to tell me what the devil this is all about?" Brasseur demanded as Aristide returned to the porte cochère and the porter closed the wicket gate behind them.

"I know what happened. At least—I know what's been going on here. But—"

"Ravel!" someone said behind him. Thinking that perhaps Moreau had hurried after him and hailed him, he turned. Immediately a short, powerfully built man stepped out from the shadow of a standing carriage and grasped his arm.

"Monsieur Ravel, don't make any fuss, now, and kindly come with me, if you please."

"What?"

"Just come with me, please," the man repeated, in a hoarse undertone that Aristide thought he recognized.

"I think you're mistaken," he said, fumbling in his pocket for the police card Brasseur had given him. The man, though dressed inconspicuously in a drab suit, was not wearing the customary black of the police. "I'm working for Inspector—"

"We know who you're working for," the man said, keeping a firm grip on Aristide's arm. "Would you just come along this way."

"Here, what do you think you're doing?" Brasseur snapped, holding up his own card. The man glanced at him and scowled.

"You're Brasseur? Well, you can either quietly remove yourself and keep your mouth shut, or you can come along with your nosy friend here."

Aristide and Brasseur exchanged a glance. Feeling it was wiser not to resist, Aristide allowed the man to propel him the few steps to the closed carriage. The man thrust him inside, stood aside to let Brasseur follow him, climbed in himself, tugged down the blinds, and thumped with a cane on the roof to signal the driver.

"You're the same friendly fellow who warned me off the other night," Aristide said, after several minutes of oppressive silence as the unlit carriage jolted along. "Who are *you* working for? Not the police, I imagine."

"I expect you'll find out shortly," said the man. He folded his arms and leaned back in his seat without further words. Brasseur glowered but said nothing.

The carriage proceeded onward, at the usual slow pace of the crowded city streets, for a quarter hour. They must be driving along Rue St. Dominique toward Rue des Saints Pères, Aristide thought, but shortly the carriage swerved northward. Soon afterward, the familiar clamor of the city streets grew suddenly softer and the clatter of the hooves and wheels rang hollow on a wooden bridge. Finally, after another quarter hour, the carriage rolled to a stop in what he guessed, from the echo of hooves on cobblestones, must be an enclosed courtyard. The man threw open the carriage door and gestured them out, but before Aristide could look about and deduce where he might be, his captor had seized his arm once more and was pushing him toward the nearest door, a small one at ground level.

"Follow me, please, messieurs," the man said, once they were inside. Baffled, Aristide followed him through a long, dark corridor and finally upstairs to the first floor, where a few candles burned in sconces here and there. He could tell at once from the delicate *boiseries* on the walls, the carved details of the panels and central trophies not painted but gilded, that they were in a very grand mansion indeed, but his captor remained uncommunicative and merely led the way through three opulent formal rooms.

The man stopped before a pair of high white double doors. A waiting footman, whose buckled shoes and powdered peruke must have cost more than Aristide's entire wardrobe, silently opened one door as Aristide's companion stood back.

"In there. I'll be right out here, by the way," he added, "so don't try anything silly."

"I wouldn't dream of it." Aristide entered the room, trying to tread lightly as the intricate oak parquet beneath his feet gave a series of loud creaks.

"I could have that repaired, of course," said a man's voice at the far end of the chamber, "but I find it useful for announcing guests. Ravel, is it?"

"Yes, monsieur." He approached, mystified, Brasseur behind him, until he could see the other man clearly in the candlelight. The man who had addressed him stood at a bookcase in the opposite wall, a book in his hand; richly clothed in an embroidered silk suit and elaborate wig, he was tall and handsome, though his patrician features were growing blurred from good living and the advance of early middle age. Aristide thought he seemed vaguely familiar, but could not place him.

"My, my," said the man, "another fish in the net? I suppose you'll be Brasseur?"

"*Inspector* Brasseur of the Eighteenth District," Brasseur growled.

"I understand you both have been meddling in matters that shouldn't concern you," the man continued, unimpressed.

"Forgive me, monsieur," Aristide said, wondering who he could be, "but I'm only trying to clear my name. Inspector Brasseur told me that—"

"Yes, yes, I hear there's some misapprehension regarding you. Nothing more, I suspect, than a matter of a commissaire who is, perhaps, better suited to other aspects of the law." The man replaced the book on the shelf and seated himself in an armchair, without inviting either of them to do so. He had, Aristide thought, the urbane, supremely confident air of an aristocrat accustomed to having his own way in all things. "Therefore: if I assure you that you will no longer be suspected of any criminal act, will you agree to cease interfering with my friends and their business, and other affairs that should be none of your concern?"

Aristide gazed at the man, furiously trying to remember where he had seen his face before. Whoever their mysterious host was, it was clear from his house and his manner that he was a *grand seigneur,* a powerful aristocrat, probably with connections at court, whom it would be dangerous to cross. At last he decided to speak frankly.

"Monsieur, if you mean the murder of Monsieur Saint-Landry, then, no, I won't promise you I'll stop investigating it. If, however, the Marquis de Beaupréau is one of these friends of whom you speak, then I'll certainly agree to cease prying into his business, because I already know what happened."

"Do you, now? What is it you claim to know?"

"I know we've managed to solve the wrong murder."

Despite the well-dressed man's composed, unreadable demeanor, Aristide was sure he saw him blink. "The wrong murder?" he echoed Aristide, with a delicate lift of his eyebrows. "What on earth do you mean?"

"The murder of the Vicomte de Castagnac."

A pace or two behind Aristide, Brasseur cursed softly.

"The Vicomte de Castagnac?" the man said.

Aristide nodded. "He was the cousin of Monsieur de Beaupréau's father—"

The man waved a languid, perfectly manicured hand. "Yes; I'm acquainted with the name. And what has he to do with this Saint-Landry?"

"Nothing at all, in life."

"You're beginning to test my patience, Monsieur Ravel," the man said, a faint frown playing across his smooth features. "Kindly explain yourself."

Aristide hesitated, wondering why he should explain what was strictly a police matter to a man whose name he did not even know, but Brasseur, behind him, tapped his elbow.

"Go on, tell him whatever you can," he murmured. "He'll have our skins if we don't cooperate."

The aristocratic man smiled but said nothing. Brasseur, evidently, had recognized him, but Aristide was no more enlightened than before. He paused for an instant, setting his thoughts in order, and nodded.

"If you'll be patient with me, monsieur . . . we have to go back to the day that Inspector Brasseur and I began investigating this whole affair. I think this is what happened." He clasped his hands behind his back to keep himself from fidgeting and began, feeling absurdly as if he were fourteen years old and back at St. Barthélemy, practicing Latin declamation before a class of yawning, squirming schoolfellows.

"Jean-Lambert Saint-Landry was found murdered, his throat cut, early in the morning on the tenth. Inspector Brasseur and I saw Saint-Landry's corpse again at the Basse-Geôle de la Seine, the next morning. The attendant there pointed out some strange marks on the body that seemed to refer to Freemasonry, and also showed us that someone— presumably the murderer—had cut out Saint-Landry's tongue." He paused briefly as a gleam of surprise flickered in the aristocratic man's eyes.

"At that point, monsieur, the corpse was unidentified. So we tracked the man's identity down by way of his clothes. Monsieur Derville, an acquaintance of mine, knows who all the best tailors are, so we showed him the dead man's waistcoat and he gave us the name of the tailor most likely to have created it.

"We didn't know it at the time, but Derville recognized the waistcoat as one that might belong to Saint-Landry, who was a close friend of his. Wanting to be sure before he brought such frightful news to Madame Saint-Landry, he secretly went to the morgue himself to see the body. He recognized Saint-Landry immediately. What's more, because Derville is a Freemason himself, he recognized the marks on Saint-Landry's body, and the fact that his throat had been slit and his tongue torn out, as signs pointing to Freemasonry. He feared they were either the work of a deranged member of the fraternity, or of someone who wished to cast blame on the Freemasons for the murder of one of their own—for Saint-Landry was not only Derville's friend, he was a brother Mason and, in fact, the Worshipful Master—that's the president—of the lodge of which Derville was a member—"

"I'm well acquainted with the titles and symbols of Freemasonry," the man said coolly. "Pray continue."

"Yes, monsieur. As I said, Saint-Landry was the master of the Lodge of the Sacred Trinity, and Derville was a junior member of that same lodge. Recognizing the Masonic symbolism connected to Saint-Landry's murder, Derville grew worried and went to ask the Senior Warden of his lodge what it might mean, and what should be done.

"If the Marquis de Beaupréau is one of your intimates, monsieur, then I expect you already know that it's he who is Senior Warden at the Lodge of the Sacred Trinity, and also that he's a man of the most advanced and liberal ideas. Beaupréau, and many of his closest friends at the lodge, have one fixed idea above all: that France is sorely in need of reform." The aristocratic man smiled slightly, but said nothing, and Aristide continued.

"Nearly everyone would agree that we need a strong and decisive king to initiate those reforms, in the face of all the opposition he'd undoubtedly receive from the nobility and clergy who want to keep a firm grip on their privileges; and plenty of people are hinting that the Duc d'Orléans would make a much better . . ."

He stopped, feeling his face grow hot, and swallowed hard. A quick glance out of the tall windows at his left immediately confirmed his suspicions; below him, beyond the gated rear courtyard, lay the brightly lit gardens of the Palais-Royal. Now he could recognize his host's features from the dozens of cheap portrait prints he could see every day hanging for sale, together with those of the king and queen, from every bookstall on the Pont-Neuf.

"Forgive me, monseigneur," he said, after a moment's uncomfortable pause. "I'm addressing the Duc d'Orléans himself, am I not?"

Orléans nodded, watching him. "Please continue; your story is most intriguing."

Aristide struggled to collect his thoughts and the duke raised his eyebrows again.

"I believe you were saying that certain people are whispering that I would make a better king than my undoubtedly well-meaning cousin Louis."

"Yes, monseigneur. They are. And as Monsieur de Beaupréau is linked to a thousand other highly placed and influential people through Freemasonry, or one of its variants, he knows both you—as Grand Master of all the Masons of France—and Count Cagliostro. Through Cagliostro, he learned of Cardinal de Rohan's possible plan to buy the court jewelers' diamond necklace as the queen's proxy. He—and Saint-Landry—urged Cagliostro to advise Rohan to enter into the scheme, never dreaming that it would end in a far greater scandal than the relatively minor one they'd planned."

"And how does the Vicomte de Castagnac come into this?" Orléans inquired.

"He doesn't, monseigneur, not yet."

"And yet you claim he was murdered."

"Bear with me a moment more. As I said, Derville told Monsieur de Beaupréau about Saint-Landry's murder, and I think Beaupréau panicked. Saint-Landry, as Worshipful Master of the lodge, was close to Beaupréau and was part of the scheme to influence Rohan's decision, and when he suddenly turned up brutally murdered, with the symbols of Freemasonry on him for all to see, Beaupréau immediately feared that someone—some outsider—knew about the plot. So he stole the body: not to keep the body itself from being identified, but to keep the symbolism of the wounds from being identified, and thus doing away with any connection between Saint-Landry's murder and a conspiracy among a handful of high-ranking Masons.

"Of course, now he had the dilemma of—"

"What to do with the body," said the duke, nodding.

"Yes, monseigneur, exactly. How do you rid yourself of a corpse, with its throat slit, in the middle of Paris in January during a particularly harsh winter, when the ground is like iron, and ensure that no one will ever see it again?"

He fell silent. Orléans coughed gently.

"Well?"

"I've only been sure since this afternoon, monseigneur, just a few minutes before that amiable gentleman in the gray coat brought us here. But I do know that Monsieur de Beaupréau, in the past, has conducted business with a certain Fragonard, an anatomist. He was sacked from the Royal Veterinary School fifteen years ago and now earns his living preparing anatomical curiosities for wealthy collectors. Perhaps you've heard of him?"

"Cousin of Fragonard the painter? Yes, I believe I have a small specimen in my own collection."

"Is it too much of a stretch of the imagination, monseigneur, for Beaupréau to conceive of ridding himself of a corpse by delivering it to Fragonard—the same man who'd dissected and preserved his sister's pet monkey a few years ago—who, naturally, would proceed to make the corpse completely unrecognizable?"

Orléans frowned. "Surely Fragonard's suspicions would have been raised when he received a corpse with a slit throat."

"Yes. That's what baffled me. It's one thing to buy cadavers from hangmen or grave robbers; quite another to collude with murderers by obligingly disposing of their victims. I'm not sure that even Fragonard, who is more than a little eccentric, would have gone that far, and I expect Beaupréau wondered about that, too. But then, I think, chance favored Beaupréau. His cousin, Castagnac, must have been out making the rounds of the fleshpots, and came blundering into the stables in the small hours of the morning, just as Beaupréau and his companions were secreting Saint-Landry's body away. They told me at the Hôtel de Beaupréau, you see, that Monsieur de Castagnac had died in an accident; that he'd been found early the next day with his neck broken, his horse beside him, in his own stableyard."

"And did he die in such a manner?"

"I don't know, monseigneur. But it seems very convenient that Castagnac should die in a fall just when Monsieur de Beaupréau had a corpse to dispose of. And there, you see, lay the solution to the problem: the best place to hide a dead body, where no one will question its presence or think of looking at it again, is in a tomb."

Orléans nodded. "Ah."

"With Castagnac dead—I'm sure to the great relief of his family—Beaupréau and his friends could simply switch the bodies. Hide Saint-Landry's body in the hayloft for a day or two—no difficulty with that in this weather—and then, after Castagnac's coffin was closed, merely reopen it, take Castagnac out of it, put Saint-Landry in, and nail down the lid again for good, to respectably shut him away forever in the Beaupréau family vault. And then, well disguised as a resurrectionist or an executioner—according to his valet, Beaupréau was a talented actor in private theatricals in his youth—he could easily do away with Castagnac's body by delivering it to Fragonard's workshop. Fragonard, not recognizing him after three or four years, suspecting nothing, would willingly pay him for it and proceed to turn it into medical specimens or even one of those skinless horrors that he produced at the veterinary school.

"I saw the body myself; Fragonard told me it was the body of a man who had been hanged. But it was also, certainly, the body of a man who had led a life of excessive drunkenness and debauchery, and I gather Castagnac's reputation was well-known. What's more, Monsieur de Beaupréau's valet accompanied me to Fragonard's workshop, and I'm sure he recognized the corpse, though he said nothing, probably out of loyalty to his master."

"So you think," said Orléans, "that Monsieur de Beaupréau murdered his cousin in order to hush up the manner of Saint-Landry's death?"

"Yes, monseigneur. As I said, Castagnac's accidental death seems really too convenient."

Orléans nodded. Suddenly he rose to his feet, strode to a door concealed amid the gilded *boiseries*, and threw it open.

"Inside. Now."

23

The duke returned with a lean young man following a pace behind him. Aristide recognized him immediately by his resemblance to Moreau, though he was clad not in an army officer's uniform, as in his portrait, but in an informal, English-style redingote and top boots.

"Beaupréau," said Orléans, seating himself comfortably in his armchair once more, "you must have guessed by now that this is the inquisitive fellow who's been hanging about your household lately. Ravel—my friend Ferdinand-Alexis de La Roche, Marquis de Beaupréau and Chevalier d'Andrezé, who has been my guest for the past week.

"So," he continued, to Beaupréau, "you heard everything, I presume? What have you to say for yourself? Is he speaking the truth?"

The young man's lips slowly curved into a slight smile. "Yes, monseigneur." He glanced over at Aristide, appraisingly, but with a measure of respect. "Yes, he is."

"It all happened just as he described?"

"Castagnac's horse threw him," Beaupréau said evenly. "Or rather, he slid out of the saddle. He was hopelessly drunk; it had happened before."

Orléans sighed. "Now, you see, I find that just a trifle too coincidental. Tell me the truth, Alexis."

"The truth, monseigneur . . ." The young man paused and then seemed to come to a decision. "The truth is that he did blunder into the stableyard, just at the wrong moment, when the back gate was still open, and nearly rode down one of my companions. Then his horse shied and threw him, right there in the courtyard, in front of us. And I, like everybody else in my family for years, devoutly hoped that this time, perhaps, he'd broken his neck. But God preserves drunkards and idiots, they say, and he managed to sit up without anything worse than a knock on the head and a sprained shoulder."

"And then?"

"Then he saw us—"

"Who?"

"Myself and two other brothers from my lodge, monseigneur. Forgive me if I refuse to divulge their names; they volunteered to help me, but it was I who gave the orders."

"Go on."

"He saw us, and he saw Saint-Landry's body, which we hadn't yet carried up to the hayloft, and I knew we couldn't risk his making a commotion and waking the stablehands, or blurting it out later to anyone who would listen to his drunken babbling. So I . . . I finished what Nature had failed to do."

"You broke his neck?"

"Yes, monseigneur."

"Go on," Orléans said, expressionless.

"Then I realized what an opportunity it was to conceal Saint-Landry's body and eradicate any links to Freemasonry, and the rest happened just as Monsieur Ravel said." He glanced at Aristide again, without rancor. "I salute your ingenuity, monsieur."

"What about Saint-Landry?" Orléans inquired.

"He's safely inside a coffin, monseigneur, decently buried with all the appropriate rites—"

"You misapprehend me. What did you have to do with his death?"

Beaupréau stared. "Nothing, monseigneur. Nothing at all."

"Quite sure?"

"I swear by God and all the saints, I have no idea who murdered him, or why. I was horrified when Derville brought me the news."

"Monseigneur," Aristide said, "even if Saint-Landry had been an enemy rather than an ally, it scarcely seems likely that Monsieur de Beaupréau would have murdered him, slashed Masonic symbols into his flesh, left his body in a churchyard for anyone to find, and then gone to such extreme lengths to conceal the body well after it had been found. I believe he's completely innocent of Saint-Landry's murder."

Orléans nodded and relaxed back into his armchair. Beaupréau turned to Aristide with a cautious smile. "You're a fair man, Monsieur Ravel. I appreciate—"

"Do you think I ought to ignore everything else, now," Aristide said, "because you're guilty only of murdering your cousin and not Saint-Landry?"

"Castagnac?" Beaupréau said, taken aback, but promptly recovered his poise. "Small loss, I assure you."

"I see . . . you believe one matters more than the other; or perhaps you believe that your cause is more important than one man's life."

"Yes," Beaupréau said, "I do." He turned back to the duke. "Monseigneur, you know why I devised this plot around the cardinal and the diamond necklace. For the country I love, and for our sacred trinity: liberty, equality, and brotherhood. The reform and justice our land is crying out for, and which you can provide. Everything I've done in this affair has been with the goal of making my country greater and my countrymen happier, by smashing the barriers to progress that greedy, corrupt men and institutions throw up before us. And the only way to do that was to disgrace those who are now in power, and show them for the fools and scoundrels they are. How will we ever get anywhere with a weakling like Louis on the throne?"

"Be careful, Beaupréau," Orléans said, without moving, "such reckless talk could take you to the Bastille."

"You prove my point for me, monsieur the duke. In a truly free nation ruled by justice, there would be no Bastille, and no one could be prosecuted for speaking his mind, no matter how disagreeable and unwelcome his opinions. *That* is what I want, a nation ruled by justice and fairness and not by inherited privilege; and that's what I've actively worked for, every step of the way. You, monseigneur, *you* are this kingdom's best hope; and to put you on the throne I would do anything, anything at all, to throw Louis down from it." He paused, with a scornful smile. "You know him, monseigneur."

Orléans sighed. "Alas, yes, all too well . . ."

"He's well-meaning, intelligent, and enlightened, to be sure, but he's abysmally ill suited for kingship, and because of that, he's a weak and passive ruler, and such a man will never accomplish anything more than trifles. Name me one reform he's enacted, one great measure he's taken, that will forever benefit our people, and that isn't just, in the end, for the greater power and profit of the aristocracy and the Church."

"Well, he did abolish torture—"

"Trivial, monseigneur, a mere sop to placate reformers, in the face of all the daily inequities that shackle every ordinary Frenchman. What about inherited privilege? Do you imagine he'd ever abolish that?"

"He sent our forces to help the American colonists . . ." Aristide could not help murmuring.

"The American war?" Beaupréau echoed him scornfully. "You forget, monsieur; I was there. It was a grand gesture in the name of liberty, to be sure, but not *our* liberty." He turned back to Orléans. "You and I both know, monseigneur, that his ministers decided to fight the British because they wanted revenge for losing Canada in 'sixty-three. You don't honestly think, do you, that they cared one particle about American independence? And what earthly good has it done France? The war may have benefited the Americans and humbled the British, but it's bankrupted our treasury and, as usual, the burden of paying for it falls on the common people, who are already overtaxed, while the nobility and the clergy pay not a single denier. I see no progress or reform in that."

Orléans coughed. "Alexis, calm yourself. You say nothing I've not heard before. And haven't I said myself, before now, that I have no desire to be king, to take on the responsibilities of ruling?"

"Yes, monseigneur, you have; but it's your duty. Take Louis from the throne in favor of his son, and install one of his brothers as regent for the boy, and we'll be worse off than when we began. Imagine Provence or Artois as king—my God! They'd have us back in the Middle Ages. No, the only way is to make a clean sweep—throw them all out, the whole pack of them, and start afresh with a new, enlightened royal line that's far more in step with the times. Because change *is* coming—I saw it begin in America and it's not going to end there—it's in the air, it's as inevitable and unstoppable as a flood."

Watching him, suddenly Aristide remembered Fragonard's skeletal rider. War, Famine, Pestilence, Death: all of them just as inexorable. And he knew that thousands of people with hopes just as bright and intense and fierce as Beaupréau's—perhaps hundreds of thousands across France—aristocrats and bourgeois, philosophers and businessmen, clerics and scribblers, also dreamed about reform and a new era, demanded them in a torrent of illegal writings, whispered their hopes and schemes and dreams incessantly back and forth in countless cafés and salons and street corners, despite the most energetic efforts of the absolutist regime to suppress them. Were such men, waiting for their opportunity to effect change, all convinced of the rightness of their cause, equally as unstoppable as the flood or the Four Horsemen?

The handsome young man who stood beside him, flushed with visionary zeal, could be a sign of what might come—an impassioned cavalier whipping his mount at full speed toward an approaching apocalypse . . .

"You, monseigneur," Beaupréau continued, shaking Aristide out of his hectic flight of imagination, "you are the best hope we have for the future, and for a new order. You *must* take the throne. For the sake of our country."

"What do *you* think, Monsieur Ravel?" Orléans said suddenly, turning to Aristide.

"Me, monseigneur?"

"Do you think I ought to be king? You've written more than a few uncomplimentary words about my cousin and his queen. No fear—you can be frank here. Nothing we say goes beyond this room."

"Monseigneur," Aristide said, choosing his words carefully, "I believe, as does Monsieur de Beaupréau, that affairs can't go on as they are for much longer. And His Majesty, though he wishes the best for France, is far too weak, indecisive, and easily led to be the right man to guide us through the changes which eventually are going to come. I see you as someone of a more independent and liberal character, who would be more open to reforms, and more willing to force the privileged orders to stomach them. But whatever the case, I fear that the means Monsieur de Beaupréau took, to further him in disgracing the monarchy to your benefit, is a step down the wrong path."

"The wrong path?" Beaupréau said, nettled. "Everything I do is for the sake of my country, not for any personal gain—"

"I appreciate that, monsieur. But you've just admitted you murdered your own cousin for the sake of your great cause. Is that how you want to begin your new reign of reform and justice—with snapping an innocent man's neck?"

"If you had ever known Castagnac," Beaupréau declared, "you would agree with me that his death was no loss to the world. How can you compare the death of one worthless, drunken sot to the advance of progress? Surely it's a small price to pay!"

"I understand your reasoning. But what disturbs me is your apparent willingness to let the ends for which you're striving justify less than honorable means. Today, Castagnac, who may very well have been no loss to the world; but once you've set foot on that path, how many other people will you decide are disposable, as well? How many murders do you think are worth committing for the sake of your ideals? If one, then why not ten; if ten, then why not a hundred, or a thousand? I can't believe that reform and justice can be achieved by means that are contrary to reform and justice." With a sigh, he turned again to Orléans. "You asked me for my honest opinion, monseigneur."

"So," Orléans mused aloud, "what am I to do with the two of you?"

He was silent for a moment, glancing back and forth between Aristide and Beaupréau. "Go home, Alexis," he said at last. "No—not home, I think; I want you out of Paris for a while. Go to the country, to Andrezé, and stay there; do you understand me?"

"Completely, monseigneur."

"Go hunting; ride your acres; chase some village girls; mend the roof on the château. Yes," he added, as Beaupréau seemed about to protest, "I know that being condemned to one's country estate in the middle of January is a harsh punishment, but I think you'll survive it. I don't want to see you in Paris again until autumn. Is that clear?"

Beaupréau gave the duke a deep, formal bow. "Monseigneur."

"And what about you?" Orléans said, when Beaupréau had left them. "You're a devilishly inquisitive fellow, Ravel. You, too, Inspector. If I let the two of you walk out of here, what are you going to do?"

"Keep on looking for the murderer of Monsieur Saint-Landry, monseigneur," Brasseur said. "We hoped Monsieur de Beaupréau knew who'd done it—"

"He says not."

"No, monseigneur. I expect he's telling the truth. As for this other matter—"

"The police won't be looking into the death of Monsieur de Castagnac," Orléans interrupted him, "because it was a mere accident that might have happened to anyone, especially a notorious drunkard, and there was nothing suspicious about it. Don't you agree?"

"If you say so, monseigneur," said Brasseur, unsmiling.

"I see no need to raise any concerns," the duke said composedly.

"Now that we know Monsieur de Beaupréau's part in all this is a dead end," Aristide said, "Inspector Brasseur and I will have to start at the beginning again, this time without even a corpse. Because I imagine that Saint-Landry's body will remain where it is, and any attempts to question the Beaupréau family, or to have the vault opened, would be met with opposition from some highly placed but anonymous personage."

"You imagine correctly. Always keep in mind, messieurs, as you pursue your investigations, that Monsieur de Beaupréau is under my protection and is not to be harassed by the police. Is that clear?"

Aristide nodded curtly and the duke smiled.

"You don't approve of this one bit, do you? You believe justice ought to take its course, no matter what. But I tend to share my friend's opinion, that many errors may be forgiven for the sake of a noble purpose. So do not attempt to impose your bourgeois sanctimony upon *me*, monsieur."

"As you wish, monseigneur," Aristide said. He shifted his hands behind his back and found that his fists were clenched. "Though I'd ask one favor of you: Use your influence to have Monsieur Saint-Landry's death officially confirmed, for the sake of his family and their affairs, so they aren't living in a sort of legal limbo."

Funny, he thought, how the rush and scramble, and the bizarre revelations, of the past days had completely eclipsed his bitterness and disappointment over losing Sophie to Derville. The ache was still there, to be sure, but it seemed a little less painful now.

"I see no difficulty with that," said Orléans, nodding. "So you intend to keep on as a police spy, do you, Ravel?"

"I'm not an informer, monseigneur."

"A subinspector, then, or a free agent? Clearly you have an aptitude for this sort of thing. More, perhaps," he said dryly, "than you have as an author. Oh, yes, I've read one or two of your more venomous compositions. They show talent, I grant you that; but perhaps not exceptional talent, and it takes exceptional talent to succeed in the literary life, which, as you undoubtedly know, is merciless to the mediocre. Or are you committed to literature?"

"I . . . I'm not sure."

Orléans reached for a dainty enamel and gold snuffbox, helped himself to a pinch of snuff, and produced a pair of satisfying sneezes before continuing. "I'll offer you another option, Ravel. In truth, I'd rather have a clever fellow like you working for me than against me."

"You want me to be one of your agents, like the man who brought me here?"

"Oh, no, no; oh dear no. Nothing as unsubtle as that. That would be a waste of your gifts. What I need are people who can provide me with useful information from all walks of life, and who can carry out discreet . . . errands, shall we say, to influence others, also in all walks of life."

"In other words, an informer and an agitator, and, if I'm not mistaken, an agent provocateur," Aristide said. "What makes that any different from spying for the police, monseigneur?"

Orléans smiled. "Well, for one thing, the police are generally devoted to maintaining, not only public order, but also the established order—don't you agree, Inspector?—while you, like my friend Beaupréau, are, in the end, devoted to stirring up the established order for the sake of bringing forth something better. You heard Beaupréau; the times are changing. Unlike my cousin Louis, and nine-tenths of his court, I understand that they're changing, and I intend to remain at the forefront of that change. Work for me, and you may yet achieve the reforms you've advocated in your gutter-press scribbling, perhaps with more immediate and tangible success. What do you say?"

"Monseigneur," Aristide said after a moment's hard thought, "I prefer to remain my own man, and wear no labels, neither 'police agent' nor 'Orléans's agent.'"

Behind him, he heard Brasseur stir. "I'd hoped to keep him, monseigneur; he's got a talent for this, all right."

He shot Brasseur a brief grateful glance before continuing. "I expect I'll be working with Inspector Brasseur again. But that's not to say, if your lordship were to invite me to perform one of those errands of which you spoke, that I would refuse the job, if I found it to my taste. I hope that's an acceptable answer?"

"I suppose I shouldn't have expected more," the duke said. "That independent streak may make you enemies, Ravel. Nevertheless," he added, "*I* am not your enemy, so long as you behave prudently and keep your mouth shut when necessary. And this matter of Alexis de Beaupréau is one of those times when it's necessary; I repeat, he is under my protection, and he's not to be harassed or threatened in any way, by anyone, do I make myself clear? To both of you?"

"Yes, monseigneur."

"Yes, monseigneur, perfectly."

"Very well." He rang a bell and a footman appeared. "Show these gentlemen out. And you might make a point of remembering Monsieur Ravel's name and face; I suspect you'll see more of him."

24

The footman let them out through a small door that led to the rear courtyard of the palace. Beyond it lay the gardens, in all their clamor and color, bright with lanterns that banished the winter dark. They passed the porter, who opened the gate for them without a word, and stepped into the busy foot traffic along the colonnade.

"At least Moreau will be pleased," Aristide said at last, "now that we know Beaupréau is alive and well." He was silent for a moment more as they trudged along.

"Brasseur," he said suddenly, "we have to consider the likelihood that this Masonic nonsense may all, as we originally thought, be the work of someone who wishes to discredit the Freemasons. Or even of someone who simply wanted to lay a false trail."

"And you and I," Brasseur grunted, "like good bloodhounds, went bounding after that trail in the approved fashion. Hell and damnation—"

"We might not have, though," Aristide said, "if Beaupréau hadn't complicated matters. After all, a few crude symbols, haphazardly scattered about, do not necessarily make a Mason. I think that, without monsieur the marquis's interference, we'd have suspected fairly soon that the trail led nowhere."

He stopped and faced his companion. "Isn't it possible that the solution to this murder is actually a very simple one, dressed up in irrelevant, outlandish trappings so that we wouldn't see how straightforward it really was?"

"A moment of your time, messieurs?" someone said behind them, before Brasseur could reply. Aristide turned to find Beaupréau himself, wrapped in an overcoat and a wide-brimmed hat shadowing his face, leaning against a column.

"Monsieur?"

Beaupréau stepped forward and doffed his hat. "I wished to apologize to you both, gentlemen, for leading you on such a wild-goose chase. And to you in particular, Monsieur Ravel, for dispatching one of the duke's agents to warn you away from me and my household—though clearly the man didn't do his job as effectively as he should have. Regrettably, it was all necessary. I trust there's no lingering ill will between us?"

Aristide glanced at Brasseur and, after an instant's pause, they both inclined their heads in the slightest of nods.

"Inspector," Beaupréau continued, lowering his voice, "I also trust that this matter of my cousin—for which I do *not* apologize—is now closed."

"If the duke says it is, I suppose I have to accept it," Brasseur said stiffly.

"Let me assure you once again, nonetheless, that I had nothing whatsoever to do with Saint-Landry's death. He was my brother in Freemasonry and my friend. I want his killer brought to justice as sincerely as you do."

"Any ideas about who might have done it?" said Brasseur. "Somebody in your lodge, maybe, who sniffed out your little plan to stir things up?"

"I cannot conceive that any member of the Lodge of the Sacred Trinity would wish to work against such a plan, much less murder Saint-Landry. He was universally respected, and well liked."

"It's only permissible to murder non-Masons, then, is it?" Aristide snapped, before he could prevent himself.

Beaupréau shot him a scathing look. "For the sake of the greater good—"

"Please, Ravel, monsieur," Brasseur said, holding up a hand, "the matter's closed, as you say, whether we like it or not. Monsieur, is it possible that it was someone outside your own lodge, then? Some other Freemason who thought you gentlemen were going a bit too far?"

Beaupréau sighed. "Inspector Brasseur, in the days since I . . . took steps to conceal Saint-Landry's whereabouts, I've come to the conclusion that I overreacted at hearing what Monsieur Derville had to tell me. I've searched my memory and I cannot think of any possible way in which an outsider could have learned of our strategy regarding Count Cagliostro and the—the jewel. The four of us who discussed these matters—no," he added, as Brasseur opened his mouth to speak, "I'm not telling you the names of the others—"

"Joubert the bookseller," Aristide murmured, as if to himself. Beaupréau darted him a sharp glance before continuing.

"Our sacred word of honor bound the four of us to silence. No one could have learned of our plans regarding the diamonds. Besides, no sane Freemason would commit such outrages as the desecration of churches or the needless violation of a corpse. The principle of Freemasonry is that it makes good men better. If I were you, messieurs, I'd cease such fruitless investigation and try to learn who else had a motive to see Saint-Landry into his grave."

"Oh, we have, you can be sure of that," Brasseur said, bristling.

"The police aren't quite that stupid, you know. It wasn't anybody in his household."

Beaupréau smiled slightly. "I'm sure none of the ladies could have done the deed themselves. But I ought to advise you, I know from experience that Madame Saint-Landry is not quite the demure wife that she appears."

"I suspect," Aristide said, suddenly enlightened, remembering encounters with Eugénie, "she once cast her eye your way, monsieur?"

"That woman," Beaupréau declared, "would cast her eye at anything in breeches. She certainly tried to appeal to me with that wide-eyed, helpless gaze of hers, until I made it abundantly clear to her that, while I found her desirable—and who would not?—I would never betray my friend and fellow Mason in such a fashion. But I assure you that she's not the kind of woman who is content for long with an earnest, dependable, stolid sort of husband, a man of simple tastes, like my late friend." He bowed. "Good evening to you, messieurs, and good luck."

"A moment, monsieur," Aristide said as Beaupréau turned away. "Please satisfy my curiosity—why did you disappear as you did, with no word to your household? Merely to confound the police?"

Beaupréau smiled. "To be sure. I was spending a few days, as I often do, in my mistress's company. From there I went on to my lodge, where Monsieur Derville found me and told me about Saint-Landry's death. After we took steps to conceal my unfortunate friend's remains, I concluded that, since I'd already been absent from home for two days, it would obscure matters quite nicely, and thwart any possible attempts on my own life, if I were to inexplicably disappear for a while. So I told Mademoiselle Sédillot to say she hadn't seen me to anyone who asked, spent a few hours lying low at Joubert's printing works, and then came here, in secret, late Wednesday night, and appealed to Monsieur d'Orléans's hospitality. Nothing more than that."

"Oh, hell," Brasseur said wearily as Beaupréau melted into the crowds. "I don't like being taught my job by a self-righteous little sprig of the nobility who's going to quote *The Social Contract* at me with every other sentence, but he's probably right. All the Masonic symbolism—it *could* have been so much window dressing, after all."

"Someone wanted us to go haring after mad Freemasons," Aristide agreed as they trudged along the colonnade toward the passage to Rue St. Honoré. "And one mad Freemason—or one obsessed with an ideal, at least—inadvertently obliged him by hopelessly confusing matters."

"A couple of credulous fools, that's what we are . . ."

"So what about the alternative? Could it have been madame all the time?"

"If Beaupréau is right," Brasseur said slowly, "and Eugénie Saint-Landry is actually far from being a grief-stricken widow . . . but people rarely do away with their spouses just because they're tired of them; usually there's an incentive, like a lover, or a prospective bride with a fat dowry, or else the husband might have been a wife-beating brute . . ."

"Mademoiselle Sophie insisted that her brother was the best of men. Between Sophie and the companion, Marguerite, who seems devoted to Eugénie—if Saint-Landry had treated his wife harshly, I think we'd have learned of it. No, I suspect Saint-Landry was exactly the dull, decent, earnest, honorable man that he seemed. And Eugénie probably grew bored to death with him and his preoccupation with Freemasonry and his cheeseparing little economies . . . come to think of it, she's refused to even think of letting the household go into formal mourning until quite recently, you know."

"Because she doesn't believe her husband's dead."

"Or so she says. It's also a convenient pretext to have the freedom to slip out and meet a lover. She'd be much more confined, for several months at least, as a new widow. Perhaps it is, indeed, as simple as that."

Brasseur nodded. "All right, so madame may have found herself a fancy man. But a woman doesn't often kill her husband, or persuade her lover to kill him, simply because she's warming someone else's bed. We'd have a murder every hour if that was so."

"She must have had some other incentive, as well," Aristide agreed, "something that suddenly became significant enough to be a motive for murder. Money?"

"Didn't you say that his fortune, aside from madame's dowry, goes to Mademoiselle Sophie?"

"Yes; that can't be it."

"And the Masonic symbols? If they were there to lay a false trail, how'd she know about them?"

"Eugénie's a Freemason herself—or at least a member of some ladies' society that probably models itself very closely on the Freemasons. Sophie told me. With a little basic knowledge, it's easy enough to scrawl a few random symbols that might mean anything. Or perhaps the lover is a Mason."

Brasseur shook his head, disgusted, as they reached the foot passage out of the gardens. "We never looked too closely at her, you know, because this Masonic business distracted us good and proper. If she's the one, she's cleverer than she looks . . ."

"What now, then?"

"We follow her. Or rather, you follow her."

"I?"

"Well, I could put one of my other subinspectors onto it, but, as you might have guessed from the way I trust you, you're by far the brightest of them. Why not you? All you have to do is look like someone with a reason to be loafing about on the street. Put on a shabby old suit of clothes, don't shave, and take care you're not recognized."

"Wednesdays and Saturdays," Aristide said suddenly.

"Eh?"

"Wednesday and Saturday afternoons—someone mentioned that

those are the days on which Madame Saint-Landry goes out to the meetings of her ladies' society. Tomorrow's Wednesday, isn't it?"

"Let's see if that's really where she's going, shall we?" Brasseur said, frowning as they dodged a pair of prostitutes who were quarreling loudly over territory. "Girls! Enough of that. Break it up, now. I don't care whose patch it is, see?" The women glowered and slunk away as Brasseur clapped Aristide on the shoulder. "Come on, Ravel. Let's call it a night; you look worn out."

Wednesday, 18 January

Insisting that his black suit made him detectable a mile off, early the next morning Brasseur escorted Aristide to an old-clothes vendor in the neighborhood and bought him a snuff-stained, frayed moss-green coat that had apparently been handed down, some years before, from a bourgeois master to a servant, and finally discarded even by the servant. "Now you look more like the average odd-job man," he said, looking Aristide over, and thrust a decrepit three-cornered hat at him. "D'you always wear your hair undressed?"

"Usually." Aristide inspected the hat, which was of doubtful cleanliness, and hoped that no stray lice lurked in it.

"Tie it back, then, as carelessly as you please. You want to look different enough so that no one'll pay attention to you at the first glance."

Well, I certainly look different, he mused glumly as he caught sight of his new, unshaven, seedier self in a shop window on the quay, before turning down Rue Pavée toward Rue de Savoie. He took up a post near the corner as the bells tolled nine o'clock and lounged against the nearest wall, not far from a pair of similar loiterers who made desultory conversation. Such odd-job men were all over Paris, idlers without regular employment who earned a few sous a day by hailing public carriages, lugging parcels, delivering messages, carrying well-dressed ladies across muddy streets during rainstorms, or lighting tipsy late-night revelers home through the dark streets.

At about ten o'clock, Marguerite Fournier and the cook left the house. They returned an hour later, their market baskets full. Aristide had been lounging on the street for over two hours, he guessed, hands in pockets, jingling the small coins he had earned from hailing a fiacre for an elderly lawyer hampered by a cane, when at last the courtyard gate opened. It was not Eugénie who appeared, however, but Sophie, with the ever-present Victoire. She wore a plain dark gown beneath her cloak and seemed silent and pensive. He watched her pass, a queer tight feeling in his chest.

An hour and a half later, they returned. Before they turned the corner, he made a rapid decision and stepped out to intercept them.

"Mademoiselle—"

"No, thank you," she said mechanically, before abruptly pausing and staring at him. "Monsieur Ravel?"

"Might I have a private word with you?" he said. "Only for a moment."

"I don't think it would be proper," she began, but he shook his head.

"It's nothing to do with that. Please?" He gestured and at last she moved a few paces away, out of the maid's hearing.

"I only . . . I thought you ought to know that your brother's body has been buried, with a proper ceremony and a priest, in consecrated ground. That's all I can tell you."

"I don't understand," she said. "Where is it, then? Can I visit his grave?"

"No. I'm sorry. But I did want you to know that much, so you could be easy in your mind about . . . about the state of his soul. And so on," he concluded lamely.

She glanced down at her skirts. "Thank you. I—I've been to the dressmaker," she added hastily. "My black gown needs to be altered. Eugénie is finally admitting that Lambert may be dead."

"Don't ask any questions, but a certain powerful personage will ensure that the courts declare your brother's death to be official, so your legal affairs can be taken care of before . . . before your marriage."

"I still don't understand . . ."

"I can't tell you anything more. I'm sorry."

"Why are you here?" she said suddenly. "You didn't come here, dressed like that, and wait in the street for a couple of hours just to exchange two sentences with me. Or did you?" she added, with a sort of desperate anger.

"Do you really need to ask me that?" he said, trying to keep his voice level. "If I'd thought it would have done any good—but since I've become untouchable—"

"Please—don't," she said. "That's all over with now. I do care for you, you know that, but it wouldn't work, it would never work. Didn't I tell you that I have distant cousins near Bordeaux? What if they recognized your name?"

"Oh, they'd recognize it all right," Aristide said bitterly. "The Tourtiers know exactly who I am. You're right—why should you take my family's disgrace upon yourself?" He wheeled about, ready to stride off.

"You're spying on us for the inspector, aren't you?" Sophie said, behind him. "Is it Eugénie you're watching? Do you think she murdered my brother, after all? You can't think that *I* would have . . ."

He hesitated, unsure of what to tell her.

"I must go," she said, after an uncomfortable moment of silence. "But Eugénie will be leaving at about half past three to go to the Order of the Dove . . . or so she says," she added, over her shoulder, before hurrying away.

25

No one else left the Saint-Landry household. At half past one, a fiacre pulled up outside the gate and Derville, carrying a small parcel and what was apparently a well-wrapped bouquet of hothouse flowers, ambled into the courtyard. Aristide tilted his hat lower over his face as he watched him. *I wish you* had *murdered Saint-Landry*, he thought venomously, *so I'd have the pleasure of seeing Brasseur arrest you*, and balled his fists inside his coat pockets, stretching them irredeemably out of shape and further tearing the already tatty lining. A quarter hour later, Brasseur, shrouded in a heavy gray overcoat, strolled up to him and beckoned him away.

"Anything?"

"She should be leaving the house around half past three. Other than that, Marguerite and the cook went to the market as usual, Sophie went to her dressmaker and returned, and Derville's evidently come to dine." *Wearing his damned expensive best suit and bringing his damned gifts like a respectable fiancé*, he could not help adding to himself. "Nothing out of the ordinary."

Brasseur glanced up at the windows, sighed, and looked at his watch. "Well, they're probably sitting down to dinner now. If I know that sort, they'll dine at two. Go get a bite to eat, and be back at three."

Aristide bought a roll from a peddler and a slice of sausage from the closest charcuterie, and returned. By the time the bells of St. André des Arts rang half past three, he was well chilled and yawning hugely, wishing he had thought to have a cup of coffee, dreadful as it would probably have been, from the woman who sold hot drinks from a cart in the nearby Place St. Michel.

Derville left the house a few minutes after the half hour, whistling and looking far too pleased with himself, Aristide thought. Not long after Derville had vanished up the street, jauntily swinging his walking stick, a smart chaise rolled up to the house and the driver sprang lightly down, tossing the reins to his companion.

Beaupréau, Aristide said to himself, recognizing him. He started forward, as Beaupréau vanished into the little courtyard, and then remembered he was supposed to remain anonymous. He retreated to the street corner and resumed his pose, the disreputable hat low over his eyes.

Moreau, waiting in the chaise, seemed restless. At last he climbed down from the seat and paced back and forth, rubbing his hands together for warmth, the reins forgotten. After some time had passed, he abruptly paused, frowned, peered straight at Aristide, and raised a tentative hand to his hat in greeting to him.

Oh, damn, Aristide thought, before warily approaching the carriage. Moreau stepped forward, a sudden smile illuminating his boyish features.

"Monsieur Ravel! Did you see? Monsieur Alexis came back last evening. We were all fit to be tied, when he walked in without so much as an explanation!"

"I saw," Aristide said, endeavoring to keep his voice low. "Is he well?"

"Yes, he's perfectly safe—told me later that he'd had to be out of Paris on important, secret business for the Duc d'Orléans himself. Something he couldn't reveal even to me."

A *delicate way of putting it*, he thought. "But what's he doing here?"

"Ah . . . well, you see," Moreau said, his smile fading, "as soon as he turned up at the house, he said he would have to be off again. To the country, to Andrezé, if you can believe it. In January!"

"Did he say why?"

"No. Only that it was something else having to do with the duke's business. So he said that, before he left Paris, he ought to call on Madame Saint-Landry. To offer her help if she needed it, and so on. I gather her husband's still missing, presumed dead." He glanced swiftly up at the first-floor windows, which were still not yet draped in black. "Then he'll have to get ready to leave; Monsieur Alexis says he must be gone by tomorrow morning. The rest of the household can follow."

"You're not going with him?" Aristide said, noting Moreau's choice of words.

"I . . . I don't know. Circumstances might keep me in Paris. This business—he said he might leave me behind in case he needs someone he can trust in town."

"Look me up, then, if you're staying," Aristide said, wondering what the duke's other mysterious business might be.

"Are you not visiting the Saint-Landrys, then?" Moreau said as Aristide began to edge away.

"No." He backed away a few steps, feeling that he had spent long enough in the valet's company; any longer and it might seem peculiar to an observer. Before he could return to the safety of the street corner, Beaupréau came hurrying down the stairs and out to the courtyard. "All right, Gabriel," he said to Moreau, "we've fulfilled our social obligations, I think." He paused for an instant as he caught sight of Aristide. One eyebrow twitched, but he passed him without a word, climbed into the chaise, and took the reins from Moreau. Aristide retreated once more to the corner as the carriage drove away toward the faubourg St. Germain.

Eugénie Saint-Landry left the house, alone and on foot, fifteen minutes after Beaupréau had quitted her. Praying she would not recognize him or notice him, Aristide strolled after her.

She proceeded at a brisk pace along the Quai des Augustins and turned northward across the Pont-Neuf. After passing the municipal pumphouse that stood at the northern end of the bridge, and the busy café at the corner, Eugénie turned westward once again onto a small street lined with modest shops. Pretending to eye the wares displayed in the shop windows, he followed her at a careful distance.

She did not go far. Halfway along the street, she paused, glanced about her, and vanished into a doorway that bore the legend HOTEL RICHEBOURG above it in flaking paint. Shaking his head, Aristide retreated across the street and waited, but she did not reappear. After a quarter of an hour had passed, he crossed the street again.

"The very attractive, fair-haired lady in the dark green figured gown," he said to the clerk at the hotel's counter, "do you know her? Has she been here before?"

"I don't know her name," the clerk said, glancing from Aristide's seedy coat and hat to the ten-sous piece he held, "but she comes here now and then."

"To meet someone?" Aristide said, adding a second coin to the first.

"She's always asked for a Monsieur Legros."

"Who's Legros?"

"How should I know?"

"Can you describe him?"

The clerk shrugged. "Thirty maybe, good-looking, fine clothes, seems to have plenty of money."

"Where does he come from?"

"Laon." He shoved the register toward Aristide.

"How long do their, er, meetings usually last?"

"Couple of hours, mostly," the clerk said, with a leer. "But if you're waiting to catch them, monsieur, if you're her husband, or working for him, I can't be responsible for any of it, understand?"

"Thanks." Aristide slid the coins toward the clerk, who deftly pocketed them. He glanced at his watch and left the hotel, thinking hard. The name and the Laon address meant nothing; the desk clerk would have conveniently forgotten to ask for identity papers, no doubt, for the sake of a small bribe.

At last he went to a modest café, half empty in the afternoon and almost directly across the street from the Hotel Richebourg, and scribbled a note to Brasseur. Errand runners were thick on the ground in the center of Paris; he soon found a shabby youth loafing outside a tavern and sent him off to Brasseur's office with the note and two sous. Returning to the café, he chose a table at the front window, which had a good view of the hotel's entrance, and warmed his hands on a cup of hot chocolate while glancing over a copy of the day's *Journal de Paris*.

Brasseur appeared shortly as the last of the daylight was failing, at half past five, and settled into a chair opposite him. "Good work. They still there?"

"I've not seen Eugénie leave."

"Excellent. Now in my experience, when a lady and gentleman meet at a hotel, usually the gentleman arrives first and leaves last, so the lady isn't left alone in the room. So I'll guess that he'll leave a quarter hour after she does. We'll collar him then, and take him back to my headquarters, I think, to give him a bit of a scare. Any idea who he might be?"

"None at all. The clerk told me his name was Legros, but that's sure to be an alias, isn't it?"

"Probably."

Aristide drank the last of his chocolate and leaned back precariously in his rickety chair. "Don't the police have the authority to arrest adulterers?"

"Only if the husband makes a formal complaint. But we ought to be able to get ourselves an ally. Back in a moment." Brasseur pushed his chair aside and strode off, returning a few minutes later. "Wonderful what a police card will do. The desk clerk, in exchange for my forgetting to mention to my superiors that he's been lax about getting the guest register filled out properly, is going to signal to us when 'Legros' leaves the hotel. So have another cup of chocolate; it's on me."

Half an hour later, as they gazed out the window, surveying the pedestrians, delivery carts, and private carriages that crawled past along the narrow street, the hotel door opened once again. Aristide stirred.

"There goes Eugénie."

They watched her glance swiftly about her before mingling with the passersby, and quickly paid their bill and exited the café. Ten minutes later, as they loitered by the hotel's front window, the desk clerk at last turned and peered through at them, with a sharp nod. Brasseur started forward as a young man in a stylish dark blue overcoat and high-crowned hat sauntered out the door and down the street in the opposite direction from Eugénie. The man soon paused to glance in a shop window and Brasseur and Aristide caught up with him.

"I'd like a word with you, monsieur," Brasseur said, holding up his police card. The man turned, puzzled, and Aristide blinked.

"I know you."

"I beg your pardon?" the young man said. "Do I know either of you gentlemen?"

"Police," said Brasseur. "Might I have your identity papers, if you please?"

"I'm sure I don't know what you want from me, monsieur the inspector; I'm a respectable man of business, my premises are just a short distance away . . ."

Brasseur unfolded the papers offered him and glanced over them, squinting, in the half-light of a street lantern above. "What's the nature of your relationship with Madame Saint-Landry . . . as if I couldn't guess . . . Monsieur Joubert?"

"Joubert!" Aristide said. "Of course. Nicolas Joubert. We met a fortnight ago, at your brother's bookshop. I see you're still chasing married women."

"Married women don't have fanatical mothers hovering about them," Nicolas said. "Monsieur the inspector, I haven't been debauching any virgins. Are you charging me with something? Has some angry husband—"

"I only need the answers to a few questions," Brasseur said blandly. "If you'd be so kind as to come with me to my office, monsieur, I expect we can sort this out soon enough."

Before Nicolas could protest, Brasseur deftly steered him into an empty fiacre, where he sat sullenly through the twenty-minute journey to Brasseur's headquarters in the Eighteenth District. As they entered the antechamber to Brasseur's office, Aristide following, the dour subinspector who sometimes took notes came forward.

"Monsieur the inspector, a young lady says she wishes to speak with you on an urgent matter. I've put her in your office."

"Very good, Paumier." Brasseur glanced at Nicolas. "Just keep an eye on this fellow, won't you, while we talk with the young lady. Make sure he doesn't disappear before we've had a chance to discuss a few things."

Nicolas seemed ready to protest, but thought better of it and retreated to a bench, where a woman was already sitting. As Aristide passed, he recognized Marguerite Fournier and was unsurprised, a moment later, to discover Sophie waiting alone inside Brasseur's office.

"Mademoiselle Saint-Landry?" Brasseur settled himself behind the desk, lit a few candles, and took up a quill. "How may I help you?"

"Good evening . . ." She quickly avoided Aristide's gaze and seemed to fix her eyes on Brasseur's quill. "Monsieur Brasseur, I had to come and speak with you," she continued in a rush, as if she feared her courage would fail her. "Because I've been thinking and thinking, and I just can't see how Eugénie could have done it. As much as I would prefer it otherwise. But I think I know who did." She stopped suddenly, reddened, and looked away.

"You don't like her much, do you, mademoiselle?" Aristide said softly.

"I used to . . . or, rather, I never disliked her. But I think Eugénie has probably been unfaithful to Lambert for some time now, and I can't forgive that." She rapidly blinked and snatched a handkerchief from her pocket. "You see, Monsieur Brasseur, I . . . I'm going to be married."

She paused infinitesimally, as if expecting one or the other of them to offer congratulations. Brasseur glanced quickly at Aristide, who said nothing and turned his gaze to the window.

"The notary visited us yesterday," Sophie hastily continued when they remained silent, "to discuss the marriage contract. He also spoke of Lambert's estate, should Lambert be declared dead. He told us that the terms of the will were that, if Lambert should die without children, Eugénie would get her dowry back, of course, and a certain amount beyond that, and Marguerite would receive a small legacy; and all the rest—quite a lot of money and shares, apparently—would come to me. But if they had children, of course they would be Lambert's heirs, instead of me, and they would get most of it, except for a generous portion for my dowry."

"Yes?" Brasseur said, when she paused. "It sounds like a perfectly straightforward document to me, mademoiselle."

"Yes, monsieur, but that's not the point. You see, I . . . if I weren't so silly and ignorant, I'd have put it together much sooner . . . It—it's growing clearer now that Eugénie is . . . expecting."

"Expecting!" said Brasseur. "Are you sure?"

"I don't know much about such things," Sophie said, staring hard at the desk, "not as if I were a married woman, but she looks tired and pale all the time, and she's been eating more than usual lately, and then sometimes, after breakfast, she suddenly looks ghastly and runs off to her boudoir. It's been going on for three or four months now. I thought she'd caught some strange sort of fever, but Victoire told me, when I asked her about it, that Eugénie's often sick in the mornings. Even I know what that means."

Fool, Aristide said to himself; he and Derville had watched Eugénie abruptly look ill and flee the room one day, and had thought nothing of it.

"Doesn't Madame Fournier attend your sister-in-law?" he inquired. "She's had a husband, knows about women's concerns . . . surely she would have guessed before anyone else . . ."

"Yes, I imagine Marguerite knows," Sophie said. She looked up at Brasseur, unsmiling. "But Marguerite adores her, you see, and whatever Eugénie did, Marguerite would keep her secrets. I can tell, when the three of us are together . . . sometimes I catch her looking at Eugénie. It's the same way Lambert would look at her: a lover's gaze. Some women are like that, aren't they?"

"Yes."

"She doesn't like men much," she continued, her voice unnaturally calm, as if she were fighting to keep her composure. "Actually, I've always wondered if perhaps Marguerite poisoned her husband. She was horribly unhappy in her marriage, you know. But I doubt anyone could ever prove it." She paused. "And I do like her, really. Marguerite's always been good to me. But she would never, ever betray Eugénie, not to anyone, not over anything.

"I can put two and two together, though. Lambert and Eugénie were married for nine years and never had any children. And now suddenly this—so I doubt the child is Lambert's. I think that Eugénie has a lover, who is the baby's real father, and that she's been meeting him on the days when she says she's going to attend ceremonies with the

Order of the Dove. It must have been her lover who murdered Lambert."

"Well, mademoiselle," Brasseur said, thoughtfully tapping his fingers on the heap of papers on his desk, "I'll tell you, in confidence, that you're certainly right about the existence of a lover. And if Madame Saint-Landry is with child, as you suggest, then she'll undoubtedly be managing her husband's fortune until the child comes of age, won't she?"

"Yes, Maître Ouvrard said that that was normally how it was arranged."

"A man who's never fathered any other children," Aristide said softly, still gazing at the window, "in nine years of marriage, might have doubts about who the child's father was, if his wife suddenly turned up in an interesting condition. Wouldn't it be to her advantage to keep him from ever denying paternity?"

"Yes," said Sophie, "that's what I thought."

She rose, curtsied formally to them, and quickly left them.

26

Hell," said Brasseur. "If it hadn't been three years already since our daughter was born, I might have remembered how my wife behaved, and what she complained of . . . damn it, if we'd been a couple of half-witted fishwives from the faubourgs, we'd have guessed long ago!" He banged a fist down on the desk and sat fuming for a moment before shouting for the subinspector to bring Nicolas Joubert in.

"All right," Brasseur said when the essential formalities of name, residence, place of birth, and age had been completed. "You're carrying on with Madame Saint-Landry, aren't you?"

"I can scarcely deny it, I suppose," Nicolas said, with a smirk.

"How d'you know her?"

"I think I can answer that," said Aristide, as he leaned against the wall by the door. "I expect Derville introduced them."

Nicolas nodded. "Derville's a friend of my brother's and he introduced us to Monsieur Saint-Landry and his family about four years ago. Saint-Landry had some connections in the papermaking industry that Pierre thought could be useful."

"How long has this affair of yours been going on?"

"Since about three months after we met."

"And you've been keeping your assignations once or twice a week, I gather? Always at that same hotel?"

"Various hotels. We stuck to the same days of the week; that way Eugénie could claim she was going to a meeting of her ladies' charitable society, the Sisters of the Dove, or whatever it was. Actually, she hadn't been to a meeting in months." He straightened in his seat and stared at Brasseur. "If you think *I* did away with Saint-Landry, then you're mistaken. Why would I have wanted to kill him?"

"You're sleeping with his wife," Brasseur pointed out. "What's more—"

"And I adore her," Nicolas interrupted, "and look forward to every hour we spend together, but that doesn't mean I want to marry her, or anyone. Monsieur the inspector, I'm quite happy with the way matters stand, thank you very much, and I'm not yet eager to settle down and produce heirs. I leave that to my brother."

"Where were you on the evening of the ninth of this month?"

"The ninth?" His face cleared. "I told you—I had nothing to do with it! I wasn't even in Paris—I was in Lyon, where Pierre sent me, haggling over the price of paper with the Montgolfiers."

"Monsieur Joubert," Aristide said, "do you think Madame Saint-Landry is as content as you are with 'the way matters stand,' as you put it? You may prefer to remain a bachelor, unburdened by a wife and family, but what about the lady?"

He watched Nicolas as the young man leaned back in his chair and pondered the question. "She did keep harping on how monotonous her marriage was, and her life," he admitted after a moment's thought. "That she was tied to the dullest man in Paris, that he had no imagination even in bed. I fancy I satisfied her in that regard," he added, with a wink.

"Might she have been picturing herself as Madame Joubert?"

"Good God," he exclaimed, "surely not." Clearly, Aristide thought, the idea had never occurred to him. "Although . . . although about four months ago, she actually began to make noises about 'If only I were free, we could be together always,' and so on. I had no intention of committing myself to being together always, so I didn't pay her much notice, and she gave up after a while. You know how women are, always hinting at things."

"You didn't take it seriously, that she might have been suggesting that you two would be happier with her husband out of the way?"

"Of course I didn't! What do you take me for?"

"Monsieur Joubert," Brasseur growled, "did you know you were soon to be a father?"

"A father?" Nicolas echoed him, astonished.

"She's pregnant."

"Who's to say it's not her husband's?"

"Her husband would probably have disagreed."

Nicolas shrugged. "Well, *I'm* certainly not going to admit paternity. Who needs that?"

"That's the last thing Madame Saint-Landry would want," Aristide said. "As long as the child's status as Saint-Landry's heir remains uncontested, she'll have control of the purse strings for twenty or twenty-five years. A persuasive reason to murder Saint-Landry before it becomes evident to anyone—especially him—that she's with child . . . don't you think?"

"Maybe you thought it would be worth giving up bachelorhood to marry the widow?" Brasseur said, fixing Nicolas with an unblinking stare.

"I had nothing to do with it," Nicolas insisted, paling. "I wasn't in Paris, and you can't prove I was. I was away in Lyon for ten days—ask my brother. Or you can write to the Montgolfier manufactory and ask them."

"Oh, you can be sure we will, monsieur," Brasseur said, making a note and shouting for Paumier.

"And don't you go trying to accuse Madame Saint-Landry of such an abominable crime. You can't imagine a woman like that taking a knife to a full-grown man!"

"If you were in Lyon that week, you can't very well give her an alibi, can you?"

"Well . . . no. No, if it comes to that, I can't. But you must see I'm right, monsieur."

Brasseur sighed as the subinspector entered. "Monsieur Joubert," he told Nicolas, "I'll have to hold you on suspicion until we get confirmation from the Montgolfier manufactory, or an innkeeper, or what have you, that you were down in Lyon on the ninth and tenth. You can give names and addresses to Paumier here."

"But that'll take days!"

"Four days or so for a letter and a reply, by the express mail van," Aristide said. "Maybe longer, depending on the schedule. You'll have plenty of time to rethink your policy of only carrying on intrigues with married women, won't you?"

"I'll send word to your brother where he can find you," Brasseur added kindly, as Paumier escorted away the fuming Nicolas.

"I'm afraid he *is* right about Eugénie," Aristide said gloomily, after they had disappeared. "We know a woman, especially one Eugénie's size, couldn't have done it, and anyway her maid can swear she never left her bedchamber that night, or any other."

"Damn," said Brasseur. "He may be lying through his teeth, of course, but I doubt he'd offer an alibi that's so easy to disprove. And if neither the wife nor the lover did it, then where are we?"

Aristide gratefully pulled off the soiled, threadbare green coat and donned his own black one before taking the chair Nicolas had vacated. "Is it possible," he said slowly, gnawing at a thumbnail, "that she could have had a second lover?"

"*Two* lovers? Where would she find the time?"

"I don't necessarily mean a long-standing liaison like this with Joubert. But if she is as calculating as we now think, what's to prevent her from ensnaring another man who would be more compliant? A lover to make use of and then discard."

"She whispers artlessly to Joubert that she'd be happier if she were free, but he doesn't take the hint," Brasseur said, nodding, adding another note to a fresh sheet of paper. "So she finds herself a cat's-paw, a man less cynical than Joubert, and she bats her eyelashes at him in the usual fashion?"

"Yes. Probably she poses as the helpless lady in distress . . . you know, she gave me the lady-in-distress look right off, the first day we interviewed her; and then later, I saw her playing the same game with Derville. More than once. And that was despite the fact that Derville admitted, out of her hearing, that he'd once made overtures to her and was rebuffed."

"Probably because she was already carrying on with Joubert," Brasseur suggested, with a leer.

"Yes. I don't think she can help it, that instinctive performance of hers, calculated to appeal to all the most chivalrous impulses. But it comes in useful, doesn't it? She sparks a fellow's gallantry with her appealing frailty and then confesses, weeping, to her admirer that her husband only married her for her dowry, and that he beats her, and is secretly a man of unnatural tastes who forces her to do unspeakable things in the bedroom—anything you like that will rouse his manly indignation and stir him into protecting her."

"And the poor fool's so besotted with her by now," Brasseur grunted, "and so worked up and convinced that this defenseless angel is tied to a fiend, that he'd do anything for her, including disposing of her vile husband."

"And Eugénie, you can be sure, will have taken care that not one scrap of evidence, not a single eyewitness, can link her with him. She'll be able to deny everything, to swear before a magistrate that although she might have, in a moment of feminine weakness, committed adultery with another gentleman entirely, a gentleman whom she truly loved, nevertheless she never dreamed poor Monsieur So-and-So, whom she barely knows, would do such a terrible thing, because she never gave him the slightest reason to think, and so on and so on. People might wonder, the authorities might have their suspicions, but there would never be enough proof, beyond the lover's wild, implausible accusations, to have her up on any kind of charge."

Brasseur scowled. "And the poor fellow is broken on the wheel for murder while Eugénie enjoys her widowhood and her husband's fortune, and continues to carry on happily with young Joubert."

"Beaupréau seemed to believe she was capable of it."

"Who is he, then?"

Aristide thought a moment. "A young man," he said at last. "Only a young man, or a very inexperienced one, would be callow enough to fall hard for a beautiful, older woman and unquestioningly believe everything she told him. And he must have ties to Freemasonry, at least enough to know something of the lore."

"All right," Brasseur said, rapidly scribbling notes, "how'd she meet him? It can't be anything too obvious, or the household would have brought him up as a family friend who visited a bit too often for propriety. It couldn't be Monsieur Derville after all, by any chance?" he said suddenly. "He seems to hang about the Saint-Landrys a bit more than most."

Aristide darted a sharp glance at him. "Derville? Callow? You must be joking."

"No, that would have been too easy, and of course he'd never have gone to Beaupréau in a panic like that if he'd committed the murder himself. Though he seemed to be a great admirer of madame, wouldn't you say?"

"It wasn't madame he went there to see," said Aristide. "Not in the end. It was Sophie. He's going to marry her."

"But I thought she was—" Brasseur began. He paused and then said, more gently: "I thought it was you she was partial to, Ravel."

"So did I. If you want to look for a callow young man," he added bitterly, "you should start with me."

He was silent for a moment, staring straight ahead at the dossiers that filled a sagging bookshelf behind Brasseur's desk.

"A young man," he repeated slowly, "rather naïve, openhearted, capable of an ardent devotion . . . superficially familiar with Freemasonry . . . yet someone whose presence would scarcely be remarked upon . . . Oh, God. It can't be. Anyone but that." He sprang up from his seat, paced across the room, and stared into the cold fireplace. "Oh, God, no."

"What's the matter?"

"*Moreau,* Brasseur. Beaupréau's valet. I think it was Moreau."

27

The *servant?*" said Brasseur.

"Aren't servants just as capable of human passions as the rest of us?" Aristide demanded. Brasseur did not answer. The soft buzz of voices from the front chamber of the office rose in the silence.

"It's true, you know," Brasseur said a moment later. "You never do remember a servant in the background. And yet they're people, too . . ."

"A servant, 'a superior young man,' as Madame Fournier put it, who is probably half brother to his master, and knows it," said Aristide, still looking away. "A favored servant and friend to a master who's an ardent Freemason and who worships equality, and who has always encouraged him to believe that he deserves as much from life as any other man. A servant who received an early education befitting a nobleman's son, and who has probably only remained a servant out of admiration and loyalty to the master—the brother—whom he adores. It all fits." He paused, as the fragments of evidence fell into place, one by one, inexorably.

"Beaupréau sometimes brought him along to the Saint-Landrys

when he called; Sophie and Madame Fournier told me as much, and—my God—he was there this afternoon, waiting on his master, when I was watching for Eugénie. And he seemed restless . . . said something about not leaving Paris with Beaupréau, that he might have to stay behind. After all this, can you imagine that he would desert Beaupréau so abruptly, unless the thought of someone else was consuming him?" He paused for an instant, trying to remember how much he had said in front of the young man.

"They—they told me, also, that he was always polite but aloof with the maids, when a privileged servant like him could have had his pick of them. A man like him, lowborn but conscious of his aristocratic blood . . . with his head full of Beaupréau's audacious ideas about equality and natural rights . . . no, he must have believed he could aspire to something much higher than a chambermaid."

"And so—with more than a little encouragement from the lady—he dared to fall in love with a married woman well above his station?"

"And, I'm sure, to believe she returned his love." He was biting his thumbnail again, and thrust his hands in his pockets to still them. "God, Brasseur, it's so cruel. Moreau must have been attending Beaupréau at the Saint Landrys', months ago, and Eugénie caught him staring at her—any man would, if he's drawn to that fragile, helpless sort of woman who arouses gallantry—"

"And she decided he was ripe for the plucking," Brasseur muttered.

"Easy enough to send Sophie and Marguerite out to amuse themselves, give the servants the afternoon off, then invite him out of the kitchen and exchange tender whispers—or more—in private with him in her own home, while Saint-Landry and Beaupréau were closeted away with their little conspiracy." Aristide felt himself trembling with anger and stalked to the window, not daring to look at Brasseur.

"But Moreau's been right beside you these past couple of days, helping you," Brasseur said suddenly. "He wouldn't willingly have investigated his own crime!"

"He didn't. He stuck by me because he was genuinely worried about Beaupréau, and he couldn't have known that Beaupréau's mysterious disappearance was directly connected to Saint-Landry's murder. Though he managed to divert any attention from himself right away, by suggesting that his master's friends might be involved in some shadowy plot. And I promptly fell for it, thanks to Beaupréau's mischief—they unwittingly helped each other in obfuscating their various schemes."

"That must be why he tried to confound us with all the sham Masonic rubbish."

"Yes. Some things you don't share with a servant, even a longtime friend and confidant like Moreau, and Beaupréau would have told him nothing about his scheme regarding the diamond necklace. Moreau's an intelligent fellow, though. He couldn't have failed to see that something suspicious was going on among his master and some of his friends, all of whom also happened to be members of the same lodge."

Brasseur pulled a dossier from the shelf and rapidly skimmed through it. "The timing fits. He knew something was up, and took advantage of it. He must have laid his plans back in October—"

"That's probably right about the time when Eugénie realized she was pregnant, and chose her pawn . . ."

"Moreau began slipping out every week or two—"

"He's a trusted servant, he has keys, he can go in or out of the *hôtel* at any time he pleases—"

"Slipping out to leave his churchyard fires and his magic symbols—"

"And it wouldn't have been hard to duck out into the back streets, by the stables—"

"—to make us think we were dealing with a madman or a sinister conspiracy," Brasseur concluded. "And then Saint-Landry's death would have seemed just an unhappy, accidental result of the other thing."

"You said the boy you found, the one who delivered the letter that lured Saint-Landry out that night, described a man who could have been Beaupréau. But it could just as easily have been Moreau." Outside, a municipal refuse cart had paused behind a grocer's wagon pulled by a bony, balking horse. Aristide stared at the shouting, swearing carters without seeing them. "The letter must have been from Beaupréau, or so Saint-Landry thought."

Brasseur nodded. "Who better to forge Beaupréau's handwriting than the man who knows him best?"

"But then Beaupréau suddenly vanished, and Moreau was frantic with anxiety for his friend's safety. He knew mad Masons hadn't killed Saint-Landry, but he knew nothing else, nothing of the marquis's whereabouts. For all Moreau knew, Beaupréau's disappearance just after Saint-Landry's death was mere coincidence, something genuinely having to do with whatever it was they were involved in, and Beaupréau was in real trouble somewhere, or even dead. He sincerely loves Beaupréau like a brother, and so he determined to try his best to find him and help him, by assisting us as well as he could. Even if it meant taking the chance of being found out himself."

"That poor young fool . . ."

Aristide shook his head vigorously. "No. The tragedy of it is, he's *not* a fool. God, it's so heartbreaking. He's a thoroughly decent man, intelligent, agreeable . . . capable of such love and loyalty . . . and she took full advantage of those qualities and convinced him to throw his life away for her." He closed his eyes for a moment. "You were right, you know, about people who commit murder for love."

"We'll have to take him in to the commissaire for questioning right now, you know," Brasseur said, as he rose from his desk. "I'm sorry."

"I know."

"You needn't come along if you don't want to; I know you've taken a liking to him."

"No—I'll come," Aristide said reluctantly. "I think he'd want a friend present."

After scrawling down a brief message to be sent to the commissaire, Brasseur called for his subinspector, Paumier, and they hurried out to the street and commandeered the first fiacre that passed. Neither Aristide nor Brasseur said anything more as the crowded cab jolted out through the short, winding streets of the Latin Quarter toward Rue St. Dominique.

They paused at a local watchpost near St. Germain des Prés and requested two guardsmen to accompany them. A barked order let them past the porter at the gates of the Hôtel de Beaupréau. After setting his men at the servants' door and at the doors to the rear of the mansion that led out to the formal gardens, Brasseur rang the bell at the front door.

"My apologies to Monsieur de Beaupréau and to his family," he said to the footman who answered, "and I understand this is a household in mourning, but I'm under orders to take in the valet Gabriel Moreau for questioning regarding a police matter. Stand aside, please."

Cowed, the footman shrank back. "His—his room's in the attics, monsieur. But I haven't seen him for some time—not since Monsieur de Beaupréau went out this afternoon."

Beaupréau himself descended the sweeping staircase to the foyer a moment later, surprised and bemused. "Inspector Brasseur! How charming to see you again, and so soon. I trust you're not hounding me in regard to that little matter we've already talked about. Because I should have to discuss your officious conduct with Monsieur d'Orléans, you know."

"Forgive me, monsieur," Brasseur said, glowering, "for disturbing your household, but if you'll recall what you said to me and my associate about Madame Saint-Landry—"

"Don't tell me you suspect *me* of being her confederate, Inspector. We've been through this."

"No, monsieur. Your valet."

"*Gabriel?*"

Beaupréau stared at him for an instant, stunned, before his expression abruptly changed and he paled. "Oh, dear God. I must have been blind."

"You never imagined him falling in love?" Aristide said, joining Brasseur.

"Of course I did—but with some shopgirl or lady's maid. Not with a bourgeoise. And yet of course it must have been my own doing," he added bitterly. "Me and my endless, hollow talk of natural rights, in a world where equality and natural rights are still no more than pretty theories!"

"Is he here, monsieur?" said Brasseur.

"No, he didn't re—Oh, sweet heaven." Beaupréau paused, marshaled his thoughts, and began again. "Inspector, I must tell you something, although I hope to God I'm wrong about all of it. I called on the Saint-Landrys this afternoon, bringing Gabr—Moreau—with me. On my way back to my carriage, I caught sight of Monsieur Ravel here, hanging about the street corner in a particularly hideous coat and hat."

Aristide nodded in confirmation as Beaupréau continued. "As we left, I remarked to Moreau, almost without thinking about it, that Ravel was probably waiting to tail Madame Saint-Landry, because I had mentioned to you yesterday that I had my suspicions of the lady's conduct."

"You told him you thought Madame Saint-Landry had a lover, who might have murdered her husband, and that we were likely to suspect both of them?"

"Yes—like a fool. He seemed unaffected by what I said, but five minutes later he unexpectedly asked me for a few hours off, so he could say his good-byes to a certain girl before we left Paris. I let him go, of course, though he hadn't spoken of any sweetheart to me for months. And I've not seen him since."

"And you think now," Aristide said, "that, instead of visiting some girl he made up on the spur of the moment—"

"He must have decided, then and there, to make a run for it. If he knew that the police were shadowing Madame Saint-Landry, then he would also have guessed that eventually they would learn who her lover was. He knew the game was up and that his only hope was in fleeing the city."

"I expect you're right," said Brasseur, "but with your permission, monsieur, we'll still have to search the house."

Beaupréau nodded. "If you must. Though I pray you don't find him."

Moreau was nowhere in the attics, neither in his own simply but comfortably furnished chamber nor in the other servants' tiny rooms. Brasseur looked into his wardrobe and shook his head.

"Doesn't look like anything's missing. If he's decided to run, he didn't come back and collect anything. Spread out, lads, and find him if he's in the house."

A quarter hour's search proved that Moreau was not in the servants' quarters, nor was he in Beaupréau's apartments or in any of the formal rooms or bedchambers. They converged in the cellars, the subinspector and guardsmen shaking their heads.

"Round up the other servants and question them," Brasseur ordered them. He strode into the busy kitchen, Aristide following, and confronted the cook, a stout, surly middle-aged man.

"Have you seen the valet Moreau this afternoon?"

The cook shook his head impatiently but one of the kitchen boys laid down his knife.

"Maybe a couple of hours ago," he said. "He came down to the kitchen, and asked me what was for supper. The last of the cold roast pheasant from Monsieur de Castagnac's funeral supper, I told him—only for the upper servants of course—and pot-au-feu, like always, if anybody wanted something hot. He said that would do, and went off again."

"Cold roast pheasant," Brasseur echoed him, mystified. Aristide frowned. Why, indeed, at such a time, would Moreau return to the

Hôtel de Beaupréau but not gather any of his effects, yet concern himself with trivialities like the evening menu in the servants' hall?

Brasseur dismissed the kitchen staff with a grunt and stomped back along the corridor to the tunnel. "I'm off," he said to Aristide. "I have to send a message to all the barriers to have him stopped, though he's probably long gone by now."

"But why on earth would Moreau be asking about cold roast pheasant?" Aristide said, hurrying at his heels, as the subterranean door to the courtyard banged behind them. "He must have had other things on his mind than a chat with the cook!"

A vision of the kitchen and the worktable, where the kitchen boy and an undercook had been chopping winter vegetables, abruptly sprang to his mind and he realized, with an icy jolt, where Moreau would be.

"Perhaps . . . perhaps it was merely an excuse to visit the kitchen." He raced up the steps to the terrace and courtyard, toward the waiting fiacre. "Brasseur, when he left Beaupréau with the excuse of wanting to say good-bye to a girlfriend—"

"He would have made straight for the barrier, I expect—"

"But maybe he didn't. Maybe, with his suspicions aroused, he chose to go straight back to Rue de Savoie, skulk there out of my sight, and trail Eugénie himself. He might have been shadowing both of us all the way to that hotel. So much for my talent for trailing a suspect, when the follower can't even tell he's being followed!"

"So you think he might know about the other fellow, then?"

"I'm sure of it," Aristide said, flinging the door of the fiacre open. "Because I can guess why he went to the kitchens, later. Come on!"

"Where the devil are you off to?" Brasseur demanded.

"To find Moreau!"

Marguerite Fournier answered the door at the apartment on Rue de Savoie. "Is Madame Saint-Landry at home?" Brasseur demanded.

She shook her head. "I believe she's not at home to visitors—"

"But she's at home?" he repeated. "Official police business, madame. Where is she?"

"She must be resting in her boudoir, monsieur. I've not seen her, but Mademoiselle Saint-Landry and I only returned a short while ago."

"Any callers since then?"

"Only Monsieur Derville, who arrived about ten minutes ago—"

"Where are the servants? Did they let anyone in while you were out?"

"None of the servants seem to be here, monsieur," Marguerite said, stepping aside to let them in. "Madame Saint-Landry must have given them the evening off, for what reason I have no—"

"Where's her boudoir?"

She blinked, scandalized. "I beg your pardon?"

"Her boudoir!" he insisted. "Quick, madame!"

"He comes here, says anything that will get him inside," Aristide said feverishly to Brasseur as they strode through the foyer, past Sophie and Derville who appeared, looking bewildered, from the adjoining parlor. "Perhaps he claims that he has a message from Beaupréau for madame . . . they know him and let him in . . . Eugénie sees who it is, doesn't want the servants to overhear anything compromising, and promptly gets rid of them—they were alone here, Brasseur—"

They hurried through the salons, Brasseur close behind Aristide with Marguerite and Sophie scuttling after them. Marguerite pointed to a door at the far side of a daintily decorated little antechamber.

"Madame Saint-Landry?" Aristide said, rapping on the door. "Moreau?"

No one answered him. He rapped again and tried the handle, without success. Brasseur gestured to Marguerite.

"You have a key? Open it."

Aristide pushed past her as the door swung open. Behind him,

Brasseur swore and Marguerite sucked in her breath with a sharp gasp.

Eugénie Saint-Landry lay on a day bed beneath the window, one arm flung wide. The blood had soaked into her gown, and into the upholstery and cushions beneath her, in a vast crimson blotch. She had been stabbed, he judged, at least a dozen times.

Moreau lay in a huddled heap on the floor beside her, the kitchen knife clutched in his hand. Aristide touched his shoulder and turned him slightly; his blood, too, had gushed out from his throat, his chest, his wrists, and stained everything around him. The metallic reek of it rose to Aristide's nostrils like the smell of the slaughterhouses and he swallowed back a sudden twinge of nausea.

A sheet of paper, smudged with blood, lay on the dainty lady's writing-desk in the corner of the room. He paused a moment to close Moreau's half-open eyes, then went to the desk, took the note, and silently handed it to Brasseur.

"'Madame Saint-Landry shares my guilt in the death of her husband,'" Brasseur read, "'but the law might never have touched her. She gave me to know, by word and deed, that she loved me. Now I know she lied. She loves another, and she lied to me until I committed that terrible crime for her sake. This she admitted to me a quarter hour ago, when I challenged her with it. She laughed at me, saying that I would not dare denounce her, for fear of justice; that if I did, I would be the one to suffer and she would escape the penalty. But she has paid for her lies. We both will pay the price, as it should be. May God forgive me for all I have done and am about to do. Adieu.' Signed Gabriel Moreau."

He paused a moment, looking down at the bodies.

"Poor lad . . ."

Aristide did not reply. Instead he left the room, stumbling past the weeping Marguerite, and Sophie, white-faced and staring. Derville, coming up behind her, slid his arm about her shoulders and bent to murmur something in her ear. Aristide exchanged a frigid, silent glance with him as he passed and at last found his way through the salons and out the door to the unlit staircase beyond.

A moment later Brasseur, carrying a candle, joined him on the landing. "I'm so sorry, Ravel."

"It's better than the executioner and the wheel," Aristide whispered, avoiding his eyes. "At least—this way—there was some justice done . . ."

"There's no reason you should stay here," Brasseur said after a brief silence. "Listen," he added, taking hold of Aristide's shoulder in a firm grip, "laying hold of a murderer is never pretty, and this affair ended up uglier and sadder than most. But you'll mend." He pushed a coin into his hand. "There's a brandy seller at the quay by the Place St. Michel, last I saw. Go get yourself a stiff drink. Maybe two."

Aristide slowly nodded. Brasseur gave his shoulder an encouraging squeeze before reaching for the door handle.

"Go on. Have a drink and go home, get some sleep. But come by my headquarters in a day or two; you're owed some pay."

"Pay?" Aristide repeated dully. Grief choked him for a moment. At last he rubbed the back of his hand across his eyes and nodded again as he felt for the stairs.

In the street, the hurrying passersby swirled about him in the half-light of the overhead lanterns. He paused for an instant by the courtyard gate and drew in deep lungfuls of the icy air, ridding his senses of the stink of blood, and then trudged away toward the quay where the river flowed ever onward through the dark.

HISTORICAL NOTE

Honoré Fragonard (1732–1799), the anatomist, was a real person. A scientist far ahead of his time, he was dismissed from his directorship at the Royal Veterinary School in 1771 and lived for the next two decades in semiobscurity, until he regained his status as a reputable man of science during the French Revolution. He then donated the specimens he had preserved during the past twenty years to the Academy of Sciences, enthusiastically proposed the establishment of a national collection of anatomical specimens (which he, naturally, would organize and produce), and sat on various government committees for the arts, together with his cousin, painter Jean-Honoré Fragonard, and Jacques-Louis David.

His surviving *écorchés* created during his tenure as director, including the dancing fetuses, *Man with a Jawbone*, and *The Cavalier of the Apocalypse*, may still be seen today in their original home at the Musée de l'École Vétérinaire de Maisons-Alfort, just outside Paris. The small museum, one of greater Paris's most bizarre and least-known, also houses a fascinating display of veterinary oddities, freaks, and preserved body parts. Though most of the existing collection dates from the nineteenth and early twentieth centuries, the original eighteenth-century "royal cabinet of curiosities" must have been fairly similar.

To visit the museum, take the Paris Métro line number 8 eastward to the École Vétérinaire de Maisons-Alfort stop, or visit the Web site at http://musee.vet-alfort.fr/ (site in French and English).

The fallout from the Diamond Necklace Affair, one of the greatest confidence games in history, further blackened the already shaky reputation of Marie-Antoinette, and the French monarchy never fully recovered from the scandal. Although it paints far too flattering a picture of both Jeanne de La Motte, the adventuress at the center of the plot to steal the diamonds, and the gullible Cardinal de Rohan, the film *The Affair of the Necklace* (2001) is a reasonably accurate portrayal of the swindle and its leading characters, for those who wish to learn more.

Many fanciful conspiracy theories about the Masonic origins of the French Revolution have sprung up during the past two centuries. Masonic influence on the political philosophy of the bourgeoisie and liberal nobility of the prerevolutionary period is undeniable, but the French Revolution was no more the direct result of a vast, calculated, continent-wide "Masonic conspiracy" to seize power and destroy monarchies or Christianity than was its earlier American counterpart.

French Freemasonry, in fact, suffered during the Revolution and nearly all the prerevolutionary Parisian lodges closed, or permanently transformed themselves into far less mystical political societies. The revolutionaries whom he had supported guillotined the Duc d'Orléans in 1793, and there was no Grand Master in France again until Napoleon's brother Joseph assumed the title.

The Lodge of the Nine Sisters did exist—members included Voltaire, Franklin, and John Paul Jones, as well as such future revolutionary figures as Desmoulins, Danton, Sieyès, Bailly, Guillotin, Pétion, and Chénier—but the Lodge of the Sacred Trinity is wholly fictional.

A WORD FROM THE AUTHOR

Would your book club like to discuss *The Cavalier of the Apocalypse* and/or any of Aristide Ravel's other adventures? Visit www.susannealleyn.com for some suggestions for discussion topics (no spoilers!), or to contact me and schedule a live chat with your group (in the United States, Canada, or the UK), in person or via your speakerphone. I look forward to our conversation.

SELECT BIBLIOGRAPHY

Birch, Una; James Wasserman, ed. *Secret Societies: Illuminati, Freemasons and the French Revolution*. Lake Worth, Fla.: Ibis Press, 2007.

Darnton, Robert. *The Literary Underground of the Old Regime*. Cambridge, Mass.: Harvard University Press, 1982.

Emsley, Clive. *Policing and Its Context, 1750–1870*. London: Macmillan, 1983.

Ellenberger, Michel. *L'Autre Fragonard*. Paris: Éditions Jupilles, 1981.

Harwood, Jeremy. *The Freemasons*. London: Hermes House, 2006.

Hillairet, Jacques. *Connaissance de Vieux Paris*. Paris: Éditions Payot & Rivages, 1993.

Manceron, Claude. *Toward the Brink: 1785–1787*. New York: Alfred A. Knopf, 1983.

McCalman, Iain. *The Last Alchemist: Count Cagliostro, Master of Magic in the Age of Reason*. New York: HarperCollins, 2003.

Restif de la Bretonne, Nicolas-Edmé; Linda Asher and Ellen Fertig, translators. *Les Nuits de Paris or the Nocturnal Spectator*. New York: Random House, 1964.

Seligmann, Kurt. *Magic, Supernaturalism and Religion*. New York: Pantheon Books, 1971.

Stead, Philip John. *The Police of Paris*. London: Staples Press, 1957.

Williams, Alan. *The Police of Paris, 1718–1789*. Baton Rouge: Louisiana State University Press, 1979.